The

SORROWING
STARS

'This beautiful and beguiling book tells a poignant and haunting
story rich in slow-burning intrigue and tender emotion.'
Jennifer Saint, author of *Ariadne*

'Perfect reading for fans of Bridget Collins and Kiran Millwood Hargrave,
The House of Sorrowing Stars is an electrifying modern fairytale
centred on a fading island home that can only be accessed
by those experiencing loss.'
Waterstones

'A transporting, delicious fairytale about loss, beauty, and love.'
Kiran Millwood Hargrave

'A haunting journey of self-discovery, bursting with metaphor,
and with the feel of a classic fairytale. Prepare to get lost in this
spellbinding world.'
Ava Reid, *Sunday Times* **bestselling author of**
The Wolf and the Woodsman

'*The House of Sorrowing Stars* is like a dream poured onto a page.
Haunting, surreal, and intricate, Cartwright has deftly crafted
a story about what we find when we believe we are lost.'
Heather Walter, author of *Malice*

'Enchanting, poetic prose that enriches a beautiful fairytale world.'
A. E. Warren, author of the Tomorrow's A̶n̶c̶e̶s̶t̶o̶r̶

'A beautiful and moving
the ve
The Bibl

Also by Beth Cartwright
Feathertide

The
HOUSE
of
SORROWING
STARS

BETH CARTWRIGHT

PENGUIN BOOKS

PENGUIN BOOKS

UK | USA | Canada | Ireland | Australia
India | New Zealand | South Africa

Penguin Books is part of the Penguin Random House group of companies
whose addresses can be found at global.penguinrandomhouse.com.

First published by Del Rey in 2022
Published in Penguin Books 2023
001

Typeset in 11.52/15.85 pt Dante MT Pro
by Integra Software Services Pvt. Ltd, Pondicherry

Printed and bound in Great Britain by Clays Ltd, Elcograf S.p.A.

The authorised representative in the EEA is Penguin Random House Ireland,
Morrison Chambers, 32 Nassau Street, Dublin D02 YH68

A CIP catalogue record for this book is available from the British Library

ISBN: 978-1-529-15781-9

www.greenpenguin.co.uk

To my parents, who made so many things possible, especially to my father Phil, with endless love and gratitude, and to Joe, his shadow, his best friend, his world.

Sixteen Years Ago

The doll had been in the lake for so long that the water had rinsed almost all the colour from her clothes. What had once been a beautiful cornflower blue was now as dull and pale as a winter sky – more rag than dress. Her feet were bare, and one of her fingers had broken away. The bouncy chestnut ringlets of her hair were now two heavy twists that wrapped around her arms like dark rope. Her face was white and cold to the touch, and the apple blush of her cheeks and the small rosebud pout of her mouth had long since washed away. With unblinking emerald eyes, she stared at the sky as the garland of white flowers and feathers adorning her head slowly loosened and drifted around her like a scattered offering.

By the time she floated towards the banks of the island, the light was beginning to fade. A young woman was walking along the edge of the lake. She came there most evenings to listen to the gentle sound of the water. That evening she heard the flute-like note of a curlew echoing through the dusk. It would not be long until the soft hoot of an owl summoned the moon. She wondered if it was the same one that she had released a few days before, after finding it sprawled on a pile of leaves in its light speckled gown, its wing bent at an odd angle. The month before, she had found a baby robin shivering on the lawn. Unable to find its nest, she had nursed it back to health, waking through the night to feed it bits of hard-boiled egg from a toothpick. She had rescued so many animals on the island – and not only birds, but also salamanders, hedgehogs, mice and even a fox that had torn its neck on a rusty wire. A piece of its fur would forever be missing, but it lived. This is where she came to release them; chosen because it was far enough from the house not to be seen and it offered the secret shade of the chestnut trees. She was thinking of keeping a leger of them all, like that of a jewel merchant or a curator of the finest museum specimens. Her work was just as important as theirs, and she was determined it would count.

The warmth of the day hadn't yet left her skin as she pulled off her stockings and walked towards the lake. Hitching up her dress, she dipped her toes into the cool blue water, then, unable to resist, she plunged in her whole foot, feeling the cold splash against her legs. There was no one there to see. Her brother was the only one who might come this way, but he was always too busy mending a broken lock or carving out a new one. She closed her eyes, tilted her face to the sky and inhaled the wispy scent of hibiscus, which every now and then caught on the gentle breeze.

On the island the dark always arrived swiftly. In a blink, the sun's dramatic red flare would vanish from the mountains and the sky would glow like a long-burning fire. It was the magic hour – the hour of water and birdsong and fast-fading light. It was her time.

Something tickled her ankle. At first she didn't give it much attention; wind-swept twigs and ferns were always finding their way into the water. She probably would have continued standing there with her eyes closed and her skirt bunched in her fists, dreaming and drifting, except that whatever it was suddenly grew insistent. It felt like the tapping of tiny impatient fingers on her skin – so strange that she finally opened her eyes and looked down. What she saw floating against her leg made her gasp in astonishment.

Gently, so as not to damage it further, she lifted the doll out of the water. It was heavier than expected, and it didn't break apart in her hands, as she had feared. Carefully she shook away the water and unpicked a twig that had tangled in its hair.

'Someone will be missing you,' she said, staring into the doll's eyes, still bright and shining.

Then she felt it, as she so often did when she touched an unfamiliar object. A vision, a connection. Only this time the feeling was difficult to explain. She waited, hoping that if she grasped the doll a little tighter with both of her hands, the meaning would come.

Usually the sense was sudden and sharp, like a pin-prick. Sometimes there was a sound or a feeling. At other times it came to her as a smell or a taste on her tongue. Her gift was an unusual one. The first time it happened she had been returning a dropped pendant to a lady in the street. As soon as she picked it up, she could hear the relentless sound of a baby crying. It was so loud that she had run away, covering her ears, before the woman even had time to thank her. A few months later she saw the same woman gazing excitedly in the window of a toy shop and, when she turned to leave, she saw the rounded swelling of her stomach, confirming what she'd already known.

Unfortunately the visions weren't always that pleasant. One winter morning she had bought a bag of chestnuts from the old peddler on the street corner. As she popped one – still warm – into her mouth and crunched it between her teeth, she knew immediately that something was wrong. Instead of the burst of sweetness she had been expecting, the metallic taste of blood filled her mouth. She began to gag in disgust, clawing at her tongue and choking as she tried to spit out all the pieces. The peddler

4

watched in confusion and guilt, but she hurried away, unable to explain. A week later, when she was standing in the bread shop, she saw a funeral procession go by. She didn't need to look inside the coffin to know she'd find the old peddler lying there.

Another time she'd found a glove, its owner long gone. She picked it up, intending to lay it on a window ledge, in case someone came looking for it. As soon as she touched it, she felt a terrible burning sensation, so hot that she dropped it back on the ground as though she held a lit coal. She was convinced that it had left scorch marks, but when she turned her hand over, the smooth, unblemished skin said otherwise. The next day she'd heard that a house in the village had burned to the ground and all the people inside had perished. She would never know for sure if one of them had lost a glove, but she was almost certain they had.

This time it was different. It wasn't a sound or a taste that came to her as she held the doll, but rather an unshake-able feeling. It made her heart lift, then fall, then lift and fall again like a choppy wave, but she couldn't tell if it was bringing her closer to the shore or sweeping her further away.

Tentatively she turned the doll over in her hand, hoping she would sense something else, something more. It would have been so beautiful once and expensively made, but now its porcelain arms and legs were stained and its face was chipped. She could see that one of its fingers was missing and its dress looked like an old dishcloth. If it had once worn shoes, they were long gone.

But it is not beyond repair, she thought, her mind turning to the paints she kept in her room. She could use them to revive the doll's cheeks and lips. Curling its hair would be simple enough – she had done her own enough times – and she could wash its dress and sprinkle lavender into the water to banish the mould. After all, she was used to rescuing things. Her brother would laugh and say she was almost grown, and far too old to play with dolls. She knew he was right, but it wasn't the doll she was interested in, it was the person who'd lost it.

The last of the light vanished, deepening the sky from lilac to indigo and, in the lake below, the petals of the sorrowing stars were stirring. It was time to leave.

That night, as she fell asleep with the doll by her side, she could feel her cheeks damp, but the tears that fell were not her own.

Across the lake a young girl was crying into her pillow. A few weeks ago she had left her doll somewhere, but couldn't remember where. Her father and her uncle had gone back to the little park they'd sat in that morning and retraced their steps to the café where they'd all eaten lunch. The following day they'd gone back to see if the doll was lying on the steps of the church they'd admired, but they were empty, aside from a pair of cooing doves. They spent days searching the village without any luck, and by the time they eventually wandered along the lakeside path, the doll had almost reached the island. Each time they returned empty-handed the little girl's heart broke all over again, and the promise of a new doll did nothing to fix it. As she lay inconsolable in her cousin's arms, her crying continued long into the night, and into the many nights that followed.

Her loss was a ripple in the water that could be felt far across the lake.

CHAPTER 1

The Marchpane Girl

Liddy spied yet another card lying in a silver tray on the hallway table. It was the fifth one in as many weeks and, just like all the others, it had her name written on the front. She instantly recognised the hand that had left it there, and her heart plummeted. It belonged to Jack Heathcote. Dipping her head to unwind her scarf, Liddy noticed that the top left-hand corner had been turned down, indicating that it had been hand-delivered. She felt a momentary flutter of panic at the thought of him still being there, sipping tea and discussing business with her father in the drawing room. She strained her ears for the sound of voices tucked deeper in the house, but none came. A quick rummage through the coat-stand confirmed that her visitor hadn't stayed and she gave a sigh of relief.

She lifted the card from the tray, a gesture that brought with it a waft of something pungent and much too sweet, like rose petals stewed in rain. His mother's perfume perhaps, or the trace of one of his many lovers. She didn't need to read it to know what it would say – the cards all had the same nauseating sentiment, which was as sickly as it was false. In the last one he described her as his *dearest creature* and declared himself to be her *most ardent pursuer.* She shuddered at the thought. As soon as her mother had discovered that Jack Heathcote was the one sending the calling cards she'd begun planning the most lavish of weddings. Her father was equally delighted by Jack's interest in his daughter; the Heathcote family came from a long line of shipping merchants and, with the right investment, he imagined his marchpane travelling to the distant corners of the world.

Liddy knew it wasn't polite to ignore the card, but she didn't care – she wasn't about to give Jack the satisfaction of a reply. It might please her parents if she became the wife of a man with more lovers than plum puddings, but it certainly wouldn't please her. Down the corridor she heard the rustling and folding of paper and then the swift shuffle of her father's approaching feet. Quick as a minnow, she slipped the card into her pocket, just as he emerged from the shadows, carrying a small bundle of boxes in his hands.

'No, no, no,' he said, shaking his head, before she had a chance to undo the first of her coat buttons. 'I need you to go out again; there is a very important sugar banquet happening right now, and our marchpane is to be the centrepiece.'

Liddy's father thrust the boxes into her hands and bundled her back onto the street.

'Hurry,' he called. 'These packages are for Jack Heathcote, and I think it's about time you answered his calls.'

'But—' Liddy began, but her father's face immediately hardened and her protestations fell away.

'I told you, good men don't wait for ever,' he said sternly. 'Especially the likes of Jack Heathcote.'

He slammed the door shut, leaving her alone on the street. Liddy wondered if there even was a sugar banquet or if it were simply a stupid ruse to bring them together. Reaching inside her pocket for the card that her father had obviously already discovered, she scrunched it into a ball. *That's my answer, and it won't change*, she thought, tossing it into the gutter.

A quiet storm brewed, and she strode across town in such a temper that the pounding of her footsteps startled a flock of pigeons into the air like a spray of bullets. She was so angry that she walked straight past her destination, and it was only when she reached the rowdy rabble of the Queen's Head that she realised she'd gone too far and had to double back.

The Heathcote house was a large stone building on the edge of the town. From the outside it was a rather drab and tired affair, with crumbling walls and chipped paintwork, but once inside it became a different place entirely. When she had been too young to make deliveries by herself, she would accompany her father on his errands, and it was in the early dark of winter that she had first glimpsed the sumptuous world within. She had gasped when the door had opened for the first time to reveal a place of breathtaking opulence, unlike anything she had ever seen before. While they had waited in the grand hallway, her eyes had hurried over everything: a sweeping staircase, a polished floor, a sparkling chandelier, gleaming elegant furnishings. Then through a large open doorway her eyes had fallen upon a boy. He was perhaps a year or two older than her and he was pulling a mewling cat along the floor by its tail. Liddy had watched in horror as the boy began to spin the cat round and round. His laughter made her furious. Her father didn't seem to notice, or perhaps he dismissed it as boyish mischief; either way, he ignored her tugs at his sleeve. Taken by surprise at seeing Liddy and her father standing there, the boy had loosened his grip and the cat seized its opportunity to escape. On frantic paws, it skittered straight for the front door, which had closed behind Liddy and her father. Without hesitation Liddy stepped back to turn the handle. A cold draught blew in and the cat brushed past her legs and was gone. The boy watched her with narrowed eyes and then smiled smugly. He didn't look at her angrily, but as though she was a new challenge, which was even more unsettling. Liddy averted her gaze and shifted her feet back until she was hidden safely behind her father's over-sized coat.

In that moment Liddy learned that wealth couldn't make everything shine and it certainly couldn't buy manners.

On reaching the top of the steps leading to the front door, she now saw her scowling face reflected in the polished brass of the door knocker. The fixture felt too heavy in her hand, and she let it drop before she was ready. A shallow, dull thud half-heartedly announced her arrival. She tutted at herself; the walk across town had done nothing to abate her temper. She stood back, ready to hand over her father's delivery quickly and scarper, but no one came. She tried again, this time with a thud loud enough to rouse the dead, but it seemed the dead were not listening – the door stayed firmly shut.

Behind her on the street, two children ran past, giggling. They were followed by a breathless woman hitching up her skirts, in slow pursuit. 'It's time you rascals were home for supper,' the woman cried to the children, shaking her head and pausing to rest against the railings. After a moment she straightened herself and hobbled away after them. Liddy's attention fell back to the door.

She knocked again and again, but still nobody answered. She felt a drop of rain on her head and looked up, to see an ominous dark sky: rain was on its way. Impatiently she placed the boxes on the step and peered through the nearest window, hoping to catch someone's attention. The room within was dark and filled with shadows, but on the other side the light through an open doorway revealed a crowded room, and she could hear the very faint sound of laughter. At that moment the front door swung open and the suddenness of it sent her stumbling backwards; her foot slipped and she fell down the steps to the street below. Unharmed but embarrassed, she looked up to see Jack Heathcote standing above her.

'Let me help,' he said, moving towards her.

Liddy scrambled to her feet; she did not welcome the weight of his hand upon her arm. Straightening her skirt, she dusted off her coat and climbed the steps, then hastily snatched up the boxes and thrust them towards him.

'You must be here for my party,' he said, letting the marchpane boxes hang between them.

'You are mistaken,' Liddy snapped. 'I came to deliver your marchpane – and only at my father's insistence.'

Jack smirked as she continued to hold the boxes out to him. Part of her wished he would just take them and close the door, but another part of her was intrigued by the laughter and the chatter, and the sound of glasses chinking that she could hear over his shoulder.

'And have you brought me anything else? Perhaps a reply to one of my many calling cards?' he asked with a smirk.

His words drew her back, and Liddy shook her head. Despite her earlier defiance, she felt a twinge of guilt at her own rudeness.

'Very well,' he said, with a touch of disappointment. 'I would like you to arrange the marchpane on the table. That is what you do, isn't it?'

No, it isn't what I do, she thought, her irritation returning. But the glow behind him held her gaze, and Liddy hesitated a beat too long. Sensing her indecision, Jack moved back and the door widened.

Ensorcelled by all the glitter, she stepped inside.

The house was warm – too warm – and the glare of so many lights hurt her eyes. Jack led her down a wide hallway with a gleaming marble floor and past a grand sweeping staircase that led to who knew how many bedrooms. A sweet scent coated the air, making her teeth tingle, and she smoothed her tongue over their ridges to make them settle. On the wall hung a portrait of the Heathcote family, and there was Jack as a boy, staring back at her with an expression of arrogance and entitlement. Even then, you could tell he was used to getting his own way. She remembered the poor cat and her skin prickled.

The voices grew louder, and Liddy suddenly regretted her decision to follow him into the house. *This was a mistake*, she thought too late, as she found herself in a room full of people. For a moment it felt like time had stopped and all eyes were upon her, cold and disapproving and full of mockery. Standing there in her drab coat with its missing button and her boots all scuffed at the toes, Liddy felt a flush of shame. She did not belong in such a polished world. Her stomp through the street had left her more dishevelled than usual and she remembered her pale reflection in the brass knocker. She swallowed hard and continued to follow Jack further into the room, trying her best to ignore all the giggles and nudges. The women in the room wore flamboyant parrot-coloured dresses and had ribbons tied in their hair. From their ears and necks dripped jewels, like molten gold. Liddy lowered her head; she felt like a beetle scuttling over treasure. Self-consciously she smoothed down a strand of loosened hair and tucked it behind her ear, and immediately hated herself for caring what these people thought of her.

'Who's this?' chortled a young man. Despite having the plump red cheeks of a farmer, his soft leather boots, without a single scratch upon them, confirmed that he had never set foot in a muddy field, much less baled any hay.

'You didn't tell us you had invited another guest, Jack,' purred a girl with large blinking eyes. She clung onto the arm of the red-cheeked man as though he was going to save her from stepping into a cowpat.

'Don't be silly, Emily, she's not a guest,' sang a voice from across the room.

The girl who had spoken – similar in age to Liddy, but far more immaculately preened – walked over and, without giving Liddy time to object, lifted the boxes from her hand.

'She's just the marchpane girl,' she said dismissively. Putting the boxes on the table, she ripped them open in greedy delight. Liddy felt herself bristle.

With a swish and a rustle, all the girls quickly arranged themselves around her like shiny baubles. They watched with wide and eager eyes as she carelessly tipped the multicoloured squares onto a large three-tiered stand in the middle of the table. Some landed on the table and others fell to the floor in an avalanche of sugar. Liddy had to resist the urge to pick them up. Instead she stepped back. The girl popped one in her mouth immediately and closed her lips around it with an undisguised squeal of pleasure, her performance captivating the men in the room. All except one – Jack Heathcote – whose eyes were still firmly fixed on Liddy. She turned away as the other girls shuffled forward, desperate for a taste of the exquisite marchpane. A wicked thought suddenly sparked in her mind: if only she had added a spoonful of salt to the mixture – that would have taught these snotty girls a lesson.

'Try one, they are truly divine!' the girl exclaimed, licking her fingers and wiping them on the fabric of her beautiful dress. *What a waste of such fine silk*, thought Liddy. On first sight she had thought the woman to be beautiful, with her shiny blue eyes and her tiny button nose, her perfectly ringletted hair tied in a pretty pink ribbon like a doll. But when she opened her mouth to laugh, all Liddy's thoughts of beauty quickly evaporated. Where her teeth should have been, there were mostly gaps, and the very few that remained wobbled from blackened gums. Liddy wouldn't have been at all surprised to find one left behind in a piece of marchpane, and she wrinkled her nose in disgust at the thought. Holding another marchpane square between sticky fingers, the girl skipped over to where Jack was sitting and bounced onto his knee with a giggle.

'You simply have to taste them,' she insisted, forcing one into his mouth.

Jack seemed to have finally forgotten all about Liddy and happily played along, nodding his agreement, *oohing* and *aahing* and closing his eyes as the marchpane sat on his tongue. Liddy watched as his jaw ground like a miller's wheel, and the thought of his mouth being anywhere near hers made her quite nauseous. The girl on his knee was laughing now and stamping her feet in a pitter-patter of excitement that made the crockery in the cabinet rattle. Liddy wondered if perhaps they were all high on sugar – the sugar mountain on the table had already been half-conquered. Watching Jack and the girl didn't fill her with envy; it simply confirmed that she would never ever want to be with someone like Jack Heathcote, and she felt only disappointment that her parents thought him to be such a suitable match.

Thankfully the whole room seemed to have forgotten she was there, including Jack, and when he opened his eyes again, the marchpane girl was long gone.

CHAPTER 2

Disappointment

Hurrying through the damp streets, Liddy was careful not to let the hem of her skirt drop in the grimy puddles. Only when she was finally back on the cobbles of Wingate Square did she release the fabric from her clenched fists. Her house was slotted right in the middle of a modest red-brick row, all tall and slender and as upright as the people who inhabited them. Their roofs were neatly assembled, their windows shone like military medals and the steps were routinely swept clean of leaves. It may not have been as grand as the Heathcote residence, but it was a respectable neighbourhood and her father had worked hard to afford it.

Upon reaching the front door, she paused at the sight of a small package. She glanced up and down the street, but no one loitered and whoever had left it there was nowhere to be seen. Liddy wondered if it was once again Jack Heathcote's doing; rather than pursuing her with simple acquaintance cards, perhaps he had decided that a gift would be a more persuasive way of gaining her affection. But as she thought about it, she realised it was impossible; she had just seen Jack at home with his sugar queen, and the package hadn't been there when she left, had it? Unwelcome thoughts of Jack Heathcote filtered back into her mind and she stomped up the steps with the same frustration as she had descended them less than an hour before. At least she could be reasonably confident that neither her father nor her mother had discovered this package yet – she was thankful for small mercies.

The paper in which it was wrapped was torn and weather-worn as though it had travelled a great distance to get there. Scooping it up, she heard its contents rattle within. She turned it over to find a perfectly square label, and written upon it in a careful but unfamiliar hand was her name, Madeleine Harchwood. She had never seen such controlled and crafted calligraphy before; the letters were a collection of fine inky swirls and loops – a little timid perhaps, as though whoever had put them there was too shy to reveal themselves fully.

If not Jack Heathcote, then who? She pondered the thought fleetingly and then her mind solved the mystery. Although she hadn't been expecting another arrival of her secret ingredients so soon, this was surely what she was holding now in her hand. For months she had been adding to her father's recipe, without telling him and without arousing his suspicions. With increasing regularity she had begun to swap the rosewater for orange-flower water to give it more of an exotic flavour: a sharp burst on the tongue. At other times it was honey that she substituted for sugar, and found that not only did the customers comment on how smooth the marchpane tasted, but she was saving them a potful of money in the process. Sugar always came at a high price.

Her father's sole heir, she had been brought into the business several years ago. She had grown up watching in wonder as her father blanched handfuls of almonds and ground them to a thick paste in a mortar. He always worked swiftly and silently, whipping egg whites, sifting sugar and mixing in the occasional spoonful of rosewater, stirring it all with a deft hand. Once it was ready, he would roll it out on the worktop and then cut it into small, equal squares, placing each one on little wafers and setting them to bake. She would wait for him to give her the sliced-off edges, so that she could make weird and wonderful patterns and shapes out of them. *Why did he only choose squares?* she often wondered. How boring! Where was his imagination? Once she had tried to make a seahorse, because she'd seen one in a book and thought it was pretty, but it had looked more like a serpent and, with a stab of disappointment, she squished the marchpane back into a gooey ball and then reshaped it into a slightly more convincing heart.

Now that she was older, her father trusted her with more responsibility and sometimes, when he was busy with his accounts, he let her make the paste all by herself. He had even been convinced to let her shape it into fruit: pears and cherries and apples, with a clove for a calyx. Her favourites were strawberries, which she'd roll in fine sugar to create a dimpled finish. He knew nothing about Liddy's experimentation with ingredients, however, and she knew he wouldn't be pleased. Any money she saved she invested straight back into the business, to fund the purchase of other fine ingredients. Her deception was profiting them well. Once she'd daringly added cherry liqueur to a batch of almond paste, much to the delight of Lady Goldman, who gobbled it up in a single evening, proclaiming it was the most wonderful thing she had ever tasted. Liddy promptly ordered a month's supply and did so every month thereafter. Whenever her father queried the arrival of these strange packages, she told him they were oils to perfume her bath water and creams to soften her skin. He was quick to accept the lie, satisfied that his daughter was making herself desirable. But if he'd looked more closely, he would have seen that her skin was no softer than before and carried the simple scent of soap and nothing more.

Liddy dropped the package soundlessly into the deep dark of her pocket, where it was quickly forgotten.

She hurried into the house and out of the cold, but before she had even slipped off her shoes, she heard her father's voice summoning her to the drawing room. Taking a deep breath, she pushed down the handle and entered the room.

'Ah, here she is at last. Tell us everything!' her mother cried joyfully, rushing over to greet her. Liddy knew her mother's delight had nothing whatsoever to do with her return, and everything to do with Jack Heathcote. She pulled Liddy's hands into hers and opened her eyes wide in anticipation. Liddy offered nothing.

'How is Jack?' her father prompted.

'A flirt and a philanderer at best,' she announced loudly.

There was a sharp intake of breath and Liddy's mother dropped her hands as if burned. 'Really, Madeleine!' she exclaimed, looking to her husband for support.

Liddy took the opportunity to move quickly away from her hysterics. She slid a book off her father's shelf and settled into a chair in the corner. It was where she went to escape. From the corner of her eye, she saw her father shake his head at her mother; the gesture was enough to return her to her chair, where she quietly pulled her knitting onto her lap. *Thankfully I am nothing like her*, she thought, opening her book.

'So, have you given him your answer?' Her father tried to sound nonchalant, with his eyes still focused on his newspaper.

Liddy hesitated, wondering if she should feign ignorance, but it would only prolong the inevitable and provoke them both further.

'Jack is not a serious man,' she protested. 'His eye is turned too easily by ribbons and curls, and his ear loves nothing more than the tune of a playful giggle—'

'What man doesn't?' interrupted her mother, quick as ever to come to Jack's defence.

Liddy rolled her eyes in despair. 'Mother, please!'

'He is from a fine, respectable family,' said her father evenly.

'So am I.'

Her father half-smiled and his voice softened, almost to a whisper. 'You are different from most other girls – more intelligent, more thoughtful and much more capable. Jack told me so himself.'

Liddy shook her head. She knew what Jack really thought – that she was a novelty, a challenge, someone who needed to be put in her place. She didn't bow to his every whim and so she must be conquered. Her father might be a successful businessman who had earned himself a good reputation, but they were still a world away from people like the Heathcotes. She wondered if his parents would even agree to such a union, but then he was incredibly spoiled. Whatever Jack Heathcote wanted, Jack Heathcote got.

'You will never have to struggle for anything,' said her father, interrupting her thoughts.

Maybe not for money, she thought. Her mother's heavy sighs grew louder and the gaps between them closer together, like the count between the thunder and the lightning – a storm was rolling in.

'I will not accept his invitation,' said Liddy firmly.

'You will never get a better one,' snapped her mother.

'I have no interest in Jack Heathcote or his whims,' she protested.

'This is not just about you,' she continued. 'There is a lot to be gained from this union. Can you not for one moment think of anyone but yourself?'

'I don't care what is to be gained. I will not be spending a single second with Jack Heathcote. I would rather contract cholera.' Liddy's voice was growing more defiant.

Her mother whitened, and her knitting slipped from her lap to her feet. 'Madeleine! What did I do to deserve such a selfish, stubborn child as you?' Her voice had taken on the rising pitch of helium gas. 'Less than a year separates you from Tabitha, and yet Matthew's proposal came three years ago, and we were all blessed with such a beautiful summer wedding. Why can't you be more like your cousin? So gentle and sweet.'

Tabitha was the daughter of her mother's sister. She had known her husband Matthew since they were both children and had always been in love with him. She had shared her feelings with Liddy behind closed doors and they'd giggled over the poems he'd written for her, which she'd kept locked in a little pink box. Tabitha had longed for marriage and, when the proposal had finally come, she cried with happiness and couldn't wait to announce it to the world.

'Tabitha would have married Matthew at sixteen if she could!' declared Liddy.

Her father loved his niece – her theatrical performances amused him greatly – and Liddy saw the sides of his mouth lift ever so slightly to form a secret smile at the mention of Tabitha. It was all the encouragement she needed and so she changed track, instead arguing that she should be able to choose not for convenience or money, or for any reason other than love. After all, wasn't that why Tabitha had chosen Matthew – because she loved him, and he loved her too? Liddy's vehement words somersaulted through the air, leaving her mother shaking and on the verge of tears; and, too late, Liddy realised that the smile had gone from her father's lips, leaving his face dark with anger. She finally bit her tongue.

Anxiously she waited for him to break the silence – for the sound of his words to heal the stricken air – but nothing came. Instead he paced quietly across the room, stopping when he reached the window. If it had been an open door, she was quite sure he would have continued walking, ousted from his home by the disobedience of his daughter and the hysterics of his wife. He stared into the darkness as though the answer to all his problems lay far beyond the confines of the house. He kept his face turned away from her, and she was grateful not to see it.

When the words came, they were not the ones she was expecting.

'I have allowed you too much freedom.' He sighed, as though this were all his fault and he was the one to blame. His disappointment was even worse than the anger Liddy had expected. 'Do you think I didn't realise what the honey and the orange-flower water were really for?'

Her heart sank. She should have known he would guess – he was not an easy man to deceive. At least the look of astonishment upon her mother's face told her that she had fooled one person in this house.

'Please, Father—' she began, but he held up his hand and Liddy fell into the safety of silence.

'Nobody takes that many baths.' He shook his head despairingly. 'I allowed you to continue your charade, and in many ways I admired your ingenuity, but I can see now that it was a mistake. *My* mistake.'

'Were there complaints?' she asked, suddenly appalled by her own transgression. She could not stand the thought that she had put her father's business in jeopardy.

Her father sighed. 'There were many complaints.'

Liddy felt her heart sink at the thought of her impulsive stupidity. How much damage had she caused?

'But the complaints weren't about your marchpane; they were about mine.'

Liddy frowned in confusion, waiting for him to explain.

'It seems our customers prefer their marchpane to taste of oranges.' He turned to her and smiled then. 'It is *your* recipes they want, not mine. That's why I left you alone in the kitchen; it had nothing to do with my paperwork.'

'But I thought—'

His smile faded. 'Yes, that's the problem: you thought ... And now your head is filled with magic and daydreams, from reading too many books. Because I gave you free rein, and it worked, you think you know everything and you can do as you like. But I'm afraid there is no choice now. We will no longer live with the shame of an unmarried daughter – the time has come for you to accept Jack Heathcote's invitation, and whatever may follow it. He is a worthy match and, with his support, the business will grow even more and you can keep creating marchpane. Unless you can think of another way to leave this house, then you will take what is being offered to you. I am your father, and my word is final.'

'Please,' she begged. 'My heart feels nothing for him. Nothing at all!'

'Then we must fetch a doctor,' said her mother, who until then had remained in watchful silence. 'A heart that feels nothing for a man such as Jack Heathcote must surely be suffering from some grave malady.' There was a quiet tut.

Panic-stricken, Liddy looked back at her father, desperate for some reprieve, but none was forthcoming.

'It is getting late,' said her father quietly. 'We have a large wedding order to prepare tomorrow, and you will need to rest.'

Thus dismissed, she ran from the room before her distress turned to tears; a sight that would surely have given her mother great satisfaction. For her this was a small triumph, but for Liddy it was the painful stab of defeat.

'A wedding!' harrumphed her mother. 'Chance would be a fine thing.'

Interlude

*T*he quiet is deep this evening. It arrives on tiptoes, but if you listen carefully enough you can still hear what it leaves behind. Fading light holds the wispy notes of birds as they finally settle to sleep. The water is calm, but it gently laps the shore. Her window is ajar and the scents of hibiscus and oleander drift in from the garden below. I listen for every small sound she makes: a gentle sigh, the shuffle of paper on the desk where she is sitting, the tapping that her feet make upon the wooden floorboards. She is restless, and uncertain; I can tell.

She is taking her time. She picks up her pen and dips it into a pot of the finest blue ink. After a moment's hesitation, she begins. She has written letters before, but something about this one is different. There is more thought and deliberation, as though she is hoping to impress the recipient, or perhaps convince them of something. Usually a letter is finished faster than it takes a pot to boil on the stove, or for the leaves to be swept from the path, but not this one. I can hear the scratches made by the nib as the words emerge across the thick vellum paper; it is like the quiet, purposeful rustle of a nesting mouse. There is a deftness, an assuredness to her stroke, but then abruptly she stops. The pen lingers a little too long on the page, leaving a dark clot of ink behind. I hear her tut as she lifts the pen from the paper and sets it down. It rolls along the desk and she is too slow to catch it before it clatters to the floor. Instead of stooping to search for it, she leans back in her chair and closes her eyes, exhausted by her own words. Fine lines pattern her pale marble face and speak of things lost. She lifts her hands and wipes them across her cheeks as though she could rub the lines away, but grief cannot be erased so easily. Her once-bright eyes are tarnished, dulled by anguish, and I can see the swift clenching and unclenching of muscles in her firm jaw. There are so many words to be spoken, but there is no one to hear them.

Eventually the quiet music of the garden interrupts her thoughts; she opens her eyes, reaches down to retrieve her pen and continues her task. When she has finished, she pushes her chair back to stand. It scrapes noisily against the floor, disturbing the now-resting birds, and a squabble and a flutter of annoyance come from the tree outside. Allowing the ink to dry, she walks across the room to the window and pushes it wide open. The air is still, warm and heavy with fragrance. There is little relief or, if there is, she cannot find it. She rests her elbows on the ledge and listens to the evening's quiet incantations, breathing it all in, wondering.

She looks more tired than usual – there is a strange transparency to her eyes, and the skin below them is a mottled lilac. Suddenly she splutters and then coughs, and then the cough turns into a spasm. Covering her mouth with the crook of her arm, she tries to muffle the sound, in case the Keymaker hears her. It is unlikely that he will come to see if she is well, but if he does, he could find the letter and she can't let that happen. She waits for the coughing to pass. For a while it sounds like there are peppercorns loose in her chest, but eventually the rattling settles. When it does so, she pulls the window sharply closed and drops the latch with a gentle thud.

Crossing back to the desk, she sees the little square of marzipan sitting there and holds it up between her fingers. She spends the next few minutes inspecting it carefully from all its different angles. To anybody else, it is quite ordinary and unremarkable – a table decoration, a birthday gift, a sweet treat – but to her it is so much more. When she puts it back on the desk there are small sugary granules still on her fingers and she brushes them away in mild irritation. Then she picks up the letter and wafts it in the air, like a white flag of surrender, before folding it and placing it carefully into a waiting envelope. She pauses. I can almost hear her mind whirring, as she wonders whether to read it one last time. Deciding against it, she reaches hastily for a taper. Like a drop of blood impressed with the image of a key, the wax safely seals the message within. The thrum of her heartbeat is soft and expectant, like the wings of a bird waiting for release, suddenly alive with possibility. She mutters something, half-prayer, half-spell, and I feel a strange flutter of hope.

Letter in hand, she leaves the room. All we can do now is wait.

CHAPTER 3

Forgotten Package

Usually Liddy slept quickly and without interruption, but that night she lay wide-eyed, finding little comfort in her bed. Her father's disappointed tone had chased away any hope of slumber. He hadn't given her an ultimatum – there was no need. He was her father, and if it were his will that she marry Jack Heathcote, then she had little choice other than to obey. She wished she could change his mind, make him see that Jack was no more in love with her than she was with him. His pursuit was no more than a game that had started when she opened the door for the cat all those years ago. She wouldn't be at all surprised if he planned to jilt her at the altar, just to bring shame on her and her family. The thought turned her mind into a tangle of misery and desperation. She pushed her head into the pillow so that no one would hear her muffled scream of frustration.

In the distance she heard the church bell chime twice, followed by the gekkering of a fox down in the dust yard. With a heavy sigh she kicked away the quilt and stepped onto the wooden floorboards in search of a distraction. At the bedroom door she quietly lifted the latch and crept onto the landing. She knew the house well enough to avoid all its creaks and groans and she trod where its betrayal was the quietest. She could easily find her way down to the kitchen, unheard, in the dark, where sometimes she'd start blanching almonds before the bread in the town's bakery had begun to rise.

Downstairs the hallway stretched out before her; it was filled with night-time shadows and Liddy flinched, mistaking them for silent intruders. She stifled a giggle at her foolish imagination and hurried towards the kitchen, where the welcoming smell of almonds lingered long after the marchpane had gone. After brewing a small pot of tea, she took her mug and sat at the table. The ticking of the hallway clock filled the whole house and she tried to match her breaths to its rhythm, so steady and constant, hoping it would be enough to summon the sleep she wanted.

As she sat there, her thoughts returned once more to Jack Heathcote. Was she overreacting? Was the idea of marrying him so utterly terrible? After all, he had wealth, status and a face that wasn't displeasing to the eye. But he had another side too – arrogant and over-confident; he saw women as toys, playthings for his own amusement. She knew that the woman from the sugar banquet was just one of many, and Jack would soon grow tired of her and move on to the next. Liddy held his interest simply because she didn't return it. It was a game, and she was a trophy. If he caught her, then he would have won and the game would be over. Maybe that was the answer – to surrender – but the thought of it nearly made her choke on her tea.

Her mother had been right about one thing: there were no other offers, and no other interest. When she had first run errands, the barrow-boys in the marketplace would holler and whistle as she hurried past, but she quickened her pace and never once turned her face to theirs. She could tell you the colour of their shoes, but not of their eyes. Once, when a boy had dared to block her way, she had stamped so hard on his foot that he'd yowled in pain. Impatience soon turned their desire to mockery, and their taunts followed her from stall to stall, until finally their voices fell silent and they didn't call her anything at all. To them, and to everyone else, she had become invisible. Perhaps Jack Heathcote's wretched sugar queen had been right and she was merely the marchpane girl after all – nothing more and nothing less.

To quieten her mind, she lit a lamp and began to search for the utensils she needed to make the first batch of marchpane: the pestle and mortar, the stirring spoon, several large baking pans and cooking parchment, a mixing bowl and a rolling pin. From the shelf she took down a sack of almonds, a bag of sugar. Hidden right at the back of the cupboard she found her stash of honey and orange-blossom water. Then she waited for the kettle to finish warming on the stove. Working through the night meant that her father would wake to find the wedding order already packaged and waiting, and perhaps it would be enough to make up for her disobedience.

Liddy worked quickly, grinding and mixing and stirring and rolling. Then she carefully cut out the dough, moulding shapes that she thought lovers would appreciate: hearts, birds, strawberries and rose petals folded around one another. More often than not, she left the shapes to harden by themselves, but she liked the way the heat turned them into crispy bites with a delicious chewy centre, and so today she placed them on the parchment paper and lifted the baking tray into the oven. Washing her hands, she gazed up through the high window, glimpsing the sky between the roofs, a deep midnight blue, yet sleep still felt so very far away.

A sound from the hallway, sudden and muffled, made her turn. Liddy crossed the kitchen and peered into the shadows. It took a few moments for her eyes to adjust to the gloom, and then she noticed a tall shape standing by the door. She could make out the curved rims of several hats and the backs of long cloaks, like a group of men huddled in conspiracy. Not daring to breathe, she watched and waited, but they remained motionless, lifeless. Suddenly a burst of mirth escaped from her mouth as she realised what she was looking at. She quickly clamped both hands firmly over her mouth before she alerted the whole house. Her mind had played another trick on her, and what she had feared to be some sort of espionage was nothing more than an innocuous coat-stand. Perhaps she was sleepier than she thought. But what of the sound she had heard? Probably just a mouse in the wall, the scavenger fox she had heard earlier or the footsteps of somebody passing by outside.

As though a cloud had floated away, a moonbeam suddenly shone though the fanlight, illuminating the coat-stand perfectly, and her own coat on top. It brought with it a trickle of memory, a whisper. The package!

In four strides she had reached the stand and was rummaging through her coat pockets. She felt her finger-tips brush against the small object and she quickly lifted it out. Earlier she had dismissed it as another delivery of honey or orange-blossom water, but now she could see her mistake – it was much too small to be either of those things. Moving towards the stairs, she sat and read her name again, then, compelled by some strange force, she lifted it to her nose and inhaled. At first she detected nothing more than the faint smell of damp, as though the package had been left in the rain – perhaps that explained why the paper was so damaged and torn at the edges. Inhaling again as deeply as she could, she caught the unmistakeable scent of pine trees; of air so clean it made her lungs sparkle; of crisp snow and resinous rain; of hibiscus and violets. Lowering the package, she tried to unpick the knot first with her fingers and then with her teeth, but it was as tight as a clenched knuckle. Just as she was about to give up and go in search of a kitchen knife, she felt the frayed string begin to loosen its hold.

Carefully, so as not to cause any further damage, she unwrapped the paper, revealing a light wooden box. With growing curiosity, she unfastened the little metal clasp and lifted the lid. The first thing she saw was a plain white envelope sealed with an oval of red wax. How old-fashioned! Pressed into the middle was the image of a key. But it was what she saw when she lifted the letter that intrigued her more. At first she couldn't make sense of the solitary object beneath; it had a misshapen and bulbous appearance, like the nose of a drunkard severed from his face in a tavern brawl. Peering closer, she realised it was a root or some kind of bulb. It felt as silky as onion skin in the palm of her hand. As she closed her fingers around it, an image emerged: a crumbling house surrounded by a garden in full flourish, despite the gently falling snow. Flowers bloomed down towards the water's edge and she saw that the house and the garden stood in the middle of a great lake. It reminded her of a beautiful cake decoration, or one of those scenes captured for ever inside a snow globe. She thought there was a flicker of movement in one of the upper windows. An uneasy feeling crept over her and she felt as if she was being watched. Then she heard a voice calling her name, over and over again.

When she opened her eyes, Liddy was no longer sitting on the stairs in the dark; she was back in her bed. Her whole body ached, and her head felt too heavy to leave the pillow. Reaching up, she felt a damp flannel pressed against her forehead and then she remembered.

'The marchpane!' she mumbled in dismay. The batches she had left in the oven would have burned to a crisp by now.

She saw her mother's face swimming in front of her. 'She's awake! Edward, come quick,' she cried through the open door. Her words brought the sound of running feet, and her father appeared. They both clutched her hands and stared at her with sad, red-rimmed eyes.

'The marchpane!' repeated Liddy, trying to make them understand.

'Shh, it's okay,' her mother said, turning the flannel and clasping Liddy's hand even more tightly.

Her parents explained that in the early morning an acrid burning smell had roused them from sleep – a smell that still lingered in the walls and the curtains and the bed sheets. Driven from their beds, they had found her lying at the bottom of the stairs and believed she must have stumbled and fallen in the night. A doctor confirmed there were no broken bones, but that she had probably suffered mild concussion. Liddy had slept for two days. By the time she had been discovered, the marchpane had resembled lumps of charcoal and the scorch marks were impossible to scrub from the baking pans. Everything had to be thrown away and new utensils bought.

CHAPTER 4

Lost Doll

The following Saturday, her cousin Tabby arrived in her usual bustle of ruffles and ribbons. The scent of roses exploded into the air as soon as she bounced herself onto the bed. Liddy loved her cousin like a sister, but they couldn't be more different in both appearance and temperament. Liddy's hair was dark as a raven's wing, whereas Tabby's was the warm yellow of a caged canary. When she grew angry, Liddy cawed and rattled from the rooftops, whereas Tabby was more inclined to sit quietly and warble in the corner. She had a simple sweetness about her and sometimes Liddy wished she herself could accept everything the way her cousin did; it would make things so much easier. Tabby was giggly enough to delight, yet demure enough to reassure, and it was no surprise that she had received a marriage proposal by her eighteenth birthday. A year later she had married Matthew Clements, who was a kind, but rather dull man, who made his living as a tailor on the high street. More than two years had passed, and still Tabby seemed as infatuated with him as ever.

'So, I heard there's going to be another wedding,' said Tabby, fluttering her long eyelashes at Liddy and then, without waiting for confirmation, she flung her arms around her in excitement. 'Jack is such a dish. I simply cannot wait!'

'You sound just like Mother,' snapped Liddy, making no attempt to hide her scowl. 'He hasn't even proposed yet.'

'Oh, but he will – I am absolutely sure of that.' Tabby rolled her eyes in mock despair. 'How many acquaintance cards has he sent you? You must have dozens of them by now. I've still got the *one* Matthew sent me.' She held up a single finger for emphasis.

'They make me feel like a hunted animal,' said Liddy with a grimace. '"My little creature" this and "your devoted pursuer" that.'

'But it's so much fun to be chased,' replied Tabby, hopping down from the bed. 'Where do you keep all Jack's cards? You *do keep* his cards, don't you?' she said accusingly.

Liddy waved her cousin towards the dressing table and flopped back onto the bed. After some searching, Tabby finally lifted a piece a paper, cleared her throat and began to read from it:

Dear Ms Harchwood,

I would like to invite you to the House of Sorrowing Stars, where you will be a guest for as long as you choose to remain. In return, I request only that you make your delicious marchpane. Our shelves are well stocked, and the garden is plentiful. Anything else you might need can be found in the village. I hope that being here will bring you much happiness and open your mind to new possibilities. Our guests are usually asked to bring three taglocks with them, but in your case this will not be necessary; you need only bring yourself. In the box you will also find a bulb. Please plant this as soon as possible and, once the shoot appears, you must depart immediately. There will be someone ready to meet you when you arrive. I look forward to meeting you.

Regards,

Vivienne Castellini

Tabby looked up, in scrunched-nose confusion. 'This isn't from Jack.'

Liddy was just as confused as Tabby. 'Where did you get that?'

'Over there,' she said, pointing towards the dressing table.

Next to Liddy's hairbrush sat the strange package, still half-wrapped. Snatching the letter from her cousin's grasp, Liddy slowly read the words herself, trying to make sense of them. She had never heard of the House of Sorrowing Stars, and the name Vivienne Castellini sounded equally unfamiliar. She checked again to make sure she was the intended recipient and saw her name clearly written at the top, just as her cousin had read it to her. Halfway down, her eyes faltered. There was a thick blot of ink, which made the word 'happiness' blurred, as though the writer had thought too long about what to write. What other word could she have intended? The alpine scent of mountains overwhelmed her then, as it had done the night she'd fainted on the stairs. Quietly she folded the letter over and placed it back into the box with the strange bulb. Then she closed the lid.

'Who is Vivienne Castellini?' asked Tabitha.

'I have no idea, Tabby Cat, but it doesn't matter.' A smile slowly spread across Liddy's face. 'I think I have just found a way to leave this house without marrying Jack Heathcote.'

Tabitha's eyes widened as she realised what Liddy was suggesting. 'What? Why on earth would you ever consider accepting this invitation instead of Jack's? His is the only one that matters.'

'To who – my mother?' scoffed Liddy. 'Besides, I do not love Jack – I don't even like him.'

'But why not? He is *so* handsome.' Tabby beamed at the thought of him. 'And rich.'

'What pleases the eye doesn't always please the heart,' Liddy replied. 'Besides, don't you remember what happened to poor Charlotte Swan? She thought they were to be married and then Jack broke it all off without a word: no apology, no explanation, nothing. She hasn't been the same since.'

Tabby's face crumpled. Charlotte Swan had been a gentle, pretty little thing; sweet as sherbet and bright as a nut. Now, whenever they saw her, she kept her head to the ground and quickened her pace. Whatever rumours Jack Heathcote had spread, it meant that all the men avoided her like the plague. The nut had been crushed and only the shell remained.

'But what will I do without you!' Tabitha sounded close to tears.

Liddy laughed and nodded at the rounded swell of her cousin's stomach. 'I think you will have plenty to do, soon enough.'

The reminder soothed Tabby at once and she began to stroke her hand over the bulging fabric of her dress.

'Besides, I'm dreaming. I don't even know where this house is, and without a map it would be impossible to find,' said Liddy, feeling the weight of disappointment. She had already checked and, aside from the bulb and the letter, the box was empty.

'Of course you know where it is – don't you remember?' asked Tabby, sinking back onto the bed.

Liddy frowned. 'Remember what?'

'When I was about five or six I was so ill that I nearly died. Mother said it was like someone had tied my lungs into knots, and I lay in bed for weeks, afraid to breathe.'

'Yes, of course I remember,' replied Liddy, feeling solemn at the memory of her parents' frightful whispers and her aunt's tearful sobs. Nobody knew whether to call a doctor or a coffin-maker.

'But do you remember what happened after that?'

'You got better,' replied Liddy, glad to have been pulled away from the horror of what might have been.

'Eventually I did, but as part of my recuperation the doctors told my father to take me away from the town – away from the smoky factories and the terrible stink of the river. They described a place far from here at the foot of the mountains, where the air was so pure and clear that it would rinse my lungs clean again. We were there for nearly a month and, when we came back, I could breathe again without wheezing or chest pain. They said it was a miracle.'

Liddy shook her head, 'I don't remember you going on a trip.'

Tabby looked at her in disbelief. 'It wasn't only me who went – we all did: me, you, Mother and Father, Auntie Catherine and Uncle Edward. How can you not remember? Especially after what happened with that doll. I thought it would scar you for life.'

'What doll?' Nothing of what her cousin was telling Liddy seemed at all familiar.

'The doll you begged your father to buy for you. It was in the window of a dusty old shop and you refused to move until he went inside and came back out, holding it in his hand. It was such a beautiful doll and I wanted her too, but not as much as you did. You stamped your feet until your father threw his arms up in the air in defeat and went inside to buy it for you.'

A memory began to take shape in Liddy's mind, but just as she reached for it, it slipped away again. 'Did it have a porcelain face?'

'So you do remember!' said Tabby, clapping her hands together. 'Yes, that's right, a porcelain face and big green eyes. It was her hair I loved most – all those perfect shiny ringlets, stuffed full of blossoms and feathers. And she wore a dress to rival any one of mine.'

'It was blue, wasn't it?' said Liddy, suddenly seeing the colour in her mind.

'You spent days crying after you lost her. I thought you would never stop. Even when Uncle Edward tried to cheer you up, by buying you another one, you just threw it to the ground in a fit of temper and told him to bring the other one back.'

Liddy couldn't imagine herself ever crying over a lost doll and she could only remember fragments of the one her cousin so vividly described to her.

'I don't really remember the doll, never mind losing it,' she admitted.

'Isn't it strange that I remember it all, and it wasn't even my doll? Well, they say trauma can make you forget things,' she said, laughing. 'We honestly didn't think you'd come home without it.'

'I don't understand,' said Liddy. 'What has losing a doll all those years ago got to do with this letter?'

Tabby stared at her. 'Because you lost your doll by the Lake of Sorrowing Stars, and that's the same name as the house that's mentioned in that letter. Don't you see? It might have been a long time ago, but you have been to the area before. We all have.'

'What else do you remember – about the place, I mean?' asked Liddy, urgent for more answers. 'Have you ever heard of the House of Sorrowing Stars?'

Tabby nodded. 'Father told me about it: a house in the middle of the lake. He said it was a place where people go to say goodbye to the souls of their loved ones. He talked about a room filled with sad stories, and of flowers that shone so brightly they could chase away the dark, but you know my father – if you believe anything he says, then you might as well believe the moon is made of cheese, and that witches fly over roofs on their broomsticks.'

'But how does this Vivienne' – Liddy paused and scanned the letter – 'Castellini know about my marchpane? And what are taglocks?' She let the strangeness of it all settle.

Tabby looked at her and smiled. 'I don't know, but perhaps you'll find out.'

CHAPTER 5

Lady Chamberlain

The following day brought with it low, grey skies and the threat of rain. Liddy had been busy in the kitchen all morning helping her father make marchpane for Lady Chamberlain's party. There was so much sweetness in the air that it clung to her hair and she could smell it on her hands as she boxed up square after square, each one so bright and yellow that they reminded her of slices of sunshine.

As afternoon approached, the rain finally dwindled, leaving behind a fine drizzle in the air, the kind that made delicate patterns wherever it landed. Pulling on their coats, Liddy and her father stepped out of the house and made their way through the streets. Soon they were leaving the brickwork and the chimneypots, and the rabble and chaos of the town, far behind. On such walks Liddy's father would take the opportunity to light his pipe, away from the complaints of her mother. She loathed him smoking in the house, save for the occasional cigar at Christmas. Of course he could do as he pleased – it was his house, after all – but because his ears sought peace, he kept the pipe deep in his pocket. Once outside, he was free to enjoy it at his leisure, and it gave him such an enormous sense of relief to do so.

Just past the cemetery the street narrowed into a leafy lane and about half a mile after that was the turnstile. It was here that the lane dwindled into a mossy track, more suited to cows than carts. A short stroll was all it took for the world to shift. The air no longer swirled with filth and smoke, and the only sound came from the birds tucked deep into the hedgerows. In less than two miles they would reach the old sprawling house and its single occupant.

Beyond the swinging iron gate they began their walk up the long driveway towards Lady Chamberlain's house, which wound its way between the rhododendrons and the large, looming trees. This part of the journey seemed to take her twice as long as any other because Liddy dawdled behind, lost in a dream or a fairy tale. But where the shadows patterned the ground and the leaves grew thicker, she found herself watching for the gleaming eyes of a hungry wolf or the gnarled hand of a cloaked woman who might reach out and pull her in. Her father pretended to hurry her, but really he didn't mind; her child-like ways amused him – a reminder that she was still his little girl.

Still, her feet carried Liddy faster then, and they only slowed once the house came into view, with its ivy-scribbled walls and its many hidden windows, all but one shuttered against the light.

The house had been undeniably neglected over the years, but the same could not be said for the garden, which was pruned to perfection. Due to its enormous size, several gardeners were employed to mow and clip and sweep away the debris. The borders were always bursting with colour and scent, and Liddy felt certain that people would pay an admittance fee just for a glimpse of the roses, even in autumn.

The interior of the house was a different story. It always smelled the same: dank and stale with disuse. Each room was cluttered with the remains of a life no longer lived, and the objects within them had all become faded relics coated with dust. Liddy's father moved from room to room, unlatching all the shutters to let in the smells and sounds of the outside world.

Lady Chamberlain was the only person to inhabit this ruin. She was an ethereal wisp of a woman, who was known for hosting extravagant parties that she herself never attended. From her bed upstairs she would lie with her eyes closed and listen to the mingling voices of her guests below. She could hear them chattering on the lawn like birds. It seemed such a strange comfort, but it was a comfort, nonetheless. Lady Chamberlain insisted that there couldn't be a party without marchpane, and so Liddy and her father would arrive before anyone else, to prepare the table. She left her father piling pyramids of sticky edible jewels onto plates, while she climbed the stairs to Lady Chamberlain's bedroom. Pushing open the door, she was always a little hesitant, never knowing if she would find her still breathing or vanished with the fae.

Lady Chamberlain was lying in bed today, her spindle-thin arms flat above the counterpane and her hair swirling around her like snow crystals ready to dissolve. Her eyes were closed, but to her relief, Liddy could see the gentle rise and fall of her chest; she was just sleeping. Well over ten years had passed since Liddy first met her. From that first meeting she remembered Lady Chamberlain's cherry-red lips and bright brown eyes, and the way her hair fell in midnight waves down her back, but age had since stripped her of all colour. When she spoke, the words seemed to dance off her tongue, and sometimes they sounded so strange that Liddy couldn't tell what she was saying. She knew she had come from a faraway place, but every time she asked her about it, Lady Chamberlain would simply sigh heavily and say that marriage had meant leaving behind more than merely her name. Ten years after their wedding her husband had died from a fever, leaving her all alone in a rambling house that she had never wanted. Liddy wondered why she didn't return to her faraway place, but whenever she mentioned it, Lady Chamberlain turned away and never offered any answer. *Perhaps it is too far away*, Liddy thought.

She replaced the vase of wilted flowers with the ones she'd picked in the garden, and Lady Chamberlain opened her eyes and smiled at the sight of the fresh flowers. She loved bluebells most of all, but they had long since died away, and so today Liddy had brought asters instead.

'The garden is especially beautiful today after the rain,' said Liddy.

'The nests will need clearing birds have been busy nesting,' said Lady Chamberlain in a tiny whisper.

She pointed a shaky finger outside to the bird-box on the tree. It was so old that it should have been thrown away years ago. Its roof was falling to pieces, and its walls were lopsided and cracked, but still the birds came.

She cleared her throat and spoke again, more loudly now. 'What time is it?'

'A little after five.'

'Ah.' She fell back against her pillow. Time exhausted her.

'We've brought your marchpane,' said Liddy. 'Shall I read to you a little, until the guests arrive?'

Lady Chamberlain's face softened and she gave a trembly nod. It was their usual routine.

Walking to the bookshelf, Liddy tilted her head to read the spines, even though she knew them all by heart. Finally she slipped a poetry collection from the shelf and sat down next to the bed. She read aloud about places of silence and loss and enchantment; about birds and water and shadows, both real and imagined; of hearts broken and then made whole again. Her father was right: books filled her head with magic and daydreams, and she loved them for it. Sometimes it seemed as though Lady Chamberlain had fallen back to sleep, but just as Liddy was ready to close the book, she would hear her voice urging her to continue. Time passed unnoticed and the pink light deepened to mauve, until Liddy strained to see the words on the page. Defeated by the dark, she lit the lamp and the bright flare made them both squint for a moment.

Through the open window, Liddy heard voices drifting up from the path; the guests were starting to arrive.

'Shall I close the window?' she asked, already moving towards it.

'No, not yet,' Lady Chamberlain cried out in a little panicked voice.

'But there is a chill in the air. You will catch a cold,' protested Liddy, glancing at her lying there, so frail and fragile.

'Please – not yet,' she repeated.

Liddy sighed and, as a compromise, she gently lifted the woman's arms and tucked them under the covers.

'Will you help me get ready for my party now?' asked Lady Chamberlain, her eyes glistening.

'Of course.'

Liddy smiled sadly and opened the bedside drawer. One by one she took out the items within – a hairbrush, a lipstick, powder and rouge – and laid them all on the bed.

First, she ran the hairbrush through the wilted bouquet of her hair. Then she pressed the powder to her face, but it fell like flour into the lines and cracks of her skin. Even her sunken cheeks couldn't be saved by the sweep of pink that Liddy left there. The thin red slice of her mouth looked out of place. Liddy had done this countless times before, but each time it left her feeling that little bit emptier. When she had finished, she took the bottle of perfume from the shelf and sprayed its elegance into the room, inviting the past to join them.

'Wouldn't you rather be downstairs with everyone else?' Liddy asked every time.

Lady Chamberlain's reply was always the same. 'No, I'd rather be somewhere else entirely.' Then she would gaze longingly at the garden, as though it was all she had left.

'Why do you have these parties, if you want to be somewhere else?'

Lady Chamberlain thought for a moment. 'I like to hear the sound of happiness, even if it's not my own.'

Liddy often wondered what thoughts occupied her in those long evenings filled with distant laughter and music. Perhaps it was the home she had left behind, or the husband she had learned to live without, or the garden she could only glimpse through the window. When a guest enquired about their missing host, they were always given the same answer: *Unfortunately Lady Chamberlain is not well enough to join you this evening, but she very much hopes that you enjoy the party,* and before long they stopped asking; instead they filled their mouths with marchpane and bubbles and their happiness echoed through the house.

Before leaving home, Liddy had slipped the strange bulb into the pocket of her coat, in the hope that Lady Chamberlain could solve its puzzle. Surely someone with such a beautiful garden would be able to tell her what sort of flower was waiting to unfold. But when she looked up to ask her, she had closed her eyes again. As Liddy quietly scooped up the make-up from the bed, Lady Chamberlain turned and opened her eyes.

'I thought you were sleeping,' said Liddy softly, returning the items to the drawer.

'Oh, I've been sleeping for years,' she murmured.

'I have something to show you,' said Liddy, pulling out the bulb and holding it up for them both to see. 'I was hoping you could tell me what this is.'

'Where did you get that?' Her words were wingbeat fast and she lifted her head, suddenly wide awake.

'It was left in a package on my doorstep,' replied Liddy suddenly wary. She had never seen Lady Chamberlain so alive. Her eyes so full of sparkle.

She was sitting upright, alert, and she reached out to take the bulb from her. Liddy obliged and unfurled her fingers, letting it roll into her cupped palm. For a moment Lady Chamberlain just sat staring at it in wonder, as though it was a rare treasure that had been lost for hundreds of years.

After a moment Liddy spoke. 'There was a letter with it, inviting me to the House—'

'Of Sorrowing Stars,' Lady Chamberlain replied, before falling silent once more.

'Yes, but I don't understand,' Liddy continued.

'Mira,' she whispered, finally pulling her gaze from the bulb and looking at Liddy with round, excited eyes. 'It's Fate that's inviting you there.'

'What are the sorrowing stars?'

Lady Chamberlain gave a little shake of her palm, a signal for Liddy to take back the bulb.

'Plant this and you will see.'

Then she fell back against the pillows, as though the weight of the small bulb was too much. She reached for Liddy's hand and bit her lip, the movement leaving behind a smudge of red on her front tooth. Her touch had a finality to it, making Liddy catch and hold her breath. She wondered if this would be the last time they saw each other. She wished some people could last for ever.

'Gardeners have the most sensitive souls,' Lady Chamberlain said wistfully. 'It takes such kindness and patience to grow even a single flower. Now imagine a garden that's full of them.'

'Yes, it must take a lot of dedication.'

Lady Chamberlain nodded her head. 'And a loving heart.'

Liddy laughed and began searching the drawer for the bottle of rosewater and a cloth. 'Now then, I think it's about time we got all this cleaned off your face.'

'No,' said Lady Chamberlain, tightening her grip on Liddy's hand. 'Leave it for tonight. You never know who I might meet in my dreams.'

Liddy heard her name being called from downstairs then and, with it, her father's impatience.

'I must go,' she said, quickly crossing the room to close the window; this time there was no protest.

'Take this,' said Lady Chamberlain, holding out the poetry collection she had been reading from. 'It is a long way to the House of Sorrowing Stars, and you will need a good friend to keep you company.'

'Thank you,' Liddy said, before leaning over and softly kissing her forehead. The skin was paper-thin and made her want to cry.

'Sometimes the person you end up with is not the person you love most in the world. I remember the most beautiful garden, and that is where you will find my story.'

Liddy wondered if her words were a warning against marrying Jack Heathcote, but something about the way she'd spoken them, and the dark look in her eyes, made her think that she wasn't talking about Liddy at all.

Downstairs her father was waiting for her, tapping his foot in a display of frustration. In his hand he held a lantern, ready to chase away the darkness and the wolves that might be waiting to pounce. He opened the door and together they stepped into the night.

CHAPTER 6

Leaving

Arriving home that night, Liddy found her mind swirling with thoughts of the House of Sorrowing Stars, and she was more determined than ever to find her way there. She took a little brown pot, filled it with earth and pushed the bulb deep inside.

For days nothing happened. Each morning when she woke, the earth was undisturbed and there seemed to be nothing stirring beneath. She worried that she was watering it too much, or perhaps too little. Maybe it needed the cool dark of a cupboard instead of the bright light of a window, or richer soil with more nutrients. Waiting was so frustrating; she kept herself hidden in her room, pretending to be writing a reply to Jack, when really she was contemplating her escape. Her mother couldn't understand why a simple *yes* was taking so long, but Liddy explained, through gritted teeth, that it wasn't a *simple yes*; first she had to apologise for her rudeness and hope Jack would forgive her for it. Her mother was satisfied after that and left her alone.

Of course Liddy was writing no such thing. She hadn't picked up a pen in days and had no intention of doing so. The invitation had told her to leave as soon as the shoot appeared, and day after day she stared at the pot, willing the bulb to grow before it was too late and her deception was uncovered. But what would she do when the tip eventually pushed its way through the soil? She couldn't simply pack a bag and waltz out of the front door – not unless it was on the arm of Jack Heathcote. Would it be best to leave at first light? No, the risk of finding her father already at work in the kitchen was too great. Perhaps in the middle of the night then, but the darkness could scare just as easily as it could shield. Somehow she had to find that time in between. The impossibility of it all kept her awake. What she needed was a plan.

At breakfast she asked her father about the mountain trip they'd taken with Tabby. He chatted leisurely, letting his egg go cold; by the time the plates had been cleared away Liddy knew where she would find the House of Sorrowing Stars. Lady Chamberlain was right – it was going to be a long journey.

On the ninth day Liddy gave a little squeal of excitement because finally, there in the earth, was the tip of a pale shoot. It looked like a baby's first tooth, a small and white nub, barely there at all. *Once the shoot appears . . .* the invitation had said, and Liddy's excitement quickly turned to nerves.

That day she worked side by side with her father in the kitchen, and the entire time she wanted to confess her plan to him, but she knew that he wouldn't understand. Instead she talked of Lady Chamberlain and how lonely she seemed. She didn't mention a single word about leaving; she had already disappointed him enough and didn't want to see the look in his eyes when she did it again. Jack Heathcote's name was mentioned more and more and, each time she heard it, she moved closer to the door.

Liddy willed the clock to stop, but its incessant ticking filled the house, like the tut-tut-tut of an angry schoolmaster. It knew her secret and chastised her for it. The need to leave, and the fear of doing so, overwhelmed her and at supper she pushed her plate away, untouched. Thinking that she was worried about Jack refusing her apology, her mother softened her eyes and offered words of comfort, but when her father looked at Liddy, it was with much wiser eyes, as though he knew the truth.

That night Liddy barely slept. Her mind was a somersault of thoughts, and she tumbled in and out of flickering dreams. Whenever she opened her eyes, she saw the pot with its tiny shoot, now like a drop of snow upon the dark earth. Outside came the familiar cry of a fox and she wondered if it had made its home in one of the dark, grimy alleys that ran through the town. When she opened her eyes again, it was to a watery grey sky and she knew it was almost time.

Dressing quietly, she pulled out her packed case from under the bed, picked up the pot and stepped into the hallway. As she passed her parents' room the door was ajar and through the gap she could see the shape of her mother lying under the covers, straight and unmoving, her face gentle in sleep. Liddy was suddenly overcome with a feeling of such tenderness that it made her waver on the threshold. The door was not wide enough to reveal the bulk of her father, and Liddy was glad; seeing him would have been enough to make her climb back into her warm bed, all foolish notions of running away buried beneath the blankets. But she reminded herself that it was one thing to be loved – quite another to be understood. Marrying Jack Heathcote wasn't what she wanted. She dropped her head and tiptoed down the stairs careful to avoid the creaks of the floorboards.

At the front door she set down her case and the pot and pulled her coat and scarf from its hook. Early dawn in the town always cast a cold and feeble light. Before she had fastened her buttons, a familiar voice surprised her from the dark.

'You must tell me her favourite books before you go.'

She couldn't see him, but she knew her father was standing there in the gloom.

'Whose favourite books?' she asked nervously over the thrum of her heart.

'Lady Chamberlain's.'

Liddy heard him move, bringing the sweet waft of marchpane closer.

'I will need to know which ones to read to her while you're gone.'

Her father emerged from the darkness, then pulled her into his arms and held her there for a long, long time.

'How did you know?' she asked quietly, against the warmth of his shoulder.

'Tabitha.'

Liddy rolled her eyes and laughed. She should have known better than to trust her cousin. She loved her dearly, but Tabby was too much of a blabbermouth ever to keep a secret.

'And then all those questions about a trip we'd taken so many years ago.'

'Does Mother know?' she asked, pulling away in alarm.

'Your mother only wants to know about two things: Jack Heathcote and weddings.' He arched his eyebrows. 'Besides, Tabitha spoke to me in confidence.'

At least she had some discretion, thought Liddy as she stifled a giggle in her sleeve and cast her eyes furtively up the stairs, hoping the sound had not woken her mother. 'I left her a letter – Tabitha, I mean; it's on my dressing table: will you make sure that she gets it? I wanted to say goodbye, but—'

'Of course. Goodbyes are always difficult.' Liddy's father dropped a kiss on the top of her head, then held up a small white envelope. 'Inside is a ticket for the boat train, and some money. It will get you to the place you want to go.'

'But why?' asked Liddy in disbelief. 'What made you change your mind?'

He sighed. 'A father should want his daughter to be happy. I tried to convince myself that marrying Jack would give you that happiness, but deep down I knew it wouldn't. A future with him would bring nothing but misery, and I was wrong to think otherwise. I see that now.'

'I—' Liddy faltered, overcome with a rush of gratitude, and flung herself back into his arms.

'Besides, it is better to find out what's in a person's heart, not in their pocket.' He took on a pretend stern voice, repeating his words from days ago. 'I am your father, and my word is final.' What was meant to be a laugh sounded more like a small sob. Liddy held him a little tighter.

Although she had some small savings of her own, she had no idea if it would have been enough to reach the House of Sorrowing Stars, or what she would do for money once she got there. Liddy tucked the envelope away safely in her pocket and it gave her comfort to know it was there. Her father tried to insist on accompanying her to the station, but she shook her head in refusal. If her mother woke to find them both gone, then she would accuse him of being complicit in her escape. More importantly, if he went any further with her, then she might not be brave enough to continue without him.

CHAPTER 7

The House of Sorrowing Stars

The port was only a short bus ride from the town. When Liddy was a child, her father used to take her there to feed the fish and watch the boats come and go. She'd catch him staring dreamily at the larger vessels and would half-listen as he talked of how, one day, they'd set sail for distant shores, loaded with nothing but their marchpane. Liddy tried to push the guilt from her mind now, knowing that without Jack Heathcote, her father's dream would never be realised.

Between the chimes of one bell and the other, the rooks in the rafters had been replaced with a sky full of squawking gulls, and then there was nothing to see but boats. Gathering her things, she waited until the doors opened and then alighted from the bus into the chaos and rabble below. The bracing, briny air whipped strands of her hair across her face, making it almost impossible to see. She jostled her way to the office, where she joined the back of a long queue. She didn't mind the wait; it gave her time to tidy her hair back into its pins. When her turn finally came, she showed her ticket to the guard, who quickly waved her towards a large boat at the far end of the dock – and, just like that, she was through. *It was all so easy*, she thought, striding aboard with a new-found confidence.

Almost as soon as they departed, however, Liddy was seized by such a terrible and unexpected feeling of nausea. She wasn't the only one whose stomach churned like the waves. Many of the passengers sat with paper bags held open at their mouths, and retching could be heard from the top deck. It was there that Liddy stayed, huddled deep in her coat, her wind-stung eyes fixed to the horizon. It went a little way towards quelling the rising sickness.

After that ordeal the steady rhythm of the train was an absolute delight. She quickly settled into her carriage, excited to think she was one step closer to finding the House of Sorrowing Stars. She wondered what life would be like when she got there. She imagined the house had a huge kitchen to explore, with so many utensils she'd be spoilt for choice. She relished the idea of people discovering her marchpane for the first time and telling others all about it. How the Harchwood name would soon be talked about in wider circles – synonymous with expertise and excellence.

Sitting with her face against the window, she smiled, watching the crowded blocks of buildings dwindle away until there was nothing left but stretches of bright emerald green. She considered the enormity of what she was doing – a young girl, companionless and travelling so far – yet it gave her a feeling of release and relief. Her breath had left behind a small mist on the window and she traced the word *freedom* into it with her fingertip. Even her hair had unravelled from its pins and now spread across her shoulders. The train sped under bridges and through tunnels, out into the dazzle of sunlight, before plunging back into the dark. There were snatches of light and gulps of gloom until the fields dipped into valleys and the hills rose higher, turning into snow-dusted mountains. Pine trees grew in endless clusters, and the forests looked so deep and dark that a person might never find their way back out again. *What mysteries do they keep?* she wondered, and her excitement grew.

Finally the train began to slow and gave one last exasperated sigh before coming to rest at a small station. Stepping onto the unfamiliar platform, Liddy was seized by doubt. *What am I doing here?* Passengers hurried past, throwing themselves into the welcoming arms of their loved ones, but there was no one waiting for Liddy and the feeling of uncertainty grew. For a moment she wanted to climb back onto the train and return to her life with her family, but instead she took a deep breath and pushed all thoughts of regret from her mind – it wasn't only her family who would be waiting for her if she turned back.

The doors closed behind her and the train rattled back along the track. *It's too late to change my mind now*, she thought, watching it disappear through the trees with a hiss of steam. As it departed, so too did all the people, and Liddy was standing completely alone on the platform. An attempt to find a guard or a porter proved futile, and the ticket office was nothing more than a shuttered old cabin, with no way of telling when, or even if, it would be open.

On the other side of the platform Liddy noticed a track running in the opposite direction, where a single carriage was waiting. It had the shape and shine of an orange, and it hung from an overhead cable. The upper half was made entirely of glass, and beneath it swirled a trail of painted stars and moons in all their different phases. *It needs a fresh coat of paint*, she thought.

The doors were open and inviting, and written above them in large letters were the words 'The House of Sorrowing Stars'. Liddy peered over her shoulder, hoping to find someone who could tell her what to do, but there was no one there, so she stepped inside and sat down on one of the small, rickety slatted seats. Piled opposite her were stacks of small silvery bundles. Leaning forward to get a better look, she realised it was a collection of books, all of them hand-bound and written on the same paper, which didn't really resemble paper at all. It was as thin as tissue and shone like the moon. Almost immediately the doors slid shut of their own accord and the carriage began to move forward into the trees. Then, without any warning, it tilted and swung forward, toppling Liddy to the floor and plunging her into a strange and scratching darkness. Pulling herself back onto the seat, Liddy saw that the carriage was surrounded by thick pine trees, and their heavy needles brushed against the glass like grasping fingers. The way through was narrow, and the carriage stuttered more than once, but it continued to push through the green in determined little spurts. Liddy wondered what would happen if it stopped moving altogether. She had no idea where she was – only that she could no longer see the ground below her, or the sky above, and it felt like she was floating between the trees.

To keep herself steady, she flattened her palms against the glass and, when the carriage finally burst free from the green, she wasn't jolted from the seat like before. She looked around with wide, astonished eyes, unable to believe what she was seeing. They had left the forest and she was sliding gently through the air, level with the clouds. The rest of the world had dropped away. Daring to look down, she could see the world in miniature, like scattered objects tipped from a toy box: a cluster of houses, a field of tiny goat-shaped specks, a monastery perched halfway up a mountain and endless fields of crimson and yellow, threaded together with blue. The sun crowned the tops of the pine trees as they marched down the hill in regal splendour. Liddy had no idea where she was going or how long it would take to get there, but she had to trust what Lady Chamberlain had told her: that Fate was taking her in the right direction. She settled back and felt her shoulders relax and her eyes flicker.

The gentle rocking motion must have lulled her to sleep, because when she next opened her eyes the carriage was resting back on a set of tracks, with its doors wide open. The seat opposite her lay empty and there was no sign of the books that had accompanied her. Anxiously she checked for her case and was relieved to find it was still tucked behind her feet where she'd left it, along with the potted bulb. Holding it up, she was stunned by how much the shoot had grown in the short time she'd been journeying; it was now as tall and thick as her thumb. It had a silver glow that was bright enough to light her way through the dipped shadows of the approaching evening.

Hadn't the letter mentioned that someone would be there to greet her when she arrived? The place looked deserted. Where had all the books gone? Somebody must have taken them while she was sleeping, but who? And where were they now? There was no sign of the lake or the house; the carriage seemed to have dropped her in the middle of nowhere. A short distance away, on the other side of the track, a road curved away between the trees, and Liddy thought about following it. For a moment she felt lost, unsure what to do. Her case was heavy, and she wouldn't be able to carry it far on her own. Some small movement by the wall caught her attention and she noticed there was a solitary figure leaning against it. Her glance invited his attention and he straightened as much as his body would allow and began to come towards her.

'Welcome, Ms Harchwood,' said the approaching figure, in a voice that was both slow and gentle.

Liddy was so surprised to hear her own name being spoken by a stranger so far from home that she struggled to offer a reply. He stopped in front of her, and she could see the face of an old man beneath his cap. He must be long into his seventies, with a face and hands darkened and wrinkled by the sun. He lifted his cap, patted down his hair and nodded his head in polite greeting. She could see there was something kind about him, which enabled her finally to find her words.

'Are you from the House of Sorrowing Stars? I was told there would be someone here to meet me.'

'That's right,' he said, lifting her case as though it contained nothing but feathers, and he headed towards the road with a gesture for her to follow.

'But how did you know when I'd be arriving?' asked Liddy curiously. 'I told no one. Not even I knew for certain when I'd be here, or even if I would come at all.'

'Just an inkling,' he said, nodding at the pot in Liddy's hand. 'It's easy enough to work out – give or take a day or two. Everything's written in the stars.'

'Have you been waiting long?' she asked.

'Only since yesterday.'

Liddy's eyes opened wide in surprise.

'Oh, it's no bother,' said the man, waving his hand in the air, 'I'm used to waiting.'

As he made room for her case in a large barrow, Liddy saw that it was already filled with the missing books from the carriage. She had found the book-thief.

'This way, Ms Harchwood,' he said, lifting the handles of the barrow and weaving it through the dust.

'You can call me Liddy,' she said.

'If you prefer.' Then, as an afterthought, he added, 'You can call me Ben.'

'I wasn't sure if I was in the right place.' Liddy laughed a little nervously.

'This is as far as the carriage can go,' he replied. 'The villagers would prefer it to cross the lake straight to the house.'

'Why doesn't it?'

'The island is small and full of trees. There is nowhere high enough to bring a cable across. It would be quite impossible. Don't worry, it's not far from here.'

'Don't the villagers use it?' she asked.

'They prefer the road. It takes twice as long, but still, that is the way they choose.'

There was an edge to his tone that made Liddy wonder if their choice was born out of suspicion. What exactly was waiting for her at the House of Sorrowing Stars? All her pondering had made her fall behind and she quickened her pace to catch up with Ben.

A crisp blue sky stretched away endlessly, and Liddy let her worries drift. She breathed in the fresh air, suddenly glad to have left behind the damp, drab city. Tall pine trees surrounded them in dark, feathery whispers, and nothing passed along the winding road. Who was this man whose whistle matched that of the birds? And what was he doing with all those books? She was too inquisitive to remain silent.

'Do you know Vivienne Castellini?'

Ben stopped his whistling and set down his cart. Had the name alone given him reason to pause? He lifted his cap, wiped his brow and then picked up the cart again and continued.

'Signora Castellini is the mistress of the house,' he said simply, just as Liddy was about to ask her question again.

'And what's she like?'

His face looked troubled by her question, but when he spoke it was with kindness. 'She is a quiet woman – prefers her own company – and not one that likes to be bothered.'

They continued along the somnolent road for about half a mile until patches in the trees revealed glimpses of a village up ahead. On one side houses tumbled down the hillsides, their pink-peaked roofs aflame in the fairy-tale glow of evening as they gathered to worship the great gleaming lake they overlooked. Beyond that, Liddy could see the sparkle and glimmer of the distant mountains. The place was polished in magic and Liddy was utterly mesmerised.

She smiled. It was the most beautiful place she had ever seen. The air was serene and drowsy, as though she had stepped into a dream. Forgotten memories suddenly stirred in her mind: a child holding a doll; the salty taste of tantrums and tears; then reaching for something she couldn't quite grasp, and floating and sinking and drowning.

'This way,' said Ben, heading down a leaf-strewn path.

The memory faded.

She stumbled after him until the sky suddenly widened and everything turned blue.

'The House of Sorrowing Stars is out there,' he said, pointing to a small island set in the middle of the lake.

He set down the barrow and began unloading the books into a small paddle-boat.

'Does Vivienne Castellini like reading?' she asked, handing him yet another bundle to stow safely.

'These aren't for Signora Castellini,' he replied. 'They're for Eloura to look after.'

Before Liddy had a chance to ask him who Eloura was, he had uncoiled the rope and was telling her to get in. She looked at him doubtfully.

'There's no other way to cross – not unless you want to swim there,' he said, laughing.

Lulled by the gentle rhythm of the boat, Liddy settled back and let her mind wander, as was its habit. The world had changed its colour and shape, and the sky was clear. Here majestic mountains rose into the sky instead of filthy factories. More grass than brick, more water than smoke. She had left the rowdy crowds and chaos of the streets far behind her and all she could hear were the singing trees. There was magic in the air. Her eyes drifted to the water. Beneath its surface she could make out dark shapes and strange silvery glints between them.

'What's down there?' she asked, leaning forward for a better look.

'Sorrowing stars,' replied Ben. 'Flowers that grow below the surface of the water. The lake is full of them. You can see them better at night.'

'Sorrowing stars.' Liddy repeated the name quietly and peered a little closer. 'And do they shine like the real stars?' she teased.

'Even brighter,' he replied. 'And you've got your own, right there.'

Liddy followed his gaze to the pot nestled in her lap. 'This is a sorrowing star?' she asked in amazement.

'It will be,' he replied. 'Once it's grown.'

She looked back into the water and tried to imagine the lake turned silver. *What a wonderful feeling it must be to swim among the stars*, she thought.

As they approached the island, the roof of a house rose out of the trees and she caught glimpses of its walls through the dark tangles of green. It appeared like a forgotten wish. Wildflowers poured over rocks and walls, providing goblets of honey for the bees and finding refuge among the broken stones. Despite the nearness of winter, the garden bloomed as though it was a midsummer evening. Lady Chamberlain had promised that she would find a beautiful garden, but this was beyond beautiful – it was absolutely breathtaking. Strangely, Liddy didn't feel at all cold; it was mild – warm even – yet tiny snowflakes swirled through the air and caught in her hair.

As Ben secured the boat to a small wooden jetty, she watched the mountains smoulder in the fiery light. It was the colour of fairgrounds, of candy floss and toffee apples, a welcome reminder of home.

'Be careful,' he warned as she followed him up a steep set of moss-covered steps. 'The lower ones can get a bit slippery.'

His voice startled a bird, which spluttered up through the leaves and away. They climbed higher until the steps brought them to a gravel path, which weaved its way beneath sugar-white blooms and bright magenta leaves; they were so big that Liddy had to push her way through with both hands. Finally she emerged onto a great expanse of lawn, and there at the top slouched the House of Sorrowing Stars. Smoke from a chimneypot beckoned.

With its many windows and shutters, it was more like a villa than a house. Its roof was long and sloping, and its façade blushed a timorous pink beneath the wisteria that smothered the stone walls and wept over the door frame. Liddy imagined that once upon a time it would have been a jewel of a place, majestic and elegant, but now it looked so neglected that she couldn't imagine anyone living inside. The thought filled her with an unexpected feeling of melancholy, and when she turned to ask Ben if this was really the right place, he was already at the front door.

Liddy followed him into the dark and draught-filled hallway. It was more than twice the size of hers back home, and its corners had not seen the benefit of her mother's duster. Ben told her to wait a moment, and his footsteps faded down the passage and into the dark recesses of the house. She presumed he had gone to find Vivienne Castellini and inform her of their arrival. Liddy strained to hear anything in the gloom, but all was quiet. Finally she heard footsteps returning and Ben emerged out of the darkness. She looked over his shoulder, expecting to see the face of Vivienne Castellini behind him, but there was no one there. He had come alone.

'Where is Vivienne Castellini?' she asked, perplexed that her host had not come to greet her.

'You arrived later than expected. Signora Castellini has asked that I show you to your room and she will see you in the morning.'

Liddy frowned, but was too exhausted to argue. Instead she followed him up a wide and creaking staircase.

'At least I am expected,' she mumbled to herself, still unsure how they knew when – and even if – she would come.

At the top of the stairs he led her down a corridor lit with candles.

'This is your room.' He pushed against a door and the light swept out into the corridor like a pale, welcoming ghost. Shadows hurried to embrace each other.

Inside, someone had lit the fire and there was a wooden stand waiting to warm her coat, damp with mountain mist. A candle had been left burning on a small desk, and a box of matches lay beside it. Beneath the window was a bed with a wrought-iron frame and a patchwork quilt, on top of which someone had neatly folded two towels and a facecloth. On the nightstand there was a cup and saucer and a blue plate, with a small feast of bread and cheese carefully arranged upon it.

'The bathroom is at the end of the corridor,' said Ben. 'The only door on the right.'

'Thank you.'

He turned to leave, but before he closed the door Ben stopped and slowly stepped back into the room.

'Signora Castellini is a strong woman, but grief has left its mark. Respect her privacy and I'm sure you'll be happy here.' He gave his cap a gentle tug. 'Goodnight, Liddy, sleep well.'

Then he closed the door and dropped the latch, leaving her all alone in her strange new world. Too tired to eat, she collapsed onto the bed, closed her eyes and fell into a sleep so deep that not even her dreams could reach her.

Interlude

*A*t last she has arrived, and now they are all here. But while one sleeps, another stares unblinking at the ceiling, wondering if it was a terrible mistake to invite her. Vivienne knows there will be questions, and her head hurts with the thought of them. Only she has the answers, but she does not have the certainty to give them. Not yet.

She tried to make the room as comfortable and warm as possible. She had sat for such a long time folding and unfolding towels, shaking out the damp from the quilt and smoothing away the creases in the pillowcases. She had deliberated over what food to leave, unsure what the girl would like; something light, yet satisfying – soup perhaps – or maybe a bowl of rice? In the end she decided to slice some cheese and bread onto a plate. It was fresh from the village shop and she would not need to worry about it growing cold. She used their best china cup, the one with the pretty yellow flowers, as if worried that the girl would be used to much finer things.

I watched her boil the pan and pour the water into the pot of leaves, seeking the comfort of a cup of tea while she waited. She stirred and stirred before securing the lid and gazing out of the window. I knew what she was thinking; I could hear her thoughts drumming, incessant as rain. All day she had wondered where the girl was. Was she on the train? Had she passed through the mountains? Had Ben collected her yet? She became so preoccupied by her thoughts that she completely forgot about the tea, and by the time she remembered, it was nothing more than a pulpy stew. Appalled by its bitter taste, she swiftly brewed another pot, cursing her carelessness.

Life had made it difficult for her to show kindness to others and so she did it from behind walls and closed doors. Unclaimed and faceless kindness was always easier to bear. When Ben appeared with news that the girl had finally arrived, Vivienne felt unprepared. Instead of rushing to greet her, she asked Ben to show her to her room, blaming the lateness of the hour for her absence. All that time waiting, and still she wasn't ready. She had kept the girl's imminent arrival a secret, telling no one but Ben about the invitation she had sent. She didn't want to give the Keymaker time to refuse, as she knew he would. It would be easier to explain once the girl had arrived, and more difficult to send her away then. Besides, she would welcome more help in the house, and somebody would need to be there when she no longer was.

I miss Vivienne, or I miss the way she was before. The tender side that is barely visible now. She has forgotten how to be happy and how to love, or maybe she is just fearful of such things. The guests still come, and she is welcoming, but only from a distance, moving between them like a ghost. They are too bound by their own grief to notice her, and most of them welcome the distance she keeps. But the girl won't. She isn't bound by the same grief; she will be alert and curious and aware. Unless Vivienne is careful, she will want to leave and that's the last thing that can happen. I watch as Vivienne lies awake long after the midnight hour, still thinking about the questions the girl will ask and the answers she cannot give.

Finally I hear her ragged little breaths and I know that at last she has fallen asleep, and for that I am grateful. I want her to know peace.

I like our new little guest. As soon as she looked at me, she could sense the suffering in my ancient, crumbling walls. There is too much loss here, and my rooms rumble with it. All the laughter has been silenced, and the joy has fallen through the cracks. In healing others, we forget about ourselves. We take away their sorrow, but are smothered by our own.

Perhaps Vivienne is right and the girl can mend what is broken.

Everyone is finally asleep, everyone apart from the Keymaker, who hasn't slept for more than a snatched hour in years. He *sits like a wounded animal, holding his head in his hands, mournful at his desk. He prefers the dark; it is a place of solitude and secrecy where he can be alone in his suffering. Still, a small part of him wonders when a change will come; not knowing that a change has already begun.*

CHAPTER 8
The Library of Lost Souls

Sometime during the night the fire had burned itself out. The cold crept beneath the covers and found its way into Liddy's bones, and it was this that woke her. Wrapping the blankets around her shoulders, she got up and peered through the window. Below her the garden, and the lake beyond it, were as beautiful as she remembered them. She couldn't wait to explore her new home. The sun was already a high dazzle in the sky and Liddy wondered why no one had come to wake her.

Just as she was about to turn away, she caught sight of a solitary snowflake twirling through the air, followed by another and then another. It reminded her of seeing snow for the very first time. Not understanding what it was, she'd run into her father's arms and cried that the moon was melting. Her father had wiped away her tears, reassuring her that it was merely snow falling from the sky – and that the moon was fine. Then he had taken her outside and they'd built a snowman together. A few years later she'd made snowballs and thrown them at the barrow-boys to punish them for their taunts.

The blanket was no substitute for the fire, and the cold began to nip harder. *Unpacking can wait*, she thought, hastily pulling on her clothes. She was barely able to feel her fingers as they fumbled over her buttons, and when she left the room her cardigan was still half-unfastened.

Trying to remember the way Ben had brought her last night, she wandered back along the corridor and down the staircase. At the bottom a dark panelled door had been left half-open and a welcoming warmth escaped and curled itself around her, like the long tail of a cat. Pushing the door open fully, she stepped inside. The room that greeted her was larger than her family's entire house, with floor-to-ceiling windows and glass doors in the middle that opened onto the terrace above the lawn. Near the door stood six round tables, three of which had been set for breakfast. Along the far wall stood an enormous marble fireplace, which crackled and sparked with logs. Numerous shabby old-fashioned armchairs huddled around it and there were several more, all facing the garden.

The temptation of the breakfast table was too great and, in the absence of anyone to ask, Liddy pulled out a chair and sat down. She was delighted to find that the teapot was still hot, and as she poured herself a cup, she could see the steam rising from it. She immediately felt better. The bread too was warm and delicious, and the jam was sweeter than any she had ever tasted before.

Across the room she heard someone clearing their throat and looked over to see a man sitting in the armchair closest to the fire. The angle meant that she couldn't see his face clearly, and it was no wonder she hadn't noticed him when she'd entered the room. A blanket lay crumpled at his feet as though it had once lain across his knee, but had slipped, unnoticed, to the floor. Nestled against the arm of the chair there was a large bottle half-filled with a gold-coloured liquid. Liddy had seen similar bottles in her father's drinks cabinet and guessed it was some sort of Scotch. She wondered what time it was. Her eyes flicked up to the clock on the mantelpiece, but it was too far across the room to see where the hands lay, and her attention fell back to the man as he raised a glass to his lips. Peering to the side, she saw the bush of an eyebrow hanging as heavy as a snow-cornice above his eye and the matching grey-white bristles of a moustache. She wondered if she should introduce herself, but something about his posture told her that he didn't want to be disturbed.

Tabby had mentioned that the House of Sorrowing Stars was a place for sadness, and suddenly she felt like an intruder. Finishing her breakfast quickly, she stood and pushed her chair under the table, then quietly stepped back into the darkness of the hallway. Not once, in all that time, did the man turn his head to look at her.

In the hall the cold immediately made a feast of her bones and she regretted leaving the warmth of the drawing room. *It's such a gloomy, sombre house*, she thought as she stalked down an adjacent passageway, hoping it might lead her to the mysterious Vivienne Castellini. It was impossible to see more than a few feet in front of her, so she kept close to the wall, feeling her way with her hand. Winding deeper into the crumbling house, she hesitated, unsure if she would be able to find her way back again. She felt a sudden rush of air, as though someone or something was close behind her, but when she turned round there was nothing there, or at least nothing she could see. *It was just a draught*, she told herself, and she would have to get used to them in a house as large and old as this one.

Finally the corridor curved, and glimpsing a flickering light up ahead, she hurried towards it with a great sense of relief. A few more strides brought her to a set of enormous double doors, illuminated on both sides by a cluster of candles. The floors were thick with old, bubbled wax. The doors curved out slightly, like the covers of a flattened book left open midway through a story. Into the wood someone had carved a large tree, and its leaves sprawled and flourished across both sides. Liddy ran her fingertips over the fruit bulging from its branches, round like an apple or an orange. She felt the curve of one of them smooth in her palm, so real that for a moment she believed it was possible to eat it. Over the doors arched a fanlight showing all the phases of the moon, and a thick black marker pointed to a waxing crescent. Curved above it were the words *The Library of Lost Souls*. Lifting one of the ring-pull handles, Liddy twisted and pushed and, as the door opened, the trunk of the tree split in two.

The interior took her breath away. It felt more like a cathedral than a library, with its vast space and domed roof. As she moved further into the room, her footsteps echoed on the marble and then floated away, lost in the vaulted silence. On the floor there was a huge circle, painted bright blue, and within it there were swirling patterns of luminous white. Liddy thought it was perhaps a tribute to the night sky, but she had never seen these constellations before. In the centre of the circle there was an impressively large, floor-standing globe. Its ball was the same blue as the floor and it had the same celestial pattern, twinkling like gemstones. The sphere had been mounted in a brass meridian ring and stood on top of a walnut stand. She didn't remember seeing a domed roof last night as she'd walked up to the house, but perhaps she'd been too tired to notice.

Along one wall two fires chattered happily, and she was relieved to feel the warmth radiating from them. Someone had thoughtfully left a large stack of wood in a basket and Liddy wondered if it was Ben. Two wing-backed chairs had been pushed up close to the fires, inviting visitors to stay and make themselves comfortable. On the opposite wall she discovered deep alcoves, offering secrecy and solitude to whoever sought it. Large bay windows looked onto the garden, but most of the light was obscured by a feast of green plant life, which sprawled up and over the window frames. Instead the main source of illumination came from the lamps that burned steadily along the crooked ledges.

The first section of the library had the width and length to rival any ballroom, but there wasn't a single book anywhere. It wasn't until she stepped beyond the blue circle that she saw the soaring shelves disappearing into the dome. Tilting her head upwards, she could see three stained-glass windows glowing with gold and green light, like heads bowed in circular prayer. Next to the wall she noticed a set of tall rolling ladders, but even they wouldn't reach all the way to the top.

Movement through the window caught her eye, and she turned to see Ben pushing a wheelbarrow across the garden. She waved and, seeing her, he raised his cap and dipped his head in greeting, just as he had done before. Liddy held out her arm and tapped the outside of her wrist, hoping he'd realise she was asking for the time.

He gazed at the sky for a moment and then mouthed the word 'afternoon', before trundling off into the hibiscus.

Liddy shook her head and smiled. Certainly no one seemed to be in any hurry to find her, and she was no longer sure that she wanted to be found, at least not for a little while.

If this house has a soul, then I've found it in the library, she thought, turning her attention back to the bookshelves that loomed before her like a tall forest. With no more than a shoulder-width to separate them, the only way through the foliage of books was sideways. And so, in she plunged.

The shelves curved deceptively around the walls, so that her eyes could never find the end. Every so often they dipped into a crevice, and the books hiding there were illuminated by the flickering flame of a candle or the slow burn of an oil lamp. It was a huge and sprawling collection, and it was hard to see if the books were kept in any sort of order. They looked the same as the ones that had been on her carriage, with their thin, silvery pages as delicate as pressed flowers or spiders' webs bound together with what appeared to be a knotted root. They were more like journals or letters of confession than books. Liddy guessed they had all been made by the same person and then given away, for people to fill with their stories. Was this the sad room Tabby had mentioned?

Finally she reached the end of the first row, where she noticed something glinting in the flame of a candle. Peering closer, she could see a small brass plaque nailed to the wood and engraved upon it was a single word: *Abandonment*. Beneath it someone had carved a small symbol in a beautiful feathery pattern, and Liddy brushed her fingertips along its grooves. She continued further until she noticed another plaque; this one had the word *Wounds* engraved into it, and once again a similar pattern swirled underneath. Then there was a third, which read *Sins and Lies*; again Liddy traced her fingers over the deep hexagonal ridges in the wood, wondering if they symbolised different types of grief, each with its own distinct and identifiable pattern. Strangely sad and beautiful.

Liddy was afraid to touch the books at first, but as she continued deeper into the shadows she couldn't resist letting her fingertips fall gently against their edges until, very carefully, she slipped one from the shelf and into her hand. In the dim light she could make out the outline of a cello on the cover and, without quite knowing why, she suddenly felt compelled to discover the story within. Realising it would be an impossible task to read anything between the dusty darkness of the shelves, she began to retrace her steps to the fire, taking the book with her. A quick backwards glance revealed that section was labelled *Unrequited Love and Other Devils*.

Liddy shook off her boots and curled herself into one of the large armchairs, tucking her feet beneath her to get comfy. On a small side-table there was a floral-patterned teapot and a matching cup and saucer. Reaching out, she pressed her fingers to the pot and was surprised to discover it was still hot to the touch. Although she was thrilled at the thought of more tea, she couldn't help but wonder if someone had left it there while she'd been lost between the shelves.

Other than the drawing of the cello, there was nothing to tell her about the story inside the book. Tenderly, as though it was a sleeping creature, she lifted the cover. The first page was stamped with the image of a key – just like the one that had been pressed into the seal of her letter. Written beneath it were the words: *Property of The Library of Lost Souls*.

Before she had a chance to turn another page a sound made her look up. It was like the tick, tick, tick of a clock that had unexpectedly wound back to life. At first she couldn't tell which direction it was coming from, but a movement over near the bookshelves caught her eye and she could see that the culprit wasn't a clock at all, but rather a cat. It appeared from the depths of the library and sauntered towards her without a glance. Its mane of fur was lion-long and silvery-grey, its paws a soft white, as though it had just wandered in from the garden and brought the snow with it. *All cats have a penchant for a warm fire, even this one with its thick wintery fur*, thought Liddy as it sat, perfectly poised, in front of the flames and began to lick its paws. Given all its crevices, shelves, books, cushions and windowsills, the library was certainly an ideal dwelling for a cat.

Liddy settled back and opened the next page of the book. The title of the story was *The Cellist*, which had been written in beautiful tiny letters, and Liddy sensed that those two words meant everything to the person who had put them there. Carefully she turned the next page and began to read.

The Cellist

Enveloped in the quiet hush of late afternoon, I would sit in the little square and wait. I always chose the same café, the one with the blue-and-white fluttering tablecloths facing the clock tower. I'd arrive early, when everything was silent and still, and the only sound came from the sea drifting up from the harbour below. The tables were empty at that time, apart from the waiters who strolled between them with glasses and plates. They had become so accustomed to me that they brought my coffee over without me having to utter a word. Most of the time it remained untouched, left to go cold. Sometimes I would bring a book and try to read from its pages, but always I was thinking of you.

You arrived with the seven o'clock chimes, just as the cafés were filling up and visitors were beginning to wander along the streets once again. I'd see them gazing through windows at objects they would never buy, and I understood that feeling. You came from the direction of the sea – it's where you kept your boat. You named it Fate *and I walked past it every day, hoping for another glimpse of you. Sometimes I'd see a burning lantern in the window, but never anything more.*

Walking across the square, with your case strapped to your back, you'd always choose the same spot beneath the clock tower. A kindly restaurateur would give you a chair.

Within minutes your sweet, solemn music would fill the air. I loved the tender way you held the bow, stroking it across the strings; and when you pulled the instrument close towards your body, I imagined it was really me you were holding. The idea of it made me blush and I would turn back to my book, thinking that somehow you could hear my thoughts. When I dared to look up again, you were always lost in your music. I tried not to stare at you, and instead I would close my eyes and imagine us lying together, naked in the dark. Sometimes when I went home I even dreamed about it.

When the setting sun came, it would give you a beautiful spotlight and so you performed on a gilded stage. At least that's how I saw it. You always played long into the night, and your melody would become achingly beautiful and haunting as the darkness spread its wings wider. It haunts me still. Evenings by the sea were always warm and fragrant; jasmine blossoms blew down from the hillside and the waiters were forever brushing them from the tables with frustrated sighs. I remembered one time when it rained: canopies were quickly unrolled, windows closed and people huddled together in doorways, but you continued playing until your shirt was so wet that I could see your skin underneath. I will never forget the way your hand shivered and your cello wept.

Nobody else seemed to listen. Children ran in giggling circles and stray dogs barked; people laughed and flirted at nearby tables, and beggars tried to sell crumpled roses to them, without success. The only applause was mine, quiet and grateful, but too far away to be heard.

At the end of every evening, I'd walk towards you with a fistful of warm coins and shyly drop them into your open case, before hurrying away. But that last time was different ...

Liddy glanced up from her book as she became alert to a presence in the room. Looking around, she saw a woman standing a short distance away. She was clothed from head to toe in black, making the white of her face all the more startling. Everything about her was pulled in tight: waist, lips, hair – not a wisp of which escaped from its knot. Only her cheekbones stood out, too prominent, like a pair of sharpened blades.

'I didn't hear you come in,' said Liddy apologetically. She stood to face her.

The woman didn't respond and made no sign of having understood.

'Are you Vivienne Castellini?'

The cat raised its head and yawned, before stretching its paws towards the fire and settling back to sleep. The movement broke the woman's stare, but merely for a second and then her eyes were back on Liddy, who waited patiently for an answer, but the silence lingered. Had the woman not heard her?

Liddy shifted uncomfortably as the stranger's eyes moved slowly from her face down to her feet, assessing her worth along the way. Upon seeing her stockinged feet, she frowned and a disapproving *tsk* escaped from her lips. Liddy wished that she had remembered to brush the knots from her hair, and it was too late now to roll down her sleeves, which flapped at her elbows. How slovenly she felt. She hadn't even noticed that her buttons were lopsided, but clearly the woman had.

'My name is Liddy,' she said, trying to sound more confident than she felt. 'Liddy Harchwood, and I have been invited here by Vivienne Castellini. I have the letter upstairs if you wish to see it.'

'That won't be necessary,' replied the woman in a curt, clipped tone. 'I know very well who you are.'

Yes, thought Liddy, *but who are you?* Surely this was indeed the elusive Vivienne Castellini? If so, she was almost exactly as Liddy had imagined her, from her letter. As elegant and as poised as her calligraphy. The hand that had written it was unmistakeably hers. What she hadn't expected was someone so pale and gaunt. Although she didn't look surprised to find Liddy standing there in her dishevelled state, neither did she look very pleased about it; Liddy couldn't help thinking that she wasn't what Vivienne Castellini had been expecting.

'I see you are making yourself at home.' Her eyes fell to the book Liddy had left open on the table, and the teapot beside it. There was still a small dip in the cushion from where she'd been sitting.

Liddy thought she could hear mild amusement in her voice, but a search of her face revealed no such thing, and she struggled to imagine this woman being amused by anything. She stepped closer and reached out her hand, as her father had taught her when greeting new customers.

'No!' The word came out as more of a shriek, and was so loud that Liddy immediately recoiled in horror.

Vivienne's face contorted in pain, and she pressed her hand against her breast as though to keep something buried there. She closed her eyes for a moment to recover from her sudden, strange outburst, and when she opened them again, they looked like two dull raindrops, colourless and cold and ready to break apart. The reaction felt like a slap, and Liddy could feel a flush of heat spreading across her face. There was a moment of silence and then Vivienne moved away, without speaking, towards the door.

'I have been invited here to make marchpane. Is that right?' Liddy called.

Vivienne's thin hand lingered on the door handle. 'Yes, that is correct, but first you must finish your story.'

'I can finish it another time,' she replied, eager to show willing.

From the look on Vivienne's face, Liddy realised she had said something wrong.

'All stories deserve to be finished. And once you begin, you must continue until you reach the end.' Then, as soundlessly as she had entered, she slipped back through the door and only a faint trace of violets remained. Liddy began to wonder if she had just met a ghost.

More easily than she expected, Liddy picked up the book and found her way back into the story.

At the end of every evening I'd walk towards you with a fistful of warm coins. Shyly I'd drop them into your open case and hurry away. But that last time was different. You arrived as usual just after the seven o'clock chimes, your cello strung across your back. There were so many people in the square that evening that I had to wait simply to catch a glimpse of your arm, your leg, the curls on the top of your head. Even your music seemed quiet against the moving crowds.

Frustration made me impatient, which in turn made me careless and, as I got up to leave, I knocked the leg of the table, spilling the coffee across it. One of the waiters rushed over with a cloth and I apologised, stumbling into the square. Although I couldn't see you, I knew that if I followed the giant clock tower I'd find you sitting beneath it. But when I reached you, you weren't alone. A woman was standing there, her head flung back in laughter at something you'd said; I wasn't close enough to hear what it was, but it made me bristle. She handed you something then and you lowered the bow, letting it rest against your leg. I could see it was an ice-cream cone wrapped in a napkin. A dollop had landed on the skin between her thumb and her finger and, as she licked it, her eyes never once left yours. You leaned forward on your chair, letting your hand fall lightly upon her arm; perhaps it was nothing more than a gesture of thanks, but more than anything I wanted to know what it felt like – to be touched by you. Then she moved away, and I watched her disappear through the door of a shop. Your gaze had not followed her there, and when I looked back, it was me you were staring at. The shock of it filled me with a cold panic and for a moment I was unable to move. You looked like you were about to tell me something, and suddenly I couldn't breathe. I turned away and ran into the clamour of the square, the coins scattered at my feet.

For the next three days I didn't return. Whenever I heard the seven o'clock chimes I would busy myself in the grove picking olives, or baking another tray of cheese pies, even though the first batch lay untouched on the shelf. It was shame that kept me away, but the longing that brought me back, and so I decided to write you a letter – if I couldn't say the words, then I would write them instead. The following evening, with the letter clutched in my hand, I returned to the square, anticipating the moment when I'd see you again.

I don't know how long I waited before I realised you weren't coming. As the bells chimed seven, I expected to see you appear with your cello, but the street from the sea brought only strangers. I heard the chimes at eight and then again at nine, but after that I don't remember hearing anything. Suddenly it felt like the most important thing in the world to give you that letter, so I ran down to the harbour to find you.

At first I thought I was being deceived by the darkness, because there was just an empty space where your boat should have been. I still remember running along the harbour wall, staring out across the ink-black sea, wishing I had known your name so that I could scream it out loud and maybe you would hear me. The night-fishermen thought I was mad, as I shook them by their shoulders and asked them if they'd seen the cellist. That night as I ran through the darkness my heartbeat felt too fast, but by morning it didn't feel like it was beating at all.

For a long time I still visited the square, hoping to find you there. I would sit watching the slow-moving hands of the clock, waiting for the seven o'clock chimes. Once upon a time they had brought such happiness and hope, but now they were nothing more than a cruel taunt; a reminder of a chance lost. I would stay there until the waiters had cleared away the plates and snuffed out all the candles, leaving mine to burn a little while longer.

As a way of staying close to you, I began to study music. Of course you can guess what I chose – that's right, the cello. The first time I slid the bow across the strings, I felt the hairs on my arms stand up and I couldn't stop the tears from rolling down my cheeks as every note reminded me of you. It turned out I was a natural, probably from watching you play for so many hours in the square that we both left behind. You taught me everything, without knowing what I would become. Eventually I was selected to join an orchestra and we played to sold-out theatres the world over.

Once we even played for members of the royal family, who clapped from their balcony in warm appreciation.

I kept the letter that you never read tucked inside the case of my cello, hoping that one day I'd find you again. Whenever I'm near the sea I still look for the boat called Fate, *with its little lantern burning bright in the window. My music brought me enormous wealth and even fame in certain circles, but I am too old to play now, and my fingers are old and crooked, their knuckles tight knots of pain. My cello stays locked away. I have never married, although I have not been without admirers. You see, my heart belongs to another time, another place, where the evening air is scented with jasmine and the seven o'clock chimes summon a man along a sea path with a cello strapped to his back. On the other side of the square there is a girl sitting quietly, waiting for him. He looks up and sees her and they smile, and all the longing falls away. It is the same story, but with a different ending. The one I should have chosen so many years ago.*

Liddy turned over the page and was disappointed to find there were no more words written there. The story had ended, more in a dream than in a resolution. It felt incomplete somehow, and she heard herself mutter an involuntary *No* on realising that it was over and she would never know what had become of the cellist. She flicked back to the last paragraph, read it again and absorbed its sadness. For some reason it was harder to see the words this time and they looked fainter than before. Liddy hoped her heavy-handedness hadn't smudged them away. The paper was so thin – she should have been more careful.

It took a while for her mind to return fully to the room and, when it did, she was surprised that all was the same as before: the sky outside and the garden beneath it, the walls and the two crackling fires. Only the cat had vanished – as quick as a magic trick. Liddy gently let the pages fall together and made her way across the library, trying to remember which shelf she'd taken it from.

CHAPTER 9

Vivienne Castellini

Back in the shadowy entrance hall, the cold gnawed. Nothing moved, but Liddy felt like she was being watched, as though the house were breathing down her neck. *Just another draught*, she told herself, *old houses are full of them*. She wasn't sure what she was meant to do after finishing the story – Vivienne had left without further instruction, and Liddy had no idea where to find her in such a large and rambling place.

A furtive glance into the breakfast room revealed that the bushy-browed man was still sitting in the chair by the fire, and Liddy wondered who he was. Perhaps he was a guest and, if so, were there others? The only person who seemed willing to talk to her was Ben, so she opened the front door and stepped into the garden in search of better company.

The lawn was a ferocious green and the trees were unusually thick and dark, refusing to surrender to autumn. Walking along the path, she saw a line of birch trees shimmering like silver wands, casting shadows over the grass. Dangling from their branches were hundreds of small objects, which twirled and tinkled in the gentle breeze. As she grew closer, Liddy realised they were keys. Many looked as ancient as the trees themselves; but a few still gleamed in their newness. Some were a dainty gold, the perfect fit for a trinket box, yet others were large and clunky, as if made to unlock the door of a dungeon. It was a curious sight, and hypnotic in sound.

She followed the path as it curved round, taking her past bright-blue flowers the size of dinner plates; their leaves had the same scalloped edges as her mother's giant serving platters. Occasionally snow swirled gently around her, melting into her hair and onto her skin, so light that it couldn't be felt and there was no trace of it left on the ground. *How strange*, she thought, *to see snow and flowers together.* It brought a feeling of comfort, but she didn't know why. A little gate led her out of sight of the house and into a small walled plot. The intoxicating scent in the air immediately told her she had stumbled upon a herb garden. Walking between the plants, she stopped to rub her fingers on the leaves, trying to guess what was growing there: sage, thyme, dill, rosemary, chives and other herbs she didn't recognise. Large clay pots were bursting with oregano and next to them grew neat rows of mint and, further along, a spray of lavender appeared with a flourish. A cushion and a trowel had been abandoned on the path, as though someone had recently been digging there.

Over the wall came the sound of metal scraping against stone, and Liddy hurried along the path and out through a gap in the wall. There she found another path that took her around the rose bushes and onto the lower lawn. Halfway along she saw someone standing with their foot resting on a spade. From the way he wore his cap, she knew at once who it was.

'Ben!' she called.

He tugged his cap and nodded at her approach. 'Sleep well?' he asked, plunging the spade into the flowerbed.

'So well that it seems I've missed an entire morning.'

'I thought you'd been in the library.'

'Yes, I was reading a story about two cellists.' Liddy paused, suddenly remembering again what Tabby had told her about a room full of sadness. 'Are all the stories in there like that – so sad and hopeless?'

Ben pulled a handkerchief from his pocket and began dabbing it along the back of his neck.

'I believe so, but I wouldn't really know.'

'Don't you read them?'

'Can't read them, more like.'

Liddy's eyes widened in surprise. 'You don't know how to read?'

'Not words on paper – no; at least not very well. But I can read other things – the sky and the trees, and the ways of this garden – far better than anyone else.' He looked around and Liddy could sense his pride. 'You must have met Eloura then,' he said, turning over the soil.

Liddy frowned. Had she been mistaken to think the pale apparition was Vivienne?

'She's a frightful woman,' she said.

'Frightful?' Ben looked perplexed.

'And pale as a ghost.'

The confusion cleared from Ben's face and he chuckled. 'Ah, I think the person you met was Signora Castellini.'

'So who is Eloura?'

'She is the one who looks after everything in the library. She protects the stories.'

Liddy hadn't seen anyone else while she was browsing through the shelves, but perhaps that explained the hot tea and the warm fire.

'Do you know where I can find her?' she asked.

'In the library, I should imagine.'

'No, not Eloura – I mean Vivienne.'

Ben shook his head. 'You don't find Signora Castellini, she finds you.'

For a moment he looked like he was going to say something else, but instead he pursed his lips and turned his attention back to his spade. *A garden like this one must keep him busy all day*, thought Liddy and, deciding she had already taken up too much of his time, she said goodbye and left him to his digging.

Finding her way back to the main lawn, she strode up the grass towards the house, where once again she had the uneasy feeling of being watched. She glanced about the garden. A blackbird quickly hopped across the path, before disappearing into the rhododendrons. She had almost reached the terrace when movement in an upstairs window caught her eye. At once she recognised the face with its haunted stare, and its eyes like the small sunken craters of a sickly moon. It was a reminder of the strange vision she'd had while holding the package on the stairs, just before someone had called out her name. Then the face was gone, and Liddy wondered if she had imagined it.

As she stepped into the entrance hall, a voice startled her.

'Did you finish the story?'

'Yes,' replied Liddy, watching Vivienne emerge from the gloom.

'Good. This way.'

Vivienne led her down another wood-panelled corridor, which reminded Liddy of the sides of a coffin. It was so cold and dark that she wondered if she was being taken down to a crypt.

'Isn't there any heating in this place?' she asked, but her complaint went unanswered.

'Watch your step,' ordered Vivienne.

The warning made Liddy reach for the wall and she stayed close to the sound of Vivienne's dress swishing against the stone floor. Finally she heard the rattle of something, then the lifting of a latch or the turn of a handle. A great wing of light spread over her and she followed Vivienne down a set of shallow steps into the room below. She had entered a flour-dusted kitchen with dark, uneven walls and a high, oblong window offering little light. Straight ahead there was an oven, and the heat from inside had coaxed a large doughy mound to rise from its tray; the sweet, yeasty smell of it filled the room. It reminded her of home.

Pots and pans dangled from hooks on the wall, and brightly patterned dishes and plates were stacked next to jugs filled with wooden spoons. A big copper kettle bubbled wildly on the stove, annoyed that it had been kept waiting. Vivienne crossed the room, took a cloth and whipped it from the heat, letting it simmer slowly into silence.

'So you invited me here to make marchpane?' Liddy enquired, trying to keep the doubt from her voice. Vivienne looked like someone quick to anger, and she wasn't ready for that.

A guilty expression appeared on Vivienne's face, as though she had been caught in a lie.

'It's just that there are plenty of people who can make marchpane. Why me?'

The guilt disappeared immediately, and Vivienne let the stiffness fall from her face.

'I've heard that people crave your marchpane,' she replied, after a long silence.

'But how do you know?' asked Liddy, amazed that such news had travelled so far.

'Sometimes when Ben collects the books, there is another package waiting there, one that is full of marchpane.'

'My marchpane!' exclaimed Liddy. It was her father's dream for the marchpane to cross the sea, and somehow it had happened without any of them realising. 'Have you tried it yourself?'

A strange expression flitted over Vivienne's face, as if she was deciding between a lie and the truth. 'No, I have not. They are a little too ... fanciful for my tastes,' she finally admitted.

Liddy felt a tiny stab of disappointment, followed by confusion. 'Who am I to make the marchpane for then, if not for you?'

'Some for the villagers, some for the guests.'

'What guests?' asked Liddy. 'I've only seen one other person – the old man who sits alone by the fire.' The dreams of her marchpane reaching the lips of so many were quickly dwindling.

'The Major,' she replied.

'Is it true that people come here to let go of their sadness?' asked Liddy. 'Is that the reason he's here?'

'Sit beside him and he will tell you his story. Most nights he tells it to the walls.'

'And is he the only guest staying now?'

'No, there is also a couple – John and Alice – who arrived just before you did. I'm sure you will meet them soon enough.' Vivienne gave a heavy sigh. 'What you must understand is that this is a place of sorrow, but also one of healing. It takes people time to tend to their grief. The marchpane will help them until it's time to leave.'

'How?' asked Liddy, unconvinced. Her marchpane might have been a delicious treat, but it certainly wasn't a magic potion or a miracle cure for anything, especially not the pervasive fever of grief.

'The flowers from the garden have special properties that can help ease suffering. Tomorrow I would like you to use the petals in your baking. In the meantime, you will find that the kitchen is well stocked and there is plenty of honey in the jars. Those baskets over there are filled with fruit and vegetables, and almost everything is fresh from the garden. First thing in the morning we will go to the village and buy whatever else you need.'

'But what should I do until then?'

Vivienne sighed again. 'This house seems to be getting bigger, or perhaps it is just that I am getting smaller. Either way, I need more help.'

'Help with what?' queried Liddy.

'Not much,' she replied hastily. 'Bringing in the vegetables, preparing supper, accompanying me to the village – simple things.'

Liddy didn't mind the thought of helping around the house. Besides, she would need something more than marchpane to occupy her. Vivienne's eyes flicked down to Liddy's buttons and, again, she thought she spotted a faint glint of amusement there.

'But first you must learn how to dress yourself properly.' Then Vivienne strode up the steps and out through the door, leaving her alone.

Liddy was delighted to find how well equipped the kitchen was. Every cupboard revealed a treasure trove of gleaming silver; saucepans and trays were stacked neatly on top of each other and, to her great delight, she found a large blue marble pestle and mortar in a deep drawer brimming with every imaginable utensil. Nothing looked as though it had ever been used. Apart from some spilled flour on the flagstones, the kitchen was pristine – Liddy wasn't used to working amongst such order. After a quick exploration of the pantry shelves, she found enough ingredients to make a small batch of marchpane, but as Vivienne had mentioned wanting Liddy to use flowers, which she currently didn't know anything about, she would have to wait. Instead she reached for a large brush and began sweeping away the flour into the darkened corners.

That evening she joined the Major by the fire. He was wearing a military uniform, with a row of medals pinned to his chest. Traditionally medals were polished until they gleamed, but these hung dull and dark as though from the gallows, and Liddy wondered what kind of war had brought him here, and what horror he had seen. Gazing out across the garden, she watched the dusk settle. A pair of birds flew, silhouetted against the pink sky, soaring slowly over the treetops. Her mind drifted away with them, until the sound of the Major's voice pulled her back.

'His name was David.'

When she looked across at him, he was staring into the fire and she wondered if his words were meant for her or if he was talking to himself, or to the walls, as Vivienne had said. She waited for him to speak again.

'It was his mother's choice.'

'I like that name,' she replied, in case his words were meant for her.

'He died.' The words fell quick and flat – just like that. Immediately the Major lifted his glass to his lips and drank the remains in a large gulp, as though he wanted to swallow back the words and make the truth disappear.

'I'm so sorry,' Liddy replied. He still hadn't turned his face from the fire.

'I wasn't a good father.' The Major's voice shook a little and his words broke apart. Like cracked shells. 'But he was a good boy, my David, such a good boy, I can see that now, but he wasn't—' He paused, trying to find the right words. 'He wasn't what I wanted him to be. He was a talented artist, but I wanted him to be more like me, sailing halfway around the world and leading men into battle. *There's nothing brave about standing in front of an easel*, I told him. *I've held dying men in my arms and washed their blood from my hands.* I wore my medals as proudly as he wore his jewelled cufflinks. I ridiculed him for that.'

The Major laughed bitterly and groped under his chair. He pulled out a crystal bottle and shook the last drops into his glass. Then he tossed it into the open fire, where it shattered into the crackling flames. The sound made Liddy gasp.

'It was November the twenty-first – the first day it hadn't rained for weeks.' He sighed. 'It's funny the things you remember. David announced that some of his pieces had been chosen for a big exhibition, and I lost my temper. You see, to me, art wasn't an achievement, it was a failure. That night I took all the paintings from his studio and burned every single one of them, all his paintbrushes too. That night the sky burned orange. When he discovered what I'd done, he didn't pound his fists into my flesh or rant into my face; it would have been easier if he had. Instead he collapsed, sobbing, into his mother's arms. You see, she knew what I didn't: David was never a fighter. Still, I was triumphant in my rage. I reminded him again that real men washed blood from their hands, not paint. But what I should have said was that I was sorry – sorry for not loving him the way I was supposed to, the way David deserved to be loved. And that was the last time I ever saw him.'

Liddy was so angry, listening to his story, that she wanted to tell him to stop. His cruelty made him more of a monster than a man, and yet she couldn't help feeling a sense of crushing pity for the Major as he spoke.

'We heard nothing for weeks and then he sent us a letter. He sounded upbeat and happy, telling us he had enlisted in the army. *I'm going to make you proud*, he said. I felt satisfied; finally David was doing something worthwhile. My wife begged me to bring him home, but I refused. I was a stubborn old fool. Then one day we received another letter—' He stopped and stared into his glass for a very long time. 'A few months after that, a medal arrived, honouring David for his bravery, but it felt like a curse in my hand, so I opened a drawer and threw it in. That's when I found one of his old paintings, rolled up and tied with a piece of string. It was of a small farmhouse with ducks in the garden, the kind of place he would have lived if—' The Major paused again. 'I had it framed and put on the wall, imagining the life he could have had. But there was no fixing anything after that.'

Liddy could feel tears on her cheeks and quickly wiped them away. Part of her wanted to wrap her arms around the old man in comfort, and another part of her wanted to slap him hard for being so stupid, but she knew she wouldn't do either. His story had hollowed her, and everything felt too sad, too damaged and too broken. He had a conscience and that was punishment enough.

'Who have you lost?' he asked, seeming to notice her for the first time.

Liddy wasn't sure what answer to give. She suddenly felt guilty for not having a story of her own to share; it felt like she had no right to be there.

She saw the twitch of his moustache as he tried to hold his lips in a firm line, then a strange guttural sound escaped from his throat. He tried to disguise it with a quick swig from his glass, but his grief was hard to hide, and Liddy turned away, feeling his shame.

'I'm not here as a guest,' she replied at last. 'I'm here to help Vivienne Castellini.'

His face brightened a little. 'In that case, would you mind fetching me another bottle?' he asked, nodding towards the fire, where he'd thrown the last one.

The Major had been drinking all day and he couldn't even sit straight in his chair. Liddy thought it was better if they both went to bed.

'I'm afraid I've only just arrived, and I haven't been shown where things are kept yet.' Then, with a quick goodnight, she dismissed herself from the room.

CHAPTER 10

Dark Pleasure

Something woke her. Unable to see in the thick dark, Liddy stayed perfectly still and listened. If anyone was there, they didn't reveal themselves. *A dream then*, she thought, but she couldn't remember it. Perhaps the house was playing tricks on her. She pulled the covers up to her chin and waited for the strange feeling to pass, but the feeling only grew. Unable to go back to sleep, she fumbled in the darkness for the little box of matches. Sliding one out, she took a deep breath and struck it hard until the flame caught. In the dim light, the room looked just the same as it had when she'd fallen asleep. Her coat was still draped over the clothes rail, her boots were by the fireplace and there was a neat pile of clothes on the chair where she'd left them. Liddy was about to dismiss her silly imaginings when her eyes fell upon the bedroom door. She was certain that she'd dropped the latch before climbing into bed, but now the door stood open. The match flame flickered and dwindled, and she shook it out before it had chance to burn her fingertips.

Quickly she struck another and held the flame to the wick of the candle. She threw back the quilt and padded across to the door. Could a draught have blown it open? She glanced back over her shoulder to check the window, but it was fastened, and the shutters were pulled tight; besides, she didn't know of any draught that could lift the latches from their doors. Then her thoughts turned darker. Had the Major been drunk enough to lose his way and come wandering into her bedroom at night? Or what about one of the other guests – the couple Vivienne had mentioned? She knew nothing about them, only their names, Alice and John, and she shuddered at the idea that one of them might have been snooping about in her bedroom, watching her sleep.

Liddy's throat felt parched, and she realised she'd forgotten to fill the jug last night. It stood empty on the stand. Annoyed with herself, she lifted it and made her way along the corridor to the bathroom. She'd forgotten to bring her candle, and without it the bathroom was eerily dark. She kept the door open, coaxing in the light from the candle sconces in the corridor, and it crept in just enough for her to find the sink. Setting down the jug, she turned the tap, first one way and then the other, but nothing happened. Frustrated, she tried the other one and this time a low, mournful sound shook the pipes before the tap coughed and spluttered, making Liddy jump. It was loud enough to wake the whole house and she desperately turned the tap again, hoping to silence it. The rim felt dry and rusty against her fingertips, as though it hadn't known water for such a long time. Still thirsty, she headed back along the corridor towards the stairs. Passing her room, she paused and reached inside for the candle and her shawl: such flimsy protection against the surging cold.

The single flame did little to dispel the darkness. The house was still so unfamiliar to her, so unlike the one she'd left behind. At home she knew every groan of the floorboards and every creak of the stairs; she could move between the rooms unheard. She shivered, wishing she had wrapped more than a shawl over her shoulders or worn the slippers that had been left thoughtfully tucked under the bed.

Eventually she reached the kitchen and poured herself a glass of water. Gulping it down, she refilled the jug and hurried back to bed. But she must have taken a wrong turn somewhere in the dark, and instead of reaching the stairs, she found herself in an unfamiliar part of the house. Uncertain which way to go, she tried not to panic. Some way in the distance she noticed a door. It was almost closed, but pale light from within curved out like a scimitar. Suddenly all thoughts of returning to bed were forgotten, and curious feet tempted her closer. She wondered if this was where Vivienne hid herself.

It wasn't a bedroom as she'd expected, but rather some kind of workshop. And what a mess it was – as if a storm had torn through and ransacked everything. Every surface was piled with clutter: books, newspapers, sketches, fabric swatches, bundles of oily cloths and rags thrown all over the place. Bits of broken chains, loose bolts, coils and scrap iron were scattered across the floor, and hanging from hooks on the walls were keys. So many keys, just like the ones in the trees, and each had a brown tag tied to it, like a Christmas gift. All sorts of tools spilled out of a cabinet and, against the back wall, Liddy could see the glowing edges of a small furnace. She could feel its heat from where she stood. Slumped in front of it was a large sack of coal.

Without intending to, Liddy pushed her weight against the door and the gap widened slightly, revealing a man sitting hunched over a desk. His hair curled thick and dark over his brows and continued down the sides of his face into a beard flecked with grey. Above it the high ridges of his cheekbones lifted without the help of a smile. Liddy's gaze flitted across his skin; it was the colour of almonds, rich and brown, and his eyes had the shine of a wild nocturnal creature. In his hands he held a soft lavender-blue glove – velvet perhaps – and as he pressed it to his face, his nostrils flared as he took in short, quick breaths. For a moment Liddy thought there was blood on his hands, but as the light caught his fingers, she realised the stains were more the colour of rust or of varnish, a smell of which hung in the air. There was something fierce, yet wounded about him, and it intrigued her. In darkened rooms, people were less afraid to show themselves, and so she continued to watch him.

He rose from the desk and his shirt was unbuttoned. Thick, dark coils spread down his stomach, and she couldn't help wondering what was buried beneath. He wasn't as old as she'd first thought – the grey in his beard had been deceiving – but he was still maybe ten years older than her. It was hard to describe the expression he wore. Solemn? Lost? Defeated? He released an unexpected guttural sound, like an animal in pain, and Liddy watched in shock as he scrunched the glove in his hand in a sudden burst of rage. His mouth twisted into a snarl, as he slammed it onto the desk with such force that the objects there all shook in fear. His fury was not yet satisfied, and he lifted the glove back into his fist and hurled it violently across the room. Liddy gasped as it landed right at her feet.

When she looked back up, his face was still a storm, but as he stared at her his expression slowly softened into one of puzzlement. Suddenly she forgot how to breathe. A dark enchantment held her there, frozen, unwavering and lingering. For several moments his eyes did not leave hers, and not once did she want them to. When he finally looked away, she stepped back from the door and felt herself unravel.

Was it still night? It seemed like hours since she'd left the warm comfort of her bed. She had learned to decipher the sky a long time ago – a dipped moon, a purple glow, a thread of gold to stitch together the beginnings of a sunrise – but down here it was perpetual darkness, the room shuttered away from the rest of the world. From the other side of the door came the approach of footsteps and, to avoid discovery, Liddy quickly turned and ran. Only the wild shadows of her candle followed, in quick pursuit.

She found her way back to the entrance hall so quickly that she couldn't believe she had got lost in the first place. She felt ashamed of her wanderings – she knew she shouldn't have been creeping around the house in the middle of the night, peering into rooms without invitation, but what she'd seen had stirred something unfamiliar inside her, and she couldn't stop thinking about the dark-eyed stranger who'd held her with his gaze and made her tremble. *Who is he?* she wondered. The room hadn't looked like it belonged to a guest, not with all those tools and keys.

Climbing the stairs, she tried to push all thoughts from her mind. She was almost halfway to the top when she felt something warm and soft rub against her leg. The unexpectedness of it made her loose her footing for a moment and, as she twisted away, the candle dropped from her hand. It hit the floor with a small thud and knocked itself out. Liddy was plunged into sudden darkness. Slowly, with her hand steady against the wall, she felt her way up the rest of the stairs until the candles in their sconces welcomed her back into the corridor. Sitting outside her bedroom door was the cat from the library. It observed her with its slowly blinking eyes.

'Naughty cat,' she said, with a playful wag of her finger. The cat seemed almost to smile in response. As she bent to tickle its chin, she heard a sudden gushing coming from the bathroom. Running towards it, she saw the tap was fully open and the sink was close to overflowing – it seemed to be blocked. She must have left the tap on, allowing the water to finally find its way through the old pipes. Plunging in her hand, she tried to remove the blockage before the water spilled to the floor and made a waterfall of the stairs. Grappling about, her fingers felt something thick and soft like the body of a mouse. She flinched and pulled away, but whatever it was came too. In her hand she held a small, soft bundle. The dark made it impossible to identify. She moved a little closer to the door and lifted it up towards the dim light for better examination. There she froze. It was a lavender-blue glove, just like the one that had been thrown at her feet only minutes before. Surely it couldn't be the same one? She didn't understand. Were they a matching pair? Had one got lost?

She stepped into the corridor and when she looked again under a fuller flame, she realised her mistake. It wasn't a glove at all; it wasn't even remotely lavender-coloured. A trick of the shadows or a sleepy mind? She shook her head to clear it – she must be more tired than she realised. The bundle was nothing more than a sodden clump of russet leaves bound by a copper-coloured thread. That was almost as strange, she thought, unable to imagine how it had got there. The window was closed and was too high for it to have blown in. Perhaps someone had brought it there, unknowingly, from the garden, caught in the grooves under their shoes. But then surely it would have been left on the floor and not in the sink? She shook it from her fingers in disgust, relieved when it flew away into the dark. Then she went into the bathroom and began to mop up the water.

When she finally returned to her bedroom, Liddy could see the soft mound of the cat curled in contentment at the bottom of her bed. She climbed carefully under the covers, so as not to disturb it. Closing her eyes, she listened to its gentle purring, a comfort to her ears. That night she dreamed there were almonds falling from the sky.

CHAPTER 11
The Village

This time when she awoke there actually was a figure standing on the threshold.

'I hope that your nightly wanderings do not become a habit, Miss Harchwood,' said a voice she recognised.

Groggily Liddy pushed herself up on her elbows and watched as Vivienne placed her folded shawl on the table by the door. She hadn't even realised it had slipped from her shoulders. Vivienne hesitated for a moment, as though she was reluctant to let it go. 'I am glad—' she said, before pausing. When she spoke again there was a soft, teasing lilt to her voice. 'It is easy to lose your way in this house, and who knows what you might discover in the dark.'

Before she could answer, Vivienne spoke again.

'If you wish to have breakfast, then you must hurry. We will be leaving for the village in less than thirty minutes. There are things we need.' Her eyes flittered over the bed and she pressed her lips together to stifle a sneer or a smile – Liddy couldn't tell which. 'I see you've made a friend.'

In a little panic, she thought Vivienne was referring to the dark-eyed stranger she'd stumbled upon last night, but following Vivienne's eyes, Liddy realised she was talking about the cat, still sound asleep at her feet, its paws quivering in a dream. When she looked back up, Vivienne had vanished.

In the drawing room the Major was in his chair, and Liddy wondered if he'd spent the night there. She could see the mechanical rise and fall of his arm bringing the glass to his lips and away again. *He must have found another bottle after all*, she thought, struggling to understand why anyone would want whisky for breakfast. Then she remembered the story he'd told her – perhaps she could understand, after all.

It was still early when Ben rowed them across the lake, so early that the mist hadn't yet burned away. Vivienne sat apart from them in quiet contemplation, her eyes fixed on the village ahead. As they drew nearer, she leaned forward like a figurehead on the bow of a ship, willing them on.

In the daylight Vivienne appeared even sicklier, as though she had been carved out of veined marble and left to crack apart in the cold. There was something unfinished about her, as if there were pieces missing. Nestled on her knee sat a large wicker basket and, above it, she was wringing her hands together, incessantly and nervously. She had the look of someone being sent to the gallows, and Liddy began to fear what was waiting for them in the village.

What was it that made her keep her distance? Liddy recalled their strange encounter in the library. When she had got up to greet her, Vivienne had recoiled in horror. She wondered what she was hiding, and what it was that made her so fearful of being close to someone else.

The birds soared and Ben whistled, and as Liddy listened to the rhythmic dip, swoosh and lift of the oars through the water, her thoughts returned once again to the dark-eyed stranger from the night before. One minute he had seemed so tender and loving. The way he'd held the glove in a caress, breathing it in, had seemed tender. Then he'd transformed into some wild, half-formed creature without warning. It was the suddenness of it that had startled her. A gentle flame turned into a raging fire.

'A star for them?' said Ben, interrupting her.

'Pardon?' replied Liddy.

'A star for your thoughts – that's what we say here.'

Liddy laughed. 'We only offer a penny for those.' Then she lowered her hand and let her fingertips trail through the water, looking ahead to the village. Not even a star was enough to tempt the thoughts from her mind.

The village was quiet, tucked away and hidden from the rest of the world. The houses looked as if they had been sculpted out of multicoloured jewels, glittering in the morning sun. It was hard to believe that she had been there before and had forgotten its magic.

Many of the shops had shuttered windows, their awnings still wound tight this early in the morning. A grocer was laying out oranges in a noisy clatter of trays, but when he saw them approach, he hurried back through the doorway as though they'd chased him there. It was perhaps too early to be bothered by customers. Liddy could see a small bakery on the corner and through its open door came the irresistible warm wafts of rosemary bread. Vivienne didn't stop, striding straight past and into a large square.

In the middle stood three ancient olive trees, and beneath them on a bench sat two old women dressed in black. They were engaged in a loud and lively babble, rivalling that of the birds sitting above their heads, but when Vivienne and Liddy approached, their chatter ceased. The woman closest to them narrowed her eyes in suspicion and the other one nudged her arm and whispered something under her breath. Scowling, they stamped their walking sticks firmly into the stone and levered themselves to their feet before hobbling away. Liddy admired the way Vivienne dismissed them with a defiant tilt of her chin. Glancing over her shoulder, Liddy saw that one of the women had raised her walking stick high in the air and was gesticulating wildly with it. It wasn't just suspicion she saw then; it was something else, something like fear.

When she turned back, Vivienne was disappearing through the door of a glass-fronted shop and Liddy hurried after her. Inside, a woman was slicing cheese behind the counter, and when she looked up her face darkened. Without a word, she slipped through a beaded curtain and then came the sound of muffled voices, and the name Sebastian being called over and over into a distant room.

'Do you know what you need?' asked Vivienne, without mentioning the woman's strange and sudden disappearance.

'Just a bottle of rosewater and a large bag of almonds,' Liddy replied. She had found a sack full of sugar in the pantry and wouldn't be needing any more for a while. There was also a plentiful supply of honey, should she want to use it.

They continued to wait, but minutes passed and still no one appeared.

Looking round, Liddy could see they were in a delicatessen. Shelves dipped under the weight of jugs brimming with milk and yoghurt; blocks of cheese were displayed next to pots of honey and jam. Loaves of bread were stacked on the shelves, ready to topple, and Liddy wondered if they'd been brought across from the bakery. Under the counter there was a long line of wine bottles, each one corked and labelled, and further along there were vinegar pots and jars stuffed with dried leaves and brown powder. Fruit and nuts spilled from large baskets and there were buckets of figs and drums of oil in the large window. Garlands of garlic bulbs and onions dangled from hooks and there was a mound of individually wrapped biscuits, all tied with paper bows. Liddy's mouth watered as the smells mingled around her: oregano, aniseed, sun-warmed tomatoes, sliced lemons, roasted coffee and something smoked and buttery that she couldn't quite place.

The beads clattered and she looked up to see a young man, about the right age to be the woman's son – Sebastian, she presumed. He smiled shyly at Vivienne and his gentle greeting brought a pink flush to her cheeks. She lowered her eyes for a moment, abashed. Liddy frowned, looking from the man to Vivienne and back again, trying to understand what lay between them.

'Will you have the usual?' he asked softly, taking a cup and saucer down from the shelf behind him.

'It'll be two coffees today, please, Sebastian,' Vivienne replied, looking towards Liddy. 'And a bottle of rosewater.'

Sebastian shifted his gaze to Liddy. He had been too enraptured by Vivienne to notice her standing there.

'And almonds,' Liddy said to the man who had made Vivienne so forgetful.

'Go and sit outside,' Vivienne said firmly. 'I won't be long.'

Liddy went to sit at one of the little tables in the square and continued to watch them through the glass. Vivienne smiled as she handed over several pots of honey from her basket, and bundles of herbs that she laid out along the counter. Liddy had never seen her so alive; it was like she had been woken from a long sleep. It was clear that Sebastian was many years younger than Vivienne, closer in age to Liddy, and she wondered how many years separated them. Twelve? Fifteen? Maybe more. Perhaps that's why they had been shunned, walking through the village; society did not deem it acceptable for a man to want a woman old enough to be his mother. But as she watched them together, the years between them fell away until they were just two hearts beating the same pattern. Their mouths were still, and their eyes shone with longing and tentative desire, but nothing more. It seemed innocent, almost child-like, and Liddy sensed that their lips had exchanged nothing more than words and occasional laughter. It made her sad to think of so much not being shared.

About ten minutes later Vivienne stepped back outside, and Liddy noticed that her cheeks were still flushed.

'It is better to use the almonds from the garden,' said Vivienne, sitting down. 'They have a much sweeter taste.'

Liddy hadn't seen any almond trees in the garden, but there was still so much to explore, and she was excited to discover that they grew right outside the house.

Vivienne sat with her back to the shop, and she didn't look up when Sebastian brought out their coffees; her focus was entirely on the square. Occasionally Liddy noticed her eyes flick up to the clock tower, as though she was waiting for something. It left her feeling unsettled.

Liddy was reminded of the story in the library, where the woman had visited the square every evening, waiting for a glimpse of the cellist. They weren't next to the sea, so it couldn't be the same square, but perhaps her story was somewhere not too far away. Directly in front of them, across the square, was a wide sloping street of cobbles, and just before it curved up and out of sight sat a yellow-and-white-fronted church. Its stone walls captured the golden light in such a way that it glowed. A silver bell twinkled under a little peaked roof, and at the very top there was a statue of a man with his arms held high above his head. *A saint perhaps*, thought Liddy, lifting her cup to her lips to take a sip. The coffee was thick and, without her usual spoonful of sugar, it left a bitter aftertaste. But the more she drank, the more she liked it.

When she looked back at Vivienne, she saw that her eyes were closed and she was taking long, deep breaths. Her coffee sat untouched, confirming to Liddy that some other reason had brought them here. She leaned back in her chair and let her eyes wander up to the army of alpine trees that marched like soldiers up the mountain. It reminded her of the view from the floating carriage and at once she realised how long ago that felt, even though it had only been two days. Despite the strong coffee, the warmth of the sun made her feel drowsy and she closed her eyes.

Some time later, Liddy startled awake. The army of trees must still have been in her mind because she thought she could hear marching feet. But when she followed Vivienne's gaze past the shop and up the hill, she saw a procession of young girls heading towards them. There were twenty of them, lined up two by two, all dressed in the same plain yellow dress with large white collars. They walked in silence, apart from the clack of their shiny shoes on the flagstones. A tall woman led them like ducklings into the square and another, much smaller woman followed at the back. From the way they were dressed, Liddy knew the women were nuns. Suddenly Vivienne leaned forward in her chair, her face desperate and searching. She rubbed her hands up and down her thighs in a repetitive motion, as if she was rolling out dough, or in the way a cat seeks comfort.

Just as the procession reached the square, the nun at the front turned round and raised her hand. The gesture brought the girls to an abrupt standstill, and she waited patiently for the shuffle of feet to die away. The nun at the back shushed their whispers. Walking down the line, she began to inspect them one by one, pointing to a rolled-down sock, which was obediently yanked back up to the knee. Another girl quickly straightened the edge of her collar, before her warning came. This pause gave Vivienne the chance to conduct an inspection of her own. She froze, her eyes fixed on a single point. In that moment there was no word to describe the expression that lay upon her face. A mixture of longing and regret, tenderness, fear and love, hope and hopelessness. It was like seeing a beautiful jewel hanging around someone else's neck, knowing that it would never be yours – not unless you snatched it and ran. Vivienne sat with her jaw strangely slack and her lips parted. Liddy wondered if it was one of the children who had provoked such an intense reaction, but when she turned to see, they had begun to move away towards the church.

Vivienne still didn't move, not until Sebastian appeared carrying a bottle of rosewater and a handful of change. She tucked the bottle inside the basket and held out her hand. He counted the coins into her palm with deliberate slowness and Vivienne didn't exclaim at his touch, as she had when Liddy had moved to greet her. But as he was finally dropping the last coin, he let his fingers linger on hers and, as they began to entwine, Vivienne hastily pulled away as though they had been singed.

'Thank you,' she said abruptly, rising to her feet. There was a fleeting look of desperation in her eyes, followed by pleading, then denial. A forbidden flame inexplicably extinguished.

Sebastian smiled with sad acceptance and began to clear away their cups with downcast eyes.

As Ben rowed them back across the lake, Liddy felt confused by the events of the morning. Vivienne was hunched in the furthest point of the boat, holding her arm across her stomach as though in pain. She made no sound and her eyes stared deep into the water. A gentle breeze had loosened her hair. It was nothing more than a wisp gently fluttering at her neck, but it made her seem undone somehow. Liddy wondered how she was connected to the dark-eyed stranger, and if he was the cause of her sadness. She couldn't imagine Vivienne wearing anything so bright, but perhaps the glove belonged to her. She looked so utterly lost that Liddy didn't think she could ever be found.

CHAPTER 12

The Lost Object

As they stepped back into the house, Liddy heard a commotion coming from further inside. When they entered the drawing room the Major was sitting in his usual place by the fire and there were two other people in the room with him. She presumed they were Alice and John, the other guests Vivienne had mentioned.

Vivienne loitered in the doorway, but after some deliberation she walked into the room.

'Is something wrong?' she asked, from a distance.

The man began to pace in front of the window, biting his lip as though he was trying very hard to remember something important.

'We can't find it!' cried the woman, collapsing into a chair. She looked as if she had been crying and was about to begin again.

The exclamation awoke in Vivienne a spark of impatience. 'What can't you find?' she snapped.

Without looking round, the Major answered, 'They've lost one of their taglocks. The Keymaker won't make their key without it.'

Liddy felt a jolt of familiarity. The word *taglocks* had been written in the letter that Vivienne had sent, but she still had no idea what they were.

'It's not that he won't – it's that he can't,' replied Vivienne with deliberate slowness. The annoyance in her voice was clearly directed at the Major.

'But he must,' exclaimed the woman, looking at them with large, desperate eyes.

'But he cannot,' Vivienne insisted. 'Without the taglocks, it's simply not possible for a key to be made.'

The woman rose quickly and then, without warning, lunged towards Vivienne.

'Alice!' yelled John. 'Stop!'

Liddy managed to step between them, giving Vivienne time to move out of the way. The woman's rage extinguished as quickly as it had flared, and she fell sobbing into Liddy's arms. Vivienne watched from the doorway as Liddy and John helped the woman back to the chair. The Major sat in a quiet stupor and continued to drink.

John knelt on the floor beside Alice and took her hands in his. He spoke in low, soothing words until her anguished heavy sobs became nothing more than occasional shudders and little hiccups.

'It's my fault,' he said, looking up to address Liddy. 'If only I'd handed the taglocks over as soon as we'd arrived. Instead we went to bed and now ...' His words fell away into a sigh of despair.

'What exactly did you lose?' asked Liddy, still not sure what a taglock was. 'Perhaps I could help you find it.'

A loud dismissive grunt came from the direction of the Major's chair. 'Shouldn't have been so careless.' It was clear he had no intention of helping anyone.

'Oh, please find her,' said Alice, suddenly leaning forward in her chair and reaching out to clutch at Liddy's sleeve. 'It was the end of August, and two winters have passed since then. She'll be so cold by now.'

The man tried to prise his wife's fingers from her arm, but she wouldn't surrender her grip.

'Let go now, Alice,' he said firmly, as though he was talking to a child.

She released her hold and began to grapple for the locket that hung from her neck. It opened with a small click and she thrust it out for Liddy to see. A pretty fair-haired child of about four or five was smiling back at her. She looked at Alice and saw the leap of hope in her eyes; they shone like coins in a wishing well.

'But didn't you hear what she said? She can help us find what we lost.'

John gently pulled her towards him and shushed her into his chest. As he smoothed down the straggles of her hair, Alice continued to hope.

'She was wearing a satin dress; the white one with a lace trim. I made it for her myself.' Her words came out muffled through her husband's shirt. 'And you saw her hair – it's the colour of pale buttercream.'

Liddy wasn't sure if she was describing the child inside the locket or something connected to the missing taglock. Could it have been a doll they'd lost?

'Where did you last have her?' she asked, hoping to stir some memory.

'In the garden,' came the immediate reply. 'Next to the pond.' Then she laughed, a short, sharp burst of hysteria that made everybody jump.

Next to the pond, thought Liddy, *perhaps she had been describing a doll after all, and they had dropped it outside.* She hadn't noticed a pond in the garden, but then she hadn't noticed the almond trees, either. She really must ask Ben to show her around.

Suddenly Alice fell completely silent, and Liddy could see the emptiness return to her eyes.

Wrapping his arms tightly around her, John lifted Alice to her feet. 'I'm afraid you must excuse us now. My wife is exhausted, and I think it's best that she gets some rest.'

'Of course.' Liddy stepped back and watched as he half-carried her towards the door. Vivienne was no longer there; she had once again vanished into thin air.

They left so quickly that Liddy hadn't a chance to ask them properly about the missing taglock, and she still didn't know if it was a doll she was looking for or something else entirely.

The Major muttered something in his chair, and the pity she'd felt for him previously quickly dissolved. She tutted behind him, loud enough for him to hear, then set off in search of the pond and the almond trees.

CHAPTER 13

Almond Trees

Liddy expected to find Ben on the lower lawn, potting or planting or pruning, but there was no sign of him, his barrow or his spade. This time she followed the path in the opposite direction, towards a little iron gate, beyond which stood a wood of thick, dark leaves and dappled light. Bluebells drifted down the hill and it was impossible to tell where the flowers ended and the water began. Even though these trees weren't the type to bear any almonds, she couldn't resist a closer look, and she pushed open the gate and stepped through. The wood sloped down to the lake and she could see Ben's boat resting at the side of the wooden jetty. She felt an overwhelming urge to kick off her boots, unpeel her stockings and dip her toes into the cool, sparkling lake.

A moment later Liddy was standing in the water, with her skirt hitched up around her knees. The closest she had ever come to such a feeling before was when she and Tabby had dared each other to climb into the church fountain. In the end Tabby had been too afraid, so Liddy had been the one who'd pulled off her shoes, raised her dress and waded in. She had been too full of mischief and daring to hear the hymns fall away, and she was still there splashing around when the congregation piled back out through the doors. It had caused such a stir that she was made to kneel at the pulpit and apologise for her transgression. She never much cared for churches after that.

A slosh in the water made her turn, and she saw Ben standing further along the bank of the lake. They seemed to notice each other at the same time, and he greeted her with a small tug of his cap, a now-familiar gesture. Liddy returned it with a wave.

'Can you show me where the pond is?' she called.

He cupped his hand around his ear and shrugged. Then he began to climb the other side of the slope, heading back towards the garden. Wiping her feet on the grass, Liddy quickly pulled on her stockings and boots and ran back through the bluebells, hoping to catch him before he disappeared into the rhododendrons. By the time she reached the iron gate he was already there, waiting for her.

'I'm looking for the pond,' she said, trying to catch her breath.

Ben frowned in confusion. 'There's no pond here – used to be one, over there by the lemon trees – but not any more.'

'Oh,' said Liddy, feeling more confused than disappointed. She must have misunderstood what Alice had meant.

'Too many creatures would fall in and get trapped – birds especially. One morning Signora Castellini saw me drag a drowned owl onto the grass. She rushed out, but as soon as she saw it lying there with its splayed wings and blank, staring eyes, she knew there was nothing to be done. After that she asked me to fill in the pond, and by evening it was gone.'

Liddy hadn't imagined Vivienne's heart to be so gentle, but listening to Ben's story, she wondered if that was the reason she kept it so well hidden.

'One of Alice and John's taglocks is missing and I said I'd help them look for it. The problem is I'm not really sure what it is I'm looking for. Alice didn't seem—' Liddy paused. 'She seemed confused and mentioned losing something near a pond.'

Ben stopped and looked at her. 'It wasn't a taglock they lost there; it was a child.'

'A child?'

'Yes, their little girl, she fell in and drowned.' Ben shook his head. 'There is no greater tragedy than the loss of a child.'

Liddy remembered the locket that Alice had shown her and the photo inside of the smiling girl. The girl they

140

wouldn't be able to say goodbye to unless they found the missing taglock.

'I haven't seen anything in the garden,' said Ben. 'But I'm sure it will turn up. That's what often happens around here.'

She noticed him glance uneasily towards the back of the house and then quickly away again. When she followed his gaze, all she saw was a thicket of brambles and a gang of nettles leering at the window like mischievous children.

'What about the almond trees?' she asked. 'Vivienne told me they grow right here in the garden.'

'Ah, yes, there are plenty of those.'

'Can you show me where they are? I need them to make marchpane.'

Ben smiled. 'Ah, marchpane's my favourite.'

He led her back along the path and through the herb garden. On the other side Liddy could see a tumbledown building made of wood. Ben rattled at the latch and swung the door open. Inside, it was burrow-warm. There were stacks of upturned flower pots and gardening tools hanging from hooks on the wall. Gloves lay discarded on a workbench next to a myriad of watering cans, bundles of string and trays of saplings ready for planting. A jagged bunch of dandelion leaves sat in a pan, ready to be brewed into tea. Beneath a square window in the roof lay a palette covered in blankets and pillows, and Liddy wondered if that's where Ben slept at night. She could hear him rummaging around on a shelf.

'Here you are,' he said at last, handing her a salt-glazed pot. 'It's perfect for collecting almonds.'

Just then a speckled hen appeared from behind a stack of wood with a disgruntled gurgle.

'There are chickens here?' she asked. The thought delighted her, and she watched as it sauntered past her towards the door.

'About a dozen of them,' he replied. 'Good little layers.'

Liddy bent down to coax the hen towards her, but her sudden movement sent it out of the door in a flap of excitement.

'Come on,' he said, carrying a long-handled sweeping brush and a roll of tarpaulin under his arm. 'Let's go and get you those almonds.'

The island was much larger than Liddy had first thought and there was much to discover. They passed another wood, much denser than the one on the other side of the garden. The trees here were knotted together so tightly it would be impossible to glimpse the sky, and Liddy was grateful for the low wall that separated them from its plunging darkness. Although she couldn't see the keys, she could still hear them singing among the leaves. Honeysuckle raced over the stones, pursued by tangles of wild ivy caught in a game of chase. The image reminded her once more of her cousin Tabby and she wished she were here, so they could explore the place together. The track began to slope away, leaving the mournful sight of the house behind. Underfoot Liddy could hear the snap of fallen twigs, and stretching towards the sky were the giant branches of an oak tree. The noise must have disturbed some hidden creature because there was a tiny rustle from the bushes and out flew a robin.

The trees began to dwindle until at last they fell away completely and the hazy outline of the mountains appeared. They finally came to a small rectangular-shaped orchard. Here, instead of keys hanging from the branches, there was an assortment of fruit: apples and pears and oranges and even more lemon trees, just like the ones that led to the house. Walking between them, Ben stopped and dropped the tarp on the ground and leaned the brush against one of the trunks. Liddy could see they were standing beside an almond tree, its branches bursting with hulls. Behind it stood another, and another and another, until all she could see were rows of almond trees. Her father would be amazed to see so many of them growing in one place.

Ben unrolled the tarp until a mat of green lay beneath the tree. Then he lifted the sweeping brush high into the leaves and began shaking the hulls from the upper branches. Liddy heard them land with small thuds, like heavy rain.

'What are taglocks?' she asked, gathering the hulls into the pot.

'Objects that bind you to the person you've lost. Something of yours, something of theirs and something you once shared.'

'Can it be anything? Even a toy or jewellery, or a shoe?'

'That's right – even an old cap like mine,' said Ben, tapping the top of his head. He pursed his lips and squinted into the leaves, trying to see if there were any more hulls.

'But how can you make a key out of objects like that?'

Ben laughed. 'Well, that is the great mystery, and one that only the Keymaker can solve.'

The Keymaker. She had heard the title a few times now. *Of course*, thought Liddy, *that must have been who I stumbled upon last night. Who else would turn the taglocks into keys?* Immediately she wanted to know more.

'Where are the doors for all the keys?' she asked, remembering how many she had seen hanging from hooks in the Keymaker's room, and then from the trees all over the garden.

'There is only one door.'

'Only one door?' repeated Liddy in disbelief. 'But how can that be? All the keys looked so different.'

'One door can have many locks.'

'And where is it?' asked Liddy, her curiosity growing.

'Deep in the library.'

The library had such a magical, otherworldly feel to it, she should have guessed the door would be in there.

'And what's on the other side of the door?'

A place for grief to go, and the chance to be free from whatever it is you carry – be it guilt, regret, fear or shame. They are all such heavy loads.'

Liddy smiled at his answer.

'And what's his name? The Keymaker, I mean. He must have one besides "the Keymaker".'

'Raphaelle.' Ben gave her a warning look. 'And he prefers to be left alone, just like Vivienne.'

Liddy scooped up another handful of hulls and dropped them into the pot.

'They live in a different world,' he said, lifting his cap to wipe his brow.

Liddy frowned. 'Who do?'

'Signor and Signora Castellini,' he replied.

Hearing their names spoken together gave Liddy a jolt of despair. 'They're married?'

Ben laughed and waved his hand in the air. 'No, no, not married – they're brother and sister.'

Liddy could see the resemblance between them now – something about the shape of their eyes and the expression held within; the way they both clenched their jaws to lock away their secrets. Both quick to anger. But while Vivienne's hair was stripped of colour and her face was harsh and pale, the Keymaker's curls were as thick and dark as midnight, and his skin was warm and inviting. Vivienne's movements were quick and sharp like a bird's, but the Keymaker reminded her of a hibernating bear: slow, dishevelled, unpredictable and not quite ready to emerge from the dark.

'I'm living here, but I barely know who with. And the house seems so' – Liddy looked back at its crumbling walls – 'like it holds so much sadness and it's ready to collapse on top of us.'

Ben stayed quiet.

'There are secrets everywhere and nobody will share them,' she continued.

'What is it you want to know?' he asked warily.

'What's wrong with Vivienne? Earlier, in the village, she seemed unwell and—'

'The village always unsettles her,' he replied quickly. 'I try to convince her not to go, but there is no telling her anything she doesn't want to hear.'

'Is it because of Sebastian? The man in the delicatessen.'

Ben shook his head.

'There was a group of children who—'

'Ah yes, it's always so sad to see those foundlings,' he replied too quickly, not giving Liddy time to finish her sentence.

She doubted that was the reason for Vivienne's strange reaction, but she saved her words for later.

Ben adjusted his tarp, so that it was lying under the next tree, and began to sweep his brush through the branches again.

'The village isn't a very welcoming place,' said Liddy, remembering the angry stares and scurrying feet.

'They are a suspicious lot, that's all. Mistrustful of this house and its occupants,' he replied.

Satisfied that he had got all the hulls, he began brushing them into the middle of the tarp. 'People fear what they don't understand.'

Liddy watched him, deep in thought.

'What made Vivienne this way?' she asked. 'She seems so ... damaged.'

Ben sighed wearily, seemingly torn between the idea of confession and concealment.

'Time is not tracked here in the same way as it is everywhere else. The seasons coexist.'

'But how is that possible?'

'How is it possible for people to live with grief inside them? It just is. There is an endlessness about it.'

'And the snow's always falling,' added Liddy. 'Even though it's barely autumn.'

Ben frowned. 'Snow?'

'Yes, look!' She pointed to a single flake that twirled through the air between them.

'Ah,' said Ben. 'That's not snow, it's pollen from the sorrowing stars.'

'Pollen!' Liddy laughed, enchanted, as another flake landed on her hand, so lightly that if she hadn't seen it fall there, she wouldn't have believed it had.

'Snow is a stranger here, apart from one time six years ago that we do not like to be reminded about.' Ben's voice faded and his face grew troubled at the thought of what he was about to reveal. 'Men arrived from the mountains, their cloaks fur-lined and heavy with snow. They kept their heads swaddled in scarves, revealing nothing but their dark, slanted eyes. They had not been invited and were not expected, but still they came, with icicles glinting from their belts. I remember them striding up the hillside towards the house and pounding on the door, yelling to be let in. When they saw me, one of them pushed me to the ground. Another one swept aside his layers and my heart froze; they were not icicles hanging from his belt, but rather a neat row of daggers, sharpened and still crusted with blood. I could smell it in the air.'

'Did they hurt you?'

Ben shook his head. 'I was no threat to half a dozen bandits, just an old man getting in their way.'

'What did they want?'

'What bandits always want – to take what isn't theirs. The bandit leader had been injured and they needed somewhere safe to stay until he recovered. They found food and shelter and a warm bed.'

'And Vivienne,' replied Liddy, with tentative understanding.

'One evening I saw them in the kitchen together, surrounded by a bloody pile of cloths and bandages. The bandit was sitting opposite her in a chair, naked from the waist up, and she was on her knees tending to the gash in his side, which was deep to the rib. I knew she had no choice, but even so her touch was gentle – a little too gentle – and neither one of them could take their eyes off the other. When he flinched, so did she, as if she could feel it too, as though his pain was her own.'

Liddy couldn't imagine Vivienne falling in love with a bandit, or with anyone else, but then she remembered the way she had looked at Sebastian and knew that everyone was capable of love.

'What happened to the bandit?'

'One morning we woke to find all the beds were empty. They'd left in the middle of the night, with food in their bellies and coins in their pockets. Bandits are never in one place for long; they stay on the run to avoid capture. I never saw them again – none of us did.'

'Couldn't the Keymaker have done something to stop them?'

'He wasn't here then,' replied Ben bitterly.

Liddy wondered where he'd been. For some reason she couldn't imagine him being anywhere else but captive in that dark, dark room.

'They left more than they took,' he said, reaching down to pull the edges of the tarp together, creating a sort of sack for the remaining hulls. He stopped and sniffed the air. 'Best be quick, there's rain coming from the mountains.' Then he swung the sack over his shoulder and headed back up the hill.

Clutching the pot, Liddy hurried after him, just as the first raindrop fell.

CHAPTER 14

Supper

Vivienne looked lost in thought when Liddy entered the kitchen carrying the pot.

'Are those almonds?' she queried.

'Yes,' replied Liddy, setting the pot on the table. 'The hulls will need removing.'

They worked together to strip the almonds from their downy cloaks. Vivienne's skeletal fingers worked twice as fast as Liddy's, despite her years of practice.

'It is too warm to keep them in here,' said Liddy once they had finished. 'Besides, they absorb other odours, and it wouldn't do for the marchpane to smell of garlic or grease. It will ruin the taste. There will be complaints.'

'People here have a lot more to worry about than the taste of marchpane.'

Liddy stayed quietly resolute. If she was here to make marchpane, then she would make it her way.

'Very well,' replied Vivienne. She stood up and quickly disappeared into the pantry.

She returned holding several large lidded jars. It didn't take long to fill them and, once the lids had been secured, they carried them from the kitchen and pushed them against the wall of the corridor. For once, it was a relief to Liddy to feel the cool draught of the house on her skin.

She knew that if she followed the wall away from the kitchen she would find the Keymaker's room, somewhere in the dark. The thought of him made her skin tingle and she quickly hurried back into the warmth of the kitchen. As she watched Vivienne sweeping away the hulls from the floor, the memory of the previous night stirred her curiosity.

'I didn't know you had a brother.'

There was a sudden hesitation to her movements, and Liddy saw the quick clench and release of her jaw.

'Ben told me he's the one who makes the keys – that they call him the Keymaker.'

'I'm aware of what he does, and who he is.' Liddy could hear the hostility in Vivienne's voice. 'What else did Ben tell you?'

'Nothing really,' she replied, feeling the need to protect him. 'Only that he prefers to be alone.' She was going to add *like you,* but thought better of it.

Vivienne stopped sweeping. 'He's busy,' she said, returning the brush to the pantry.

'Does he ever leave his room?' she called through the pantry door. Sometimes it is easier to ask questions when you cannot see the face of your listener. Liddy heard a loud clatter, as though something had been dropped, but no answer rose above it.

When Vivienne appeared again, she was holding a white dish. For a moment she could have been mistaken for a pauper with a begging bowl.

'Perhaps you should ask Ben to go to the village for you instead. It seems to have left you exhausted.'

Liddy's words loosened Vivienne's grip on the bowl, and it slipped from between her fingertips and smashed to the floor. Shards flew across the room and Liddy watched as the contents slowly fluttered around her. As they settled at her feet, she saw that they were flower petals in vibrant purples and pastel pinks. Vivienne stooped down to brush them into the curve of her palm, then she shook them onto the table.

'How careless,' she heard Vivienne mutter, picking off those that were still stuck to her fingers.

'Are those the petals for the marchpane?' asked Liddy.

Vivienne hesitated. 'Do you know what to do with them?'

Liddy nodded. Her father had only let her use flowers a few times – pretty, but pointless, he'd said, and not worth the expense. But here the flowers grew in abundance, so their petals could be plucked at no cost.

'These flowers are fresh from the garden. I told you they have healing properties.'

Liddy had heard of the healing power of food – garlic to clean the blood, and milk to strengthen the bones – but never of flowers.

'I have a pie to bake and a kitchen to clean,' Vivienne said, moving across the room towards the oven and turning her back to Liddy with finality.

As the afternoon stretched its damp paws into evening, Liddy prepared the petals. Carefully she brushed each one with egg white and then sprinkled them with caster sugar, before laying them upside down on the baking parchment. If Vivienne wanted the healing benefits of the flowers to be truly experienced, then it would be better to mix them into the dough, and so with that in mind, Liddy loosened some of the smaller petals and kept them to one side, ready to be chopped. Although neither of them spoke, Liddy was glad that she wasn't alone. The pie was made with swift precision, and once it was warming in the oven, Vivienne set about scrubbing the insides of the cupboards and refilling the jars on the shelf with sugar and salt and flour. Liddy took comfort in the rattle and clunks of the kitchen. Time passed.

'They need to be left to dry,' she said finally. She was pleased with her creations.

Vivienne turned to stare sharply at her, almost as if she'd forgotten she was there. Then her eyes gazed upon the petals and a smile appeared, so small and slight it was barely visible, but it pleased Liddy nonetheless.

'Some things are best given time,' said Liddy quietly.

Both women watched one another without saying a word, and in the silence that followed there was a tacit understanding.

'The pie!' exclaimed Vivienne suddenly, wide-eyed at her own forgetfulness.

She rushed across the room and flung open the oven door, and inside sat a giant steaming pie with a crust like a golden crown; the smell that escaped was beyond delicious. There was huge relief that it hadn't burned, but the sudden blast of heat made Vivienne step back and cough uncontrollably into her sleeve.

'Shall I make you some tea?' called Liddy.

'No,' she managed to say, her hand held up in protest.

'But your cough,' Liddy insisted, alarmed. 'I can stir in some honey and ginger, or a spoonful of raspberry vinegar and olive oil.' That was her mother's cure when a cough kept her up all night.

Vivienne's coughing continued, dry and hacking. Liddy feared she would break her ribs if she didn't stop soon. Finally the cough began to ease and her breathing returned to normal. Composed but exhausted, she clutched the edge of the counter, as though to keep herself from collapsing.

'Are you all right?' asked Liddy, frowning. She had never heard anyone cough like that before.

Vivienne's eyes were glazed over and her expression foggy.

'I have done too much for today,' she replied through ragged breaths. 'I must go and lie down for a while.'

'Yes, of course,' replied Liddy, stepping out of the way.

Vivienne walked slowly towards the door and lifted the latch.

'What about the pie?' Liddy called after her, its steamy, scented breaths still escaping into the room.

'Serve it,' she replied. 'There is enough for everyone. Take the plates through to the drawing room and leave them there. The guests will come if they find their appetites.'

Liddy nodded.

'I must ask that you also take a plate to my brother. Just follow the corridor to the left and keep going as far as you can. But I assume you know the way already.' Then she was gone, without giving Liddy a chance to argue.

The thought of seeing the Keymaker again filled her with a small flutter of panic ... or was it excitement? How much of her had been revealed through the gap in the door? Would he recognise her? Liddy took her time preparing dinner, washing and peeling vegetables and boiling them, together with some potatoes she found in the pantry. Then she took the pie from the warming tray in the oven, sliced it into pieces and filled the plates, ready for supper. Taking them into the drawing room, she was surprised to see the Major was already sitting at one of the tables, holding his knife and fork in anticipation of his meal.

'It's late,' he slurred.

Liddy wanted to pour it into his lap, but instead she lifted one of the plates from the tray and set it down in front of him. Then she took the other plates to the adjacent table.

'I doubt they'll be wanting theirs,' he said, already stuffing a piece of pie into his mouth. 'I haven't seen them since that debacle this morning.'

Liddy gritted her teeth and left the plates there anyway. She wondered if the Major had always been so rude, or whether loss had made him that way. His tone was sharp and thorny, but thorns could also offer protection. She was surprised to feel herself soften a little at this thought.

Back in the kitchen, she took her time with the last plate, adding another couple of potatoes and then removing them, before putting them back on again. She arranged the sliced carrots carefully around the leeks before sprinkling them with salt. This was the Keymaker's plate and she made sure it had the largest slab of pie.

Suddenly needing to know what she looked like, she lifted a ladle from the hook and held it up to her face; immediately she wished she hadn't. Of course the mischievous metal had distorted her face, but the wild hair was of her own making. Being caught in the rain had left it in tangles and she ran her fingers desperately through the frizz, attempting to release the knots. Then she pinched her cheeks, trying to restore their colour. Still disappointed, she threw the ladle down with a clang and pinched her cheeks again, harder this time, before lifting the tray of food and leaving the warmth of the kitchen behind.

The aching cold of the passageway spurred her on. Steadying her hold on the tray, Liddy continued towards the door that she knew was there in the darkness. The corridor seemed longer than she remembered, and she was grateful for the occasional flickering candle on the wall. There was just enough light for her to see the way ahead.

Finally there it was, the door to the Keymaker's room. As she approached, she felt her heart skip and her pulse quicken. After a long pause and a deep breath, she clenched her fist and knocked twice upon the door. Immediately a muffled voice replied from within. She turned the handle and entered the room.

After the biting draughts of the passageway, the room felt warm. It swelled in a sickly kind of heat, as though something was festering in the corners. There was something else too, the faint scent of perfume – lilies perhaps – left behind, but then it was gone again and she wondered if she had imagined it. She knew he was there; he'd replied to her knocking, but for a moment she couldn't find him anywhere. Then a movement caught her eye, alerting her to his presence. He was standing in front of the open door of the furnace with his back to her and she felt her stomach twist and flip.

'Leave it on the desk,' he called, without turning round.

Liddy's heart pounded as she walked further into the room. The light of the fire danced upon his skin, and once more she was reminded of the golden almonds she was so used to holding in her hands. Still he didn't turn to see her. Part of her felt relieved, but the other part felt the desperate need to see his face again.

When he finally did turn to see her, no words left his mouth, but his eyes showed recognition and Liddy shifted from one foot to the other, willing him to look away. *He must have been expecting Vivienne*, she thought, still standing there with the tray in her hands.

'Hello,' he said, and Liddy could hear the word *again* left unspoken in the air. Suddenly she felt like a trespasser, like a drunk at Vespers. With trembling hands, she pushed the tray onto the desk and a little water spilled from the glass.

'Your supper,' she managed to mumble.

She felt the dark intensity of his eyes upon her and saw in them a look of disbelief, or was it curiosity at finding her there in his room again? She wanted to explain, to apologise, but no words came; instead she stood still and continued to hold his gaze. The Keymaker moved a little closer until only the desk separated them. An image from the previous night rushed through her mind and she was convinced that he knew what she was thinking.

'Where is Vivienne?' His voice was deep.

'I – er—'

Liddy took a step back and felt her hip catch against the side of a chair. He watched. He waited, wanting an explanation.

'Vivienne is not feeling well this evening,' she stuttered. 'She has gone to bed early.'

The answer seemed to satisfy him, and he pulled out a chair to sit down. The scrape of it filled the room.

Liddy knew she should leave, but something harnessed her there.

He leaned forward and frowned. 'Are you going to stand there and watch me eat?'

'I – no – I'm—' Liddy stumbled over her words, too embarrassed for them to make any sense.

'No one has given me your taglocks,' he said, suddenly interrupting her.

'I didn't bring any,' she replied quickly.

'Well, you should know that I cannot make your key without them,' he replied, plunging his fork into the pie. The crust crumbled and the sauce oozed out.

'I'm not here for a key,' she said.

That caught his attention and he slowly lowered his fork. She could see the intrigue in his eyes and felt a tiny flush of triumph.

'Why else would you be here, if not for a key?'

'To make marchpane.'

'Marchpane?'

'Yes,' replied Liddy defensively. 'Vivienne invited me to make marchpane for the villagers and the guests here.'

'Vivienne,' he muttered, throwing the fork onto the plate, as though he had tasted something bitter.

She was close enough to see the way his tousled hair curled around his neck, so dark, but with more grey flecks than she had seen last night. A small scar glistened under his eye like the silver scale of a fish, and there was another to match it on his arm. She wondered what had left them there. Like last time, his shirt was unbuttoned and untucked. The room was too warm for clothes, she thought, feeling the clamminess beneath her own.

Her eyes lingered and she felt the urge to strip him of his rags and sink him into a steaming bath. There was enough rosewater in the cupboard to freshen his skin and hair, and there were spices on the shelf that would do the rest. Then she imagined his naked body and she could feel his hands upon her; he was no longer lying alone in the bath, because she was there with him, wrapped in his arms, legs entwined, one mouth pressed to the other. She had to make it stop.

'Goodnight,' she blurted, crushing her own thoughts.

Then she turned and hurried away without waiting for his reply. She could feel his eyes following her out of the room. But what she didn't know was that he was still staring at the door long after she'd gone.

CHAPTER 15

The Locked Room

That night thoughts of the Keymaker filled Liddy's mind. He had recognised her; she was sure of that and she felt herself flush. Unfamiliar feelings of desire and longing had taken hold and left her restless, in a way she had never experienced when thinking of Jack Heathcote, or any other man. Her mother had been mistaken to think she would grow to love Jack. Had she cried, argued, stormed from the room when she'd discovered Liddy gone? What had her father told her, if anything? Liddy could see her mother sitting with her sister complaining about her wilful, wayward daughter, who hadn't shown one ounce of gratitude since the moment she was born. With no bride, there would be no wedding and her mother would simply have to find herself a new obsession to while away the hours. Liddy swallowed back the guilt. At least there would be a baby soon to help them forget.

She tried to sleep, but her thoughts returned again and again to the Keymaker. When she closed her eyes, Liddy couldn't help but imagine his naked body lying next to hers. It was so real that once or twice she found herself reaching across the bed to see if he had come to her in the night, but her hand found nothing, just the lumps and bumps of an old, cold mattress. She remembered Tabby saying that sometimes if you really, really wanted something and imagined it was yours, then one day it would be. You didn't have to drop a coin in a fountain or catch floating dandelion seeds for a wish to come true, she'd said. She'd wanted Matthew to propose and there she was, married and with a baby on the way. Liddy sighed softly in the dark. All her wishful thinking hadn't brought the Keymaker to her bed yet, but at least he was there, below her in the same house. And for now that was enough.

She was finally almost asleep when she heard it. A persistent and continuous scratching sound. Still drowsy, she wondered if her wishing really had brought the Keymaker to her door, but it was a childish thought and a foolish one; grown men don't scratch at doors, they simply open them and stride in. Sitting up, she blinked and listened again to the sound, trying to determine if it was coming from somewhere inside the room or from the corridor. *Rats*, she thought at first, but whatever was making that noise sounded much larger than that.

'The cat!' she exclaimed aloud. Of course it was just the cat wanting to be let in. Last night it had slept at the bottom of the bed, and it must have found it so comfortable that it was back again. She threw aside the quilt and the tangle of blankets that had been keeping her warm and groped against the door for the latch. Lifting it, she peered into the corridor, expecting to feel warm, soft fur brushing against her leg, but instead all she felt was the familiar cold breath of the house. The cat was nowhere to be seen. Perhaps it had grown bored of waiting for Liddy to open the door and had wandered off to seek its dreams elsewhere. She was about to shut the door and return to bed when the sound came again. More of a scuffle than a scratch this time. Perhaps the cat had got itself shut in one of the other rooms along the corridor. Pulling one of the blankets from the bed, Liddy wrapped it round her shoulders and stepped out of her room.

At first she couldn't tell which direction the noise was coming from. The house was playing its usual tricks again, only this time with skittering sounds that seemed to come from everywhere and nowhere, all at once. Liddy listened until she was as sure as she could be and then she turned away from the stairs and went in search of the noise. Beyond the bathroom, the rest of the corridor was lost in the gloom. She lifted a candle from its sconce and continued. The flame flickered wildly and then quivered as she plunged into the inscrutable darkness. She made her way very slowly, keeping her hand pressed to the wall.

The corridor seemed to wind deeper and deeper and she felt like a frightened child lost in the dark woods. The scuffling continued. In the feeble light of the candle she could see motes of dust suspended in the cobwebbed air. It made her feel claustrophobic. The dust seemed to grow thicker, tickling the back of her throat, and she stifled a cough. After steadying herself against the wall she continued along the corridor until she reached the bottom of a set of steps encased in narrow wood-panelled walls. Conscious of every creak, she climbed up to the second floor. The air was dank and mouldy with the odour of disuse. As she lifted the candle higher, the light revealed scrawled black patterns that trickled down from the ceiling. For a moment Liddy thought they were ghostly messages, warnings to turn back, but she quickly realised they were just water stains from a leaking roof or a broken pipe, and she continued before fear had the chance to pull her back.

There were only a few doors along these walls, and their handles were thick with dust as though they hadn't been opened for years. The corridor was completely empty, and Liddy guessed the floor was unoccupied. Even the strange scratching that had brought her here had ceased. Convincing herself that she should go no further, she sighed and began to retrace her steps to bed before she forgot the way. She hadn't gone very far when she heard a sound again. This time it wasn't the innocent scratch of a cat, but something much more urgent, like a child shaking a rattle or someone trying to turn the handle of a locked door. She stopped and turned.

Instinct told her she was somewhere at the back of the house, where the windows of the closed rooms would look out onto the blackened stumps and the overgrown briars that she had noticed yesterday. Everything there seemed so distant and remote. Perhaps this was the world conjured up by the Keymaker and Vivienne – a place of darkness and secrets and sorrow. A place she didn't belong. 'Hello,' she called softly, half-dreading a reply.

The corridor went quiet. Compelled by some strange unnatural force that defied explanation, Liddy hurried in the direction that the noise had come from, all thoughts of returning to bed quickly forgotten.

The corridor curved round and the noise came again, louder this time. Her feet hesitated; something in the air had changed. It wasn't anything tangible, or even know-able, but it made her tense and an uneasy feeling crawled over her skin. It was like seeing a snake slither under the door of your bedroom, knowing it's where you were to spend the night. But it wasn't a snake that made her shudder; it was something else entirely.

Up ahead, someone had lit a pair of fat candles above a set of double doors. Their light was dim, yet they beckoned her. Taking a few tentative steps towards them, Liddy felt something beneath her feet and looked down. The floor was sprinkled with silvery dust, and small piles had been swept against the walls. It must be the pollen

Ben had told her about. Perhaps it had blown in from a hole in the roof, or down a chimneypot – the place was falling to pieces around her. Crouching, she took the strange white substance and rubbed it between her fingers. It wasn't pollen – it had a fine, gritty texture and she didn't need to taste it to know that it was salt. There were those who believed it had the power to ward off the evil eye, that a pinch thrown over the left shoulder would prevent evil spirits entering the house. But those same people believed that shoes left on a table would bring misfortune, and that onion juice was a cure for baldness. Liddy had never believed a word of such tales. Still, she couldn't think of any other reason for it to be there.

She pulled the blanket around her ears and approached the door. The handles showed not a single speck of dust, and whatever this room was, it was clearly still being used. Liddy reached for the handle, turned it and pushed. Nothing happened and she slowly released her breath. She tried again, turning it the opposite way, but clearly it was locked. For a moment she wondered if this could be another door leading people to the souls of their loved ones. A room to say goodbye, without guilt or regret or fear or shame. But Ben had said there was only one such door and that was downstairs in the library.

Lowering the candle, she found the keyhole and peered through, trying to see into the room. All was black. There was no discernible shape or movement from within, just a hollow feeling that made her quickly pull away. She felt

as if she'd slipped into the pages of one of her books –
stories of mysterious houses and locked rooms, and mad
women hiding in the attic. It made her shiver.

Then the scratching began again, but this time it was
close. It was right by her feet.

CHAPTER 16

The Doll

Liddy jumped back in fright, and the flame of the candle jumped with her. She couldn't see anything, but that didn't mean there wasn't a rat lurking in the dark. The knot in her stomach tightened and twisted at the thought. It took a moment for her to steady her hand and for the flame to settle. Everything had fallen quiet again. Slowly she lowered the candle until it revealed a small bundle propped against the door. It resembled a tangle of yarn and twigs and cloth – a strange, unidentifiable object at first. But as she carefully lifted it into her hand, she realised it was a small hand-made doll. A lump of brown clay had been attached to the cloth to create a lopsided head, and someone had hastily made a face of two slanted eyes, a nose and a stab of a mouth. Black curls sprang from the top of the head, and at first Liddy thought they had been made from wool, but as she ran them through her fingers, they felt as real as her own. It made her shiver.

It was unlike any doll she had ever seen before; tatty and misshapen, it was more like kindling to start a fire than a gift for a child. She could imagine an old woman making it by candlelight – a grandmother whose fingers were riddled with age and whose eyes saw too many shadows. A careless slip here and an awkward fumble there. Liddy's sleep-starved mind wondered if it was Alice and John's missing taglock. But what was it doing all the way up here? Had it been dropped? No likely answers came, but she held it tightly, pleased that maybe she had found their daughter's doll. *They will get their key after all,* she thought. Her relief pushed from her mind all thoughts of the strange scratching sound that had led her up the stairs.

A wretched coughing startled her. She knew at once who it was, but in the dark and winding passageways of the house it was impossible to tell exactly where it was coming from. Everything was distorted, and sound was swept along as easily as birds in a storm. Things that seemed close enough to touch were too far away to be seen, and other things hid, only to appear suddenly out of nowhere. The coughing persisted, and Liddy found an odd comfort in knowing that she wasn't the only one who couldn't sleep. She half-expected to find Vivienne standing in the corridor with her admonishing stare, but when she looked, it just stretched away into the darkness. Like a ghost, Liddy moved forward.

A few minutes later she came to a set of stairs that led down through the same narrow wood-panelled walls. They were steep and wound like a helter-skelter, making her head spin with every step. She was reminded once more of the fairground at home, but this time the memory wasn't a pleasant one. She felt trapped and dazed, and penned in, and was relieved when she finally reached a small landing. On one side there was another set of stairs continuing further down into the darkness, and on the other there was a door, half-open, and it was here that the coughing grew louder.

I'm making quite a habit of peering into rooms uninvited, she thought, as she once again quietly tilted her head around the edge of the door. Liddy's mother had repeatedly told her that nothing good would come to those who listened at keyholes; but Liddy wasn't listening, she was watching. Vivienne sat on the end of her bed in a long white nightgown; its straps had loosened and fallen down her arms Her bare skin looked as smooth and pale as the flesh of a sliced apple. The familiar black dress that she usually wore was folded neatly over the back of a chair. The most captivating thing of all was her hair; Vivienne had released it from its pins and unwound it, like a ball of soft wool, until it almost reached the bottom of her spine. Most of the grey had been drowned beneath its dark waves, and Liddy wondered why she didn't wear it loose more often. She looked younger and softer, almost beautiful.

She watched Vivienne press two fingers together and dip them into a glass pot. Lifting them out, she began smoothing them over her chest in small circular motions until her skin glistened. She dipped them in once more, only this time instead of rubbing the oily mixture into her chest, she reached her arm awkwardly over her shoulder and tried to rub it between her thin, sharp shoulder blades. The effort of doing so seemed to leave her exhausted and she dropped her hand onto her lap with a heavy, defeated sigh. Liddy felt compelled to stride into the room, pick up the bottle and continue with the rubbing, but she knew that such a gesture would not be welcomed.

There was little else in the room besides the bed, a small writing desk and a wardrobe. A few shelves had been fixed to the wall, and they were filled with books and neatly arranged objects. There was less in Vivienne's room than in her own; it would be more fitting for a scullery maid than for the mistress of the house, and Liddy wondered what made her live among such emptiness, with nothing and no one for company.

The coughing came again in an agonising burst that made Vivienne clutch her side. Liddy hoped it was just a chill, the worst of which would soon be over, but something told her that Vivienne's suffering was more deeply rooted than a common cold. At least the fire was lit, and the room was warm. Tendrils of smoke rose from a shallow dish filled with herbs and oils; it scented the room with an impossibly sweet fragrance. Rosemary? Ginger? Violets again? Liddy couldn't quite place it. Her eyes followed the tendrils higher until they reached the objects on the shelf: a pocket-sized owl carved from wood, a tortoise made of plush green velvet and a small brightly painted box, closed on its secrets. There was also a thaumatrope of leaping tigers and a little stack of puzzle blocks. Liddy realised they were all toys for a child to play with. Further along the shelf she saw a glass case and, lying within it, surrounded by a sprinkle of dried flowers, was a doll. It reminded her of the tale of Sleeping Beauty, frozen in a spell.

A sudden movement drew her attention, and she saw Vivienne stand up and move towards the smoking dish. Pushing her hair back from her face, she dipped her head and inhaled deeply. Closer to the light of the fire, Liddy noticed a red tint in a few strands of her hair, bright as ribbons. As she inhaled, Vivienne sucked in sharply and winced, as though it hurt to breathe so deeply. Then she inhaled again, holding her breath for even longer. Finally she exhaled and let her hair drop back over her chest. It was only when she lay down on the bed and her head was resting against the pillow that Liddy realised the mistake she'd made – the red in her hair was blood. There was also a red smudge on Vivienne's neck and another small stain that had soaked into her nightgown, like a flowery bloom. Worse still was the crimson trickle from the corner of her mouth making its way towards her jaw.

Vivienne must have felt it there, because she reached for a tissue to try and wipe it away, but she wasn't quick enough; it had already dropped onto the white cotton pillowcase, where it shone bright as a ruby.

It was all too much: the doll, the blood, the images of death. Liddy shrank back and fled down the stairs and along the passageway that she found waiting at the bottom. At last she saw a door she recognised and knew that behind it lay the library. She breathed a sigh of relief – she knew her way from there.

Interlude

*G*reen, green, evergreen. I am stifled, suffocating and no longer able to breathe. There are people who say this poison has neither taste nor smell, but they are very much mistaken. It is cloying and acrid, like a basket of fruit slowly rotting, but of course she cannot smell it; if she could, she would cover her nose and mouth and flee from this place like a hunted rabbit, turning the key before it was too late. But instead she makes another mistake. She stays.

I watch her for weeks. She arrives every evening, just after supper, announced by the groan of the door. In she walks, cradling the weight of her stomach under one arm as though the baby was already there and needed to be coaxed and lulled to sleep. Once the fire is lit, she moves slowly around the room, quietly singing a lullaby. I don't remember all the words she sings, but there is something about a thousand stars and the round midnight moon, bright as a bauble. How peaceful she seems, not knowing that soon there will be no peace left at all, only the haunting dirges, mournful and bleak, echoing over the tops of the distant mountains while we watch the bauble break.

Every so often she pauses to pick up a toy she has so lovingly chosen: a teddy bear with a yellow bow tied round its neck, a kite and a spinning top, which she sets to the floor. She claps her hands in delight as it whirls in colourful circles towards the window, watching until it clatters against the wall and silences itself. But her favourite is the little music box. So enchanted, she bought it from an old curiosity shop months before there was any talk of a baby, but she couldn't resist its magic. It is wooden and painted all over with tiny pink mermaids, and its clasp is made from a silver shell. Inside a ballerina springs up on her toes, arms held high over her head, with her chin tilted to the sky. A few quick turns of the handle bring her to life, and the ballerina twirls to the sweetest melody she has ever heard.

'But what if we have a boy?' he'd asked.

'All babies love the sound of music,' she'd replied, dreamily.

She looked so happy that he hadn't the heart to refuse.

But the performance never lasts long enough and, after the tune winds down, she finds comfort in the rocking chair – her feet pushing her back and forth, back and forth, until its steady rhythm soothes her to sleep next to the forever-empty cradle.

All those hours spent in this room, oblivious to the danger that is lurking silent as a serpent, watchful as a hawk. If only it were so – it is much kinder to be bitten or torn to pieces, for *it to be over so quickly. Much better than all this waiting, waiting, waiting. I can hear her breathing, in and out, deep and long, until there will be no more breathing at all. I try to scream her out of the room, willing her to hear me, but I am buried, and my cries are muffled, and she was lost in contented dreams. I try to rattle the windowpanes and the floorboards, I even invite a gust of wind to loosen the soot in the flue and send it into her lap, but still she doesn't stir. All the time death is creeping ever closer on soundless feet, unnoticed, and there is nothing I can do to stop it.*

CHAPTER 17

Gifts

When Liddy opened the window the next morning birdsong filled the room, flute-throated, happy and inviting, but not enough to chase away the previous night's strangeness. What she had seen in Vivienne's room still unsettled her. She had been coughing up blood, and there was enough of it to be caught in her hair. Even her nightdress and pillowcase had bloomed with the sickness that she tried to hide. Liddy attempted to shut her mind to the horror.

The blackbird was on the lawn again and another swooped between two trees. Liddy leaned out of the window and breathed deeply. The view was spectacular, stretching over the garden, across the azure lake towards the pink-topped roofs of the village. Someone somewhere was having a bonfire – Ben, she supposed. She could smell wood-smoke in the air. The sky had an unexpected azure blue, as though it were still summer, cloudless and pristine, and she could feel the warmth on her face. It seemed the garden still refused to welcome the arrival of autumn, and Liddy was glad. She lingered for a while longer, watching the slow drift of pollen. Finally hunger got the better of her and she pulled the window closed and, not forgetting the doll she'd found in the corridor, hurried downstairs.

She hoped to find Alice and John at breakfast, but there was no sign of them in the drawing room, and all the breakfast things had already been cleared away. Only the Major was there, in his usual stupor, his grey-white hair rising above the back of the chair, as dull and thick as a plume of smoke from a factory.

In the kitchen she laid the doll on the counter; just looking at it gave her a feeling of unease. Somehow last night it had seemed less grotesque, but looking at it now, she wasn't sure if it was even a doll at all. Its mouth was perhaps the most disturbing thing about it – more of a gash or a slice made by an angry hand – and the way its wild hair twisted, like lots of tiny nooses around its lump of a head, sent shivers down her spine. Liddy couldn't imagine letting a child play with something so hideous; it repelled her. Then she scolded herself; perhaps this was all Alice and John could afford. Fine porcelain dolls swathed in bright silks with tumbling curls were expensive and far too precious for most children to play with. She remembered the street children at home, who would make entire doll families out of clothes pegs and rags. These were loved just as much. Maybe the doll had been hand-made for Alice and John as a gift, and the value was in the sentiment, not the stitching. Nevertheless Liddy reached for a tea towel and quickly pulled it over the doll, so that she could no longer see the ugliness of it, and quickly washed the smell of mould and damp from her fingers.

After a simple breakfast of bread and honey, she retreated to the kitchen. Her hands were restless to make more marchpane. She liked the feeling of turning something hard and tough into something so soft that it could melt in the mouth. In her haste, or perhaps because she was so used to making marchpane without petals, Liddy completely forgot to add them to her baking.

By mid-afternoon Alice and John still hadn't appeared. Liddy thought about knocking on all the doors upstairs until she found them, but that felt too intrusive. She wondered where Vivienne was; she hadn't seen her all morning, either, and hoped she had finally managed to get some sleep.

Everyone here had a place: Ben's was in the garden amongst the flowers; Vivienne hid in the shadows; the Major was always slumped in the armchair; and Alice and John preferred the privacy of their room, wherever it was. Grief does not take kindly to visitors. That just left the

Keymaker, who occupied not only the dark chaos of his workshop, but also the dark chaos of her mind. Liddy decided that if she were to choose a place, then it would be in the library, with its endless shelves and marbled floor and cosy reading hideaways.

Escaping from the house, she trundled out the door and down the path, her ears listening for the sound of Ben's spade or the slow plod of his boots, but she heard only birdsong. Down by the potting shed she saw the remains of a recently lit bonfire, its embers still gleaming red and an occasional spark caught on the breeze. It must have been the one she'd smelled from her room. She looked at the charred wood and leaves and, in amongst it all, she saw the scorched hem of a nightdress and other material bearing the same pattern as the pillowcase that Vivienne had been resting on last night; the red trickle from her mouth had long since burned away.

Finally she found Ben, chatting amiably to half a dozen red hens. She rested her arms across the top of the gate and watched him, unnoticed. The way he spoke to them amused her, like a patient schoolmaster with a class full of rebellious children, and she wondered if Ben was a father, or even perhaps a grandfather. He had never spoken of a family and it made her sad to think he might not have one. Such a kind and gentle man would be so easy to love.

'Good afternoon,' she called out.

He looked up and then, as always, tapped his cap by way of greeting.

'You're just in time to help me collect the eggs,' he said, looking pleased to see her. 'I'm late this morning – there are too many jobs to do.'

Liddy pushed open the gate and walked towards the small wooden hen house. She reached her hand through the door and felt her way among the warm straw beds, delighted every time her fingertips brushed against the smooth shape of an egg. After counting seven into the basket, she went back to the yard, to find Ben filling a shallow trough with water.

'Vivienne was coughing up blood last night. I saw her.'

Ben frowned, unwilling to meet her gaze.

'And those were her bed sheets thrown on the bonfire, weren't they?'

Ben stopped what he was doing and straightened his back. 'You are right to worry.'

'Why, what's wrong with her?'

Ben finally met her gaze. 'Do you remember the bandits I told you about?'

Liddy nodded.

'Well, they brought something with them – a disease – and it found its way inside her lungs and now she can't get it out. Nothing can get it out.'

'The bandits?' exclaimed Liddy. 'But that was six years ago! Has she been sick all that time?'

'For a long time she didn't know – none of us did – but then one day the coughing started and it never seemed to stop.' His voice trailed away and there was a small silence before he spoke again. 'She called it her punishment.'

'Punishment for what?' asked Liddy, confused.

Ben shook his head, but she got the sense that he knew more than he was willing to share.

'Do you believe I'm here just to make marchpane and be a general help around the place?' Liddy asked suddenly.

Ben arched his eyebrows. 'I was told to collect you from the station, the same as all the other guests, and so that's what I did.'

'I still don't understand.'

'Not everything can be understood, but it doesn't mean we shouldn't accept it.'

'But Vivienne is—' Liddy paused, unable to find the right words.

Ben laughed and she could hear the affection he had for Vivienne when he spoke. 'Signora Castellini has the ability to sense things; she always has, even as a little girl. She knows things about a person just from holding their possessions. A hairbrush or a scarf can tell her all about someone she's never met.'

Liddy thought for a moment. 'Do you think it's possible that she sensed something about me from the marchpane you brought here?'

'I imagine so,' he replied.

Liddy knew about the ability to read objects, from the time she had seen a large board on the pavement outside the Queen's Head tavern. Anyone wishing to pass could not do so without stepping around it, and she remembered her mother and aunt tutting at the inconvenience. Liddy could still picture it: the elaborate chalk lettering announcing *Madame Sydonia, world-renowned psychometrist; only one object away from revealing the truth*. Her mother and her aunt's tutting had ceased as they read the sign, and their voices had dropped to hushed whispers and nervous titters. The door had swung open and a woman hurried out, sobbing into a handkerchief. She hadn't got very far when the door was opened again, this time by a man in quick pursuit. 'She's a quack!' he'd yelled after her, trying to call the woman back to him, but by then she was already halfway down the street.

A few months later Liddy had found a book in her father's collection called *The Art of Psychometry*, which explained how a certain person could hold an object and measure the soul of its owner. She had imagined someone like Madame Sydonia with a wide red-painted mouth, gleaming emerald eyes and midnight hair beneath a scarlet veil. She most definitely had not pictured someone like Vivienne, so drab and grey and rinsed of all colour.

'Vivienne studies psychometry?'

'I'm not sure it's something that can be studied. It's a gift, and gifts are given things,' he replied, opening the gate for her.

'And her brother?' Liddy asked, trying to keep the interest from her voice. 'I thought he was the one who handled objects?'

Ben laughed. 'They both have their gifts.'

The talk of objects reminded her of the doll still lying in the kitchen.

'Have you seen Alice and John?'

'Isn't that them?' he asked, nodding in the direction of the drawing room. Through the large windows, Liddy could see them sitting together, pale-faced and motionless like two waxworks.

'I have to go,' she said, sprinting up the lawn.

'Wait!' called Ben. 'Take the eggs.'

Entering the kitchen and putting the basket on the table, Liddy went over to the counter to collect the taglock, but as she approached it, something felt wrong. It took her a moment to realise what it was – the doll was still there, but the tea towel she had used to cover it had gone. Had Vivienne come in and used it or had it slipped to the floor? A search under the table revealed nothing. When she looked again, more closely, she realised to her horror that a small piece of twine had been twisted and tied deliberately around the doll's neck, tight as a hangman's noose. Her blood froze. Who would do such a thing, and why? She hesitated before quickly loosening the twine and pulling it free from the doll's head. Then she hurried towards the drawing room, relieved to finally be getting rid of the wretched thing.

Alice and John were still sitting at the window. Their chairs were pulled together, heads lowered, huddled in their grief. Neither of them noticed Liddy approach.

'Hello,' she said quietly, so as not to surprise them. 'I found your missing taglock.' She held out the doll for them to take.

Alice looked up blankly, but as her eyes moved to the doll, her face fell. Without speaking, she turned to John as though he might offer an explanation, but his face looked just as bewildered. He stood up, and Alice's gaze returned to her lap.

'That's not ours,' he said coldly.

Liddy frowned. 'But you lost one of your objects and I thought—'

'*That* is not what we lost,' said John. His face was a twist of disgust. 'We would never have anything to do with a cursed poppet.'

Quickly Liddy dropped her hand like a caned schoolgirl. 'A poppet?'

There was a sudden whoosh of air behind her and she felt someone snatch the doll from her hand. Turning around, she came face-to-face with Vivienne, whose expression was fierce and challenging.

'Where did you get this?' she hissed.

All eyes were on her now, apart from those of Alice, who was softly weeping, too feeble for such confusion. Even the Major had turned his head to revel in the drama.

'I found it upstairs and—'

'Yes, but *where*?' demanded Vivienne, shaking the doll so violently that all its stuffing came loose, and a handful of dried flowers and leaves fell out.

'On the second floor … It was propped up against a door. I thought it was the taglock they'd lost.' Liddy's words were broken and jagged as she realised her mistake. Her instincts had been right: nobody would have given a doll like that to a child to play with. Of course it was a poppet, she could see that now, with its dark face and little ragged dress stuffed full of tiny crusted leaves and nail clippings, and who knew what else.

Vivienne glared at her and then, without another word, she turned and strode from the room, leaving Liddy frozen in her humiliation. She could hear Alice's quiet little sobs and the comforting reassurances of John as he rested his head on top of hers, like one might do with a frightened child waking from a nightmare. He shifted then and caught Liddy's gaze, giving her a stiff nod. The damage had already been done a long time before, and not by Liddy. The acknowledgement of it released her, and she mouthed the word *sorry* before rushing from the room.

CHAPTER 18

Pumpkin

Liddy thought about running up the stairs to her room, but she knew that hiding wouldn't solve anything. It certainly didn't seem to bring the Keymaker any peace. She could still see the fury in Vivienne's face as she demanded to know where the poppet had come from, and no matter how hard she tried, she couldn't shake the image away. She went in search of a distraction.

The library didn't seem to belong to the rest of the house; it had an irresistible warmth that invited its visitors inside like an old friend, and that's what Liddy needed more than anything. Besides, she wanted to meet the elusive Eloura, whom Ben had spoken of.

Back among the shelves, she felt her spirits settle as the strange madness of the poppet slowly slipped away. She enjoyed getting lost in a good story; it was the most wonderful escape. She thought back to her father's collection, so small in comparison to what surrounded her now. Here there was a banquet of stories, a feast of words, gateways, doors, hearts and souls. Her eyes flicked over the spines, the pages all bound with the same strange, tangled root – thin and wispy – like a spiral of smoke from a fairy-tale chimneypot. There was so much more to the library that she hadn't yet explored. Secret alcoves and dusty passageways that ended in nothing but mystery, and she wondered if they led into different realms. She was right below the domed ceiling and, looking up, she could see the peridot glass of its three windows. The light filtering through them made it feel oceanic, like being submerged deep, deep underwater. Through a slender crevice in the wall, a thick rooted plant had wandered in and made itself quite at home. Its white-green stems spread decoratively along the wall and went rifling through the shelves, as though in search of a story. Its large leaves were the most luscious green, and its luminous white flowers were yet to unfurl themselves and hung like large teardrops. Another of the plants had pushed through a crack in the floor and was winding its way all around the library. From beneath one of its gigantic leaves, Liddy saw an amber gleam. It blinked at her, making her gasp. Then she heard a ruffling sound, soft and feather-like, and a beautiful snow-coloured owl appeared out of nowhere and swooped away between the shelves.

Everything was so dark and green that it no longer felt as if she had dived beneath the water, but more as though she had stumbled into some strange book-filled wood. After all, woods have their own stories to tell, and plenty of them. She moved aimlessly, hoping to get lost for a while, marvelling at the vertiginous height of the shelves and the way so many books filled them, all crushed together. They had even been slotted and balanced between the beams of the rising ceiling. Liddy feared that a loud sneeze or a sudden breeze would send them plummeting to the ground or onto her head. Then she remembered the book she had read the other day, so light in her hand, almost weightless, and her fear dissipated. If anything fell through the air, it would land with a flutter, not a thud.

Every so often along the shelves she happened upon a teapot, and next to it a small cup and saucer. Fragrant steam always rose from the spout, as though the tea had been freshly brewed. Each teapot was unique; some were square, others round, some had patterns of birds or flowers or stars, and some were painted in the exotic colours of faraway places, so distant that they could only be imagined. Many of them didn't resemble teapots at all; they looked more like the magical lamps of Arabia, with their elaborately curved handles and their tiny lids attached to minute brass chains. Liddy felt the giddy excitement of childhood, as she imagined rubbing her hand against one of them and waiting for the genie to appear with the promise of three wishes. Before she'd arrived, she'd known exactly what to wish for: for her father's acceptance of her new recipes; for her mother's ridiculous notion of marriage to be forgotten; and for Jack Heathcote to give up his relentless, futile pursuit of her. Now all of that felt too far away to matter, like it belonged to a different time and place. If she closed her eyes and thought about what she wanted that very moment, the only thing that came to Liddy's mind were the dark, thought-filled eyes of the Keymaker.

One of the tea lamps made her stop. It was ordinary enough, duck-egg blue with pink blossoms and a slender spout like the graceful neck of a swan, but the steam rising from it carried the scent of a rain-soaked orchard, so appealing and refreshing that she couldn't resist. Lifting the tea lamp over the cup, she poured out a golden liquid. She wondered if the teas were blended in such a way as to complement each section of the library's sadness. In the same way that strawberries are said to bring out the taste of champagne, perhaps the teas enhanced the stories in a similar way, making each one that little bit more poignant or memorable. She noticed the plaque, which read *Abandonment*, and became even more curious about the stories she would find there. She chose one of the books at random and made her way back to the fire, trying not to spill a single drop of her tea.

Someone had illustrated the front cover with a large orange-filled circle, which she wouldn't have known was meant to be a pumpkin, had it not been for the title written above it. Something about the writing and the picture made her think the story belonged to a child.

She lifted the cup to her lips and took a sip of summer; it had a delicate rose flavour with a hint of spiced apple, and there was something else, too unfamiliar to name. She was a little disappointed that the cat hadn't joined her and wondered if the owl would swoop past again instead. She laughed – what a strange place she'd come to – but then again, all the best things in the world are a little strange. After a few more sips, she kicked off her boots, opened the book and began to read from its flimsy pages.

Pumpkin

My mummy left when I was nearly five. I don't know where she went, Daddy never told me, and he didn't like talking about her. I remember she was sick in bed a lot and then one day she just wasn't there any more, and all her clothes were gone. I don't remember the time in between. I wondered if she had chosen to leave me, but when I asked Daddy if she'd died, he said that some things are worse than death. I later learned that dying can sometimes be a choice.

To make myself feel better I would write her lots and lots of letters. I found an old tube of her lipstick and, after painting my lips pink, I kissed all the letters, so she'd know how much I loved her. I wrote so many that I had to hide them all over the place: under my pillow, at the back of the wardrobe and in drawers. I didn't want Daddy to find them and get sad. I even took them outside and stuffed them into tree trunks or left them on park benches, hoping that someone who knew Mummy would read them and bring her home. Sometimes I kept them in the pocket of my pinafore or pushed into the bottom of my shoe and forgot about them, but when I sat down at the table and heard the crumple of the paper in my pocket, I was reminded of the wish I kept there.

One day Daddy was taking me to a birthday party, and I remember slipping my foot into my shiny red shoe, but no matter how hard I tried, my foot wouldn't fit. In my excitement I had forgotten that one of my letters to Mummy was inside and, as Daddy tried to help, my secret tumbled out. I ran from the room in floods of tears, while Daddy quietly raged downstairs. There was no party that day or any other day after that. Daddy found all my letters to Mummy and burned them in the garden. I watched from the window and, when he came back inside, he told me it was time to forget about her. But there was one he didn't find; it was hidden in the lining of Mummy's jewellery box. It was where she kept her own secrets, where the little brown bottle rolled around, more precious than any of the jewels shining above it. I would read that letter over and over again until the edges had worn away. It was all I had left.

Dearest Mummy,

I miss you so much and would do anything if you would come back. I'm sorry I asked you for so many bedtime stories when you were so tired. Now I know that one story is always enough, and I shouldn't have been so greedy, asking for two. I find it really, really hard to fall asleep without your voice, and your hand in my hair. The good news is that I have grown so much I can read the stories to myself now, and what's even better is that I have started to write my own. Even though you were always tired, you never seemed to close your eyes, and perhaps my stories could help you fall asleep. I would love to read you one. When Daddy isn't around, I sit in your room and read them aloud to your empty bed, as though you are still there listening. You always said I had a big imagination.

I know I was sometimes naughty, and I will try my hardest to be good. Here is a list of all the things I will promise to do if you come back: make my bed all by myself; brush your hair the way you used to brush mine; polish all the shoes; peel the potatoes; clear away the plates; and every morning before you wake up I will fetch fresh bread, so it's still warm when you come to the kitchen. It makes it easier to spread the butter, you said.

I promise I will try my very best to be perfect for you. Please come home.

I love you, always.

Pumpkin

When I was little, Mummy used to call me Pumpkin. It made me feel so safe and special. I still go to sleep with my *fingers crossed beneath my pillow, in a room full of quiet wishes, hoping it will be enough to bring her home. But it hasn't been so far.*

One morning I came back from the fields and there was a lady's hat resting on the kitchen table. I thought that Mummy had come back, and I burst into the drawing room full of excitement, expecting to fall into her arms. Instead there was a strange woman sitting in Mummy's chair. Her dress was the colour of a sunset and her golden hair had been curled perfectly onto her shoulders. Her cheeks glowed pink, and I thought she looked like a doll. She chattered to me with a voice full of giggles and, for the first time in a long time, I felt wanted. She pulled me into her arms and asked me my name, and I told her it was Pumpkin. If Mummy wasn't there to call me Pumpkin, then I wanted her to. She exchanged a puzzled look with Daddy and then, laughing, she pinched my cheek and told me I looked nothing like a pumpkin, because pumpkins were round and orange and best served in a pie. When she left, I asked Daddy all about her, expecting him to say it was our new housekeeper or a governess, but the answer he gave made me run from the room, slamming the door behind me.

Within a week she had moved in and brought her own child with her: a girl named Bella with long, swinging plaits. And, just like that, not only had I gained a new mummy, but I had gained a sister as well. Their arrival seemed to make Daddy very happy, but I felt sad. The woman who'd appeared that day in the sunset dress had vanished, and in her place was someone whose giggles had turned to sneers. I rarely existed in the house after that. I couldn't even go to my mummy's room any more, because the new mummy was always in there. Because I was older than Bella, a space was cleared in the attic, where I slept on a mattress among the dust and spiders' webs. Sometimes I was glad, because I could be alone with my letter and my thoughts. Daddy seemed to forget about me and each morning, when he looked up from his boiled egg, he seemed surprised to find me standing in the doorway. There was never a place set for me, and his surprise would shift to guilt as he shuffled off in search of an extra plate and a spoon. I had become invisible.

About three years later another tragedy struck. Daddy and my new mummy had gone on an outing, taking Bella with them. As usual, they had left me behind. This happened a lot, but they were always back before it grew dark, so I wasn't to worry. Often Daddy would be carrying Bella up the path, fast asleep in his arms, but this time they didn't return until much, much later and I thought they'd left me, just like Mummy. I stood at the window, watching and waiting, and before long it was too dark to see anything. I must have fallen asleep and was woken by a loud wailing. At first I thought it was a woodland animal caught in a farmer's snare, but the sound was closer than that; it was coming from somewhere in the house. I climbed out of bed and inched the door open, and the wailing grew louder. I didn't dare go downstairs, and I quickly shut the door and hid under the covers.

The next morning I saw Daddy by the window and my new mummy was sitting in front of the fire. Her face looked waxy and her eyes were still, and far away. I thought she was dead, until a great shuddering sob racked her body. Bella was nowhere to be found, and Daddy told me to sit in her place at the table.

Just like with Mummy, no one told me where Bella had gone. I would never have found out if I hadn't overheard Daddy talking about the day the horse trampled his daughter to death. It didn't make sense – I hadn't been trampled by any horse – but then I understood. He didn't mean me, he meant Bella. My new mummy sat day after day in the same chair, without uttering a single word. Her arms dangled by her sides and her head rolled forward, as though it was her neck that had been broken and not her heart. Daddy talked about shock and needing more time, and for some reason it made me think about Mummy's secret brown bottle – too empty now to offer any solace.

Then one day I heard my new mummy mumbling something through the open door of the kitchen. She was watching me and beckoning me towards her. I hadn't seen her move for weeks. I was frightened, but I moved closer. She reached out and pulled me into her arms. I stayed there, with my head pressed against her breast, listening as she repeated the same words over and over again: 'Oh, Bella. My beloved Bella. My sweet, sweet girl.'

Daddy thought it might help to pretend it was true and so he allowed the charade to continue. He got his wife back

and I got my old room again, and there is always a place
set for me at the table. I have to wear Bella's clothes, even
though they are much too small for me and the sleeves barely
touch my elbows. My new mummy brushes my hair and
folds it into two plaits, like she used to do with Bella's; we
bake cakes and read stories together, and even though I
outgrew all that such a long time ago, I don't say a word.
I know what it feels like to lose someone you loved. Sometimes
I catch her looking at me with a puzzled look on her face,
as though she isn't quite sure about something. Filled with
shame, I scurry from the room before she has a chance to
remember who I really am. It feels like borrowed time. A
magic spell ready to break; the stroke of midnight going to
take it all away again.

Mostly I accept what happens, and I wonder sometimes
if we both know the truth, but find it easier to pretend. I
know I will never be Pumpkin again, but the name Bella is
better than having no name at all.

It wasn't until Liddy had finished the last sentence that
she realised she was crying. The words had blurred and
faded as she read, but as she wiped her eyes, they still
looked out of focus. She hoped her falling tears hadn't
smudged the ink, but as she ran her fingertips across the
pages, they were completely dry. Peering closer, she could
see that some of the letters had vanished completely, yet
she was sure they had been there a moment ago, otherwise
how would she have been able to follow the story? Then

suddenly the pages began to dissolve and crumble, until she was left holding a handful of white flakes and a slender dangling root. There was nothing left of the book she had just been reading.

'Well done, you have released its sadness,' called someone from behind her. The voice was warm and deep and murmuring, like the soft purr of a sleeping cat.

CHAPTER 19

Eloura

The most astonishing woman was standing in the middle of the room. Her skin was dark, and her cheeks were dusted with gold. Over her shoulders, her hair fell like a waterfall frozen in moonlight, and she was wrapped in a black velvet cape embroidered with sequins and stars. It reminded Liddy of something a magician might wear onstage – tall and resplendent. Beneath it, the woman was dressed in a saffron taffeta gown that skimmed the floor. Something glinted, drawing Liddy's eyes to her belted waist, and to the dagger that was resting there. She gasped – wasn't it only bandits who carried daggers? But this one winked at her, more in mischief than malice. Over one of her eyes the woman wore a dark patch, with a white sailing boat embroidered onto the cloth. If she were not a bandit, then perhaps she was a pirate instead. She wore gossamer fingerless gloves with silk rosebuds sewn at the knuckles, and there were soft white slippers upon her feet. Neither a bandit nor a pirate then; more like a majestic queen.

'Bring it over here,' she said, gesturing towards what was left of the book in Liddy's hand.

'I'm sorry – I don't know what happened.'

But the astonishing woman shut her eye, revealing a glittering golden wing painted on its lid, and shook her head in a way that gave gentle reassurance. Liddy folded her fingers around the remains of the pages, careful not to let the tiny crumbs of the story flutter away, then moved towards her.

She couldn't help but gaze at the woman's one visible eye; it was the colour of sunlit honey, and so clear that Liddy could see her own wondering face reflected there.

'Follow me,' said the woman softly, and she led Liddy away from the fire towards the large globe at the front of the library.

'What section was it from?' she asked, nodding once again at the remains of the book.'

'Abandonment,' Liddy replied, remembering the plaque.

She watched in fascination as the woman spun the globe, and the silvery-white gemstones that she had thought were stars looked more like snowflakes whirling past. The woman narrowed her eye in focus, searching for something, and then she must have found it because she slowed the spinning with her finger until the globe stopped. She touched one of the gemstones and gave it a little tug, and Liddy watched as a tiny drawer sprang open.

'Here,' she said, pointing. Liddy curved her hand over the top of the drawer and dusted the remaining flakes of the story safely inside. It looked like a small pile of ash left over from a blaze.

'What about the root?' asked Liddy, still holding it in her palm.

'Yes, that must go in too. All of it.'

Once everything was inside, the woman quickly closed the drawer again and the globe returned to a perfect sphere.

'What happens to it now?' asked Liddy, emboldened by her own curiosity.

She wasn't entirely sure what had just occurred, and she couldn't imagine why anyone would want to keep bits of a book that could never be read again.

The woman's eye widened, as though the answer should have been an obvious one. 'We use it to make the best drink of them all – tea!'

Liddy's thoughts rushed back to the warm golden liquid she had been quietly sipping and it made her feel slightly peculiar, realising it had been brewed from the pages of a book. The flavour had been a strange one, but not at all unpleasant.

'So how did it feel to release the sadness?' the woman asked.

'What do you mean, release the sadness?'

'Each time a story is read, the sadness of its writer lessens little by little, until eventually it fades away to nothing and can no longer be felt. But of course a story has to be read many, many times for that to happen.'

'By who?' asked Liddy, not really understanding a word of what the woman was telling her.

'Anyone,' she replied, with a quick shrug.

'But who here can read all these stories?' Liddy's eyes roamed around the thousands of books. Reading them all would be an impossible task, even if the entire village was brought to the library.

'Me mostly, you sometimes; and anyone else who wanders this way.'

'But there are so many of them, and I've never seen anyone else in here.'

'Ah yes, but the writers send their stories in the hope that they will be read and read, and read again, and maybe – just maybe – they will receive an invitation to come here. It is hope that keeps them coming.'

'I feel like a trespasser,' confessed Liddy, quietly remembering the sadness of Pumpkin's tale.

The woman's large triangular-shaped face filled with confusion.

'A book is an invitation into another person's world – real or imagined – so how can you be a trespasser when you have been invited in?

Liddy remained doubtful. 'I don't know. The story I read felt so ... so personal, like it wasn't for me to read.'

The woman stepped closer to Liddy, and she could feel the softness of her cape brush against her hand like the warm fur of a cat. She spoke in cool, lilac whispers. 'Once stories are told they cannot be stolen, only shared. You are not a thief, Liddy, you are a sentinel.'

'How do you know my name?' she asked in surprise.

'I know the names of all the people here,' she replied, moving away again.

'And will you tell me yours?' But Liddy had already guessed that this mysterious woman was the one Ben had mentioned.

The woman tipped her head back and laughed. 'Of course I will – my name is not a secret. I am Eloura; I am a book-weaver, a story-spinner, a protector, a collector and a brewer of fine tea. I navigate vast stretches of water to find my way onto different shores, each one an unopened book. Decades might pass between one journey and the next, sometimes centuries, but I always find my way between the stories and back again.'

Liddy wondered if Eloura was speaking in metaphors. It seemed unlikely that she could be hundreds of years old. Her skin was dark and smooth, untouched by time, and her eye still had the wide-open sparkle of youth. Perhaps the journeys she spoke of were the ones spent between the pages of a book. Some books were so old, they were faded and yellow and their words almost impossible to read; others were shiny and expectant, with pages not yet turned.

'Did you make all these books?' Liddy asked, once again scanning the rows of stories and tunnels of tales, which disappeared without end.

Eloura smiled. 'I merely gather the pages together and bind them. The books are only truly made once the stories are written in them. And the stories are not mine to tell.'

'So who writes them?'

Eloura lifted her arms, spreading her cape, dark and wing-like. 'Ordinary people who need to tell their story. The books are then returned to me, and I keep them here on the shelves, knowing that for many that's the last time they will ever be touched.' Liddy felt her own heart sink at the impossibility of trying to read them all, not merely once, but enough times to take away the sadness.

Eloura saw the sorrow glitter behind Liddy's eyes, then she smiled. 'But that doesn't mean we shouldn't at least try,' she said gently.

'What about Pumpkin?' asked Liddy, remembering the book that had turned to dust in her hand. 'The writer of the book I was reading. You said I had released her from her sadness.'

'Yes, that's right. Grief is like an anchor for the soul; it keeps you safe, but unmoving. Some people shut themselves in a room with their grief, because it has become a familiar companion to them; it is all they have left. By reading these stories many times, we can help to lift the anchor and free the soul. Pumpkin is one such soul. She has escaped the shackles of her sorrow, thanks in part to you.'

Liddy wrinkled her nose in scepticism. 'Just because I read her story?'

'It is never *just because*,' Eloura replied fiercely. 'Reading her story – reading anyone's story – is such an honour. It has the power to change things, and it is the most important thing you can do. Wherever she is, she will wake up happier today; she will smile again, without really knowing why, and for the first time in such a long time she may be startled by the sound of her own laughter.'

'So reading is a cure?' Liddy asked.

'For most ailments it is, yes,' replied Eloura, with utter conviction, and Liddy couldn't help but be enchanted. Eloura hadn't been talking in metaphors at all; every word she spoke was real and true, and Liddy found herself easily believing in the magic of sharing stories. She promised herself that she would come back often and read as much as she could, especially if it meant bringing some happiness back to the world.

'Come with me, I want to show you something,' said Eloura, seizing on Liddy's excitement.

She turned and swished towards the bookshelves, and Liddy followed her into the deep, dark wood of words. Eloura didn't look back once – she didn't need to glance over her shoulder to know Liddy was there.

They went further into the inky darkness, under the watchful gaze of the owl sitting high on a shelf. Liddy really would need her breadcrumbs now, if she was going to find her way back out, and she began to wonder if they would stumble upon a gingerbread house or hear the panting of a prowling wolf. After that, her nerves wouldn't settle. She understood the fierce heart of fairy tales, and they made her own beat so much faster.

Eloura came to an abrupt halt outside a small archway, framed by a tangle of the same white flowers that had made themselves at home in other parts of the library. Carefully she lifted a handful of stems and tendrils aside and pushed her way through. Liddy followed her into the room, knowing that she would never be able to find this place again without Eloura to guide her. To her amazement, she saw that she was in a turret room and that it was snowing inside. Then she realised that, of course, it wasn't snow here either, but the pollen from the sorrowing stars. It felt as if she was standing inside a snow globe.

Liddy's eyes didn't know where to look first: the silver swirling air or the luminous white flowers that climbed the walls. In the main room of the library the buds had yet to open, but here they gleamed and glinted at her like protective shields. Liddy gazed up and saw the walls of the room were filled with books, but they weren't sitting on shelves, instead, thick flower stems kept them strapped to the stone.

The flakes were tiny and fleeting, vanishing before they had even reached the floor. As they spun their colour pulsed and changed: silver, lilac, opalescent, then back to silver.

Liddy cupped her hand to catch them as they fell, but just as they had melted into the warmth of Eloura's cape, so they did the same in the warmth of her palm.

'Does it have a special name?' asked Liddy. 'The pollen, I mean.'

A small smile tugged at the corners of her mouth. 'I call it stardust.'

Stardust belonged in magical realms and distant dreams. Liddy hadn't thought it existed anywhere else, but now she wasn't so sure.

Eloura swept across the room and gathered up an armful of petals from the long table. They were so large that they hid her from view as she carried them over to a desk. There were petals everywhere, filling the room with their strange light: spread flat across tables like documents, or maps, and draped over racks, like sheets left to dry.

So these are sorrowing stars? thought Liddy, staring around the room in fascination. Her eyes danced, unable to settle for a moment, as she followed their shine high into the turret. 'I thought the sorrowing stars only grew in the water,' she said.

Eloura nodded. 'It's where their roots begin – buried deep in the bed of the lake. The flowers bloom a little below the surface of the water, polished by the light of the moon and nourished by the shine of the stars. It's where all the stories start.'

'How are they glowing in here then?' whispered Liddy, stroking the tips of her fingers along one of the petal's smooth edges. It felt fleshy and fibrous, like waxy skin.

'From the tea,' she replied. 'I use it to polish the leaves. And of course the moon and the stars are just up there.'

Liddy tilted her head back and tried to see all the way to the very top, but where the walls began to narrow, the sorrowing stars tangled together in thick, secretive knots. It was strange to see books fastened behind the stems and tendrils; without any shelves, it looked as if they were simply floating there.

'Why are these books not with the others in the library?'

'Because they are different,' replied Eloura. 'The sadness in these stories is deeper than the rest, and the words are wounds on the pages. There will be no solace without the Keymaker's key.'

'So these are the stories of the people who are invited here?'

'Some of them.'

'But how can you possibly choose between them all?' asked Liddy. Although there were a lot fewer in the turret room than in the library, there were still too many to count.

'It is not me who has to choose, it is the sorrowing stars.'

Just when Liddy thought she was beginning to understand things a little more, the confusion returned and doubled. 'What do you mean? How can the flowers choose anything?'

Eloura pointed to one of the large open flowers, and Liddy noticed it was shining a little brighter than the others. Its petals were curved around one of the books, like a protective hand around whispering lips, and the book shone bright beneath its quivering light.

'It's like a spotlight,' exclaimed Liddy.

'That's how they choose.'

Eloura whooshed past her and sprang, cat-like, into the air, pulling herself up using the stems of the flowers as a rope. Before Liddy had time to blink, she had reached the book, unravelled it from its moorings and was back on her feet again. 'One of our next guests,' she said, tapping the cover and leaving the book on the table for later.

She went back to the desk and began pulling the petals apart. She loosened the pin that held her cape together and threw the sides over both shoulders, out of the way. Her dress underneath was sleeveless, leaving her shoulders and arms bare. Liddy stared, entranced. Bright white stars had been inked onto her dark skin, and constellations journeyed up from her wrists, along her arms, over her shoulders and down her back. It was as though she carried a map of the night sky on her body.

Loosening her knife, Eloura sliced into a petal. She worked quickly and carefully with an expert hand until she had a pile of square pages in front of her, just enough to make a book. She reached for a small earthenware pot and lifted the lid – from within she retrieved a root and, once more with the knife, she began to slice into it until half a dozen coiled pieces dropped onto the desk. Taking a hooked needle from the tray, Eloura made four small incisions and began to thread the pages together with the root tendrils until they were secured in tiny knots. The bulb itself was made into a button clasp. The work was quick, precise and mesmerising, like a wound that needed to be healed. Liddy thought she could watch her work all day. In less than ten minutes a petal from a sorrowing star had been transformed into a book, which Eloura held in her hand.

Liddy looked at it in amazement. 'What happens now?' Eloura smiled. 'Now we drink tea.'

Pushing back through the tangled archway, Eloura led her through the bookshelves once more. The soft swishing of wings came from somewhere in the darkness and Liddy knew the snowy owl was close. Then another sound tiptoed in, like quietly popping bubbles. Little by little, the sound grew louder until finally Liddy could see a well-lit chamber up ahead. From the middle of it came the splash of a fountain. Beside it grew a tree full of oranges, almost too bright to be real, each one the colour of a hot evening sun. An image of a woman sitting in a boat was carved large into the wall behind the tree. She reminded Liddy of Eloura. Her hair flew all around her and it was tangled with objects: a book, a chalice, a wand, a flower, the moon and other things too small to make out. The sky behind her was filled with night-time creatures: bats and moths and wide-winged owls. Eloura stepped forward and knelt beside the fountain. From beneath her cape, she conjured up a teapot and filled it with water. Liddy leaned over her shoulder and saw steam rising from the surface.

'Is the water hot?' she asked.

'We are standing right above the centre of the lake, where the water is thermal. It's the perfect temperature for brewing tea,' Eloura announced, holding the teapot aloft like a trophy.

Back at the globe, she lifted out the drawer where she'd left the remains of Pumpkin's story and shook the contents into the teapot, then gave it a quick swirl with the tip of the root, dropped that in too and replaced the lid.

'Let's sit,' she said, walking towards the two armchairs by the fire.

Eloura took an orange from her pocket and sank her knife's blade into its thick skin. Juice trickled down her fingers and became a beaded bracelet around her wrist. A warm, sweet aroma burst into the air as she peeled back the skin and pulled apart the segments. Then she lifted the lid of the teapot and dropped them in, one by one.

'Tea and persimmons,' she said. 'Delicious.'

'Persimmons?' queried Liddy. 'I thought they were oranges.'

Eloura shook her head. 'Only persimmons can help you forget the sadness that you read. Sometimes it can take its toll.'

She waited a few moments for the flavours to infuse before she began to pour the tea into the cups that had appeared on the table. Taking one of them, she curled herself into the opposite armchair and Liddy did the same.

'A toast to Pumpkin,' she announced, raising her cup.

'To Pumpkin.'

There was a girl out there somewhere who suddenly felt a little lighter because of Liddy, and the thought of it made her smile.

The tea tasted buttery and smooth and there was a definite hint of something sweet like a peach. That must be what persimmons tasted like, she supposed, never having tried one before.

The warmth of the fire had coaxed Eloura to remove her cape and it now lay warming her lap. Liddy was once again mesmerised by the white stars inked all over her dark skin. They shone and glittered and spiralled, and whirled like tiny pinwheels, and Liddy tried to recall the names of the constellations she had learned as a child. She remembered sitting on her father's knee when she was very young while he showed her books filled with beautiful patterns of twinkling light. Each one had a faraway-sounding name that she couldn't pronounce, no matter how many times he repeated it for her: Cassiopeia, Andromeda, Pollux and, her favourite one of all, Pegasus, the winged horse of the sky. She didn't recognise any of the constellations on Eloura's arms, though – they certainly hadn't appeared in her father's books. Perhaps they belonged to a different sky, one she had never seen before, in a world she had yet to discover.

'Why do you have a galaxy inked on your arms?' she asked, her curiosity forcing the question from her mouth.

'It's a map,' Eloura replied.

A *map*, mused Liddy quietly for a moment. 'Why do you need a map of the stars?'

Eloura smiled. 'It is not a map of the stars in the night sky. It is a map of the sorrowing stars. It helps me find my way into the stories.'

Liddy's eyes fell back to the strange and unfamiliar patterns and she searched again for their meaning. Each sorrowing star was as wonderful and unique as a snowflake, just like the carvings on the library's shelves, and exactly the same as the ones painted onto the spinning globe. Everything was connected. The stars weren't stars at all; they were stories waiting to be told.

'Do you know why I'm here?' Liddy asked. Eloura seemed to know about everything else, so perhaps she'd know about that too. 'I don't believe it's simply to make marchpane.'

Eloura peered at her over the top of her teacup and slowly lowered it onto her lap.

'You're here to mend what is broken.'

Liddy scrunched up her face. 'Mend what is broken? I've never fixed anything in my life.'

'Not the things you are probably thinking of – not what you can see and touch,' she replied, tapping the side of the teacup twice with a long indigo nail.

'Then what?'

'This house is weary and sorrow-filled. Its occupants are mourners whose footsteps leave behind trails of sadness in every room. Its walls have kept too many secrets for far too long. People come and go, but the greatest weight is carried by those who don't move on. They are the broken ones, the ones you are here to mend.'

'Vivienne and the Keymaker?'

Eloura nodded.

'So it had nothing to do with marchpane,' said Liddy triumphantly. 'I knew it!'

'Well, it did a little,' she replied, blowing on her tea before taking another sip.

In the quiet interlude that followed, Liddy wondered what the secrets were. A brother and sister so locked in their grief that they had shut themselves away from the rest of the world. She still knew so little about them and this strange place they inhabited. What made the Keymaker so withdrawn that he stayed in his room all day and made keys to release others from pain, but not himself? The people of the village might shun Vivienne, but Liddy didn't feel she was the sort of person to let gossip and judgement defeat her. There was another reason she hid – one that she wasn't willing to share. Liddy remembered her head on the pillow and the crimson trickle that stained it. Was her illness contagious? Was that the reason she kept away?

'Ben told me that Vivienne has a disease in her lungs. Her coughing is getting worse.'

'Yes, she is very sick.'

Liddy heard the gravity of Eloura's words and the undercurrent of acceptance that carried them. She felt suddenly stricken, as though the diagnosis had been made for her own lungs, and she realised to her surprise how much fondness she had developed for Vivienne in the few days since she'd arrived, despite her withdrawn nature. Then she was consumed with doubt and worry. 'How can I mend her? I'm not a nurse or a doctor, I have no medicine. The only thing I know how to do is make marchpane.'

Eloura continued to quietly sip her tea, and then she spoke. 'It is not her lungs you are here to mend; it is her heart.'

That seemed to make even less sense. 'Am I meant to mend the Keymaker's heart as well?' Liddy tried to laugh at the idea, as though the thought of it was ridiculous, but she couldn't keep the hope from wrapping itself around her words and she quickly lowered her eyes before she gave herself away.

'It's one and the same,' replied Eloura.

The tea leaves had come to settle in the bottom of the cup, and Liddy tried to decipher the pattern that lay there: circles or coins, or an abundant moon. She twisted the cup round and tilted her head slightly. This time they looked more like dark clouds, and there was no sign of the heart she'd hoped to find.

'You will learn more from a conversation over a cup of tea than you will from staring at the bottom of a drained cup.'

Liddy smiled and put the empty teacup back on the table. A gentle patter fell against the window and she looked up to see there was a fine rain outside, misting the garden. She wondered if Ben had sought shelter in his shed or if he was still out there somewhere, digging in the rain-soaked earth. *He is always busy doing something*, she thought. When she turned her gaze back to the room, Eloura had closed her eye, and Liddy could tell by the shallow rise and fall of her chest that she was asleep. The wing on her eyelid glittered like an alicanto bird and, next to the white sails of the boat, Liddy was reminded of mythical journeys and discoveries.

Closing her own eyes, she tried to remember the way back to the turret room behind the tangled arch, but her mind was already lost before she got past the second row of bookshelves and she realised the impossibility of it. Instead she thought of maps and stars and fountains and persimmons, and somewhere along the way her thoughts turned themselves into dreams.

When she awoke, Eloura had vanished and on the chair opposite she saw the cat curled into a ball. It was too deep in a dream to purr. Unable to resist, Liddy tickled the top of its soft head and then left the cat to its peaceful slumber.

The dark depths of the library had left her feeling dazed, as if she'd been on a long journey and had not slept at all. Outside, the rain had brought out the smell of wet earth and she breathed it deep into her lungs. The birds babbled from the trees, waiting for the brightening sun to restore their damp feathers. She expected Ben to be there, but after a lengthy search of the garden, and a glance in his shed, she couldn't find him anywhere.

The charred remains of the bonfire still hadn't been cleared away and someone had made another much smaller fire beside it. The smoke-scent lingered in the air and, as Liddy drew closer, she saw that it was still smouldering. Whoever had made it had done so hastily out of a mound of broken twigs. She would have walked straight past it, if her eye hadn't noticed the object lying on the very top. She stopped long enough to see the scorched remains of the poppet quietly seething in the rain. Then, hitching up her skirt, Liddy hurried back inside, bringing the raindrops from the garden with her.

In the kitchen, Vivienne greeted her solemnly. Liddy still felt awkward and embarrassed about the earlier incident and wanted to forget all about the wretched poppet and the misery it had brought.

'You'll be glad to know that Alice and John's missing taglock has been recovered,' said Vivienne.

'It has?' Liddy felt a surge of relief. 'Where was it?'

'It had been folded between some clothes and neither of them had noticed it there.'

'What is it?' asked Liddy, curiously.

'A butterfly hair clasp,' she replied brusquely.

'So they will get their key?'

'Yes, they will.' Vivienne's jaw tightened. 'I see you couldn't wait to make your marchpane.'

Her voice was neutral, and Liddy couldn't tell if this discovery pleased her or not.

'I thought I should, since that's the reason you brought me here?' There was a question in there, but Vivienne chose to dismiss it.

'In haste you waste,' she said, picking up the tray and moving over to the bin. 'You have not mixed in the petals, as I instructed. The marchpane is useless without them.'

'Wait!' cried Liddy, wanting to snatch the tray from her grasp. She couldn't bear to watch her marchpane being thrown away.

Vivienne's hand hovered and the tray tipped forward. There was a small look of satisfaction on her face.

'Useless maybe, but not tasteless,' Liddy reasoned, trying to keep her voice calm. She couldn't let Vivienne see how desperate she was; that would make her tip the whole lot in, just out of spite.

Vivienne stared down at the little yellow squares and pursed her lips. 'I do not care for sweet things – they are too sickly – but perhaps my brother will find them harder to resist.'

Liddy breathed a sigh of relief as Vivienne crossed the room and put the tray back on the table.

'I met Eloura in the library,' said Liddy, quickly changing the subject.

'I see,' said Vivienne.

'She showed me around the library. I can't believe there are so many books in there, and that all of them are made from the petals of sorrowing stars.'

'What else did she tell you?' asked Vivienne, as though she was barely tolerating a whimsical child.

'She said that this house knows so many secrets that it can't breathe, and that you' – Liddy paused, wondering if she should be saying these things – 'that you're unwell.'

'Eloura speaks too much,' Vivienne replied hastily. There wasn't any anger or bitterness in her words, only calm acceptance of a shared truth. Her skin looked as if it was made of an ancient shell, and her eyes were red-rimmed and sunken into her skull as deep as lost shipwrecks.

'She told me she is the keeper of the library and a book-weaver and a story-spinner, and lots of other things that I can barely even remember.' Liddy laughed. 'Maybe I imagined her.'

Vivienne puffed out her cheeks and rolled her eyes. 'She is not the only one who speaks too much.'

Liddy smiled. 'But who is Eloura really?'

'She is every story you have ever read. Voyaging between the chapters. A compass leading the way towards new worlds. A storyfarer. She is the beginning, the middle and the end.'

Liddy hadn't heard Vivienne speak in such a way before, or for so long. Her utterances were always brief and sharp, like the angry stabs of little thorns, but now her words bloomed with eloquence, and her hard edges softened.

'I haven't seen her for such a long time.'

'Really?' Liddy exclaimed in disbelief. 'But she's right there in the library.'

'Perhaps it's because there is nothing left of my story.' Vivienne sighed. 'No more now – all this talking makes me tired.' Her words fell hard and fast like the blade of a guillotine, chopping off the conversation. 'Come, there is still much work to be done.'

All afternoon they made marchpane together. Liddy watched as Vivienne sprinkled some of the petals into the paste she'd made, and left other petals to one side, ready to adorn the tops of each slab once they were ready. She was pleasantly surprised by Vivienne's proficiency. When Liddy asked why they were making so much, with so few guests in the house, Vivienne revealed that most of the marchpane would be sold in the village. Liddy wasn't sure that anyone there would want anything Vivienne tried to sell them. Then she remembered Sebastian, and the pots of honey and bundles of herbs, and knew that he would buy whatever she brought him, even if he couldn't sell it to anyone else. It was a bittersweet thought.

CHAPTER 20

The Girl in the Square

The following morning Liddy and Vivienne arrived in the village with their wares before the nine o'clock chimes had been released over the rooftops. Liddy was glad to be back; it reminded her that there was another world away from the house. Somewhere in between.

Vivienne strode purposefully towards the little square, with her head held high, dismissive of the scornful eyes and judgemental tongues that she knew would be waiting for her. Liddy wasn't sure she would have been so brave. She fell behind to gaze into sleepy shop windows. It was still early enough for the bread to be warm and the streets to be empty. Soon she realised that she had lost sight of Vivienne, and even the sound of her shoes on the stone had faded away to silence. She didn't mind; the village was small, and she would find her way. In one of the shop windows there were beautiful paintings hanging on the walls: the wild sea, a bird with exquisite, vivid feathers, a summer sky, the face of a beaming child holding a yellow balloon. Moving along the window, Liddy saw an organised display of oil palettes and paint pots; unblemished brushes of varying sizes spread out in a fan, and behind them stood easels and canvas stacks, disappearing into the darkness. It was tempting to think that if she bought these things, then she too could create such skilful artwork, but Liddy knew she had no talent for painting. Disappointed, she moved away.

The street led her into a tiny square that felt like a dark, secret cupboard. There was only one shop, and its single murky window made it almost impossible to see inside. Liddy stepped closer and, peering through the strangely mottled glass, saw a mournful display of toys: horses, trains frozen on a track, clockwork toys, trays of marbles and skipping ropes tightly bundled in a box. High on a shelf she saw a doll's house with a faded pink door, its roof half-eaten by damp or by mice, and next to it another box, this one was filled with miniature furniture – chairs, beds, tables, and there was even a tiny painted dog, with its ear poking out. In the corner Liddy saw a jumble of instruments: triangles, tin-whistles, harmonicas, castanets and tambourines. There was even a violin propped up against the wall; one of its strings was broken and sprang out like the whisker of a cat. Everything was grey with dust, as though nothing had been touched for years, and time had stopped ticking. She pressed her nose to the glass and squinted to see further within. It took a moment or two for her eyes to make out the outlines of a large glass cabinet, from which two unblinking eyes stared back at her. Startled, she gasped and snapped her head back from the window. When she looked again, she realised that the eyes belonged to a doll and she laughed in relief.

It was clear the shop hadn't been open for years. Scanning the shelves of the cabinet, Liddy saw they were all filled with dolls. Some with porcelain faces, others made of wax or cloth. They all had big eyes and pouting mouths. Their dresses had long ago faded to yellow, and where once there had been curls bouncing on top of their shoulders, there were now only tangles. Some of the dolls had lost their shoes and others stared out pitifully, as though waiting to be rescued. *What a waste*, Liddy thought sadly, imagining the joy they could have brought to children. Then her eyes fell upon the last doll, with satin slippers dangling from its feet, and a memory suddenly shifted and came hurtling back towards her with such unmistakeable clarity that she felt a jolt. The shimmering lake, the dusty shop, the beautiful doll she had begged her father to buy for her, all of it now so familiar. Tabby had been right – she had been here before, to this very spot. Staring into the window had returned her to a place in her childhood, but it was merely a glimpse and then the memory folded itself away, until all she remembered was the pain of losing the doll.

Eager to leave the shop behind, she followed the smell of bread into the main square and headed towards the delicatessen. Inside, Vivienne was standing at the counter talking to Sebastian, the marchpane laid out between them. He smiled as Liddy approached, but when he saw that she had brought more packages, his smile wavered. She knew instantly what he was thinking: he could have eaten the contents of the first lot by himself, but there was far too much for one person to manage alone. Still, he beckoned her over and she placed her packages on top of the others; so high that he was almost hidden behind them.

She and Vivienne moved outside to sit at the table and drink coffee once again. Vivienne was poised and alert, like a bird waiting for dropped crumbs; her eyes were fixed on the sloping street that ran up past the delicatessen. When the church bells rang, Vivienne straightened, and a look of hope and fear crossed her face. It was such a strange expression that it made Liddy nervous. Vivienne's hand was shaking, and she quickly tucked it away in the folds of her skirt, obviously hoping it had gone unnoticed. Her breathing deepened. Liddy watched.

Then, as before, came the pitter-patter of marching feet and the same procession of girls appeared, wearing their little yellow dresses and shiny shoes. After her conversation with Ben, Liddy knew that the girls were foundlings. It made her wonder what reasons a parent would have to give their child away, but such reasons were often shrouded in secrecy and never spoken of again. Vivienne's eyes darted between the girls, and Liddy wondered what she was looking for. Then her eyes stopped moving and her shoulders relaxed, and Liddy finally saw what Vivienne saw. A girl of about six was walking near the back of the line. Her hair was black and sprang from her head in unruly coils. Her skin was a shade darker than that of the other girls and her limbs were longer and thinner. Liddy couldn't see what connection Vivienne would have to her, but there was no mistake that it was this girl – and this girl alone – who captivated her. The nun at the front called out and they came to an abrupt stop, listening as she delivered a lengthy sermon about obedience and discipline. It gave both Liddy and Vivienne time to watch the girl at the back. She shifted from one foot to the other and stifled a yawn. She wasn't listening, she was too preoccupied by something in the sky – *a bird*, thought Liddy, but when she lifted her own eyes, she saw nothing but clouds. The girl was certainly a daydreamer, with a little rebellious streak. When the procession set off again towards the church, the girl near the back was too lost in her own thoughts to realise. As she continued standing there, the girl behind walked straight into her, pushing her to the ground. It wasn't a serious tumble, as she had managed to save herself by putting her hands down first, but Vivienne rose abruptly and cried out, as though witnessing a tragedy.

'Go,' she said to Liddy, with a tone of urgency. 'Help her.'

Liddy knew the girl didn't need any help, but the fierce look on Vivienne's face told her not to argue and, without questioning it, she stepped forward. By the time she reached her, the girl was already back on her feet and there wasn't a tear in sight. One of the nuns was brushing tiny stones from her knee, to reveal a small graze beneath. At first nothing about the girl's face was familiar, but as soon as she looked up, all sloe-eyed and solemn, Liddy recognised her expression at once. The same clenched jaw, the same pressed lips and the same thoughtful eyes; it was like staring into the face of a younger Vivienne. The nun took the girl by the hand and they hurried after the others, who had already disappeared inside the church.

The similarity had been so striking, and so unexpected, that for a moment Liddy couldn't move. Before she could pull herself together, she heard a loud clatter and the sound of breaking glass. She turned to see that Vivienne was hunched over, clutching the edge of the table with one hand, and her chest with the other. The coffee had spilled across the table and was dripping onto the ground, where the cups lay in broken pieces. Liddy rushed to help, but Vivienne raised her hand to keep her away. She opened her mouth as though to speak, or maybe it was to let herself breathe more easily, but all that came out was a cough, then a splutter, followed by more coughing – relentless and determined, hacking and tormenting. It seized her whole body and she stumbled against the table, and her legs collapsed beneath her. Liddy ignored her protestations and reached out to catch Vivienne before she hit the ground.

Sebastian hurried over with a blanket and a glass of water. He held the glass gently to Vivienne's lips, but as she tried to swallow, she made a gagging, retching sound and the water began to swirl like crimson smoke. Exhausted, she fell back in her chair. Little beads of sweat were glistening on her forehead, dampening her hair. She closed her eyes and for a moment she was so completely still and pale that Liddy feared she wouldn't ever open them again.

'Bea,' she wheezed between sudden sharp breaths. 'My little Bea.'

Liddy had thought she'd heard the woman call the little girl Neve, but she couldn't be sure. Looking up the hill, she was relieved to see that the church doors were shut and the girl hadn't seen any of the commotion unfold.

'It's okay,' said Liddy, placing a gentle hand on Vivienne's arm, shocked to feel her trembling beneath. 'She's gone inside now. She didn't see.'

She wasn't sure if it was the terrible wheezing she could still hear or the sound of tiny, anguished sobs. At least the worst of it had passed. Vivienne mumbled something as Liddy wrapped the blanket around her brittle shoulders, but she was too weak to refuse help and her arms fell limply to her sides. Distracted by the noise, a small crowd had gathered at the other end of the square, huddled in their gossip. Sebastian scowled and waved his hand angrily at them, as though shooing away a pack of stray dogs, and guiltily they turned their heads. Vivienne moved back to the boat on slow, unsteady feet and Liddy bore her weight, no more than that of a small child.

Glancing behind her, Liddy saw Sebastian staring hopelessly at the marchpane he'd bought, but would never be able to sell. He looked so sad that it made Liddy's heart hurt and she quickly looked away.

CHAPTER 21

The Woman in the Leaves

Back on the island, Ben helped Vivienne along the lawn and up the steps. By the time they had reached the door, she was gently pushing him away and straightening her skirt, insisting that all she needed was a little rest. Reluctantly Ben stepped back, and they watched her slip into the shadows of the house.

'We need to call a doctor,' said Liddy, turning to Ben. 'She's getting worse.'

'She won't have one,' he replied sadly. 'Not yet.'

'But that's ridiculous! She needs medicine.' Liddy looked up towards Vivienne's window and wondered if she had managed to get to her room before collapsing on the stairs. 'I should go and check on her.'

'No,' said Ben. His voice was so firm that it made her hesitate at the door. 'She'll not thank you for it. Best if you leave her be for now.'

Liddy frowned. It felt wrong to leave her alone, but he knew Vivienne better than anyone, and so she stepped back from the door.

'It's too warm to be inside anyway,' he said, turning to leave. 'It's a perfect day to explore more of the garden.'

Trying to forget her concern, she took his suggestion and wandered along the path in the opposite direction, in search of new discoveries. Almost immediately she was greeted by the wild rose bush that threw its tangle of branches over the path. *The rose is such a dramatic actress,* she thought, *always flouncing its way around the garden.* She pushed her way through to discover wild foxgloves, honeysuckle and hibiscus growing in abundance. She ran her fingers along the periwinkle walls, where explosions of jasmine and bursts of oleander scented the air. A heady, intoxicating blend, stronger than a potion. No wonder their petals had such healing properties. Here everything mingled, even the seasons. She lay down in a patch of warm grass and closed her eyes. Her thoughts returned to the village and the girl, and to Vivienne's reaction when the girl had tumbled and grazed her knee. They had to be related somehow. Her niece? Her daughter? She couldn't imagine Vivienne being able to nurture a plant, let alone a child, but as she lay there in the sun, the idea padded softly around her mind and wouldn't leave her alone. If she really was the girl's mother, then why had she given her away to a foundling home, and why did she continue to sit and watch her every morning from the square?

As she lay there, the story of the bandits in the snow came back to her and once more she heard Ben's words: *They left more than they took.* She pictured the little girl's face, her swarthy skin and almond eyes, her straight nose and wild black hair, and suddenly Ben's words took on new meaning.

Unable to settle, Liddy stood and walked back along the path, past the top terrace and the rectangular lawn. Instead of turning right by the long tunnel of lemon trees, she veered left towards less familiar territory.

In front of her stood a set of wrought-iron railings sunk deep into the ground, their rusted tips taking aim against the sky. Here the well-kept grass and the perfectly trimmed hedges gave way to wilderness. There were no flowers, aside from the weeds that straggled the ground, disguising the path – if indeed there was a path any more; she couldn't tell. Ferns as high as her head and fat stinging nettles barred her way – a warning to turn back or suffer the consequences – but Liddy crept carefully into the darkening green. She was in the mood to explore. The ground beneath her feet began to sink, making her shriek, and she quickly scrambled up a small grassy bank. With no sun to dry up the rain, the garden here was nothing more than boggy marshland. Liddy had moved just in time, managing to avoid the worst of it, but she could feel her foot growing cold and damp and when she looked down, her boot was oozing with muddy water. Searching for somewhere to clean it, she spotted a clump of leaves at the bottom of a tree and did her best to wipe away the mud. She shivered, suddenly overcome with apprehension. It was too quiet. From anywhere else in the garden she could always hear birdsong, sweet and clear, but here it was silent. For some reason the birds refused to sing. And there was something else. The drifting pollen that had become so familiar was nowhere to be seen. Everything kept away.

The back of the house was truly a bleak and eerie place; it seemed so far removed from the rest of the garden that Liddy almost felt she had entered a different place entirely. The air was misty and cold and unforgiving. Autumn seemed to have finally crept in here. She kicked her way through the tangled ground, avoiding further bogs, until another obstacle appeared. This time a fallen tree blocked her way – a giant uprooted by a storm, its gnarled roots clinging desperately to the soil, still growing. Liddy clambered over the trunk, but the drop on the other side was further than she had anticipated and she nearly fell as she landed. She felt her skirt snag and there came the sound of ripping cloth; her hem had torn away and she tutted at her clumsiness. She would have to tread more carefully, for the ground was littered with large stones and one misstep could twist her ankle, or worse.

She headed towards a ridge lined with three blackened trees, their branches reaching out like charred bones. She had never seen a place so neglected and wondered why Ben didn't venture there with his tools. He worked so hard all day, pruning and digging and raking the pathways to perfection, that it seemed strange for him to neglect this part, allowing it to become so overgrown. She supposed it would be difficult for one person to manage such a large garden alone. Ben's back probably wasn't as straight as it had been, and his legs moved more slowly than he would have liked; his barrow looked heavy in his hands as he wheeled it around the garden. She imagined this section had simply been left for too long and was now impossible to tame.

Below the ridge, the hill sloped steeply into thickets and the brambles were flattened by thick snakes of ivy. Liddy caught sight of the lake through a gap in the tangles, and it gleamed at her like a wicked eye. Stepping away from the edge, she turned back to the crumbling wall of the house and the dark shadow it cast, like a grasping hand over the long grass. Looking up, she saw a dark, square window high in the wall and, without knowing why, it filled her with an unmistakeable feeling of despair. Her skin prickled. The wall beneath was cracked and infected with damp and age. An imaginative mind might describe it as tear-stained, as though the window itself had been weeping.

Not wanting to spend a moment longer in such a gloomy, melancholy place, Liddy turned to leave, but as she did so, her attention was drawn by a movement across the ragged tufts. Immediately her senses were heightened – had it had been a bird or a small creature stirring in the bushes or something else? Then her eyes fell to a strange object jutting out from the ground. It was only a short distance away and resembled a wooden cross stabbed into the earth, half-claimed by weeds. Something bright lay before it and, stepping closer, she could see a small bunch of lilies lying on the ground. Someone must have left them there on purpose.

Liddy felt wary, as though she was being watched, and the hairs on her arms lifted. Something in the air smelled … wrong. Looking around for an intruder, she saw no one, then there was a sudden flash of red in the leaves, like a flare. She saw nothing more, but it was enough to convince her that she was not alone. Looking through the deep, dark green once more, she saw the eye of a woman staring back at her. She was dressed in the deepest, darkest red, and her thick copper-coloured hair fell over one shoulder and twisted to her waist like a rope. Her face was almost translucent and there was barely any flesh to it. But it was her eyes that frightened Liddy the most; the way they burned with scorn and disgust. Her appearance was so disturbing that Liddy stumbled to get away, but before she could move, the woman vanished, quick as a snuffed flame. When the wind parted the leaves again there was nothing there, only a terrible feeling of rot and decay.

A hand on her arm made her cry out.

'Sorry, I didn't mean to scare you.' It was Ben. 'You really shouldn't be round here. It's not safe.' There was no anger in his voice; it wasn't a reprimand, more of a warning.

'I saw someone over there,' replied Liddy excitedly. 'A woman – standing behind those leaves.' She pointed wildly in the direction of the trees.

'There's no one there,' he said, but his eyes hadn't followed her finger; instead they were fixed on the high window, the one that had filled her with such dread. 'Come on, we should get back.'

Liddy stood still. 'There was a woman,' she repeated, more insistently this time.

Ben sighed and then reluctantly trudged over to the trees. Half-heartedly he began to part the leaves in several different places and peered in.

'Her hair was bright as copper,' she called, 'and she was wearing a red dress.'

'That's just the colour of the leaves,' he replied.

It was true, the leaves held the deep, rich colours of autumn – reds and ambers and shades of purple – but Liddy knew she had seen something else hiding between them. Ben continued to rustle through the leaves, but his search revealed nothing and he let them spring back into place. 'Well, whatever you saw, it's gone now.'

He approached, picking thorns and burrs from his coat. 'Bright as copper, did you say?'

Liddy nodded, wondering if the description was familiar.

'Then I imagine it was a fox you saw.'

Heading back to the sunlit part of the garden, Liddy found the woman's haunted face still plaguing her mind. She knew it hadn't been a fox that she'd seen, and something told her Ben didn't believe that, either.

Back on the front terrace, everything felt wonderfully familiar, as though normality had been restored, and the birdsong filled the sky. 'Whose grave is down there?' she asked before Ben could disappear into his potting shed.

'Grave?' He tried to feign confusion, but what Liddy saw in his eyes wasn't confusion, it was fear. 'What grave?' he asked, continuing with his pretence.

Liddy refused to be deterred. 'There's a cross in the ground and someone left flowers on it – fresh flowers.'

Ben lifted his cap, wiped the sweat off his brow and gave a slight shake of his head. Liddy felt certain he was hiding something from her, but secrets made him uncomfortable and she felt guilty for prying.

'When Signora Castellini was a child, she would find all sorts of half-broken creatures and try and rescue them. But not all things can be rescued, and it broke her heart to have to bury them. I imagine it's the final resting place of one of those poor creatures she couldn't save.'

Ben's face looked strained, heavy with turmoil, and although she wanted to ask him more about the mysterious grave, and the child in the village, and the room with the locked door, Liddy knew better than to push him further. Such questions would have to wait.

CHAPTER 22

Sweet Treats

It was part desire, part duty that brought Liddy back to the Keymaker's door. The meal she carried was a simple one of cheese and leftover pie. Taking a deep breath, she knocked loudly and waited. A moment passed, then another, and just as she was about to leave, disappointed, the door was flung open and there he was, staring at her. He was so close she could breathe in his scent of pine needles. Her heart gave a flurry of little beats, and for a minute all words were lost.

'I brought your supper,' she stammered, holding the tray up as though he had asked for proof.

His eyes lingered on her and she felt her cheeks flush, then he looked over her shoulder into the corridor.

'Where is Vivienne?' he asked. His voice was quieter and gentler than she remembered.

'I'm afraid she's not feeling well.'

'This is becoming a habit,' he complained. His eyes had drifted back to hers, and she felt his scrutiny.

Liddy wasn't sure what was becoming a habit – her turning up at his door or Vivienne feeling unwell. She stood on the threshold, waiting for him to relieve her of the tray.

'I think I will have supper in the kitchen tonight.'

'In the kitchen?' Liddy asked in surprise.

'Is that a problem?'

His response was so unexpected that she was unable to find an appropriate response and simply shook her head and returned with the tray to the kitchen, where her own food was waiting.

Nervously she waited by the table, but after five minutes he still hadn't arrived. *Perhaps he has changed his mind*, she thought, and disappointment welled up in her. After ten minutes she gave up and began tidying away a stack of plates. Her head was half-buried in a cupboard when she finally heard the latch lift, and she felt her heart lift with it. She hurried to her feet just in time to see the Keymaker stride in. Pulling out a stool, he sat hunched over the table, then took a piece of bread from a plate and ripped into it like a bear, half-starved and wild. Liddy couldn't tear her eyes away and watched him through furtive sidelong glances, hoping he wouldn't feel her gaze. There were shadows around his eyes. His small scar glinted there, reminding her once more of a tiny fish washed up on the damp sand of his skin. Her eyes left his face and travelled further down his body, taking in the width of his shoulders and his firm chest. His skin was dark, his incarnadine hands washed clean.

'Won't you join me?' he asked, through noisy mouthfuls. Still he didn't look up.

'I – I've already eaten,' Liddy lied, knowing it would be impossible to eat in front of him.

'Then whose is that?' he demanded, waving a fork at the plate, which sat untouched on the counter.

'I—'

'Come on, I won't bite.' There was mischief in his eye.

Liddy hesitated and then, retrieving her plate, she joined him at the table. Her stomach clenched and her mouth was too dry to swallow. Instead of eating, she rolled a grape aimlessly around her plate. If she moved her hand a little way along the table, then her finger would brush against his and the thought of it held her like a magnet. He caught her eye once more and she turned away a moment too late.

'What's your name?' he asked.

'Liddy,' she replied.

'Well, Liddy, my sister was wrong to invite you here.'

Is he being deliberately mean? she wondered, angry at herself for thinking he had any interest in her.

'It is not up to her to invite whomever she chooses here on a whim.'

So he hadn't come to the kitchen for the pleasure of her company, as she had so foolishly hoped. It was clear he didn't want her there. She bit her tongue and pushed the grape with more force than she had intended, and it bounced off her plate and onto the floor.

'And who are you to decide that?' she blurted out, unable to hold back her anger.

Rather than being insulted by her directness, he seemed to relish the challenge it presented. 'I don't decide,' he said flatly, 'but neither does she.'

'Then who does – Eloura?' She remembered their conversation earlier. Eloura was the one who made the books and the one who went in search of the stories.

'You met the story-spinner then?' The Keymaker arched his eyebrows. 'She's not always easy to find.'

'Yes, in the library. We sat and drank tea together.'

The dark mask slipped back over his face. It was the same one Vivienne wore, as though they had been made by the same cruel hand. 'Still, you shouldn't be here,' he said resolutely.

Liddy fell quiet. A moment passed and then another. A tap dripped, but it sounded far away. She wondered if he had hidden in the dark for so long that he had forgotten how to be around other people. Half of her hoped he would get up and leave her alone, but when she felt his everlasting-eyes upon her, it brought fear and excitement in equal measure.

'Perhaps I should try some of your marchpane, since it comes so highly recommended.' His words sounded kinder now, but she still couldn't bring herself to respond. The tap dripped again. 'Please,' he added at last, and the word seemed to get stuck in his throat.

Without speaking, Liddy crossed the room and went into the pantry. She emerged carrying the small baking tray of marchpane that Vivienne had almost thrown away and placed it on the table before him. For the first time his face visibly brightened.

'May I?' he asked.

Liddy nodded shyly.

As he lifted one square to his mouth, she dropped her eyes, hoping for his approval, but fearing it wouldn't come. When she finally dared to look up, all but one of the marchpane squares were gone. Picking up the last one, he popped it into his mouth, leaving the tray completely empty. Vivienne was right: he certainly couldn't resist sweet things.

'Well, you really are the marchpane girl.'

Liddy blushed, her heart flipped and her courage soared. 'Oh, but I can assure you I am very much more than that.' And she wasn't sure whose eyes widened more at her unexpected daring: hers or the Keymaker's. For the briefest moment there was laughter. He had stepped out of the terrible dark and revealed himself to her.

'You should come to the kitchen more often,' she teased.

Immediately his face changed from spring to winter, and she knew that she had overstepped the mark. He stood and moved towards the door. Liddy desperately tried to think of something to say – some reason to make him stay, to pull him back – but her mind was blank and the words wouldn't come. Reaching for the latch, he paused and then, without turning to bid her goodnight, he was gone.

Liddy sank back onto her stool. She felt so confused. He was both enigmatic and frustrating. How quickly parts of him appeared and then disappeared like an unexpected tide, taking her mind with him each time he went.

Whenever her cousin Tabby had spoken of love, it sounded soft and comforting, like a basket of wool knitted into something cosy and warm, or a favourite cushion, or a coat that kept out the cold. What she felt now offered no such comfort; it felt fierce and unfamiliar and compelled her to the Keymaker like a curse that she couldn't escape. She tried to release her tangled feelings, to free herself from the endless knotted thoughts of him, but it was impossible. She had reached the unreachable and she had found him, just for a moment, but a moment nonetheless, and she was determined that she would find him again.

As she sat late into the evening she recalled his words: *the marchpane girl* – not meant unkindly, but a jarring reminder of home. She was so much more than merely the marchpane girl, with more to offer than simple marzipan treats. But, staring down at the empty tray, Liddy couldn't help but feel a small sense of satisfaction. He'd eaten every one of the sweet squares she'd made, and his eyes had delighted at the taste of them. She smiled and for a moment she didn't mind being the marchpane girl again. It felt like a triumph.

CHAPTER 23

The Nursery

The next morning Liddy felt the small weight of the cat against her feet even before she opened her eyes. Trying not to disturb the fluffy bundle, she hoisted herself up on both elbows and caught a glimpse of her ghostly grey reflection in the dressing-table mirror. Her hair had become a nest around her head and the dark circles round her eyes made her think she should be climbing into bed rather than out of one. She leaned forward and tickled the cat's head; it lifted its chin and blinked.

'Good morning,' she said. 'How on earth did you get in here?'

She remembered lifting the latch of the door last night and listening to the satisfying clink as it dropped back into place. She frowned. Someone must have let it in.

Reaching for her brush, she noticed the sorrowing star on the dresser. She had forgotten all about it and was surprised by how much it had grown. The single stem had broken clear of the soil and had deepened from spearmint to a dark jewel green. Halfway up, a leaf had begun to unfurl itself and more spectacularly, right at the top, a white bud had begun to swell. Liddy marvelled for a moment, then picked up the brush and tugged at the knots and spikes of her hair. Had her sleep been so restless that it had created such a jumble? It reminded her of the abandoned garden she'd found yesterday. She grimaced, tugging at yet another hideous clump until eventually her hair was back under control.

In the bathroom she held a damp flannel to her face and wiped the sleep away from her eyes. The cold water took her breath away, but left her feeling wide awake and alert. Then she saw it. The strangle bundle of leaves she'd pulled from the washstand was now on the floor, right next to her feet. She was sure she had thrown it much further away, but the dark was a deceptive thing. She didn't want to leave it there to fester, so she bent down and scooped it up. The leaves were still wet, and they felt heavy in her hand. Instead of the damp, earthy smell she expected, Liddy caught a whiff of something stale, like stagnant water, and she wrinkled her nose in disgust. Again she was reminded of the garden behind the house, and of being watched.

Maybe it was the tilt of her head or the way the light fell into the room that made her realise the leaves were not bound together by thread as she had first thought, but rather by hair, strand after strand of it, wound tightly. Holding it up to the window, she watched the sun from behind turn it from gold to orange, until finally it shone as bright as copper, just like the hair of the woman she'd seen hiding in the leaves. The one Ben had tried to convince her was only a fox. This was her hair – it must be. Liddy dropped the bundle into the washbasin as though the sun's light had set it aflame. Using a towel, she picked it back up, opened the window and flung it out into the garden. She didn't believe in omens, but perhaps things would have been different if she had.

When she left, the cat was sitting at the end of the corridor, watching her with its slow, blinking eyes. Liddy wondered if it was hungry and who was responsible for feeding it.

'Come on then,' she said, 'let's get you some breakfast.'

But instead of following her, the cat stood up and sauntered off in the opposite direction. *Charming*, she thought, but before she had reached the staircase there came a long, loud mewl. Liddy hurried towards it, fearful that the cat might be hurt. She expected it to be there when she turned the corner, but the corridor was empty. Softly she called out, 'Ch-ch-ch', but the cat didn't appear. She wondered if it had perhaps slipped through a door and got itself trapped in one of the many rooms, but as she pushed her hand gently against each one, none of them opened. She was close to the end of the corridor, and to the stairs that led to the second floor, when she heard that familiar, insistent little scratching sound again. Could it have been the cat all along? It was coming from somewhere above and so she began to climb.

She found herself back in the corridor with the mysterious salt piles. There was still no sign of the cat anywhere and the scratching had stopped.

Frustrated by its antics, she gave up her search and decided to spend her morning reading in the library. She knew the staircase at the other end of the corridor would take her down to Vivienne's room and from there she could find her way to the library, where a hot cup of tea would be waiting. About halfway along, Liddy hesitated. From the corner of her eye, she saw that the locked door from the previous night was now slightly ajar. Her curiosity pulled her closer and she pushed it open with a creak.

The first thing she noticed was the smell: damp and musty and pervasive, and so overwhelming that it made her splutter. Quickly she silenced her cough with the crook of her arm.

The room was immense and dismal. It was filled with old-fashioned mahogany furniture, some of which had been covered with dust sheets, perhaps to protect it from the damp. Despite the high ceiling and the wide window, the light that trickled in was cold and watery, and shadows shifted furtively around her feet as though they were not used to greeting strangers. She was glad not to have opened the door in the middle of the night, as the place unsettled her, and the feeling would have been made worse in the dark. In the centre of the room lay a thin, moth-eaten rug, its pattern no longer decipherable. The cold chewed uncomfortably at her bones.

A beautiful hand-crafted cradle stood a short distance from a small grate, the size of which would not have been enough to warm even a corner of a room as vast as this one. The cradle was the kind that rocked on a stand and, moving closer, Liddy could see that it was untouched by dust, as though someone had recently wiped it clean. The little bed within had been made ready: a cream sheet, a pink blanket, with another one carefully folded on top for colder nights. In the corner someone had embroidered the initials LC in small yellow stitching. Next to the cradle there was a rocking chair, made from the same wood – dark and solid – and it too was free of dust. Liddy could imagine someone sitting there, singing lullabies softly while a baby slept peacefully. But if there was a baby in this house, she hadn't heard it. Besides, the cradle looked as if it hadn't been used.

The shelves above were stacked full of toys so pristine that she doubted they had ever been played with. They reminded her of the shelf in Vivienne's room, but that shelf had a sense of order – every object had been care-fully chosen and meant something – whereas these shelves were a burst of chaos and clutter. There were dolls in pretty bright-buttoned dresses and lace bonnets; puppets of every animal imaginable; a spinning top painted with carousel horses; puzzles and balls; a kaleidoscope of wonder; and a music box. Liddy lifted the box and held it in her hand. When she unclicked the seashell clasp and opened the lid, no sound came, but a pink ballerina pirouetted in jerky silent circles before stopping completely.

Placing it back on the shelf, Liddy saw a flicker of movement and looked across to see a woman staring back at her. She gasped and pressed her hand to her chest before realising how silly she was being – the face staring back at her was her own. A nervous laugh escaped her throat. A mirror had been fixed to the door of a grand, imposing wardrobe and, as she approached, she could see that it stood partly open. Gripping the edge, she pulled the door towards her and peered inside. She expected to find shelves full of blankets and towels, bonnets and booties, a rail of garments to fit a baby, but instead she found a crush of dresses for a woman, their hems skimming the bottom of the dusty wardrobe. She slipped her hand in between the cool fabric, trying to push them apart for a better look, but they had been so tightly crammed in that it was almost impossible to separate them and the metal hangers screeched at her efforts. Instead she pulled out one of the skirts, spreading it into the air like the wide wing of a butterfly, and marvelled at how opulent it would have been, once upon a time. Who in this house would wear clothes like these? She couldn't imagine it was Vivienne – she would never choose anything so extravagant, preferring instead grey and black. Dresses like these would attract attention, and that was the last thing Vivienne would want.

Liddy imagined herself wearing them, and how magnificent she would have felt with the silks and velvets brushing against her skin. There was a dress in every colour, but sadly their best days were over, as the damp and dusty depths of the wardrobe had robbed them of their shine. Golden fabric was now the colour of shrivelled apples, and midnight blue had become the dull sludge of a winter puddle. Liddy imagined that another of the dresses had once shimmered a glorious crimson, but now it had faded to the faint pink stain of a stopped heart. Its style was eerily like the one worn by the woman she'd seen hiding in the leaves. Who was she? Liddy pushed the dresses back into the gloom with a quiet rustle and closed the door on the thought.

In the mirror, she could see the reflection of a large chest behind her. It was so old and shabby that Liddy wouldn't have been surprised to hear it had been dragged up from the bottom of the sea and was filled with a pirate's treasure. The lid was open and resting against the wall and, as she reached it, she could see the jumble of more toys inside. A family of white woollen mice, a skipping rope, a cloth cat with long dangling legs and a monkey on a stick. Dominoes were strewn at the bottom, and there was a wand, a box of magic tricks and a top hat, which had been flattened by dozens of puzzle bricks that someone had carelessly flung in. Chipped pieces of a miniature tea set were scattered here and there. She wondered who the toys, just like the dresses, belonged to. All that treasure was sure to give any child hours of happiness, only there were no children here, not that she'd seen. Liddy wondered if they belonged to the girl in the village. Vivienne had called out the name Bea; *my little Bea*, she'd said, so the initials LC sewn into the corner of the blanket couldn't be hers. Was there another Castellini child that she was yet to discover in this house of so many secrets?

All these unanswered questions made her restless and she sank onto the wide window ledge with a heavy sigh and gazed across the lake towards the mountains. Directly below was the forgotten wilderness and she realised that she was sitting at the same window that yesterday had filled her with such foreboding, but this time she was on the inside looking out. She wasn't sure which was worse.

The memory made her shiver and she quickly glanced over her shoulder to check that she was still alone in the room. Returning her gaze to the garden, she noticed the three black trees on the ridge standing out. Liddy thought how much they resembled three people, tangled wildly together, trying to throw each other into the lake below – or were they saving each other? It was difficult to tell. Then her eyes travelled further along to the smothering thick foliage, where she searched for a sign of the woman in the red dress. But nothing stirred. The cross looked as forlorn and forgotten as the rest of the garden, but the lilies still bloomed, and Liddy couldn't help but wonder again who had left them there. Then she noticed something else jutting out of the ground next to it. It was smaller and half-hidden among the straggling weeds – no wonder she had missed it yesterday – but from above, she could see the outline of a second grave. There was something resting on top of its cradle-sized mound. Flattening her face against the glass, she could just make out the shape of a white woollen mouse, like the ones in the toy box.

Her thoughts were interrupted by the sound of approaching feet and, in a panic, Liddy searched for somewhere to hide.

CHAPTER 24

The Wallpaper

Liddy managed to slip quickly under the dust sheet and into the narrow space between the covered chest of drawers and the darkest corner before the footsteps entered the room. They were heavy and purposeful, urgent in their mission, but from beneath the sheet she couldn't see a thing and it was a struggle to breathe. The footsteps stopped abruptly and Liddy waited, but they didn't move again. Very slowly she lifted the bottom of the sheet slightly and peered out. There was someone standing alone in the middle of the room and, from the size of the boots, she could tell it was a man.

The man moved, and Liddy dropped the dust sheet and pushed herself back as far as she could until she felt the hard, cold wall hit her spine. The footsteps stopped again, and she wondered where he was in the room. She listened for any sound, but none came, until at last she heard a small rhythmic squeak like the branches of a tree aching in the wind. She was certain then that the man had sat down and was slowly rocking himself in the chair by the cradle. Moments passed and then a soft, deep voice filled the room. Liddy was surprised by the unexpected sound of singing, and she recognised the voice straight away. It belonged to the Keymaker. She listened without understanding the words – they seemed strange to her ears, as though they came from another place, another time no longer lived, but the melody was unmistakeably that of a lullaby, gentle enough to soothe a baby to sleep. Only there was no baby, and the Keymaker was singing his song to an empty cradle.

Then came the sound of a second voice; someone else was in the room and had arrived on silent feet.

'You shouldn't be in here.' It was Vivienne; her voice sounded softer than usual, and there was a tone of apprehension that Liddy had never heard before.

The lullaby ceased at once. She could no longer hear the squeaking of the chair and wondered if he had perhaps stood up.

'Neither should you,' he countered.

This was the first time Liddy had seen them together and she was suddenly curious to know more about their relationship. *Two people so similar, yet so distant*, she thought, straining to listen to their words.

'I only came here to find you,' said Vivienne.

'And how did you know I'd be here?'

'Because I went to your room and you weren't there. I – I thought I heard something up here,' she faltered. 'Besides, where else would you be, if not in your room?'

Driven by curiosity, Liddy lifted the sheet again, a little higher than before, until she could see them both. Two dark, mournful figures, like pieces on a chessboard. The Keymaker had turned away from the room and stood in front of the window, blocking out the light. Vivienne hovered near the threshold, as though something about the room made her afraid. Finally, she stepped forward and went to place her hand on his arm – perhaps in a gesture of comfort – but he flinched at her touch and pulled himself away. She quickly retreated.

'Why do you insist on torturing yourself like this?' she said bitterly.

'Why do you insist on laying your little salt trails?' He spat out his words. 'She comes when she pleases, and all the salt in all the mines of this world won't stop her.'

'No, maybe not,' said Vivienne, recovering her composure. 'That's for you to do.'

He whirled round and glared, and for a moment Liddy thought he would strike her, but instead he turned away again and rested his brow against the glass.

'I'm only thinking of you,' she said, more gently this time. There was a sincerity to her words, but he didn't hear it.

'This is your fault – all of it.' The words sounded flat and worn, as though he had said them many times before.

No challenge came.

'And that girl – what is she doing here? And don't try to tell me it has anything to do with marchpane.'

Liddy's eyes widened. There was no question that he meant her.

'Which girl?' Vivienne feigned confusion, but the Keymaker was not so easily fooled.

'The one you've got bringing supper to my room.'

Liddy held her breath.

'I need more help around the house,' replied Vivienne. 'And in case you hadn't noticed, I am not well. I don't know how much time I have left, and then what will happen? To the house? To you?'

He mumbled something against the glass.

'Does she' – Vivienne hesitated – 'distract you too much?'

'Who, that girl? No,' he replied firmly and without hesitation. 'I've barely even noticed her.'

'She found a poppet.' Vivienne waited to see his reaction, but the room stayed quiet. 'I don't think it's safe for her here,' she continued.

A burst of scornful laughter destroyed the silence, quickly followed by the Keymaker's words. 'Well, she's here at your invitation, is she not? If you don't think it's safe for her, then send her back to wherever she came from.'

Silence hung between them; it lengthened, until it had gone on for so long that Liddy thought one or both of them must have left the room. Then she heard Vivienne's voice again, but this time it came in faltering whispers.

'There is another way ... If you were to make your own key.'

Liddy heard a bang, so loud it made the window rattle, and she covered her mouth to silence the gasp.

'No!' the Keymaker bellowed. 'How dare you say such things?'

Then, without another word, he pounded across the room and the furniture shook until he was out of the door. Up until that moment Liddy had carried a knotted ball of hope in the pit of her stomach that maybe, just maybe, there was a chance that he liked her, but now she could feel it unravelling. She shut her eyes at the stinging his words had brought. If she had peered out at that very moment, she would have seen that Vivienne's disappointment was even greater than her own. Eventually Vivienne turned and left the room. Liddy waited until she was sure they had both gone and then threw back the dust sheet and crawled out from her hiding place.

Her back ached from being cramped in one place for too long, but her heart ached even more. At least now she knew the truth – that he didn't like her at all. Why had it been so easy for her to harden herself to the likes of Jack Heathcote, and yet the Keymaker invaded her every thought and filled her head with silly desires? Never had she been made to feel like such a foolish child with so much to learn; he clearly wanted her gone.

As she angrily brushed her sleeve free of cobwebs and dust, something fluttered to the floor and came to rest across her foot. It looked like a thick, coiled snake, but as it lay there motionless, she doubted it meant her any harm. She tapped it tentatively with the tip of her boot and when the thing still didn't move, she reached down and picked it up carefully, holding it out at arm's length as if it might bite her. It was just a strip of wallpaper, with the beginnings of a swirling green pattern running from top to bottom. Where had it come from? Her eyes scanned the walls, but they were strangely bare and stripped of all colour. *How drab for a nursery*, she thought, running her fingers along the bumps of the nearest wall. There had been wallpaper there once; she could feel its rough edges and the blotches where the paper had refused to come away. Why was everything in this house so stubborn? There were strange gouges too, as if someone had dug their nails into the wall and torn at the paper.

She examined the strip in her hand and at first could make no sense of the pattern – garlands perhaps? – then, as she turned it the other way, a tree suddenly emerged, then another and another, until Liddy imagined that a whole forest had once grown across these walls. But now winter had come and left everything bare.

She returned to her hiding place and peered into the corner to see if there was any more. It was dark and murky, but after a few moments she saw another strip peeling away from the wall. She slipped sideways into the small space between the wall and the chest and then, with all her strength, she leaned her back against the dark mahogany and began to push the chest out of the way. Like everything else in the room, it probably hadn't been moved for years, and time had nailed it to the floorboards. At first it was stubborn in its refusal to move, but Liddy wasn't giving up and, wedging her feet against the skirting, she got enough traction to push again. She wasn't sure why it mattered that she saw the wallpaper, just that it did. This time she felt the chest begin to give a little and, with one last heave, it groaned across the floor. The scraping of wood against wood was amplified in the vastness of the room and Liddy stood, heart thrumming, expecting either Vivienne or the Keymaker to come rushing back through the door and discover her there. Minutes felt like hours, but to her relief no one came.

The part of the wall that had been concealed behind the chest was now fully revealed and strips of torn wallpaper sprang free like half a dozen lolling, venomous tongues. The rest was astonishing. Vivid green swirls and leafy tendrils wrapped together, framing the scene within. A repeated woodland pattern of fir trees and grazing deer and rabbits, alert on their hind legs, ears pricked to danger. A grassy path led into a forest and there was a little girl walking towards it with a basket hooked over her arm, and a brace of ducks at her feet. It looked like the beginning of a fairy tale, but Liddy knew that fairy tales were not always what they seemed. The green colour was inescapable and gave the wallpaper a nightmarish quality. It was so peculiar; how it had stayed so vivid, and been preserved so well, when everything else in the room had been claimed by either damp or dust or simply left to rot?

In places the pattern seemed to rise out of the paper as if it had been made from mossy mounds and real rabbit fur, painted green. Liddy was afraid to touch it, and she tried to calm herself with the thought that it was probably mould growing there.

With nothing left to see, she managed to push the chest of drawers back into position and was about to leave the room when she heard a soft scuttle. It was the same sound as before. Something small fell and crumbled into the grate below and so, thinking that a bird must have got trapped in the flue, she went to set it free. Often birds chose chimney breasts to make their nests until billows of smoke sent them flapping into the air, yet this hearth looked as if it hadn't known a fire for years.

Kneeling, Liddy tilted her head into the disappearing blackness. The sooty smell made her cough and she withdrew from the grate, gasping for a mouthful of air. The sound came again, like a faint scratch, and she wondered what wretched creature was stuck up there. Then her heart fell away as she remembered what had brought her there in the first place.

'The cat!' she cried. Her voice was a rising echo as she plunged her face back into the cold darkness. 'Here, Kitty, Kitty!'

Stretching her arm, she groped her way around the walls, desperately trying to feel for its soft fur, but it was only the cold stone that met her fingers, crumbling like flour. The cat had probably been chasing a mouse and got itself stuck up there. Balancing on her tiptoes and steadying herself with one hand, she thrust the other as high as she could and began again, round and round and round again, until at last the very ends of her fingers brushed against something soft. She wiggled them against it, sending more rubble into the grate at the bottom. The poor thing was probably too terrified to move.

At last she managed to dislodge it and something – too small and cold to be a cat – fell into her hand. She pulled away with a small jerk, and the thing dropped into the grate. Glaring up at her with its dark and gleaming eyes was another poppet, even more grotesque than the last one. Recoiling in horror, Liddy ran from the room without noticing that the poppet's hair, so like her own, was still caught between her fingers.

CHAPTER 25

Oranges and Bluestone Cobbles

When she eventually reached the drawing room, Liddy found that the breakfast tea had grown cold and the bread felt dry and stale in her mouth. It had probably been on the plate for hours; a punishment for her eavesdropping, she thought.

'Found any more poppets?' called the Major in cruel jest, and Liddy felt herself stiffen. She wasn't about to tell him what had fallen down the chimney.

'I was just trying to help,' she replied curtly.

'Help?' The Major laughed the word out, nearly choking on his drink. 'Is a curse your idea of helping? They both nearly died of fright.'

He stopped to take another swig, but still hadn't turned to face her. Liddy was glad. She wanted to slap him, and such was the urge that she had to sit on her hands until it passed.

'If I'd known it was a poppet, I would never—' Liddy stopped, not sure why she was trying to defend herself to him, but it was too late and he seized on her words again.

'If you'd known!' He laughed incredulously. 'What else could it have been? So black and wizened. From the look on that woman's face, I'm not sure she'll ever recover from the shock of it.'

His dismissive, almost jovial tone was a sudden trigger for her anger. She rose so abruptly that the chair tumbled backwards to the floor.

'Alice! That woman's name is Alice!' she shouted. 'Can you imagine how you'd feel, coming all this way for nothing? No key. No goodbye. No peace. All of it taken away from you, just like that.' She clicked her fingers.

The Major stared at her with bloodshot eyes, then he lifted his glass and drank deeply, while his other hand lay clenched in his lap.

'I wish it was you who had lost your taglock. All you do is sit in that chair all day, wallowing and sneering at everyone else. What about the mistakes you've made? Why don't you think about them before judging me? There are thousands of stories waiting in that library, and I'm sorry that yours was ever chosen. You don't deserve to be here.'

Liddy felt instant regret. The Major slumped in his chair, weighted by grief and too much whisky, and the truth of her words delivered the final blow. Gaping at her like a dying fish, he blinked slowly, before turning back to the only thing that gave him relief. She knew his glass would be empty before she'd even left the room.

In the hallway she closed her eyes and leaned against the wall until her hands had stopped shaking. The Major might have been a drunk and pompous old fool, but he was also a father grieving the loss of his son, battling a war that raged without end. He hadn't deserved her cruelty. Deep down, she hadn't meant any of the words she'd spoken and she took some comfort in knowing that, in a few hours, he probably wouldn't remember them. To make amends, she headed towards the library, hoping she would be able to free someone else from the burden of sadness.

From somewhere deep in the forest of books she heard the quiet hum of distant voices. They were too far away to recognise, and she couldn't even tell if they were male or female. Occasionally a word would drift past and then pop and disappear like a tiny bubble. She heard a word that sounded like *soon* and another that could have been either *door* or *dawn*. Liddy followed the words like a treasure hunt. She passed shelf after shelf, dipping in and out of shadows beneath the ethereal green glow of the domed roof. She stopped every now and then to make sure the voices were still there. By the time she'd reached the shelf labelled *Outsiders*, Liddy could hear not only words, but whole sentences and the sound of shifting feet. She was close.

'I need your sorrowing star,' said a kind and gentle voice. It belonged to Eloura.

She recognised this part of the library and knew that a few more steps would take her to the chamber with the fountain and the carved wall and the flickering lanterns. As she moved forward, she felt a little rush of air, but the shadows kept their secrets, making it impossible to see what was there. Perhaps it was the returning owl, but all she saw were dust motes disappearing into the gloom.

'Quite the little eavesdropper, aren't you?' came a quiet voice.

'Vivienne?' said Liddy to the dark.

The dark answered. 'They will need this.'

Out of the gloom only Vivienne's pale hand emerged, holding a beautiful-looking key. She slid it onto a shelf and then her hand was gone, as quick as an illusion. The key was speckled gold.

'Who is it for?' asked Liddy, but this time the dark stayed silent.

Taking the key, she stepped from behind the shelf to see there were three people standing by the fountain. Alert to the sudden movement, Eloura looked over and smiled.

'Have you brought us the key?' she asked.

Alice and John lifted their heads as she approached. They looked so broken, and yet there was hope shining in their eyes. Each held a tiny burning sun, plucked from the persimmon tree. Alice also clutched her sorrowing star – a small glimmer in the gloom of grief.

Liddy handed Eloura the key.

'Thank you,' said John.

'Yes, thank you,' repeated Alice in a soft whisper. She reminded Liddy of a rose brought in after a storm, still beautiful but more fragile than before.

Liddy stepped back as Alice shook the flower from its pot and it fell into her hand in a clump of soil, then she turned to the fountain and dropped it into the water. It sank without trace. Liddy remembered her own flower, sitting upstairs by her bed, and wondered what she was meant to do with it, since she wasn't here to say goodbye to anyone.

'One sorrowing star must replace another,' she said. 'Its roots will take hold and the map will be rewritten, and so the stories will continue to grow.'

Alice and John moved forward; perhaps it was the fear of remembering or the fear of forgetting that made them cling so tightly to one other. Liddy wasn't sure which was worse.

'Eat your persimmons,' said Eloura.

Obediently Alice and John lifted the fruit to their mouths and took tentative mouthfuls.

'Now then, where is it?' Eloura pondered to herself. She was standing in front of the carved wall moving her head one way and then the other, slowly running her fingers over the shapes and ridges before her. 'It's never in the same place.'

Liddy thought it was more puzzle than door. At last Eloura stopped with a satisfied sigh and her hand rested against one of the carved objects carried in the woman's hair. It was a butterfly, and Eloura slid the key into one of the swirls on its wing.

She turned the key three times until they all heard a gentle click.

Alice and John's eyes widened as they looked from the door to each other and then back again.

'It is time to see your daughter,' said Eloura, pulling the door open.

From the other side they heard birdsong and a sudden splash of yellow light appeared; it felt so warm. A butterfly floated in and fluttered away towards the shelves.

'I remember it was summer,' said Alice, in a small trembling voice. 'Wasn't it?' she said, tugging on John's sleeve, but John stood speechless, watching as the light fell over them.

Then through the open door they heard laughter – the happy sound of a child being chased and caught and spun through the air.

'It's Lucy,' whispered Alice, and this time John nodded.

Their eyes were bright with the sparkle of tears, but neither of them moved, as if doing so might break the spell.

'You must go now,' whispered Eloura. 'She's waiting for you.'

Picking up their few small belongings, Alice and John stepped through the door, hand-in-hand. Eloura closed it quietly behind them and turned the key in the lock.

'What happens now?' asked Liddy, feeling dazed by the light and the spectacle.

'Now we drink tea,' she replied.

Instead of sitting by the fire, this time they drank their tea in the turret room. It tasted of peppermint and sugary figs, and Liddy drank in great thirsty slurps; it was her first drink of the day – she had barely touched the cold tea at breakfast.

'What was that place on the other side of the door?' she asked. It had seemed so beautiful, but almost imaginary. The light had been so dazzling that she hadn't been able to see what lay on the other side – a garden perhaps?

'It is the place between here and there,' replied Eloura.

'And is it always the same?' Liddy pondered for a moment. 'Is it always a garden in summer?'

'No.' Eloura shook her head and her hair fell around her in a mesmerising silver drift. 'It has been a garden many times, but I have also known oceans, and hilltops, empty rooms and palaces made of gold. Sometimes there is rain behind the door and the sky is dark. Everybody's story is different – loss can happen anywhere, at any time. It is an ordinary thing.'

With a swish of her robe, Eloura moved across to the large table in the centre of the room, upon which Liddy could see an extremely long sorrowing-star petal stretched out between two wooden slabs like a huge scroll. In the far corner there were two more exactly like it. Eloura sprang onto the table and crouched above it with a purposeful look on her face. All around her there were loose pages of writing.

'Are those from the books?' asked Liddy, wondering why Eloura had unbound them and spread them out like a fan.

'Hmm,' she replied, only half-listening.

Eloura picked up one of the pages and buried her face in it. She inhaled deeply and, quickly taking her pen, she dipped its nib into a small pot of ink and let her hand glide across the petal's surface.

'What are you doing?' Liddy asked curiously.

'I'm writing my way into the next story.'

Liddy watched as flamboyant loops and curves of letters appeared. Occasionally Eloura glanced up to consult one of the pages lying around her, before continuing to fill the empty spaces.

Edging nearer, Liddy couldn't tell if the canvas was just one enormous petal or several that had been woven together; its edges looked seamless. When Eloura finally stopped and leaned back on her knees to read over what she'd written, she looked dissatisfied and held out one of the pages for Liddy to take.

'What do you imagine?'

Liddy frowned. Not sure what she was meant to do, she began to read.

'No, no,' said Eloura. 'Don't read it, breathe it in.' She closed her eyes and mimed the action.

Liddy lifted the page higher and held it to her nose, just as Eloura had done. She closed her eyes and breathed in the scent. At first there was nothing, but after taking a second much deeper breath she caught a faint trace of something warm and honeyed, and she was sure she could hear laughter and bells and music from somewhere far away.

She opened her eyes. 'I'm not sure. Some sort of funfair perhaps.'

'Hmm.' Eloura sounded uncertain as Liddy handed back the page.

'What do *you* imagine?' she asked.

Eloura answered dreamily, 'Carnival nights, brought alive by the rhythmic beat of a drum. Jangling jewels and soft feathers wrapped around skin so hot and sultry that everything burns. I imagine people gathered in doorways, smoking fat cigars that wobble between their smiling lips. There are bluestone cobbles beneath my feet and a sky filled with fireworks. And, like the ground, the nights are always blue.'

Liddy listened in amazement and wonder to her words as they created a whole new world in her mind. How she would love to go somewhere like that, if such a place existed.

'Do all the pages remind you of somewhere different?' asked Liddy.

'Not each page, no, but each story.'

'Whose story is that?' she asked, staring back at the words Eloura had written upon the sorrowing star.

'It's the story of a man who comes from a place like the one I described.'

'Where the nights are always blue?' asked Liddy, not wanting to let go of the image Eloura had spun for her.

Eloura drummed her fingers on her jaw. 'There's still something missing.'

'Missing?'

Eloura nodded thoughtfully. 'In this story there is a man who makes breakfast for his wife. He hopes that she will come, but knows that she won't. He sets her a place anyway by the window and sits down opposite to wait for her. Between them is a red rose in a vase – red for devotion, or so they say. He remembers her sitting there each morning in the sun, watching as the light slowly turned her hair to gold. But she won't come today, or any other day – you see, she died years before. Still he waits, until the sound of the carnival welcomes back the night and he realises that it is too late for her to come now. He throws away the untouched food and the fallen petals, and shuts the window to the sound of music.'

'That's so sad,' said Liddy, imagining the man sitting all alone.

'Roses!' exclaimed Eloura dramatically. 'That's what's missing: the smell of roses. Whenever their colour and scent faded, he'd go out into the garden and pick another with a hopeful hand.' She lifted the pen and dipped it back into the ink in a burst of excitement. A minute later another sentence appeared and the final full stop was blotted into place. 'That should make it easier to find him.'

Then the realisation hit Liddy, and her stomach tipped. 'So you're leaving?'

'Soon. The time has almost arrived for me to spin more stories.'

Eloura jumped down from the table and began to slide the petal carefully from beneath the wooden slabs. She indicated for Liddy to do the same at the other end and, with their arms outstretched to each corner, they carried it across the room. Eloura stopped in front of a thin rope strung low between two hooks, like a washing line, and together they heaved the petal up and over as though it was a bed sheet.

'I'll leave it there to dry,' said Eloura.

Liddy tried to read the words, but they were written in a rush of emotions like jumbled pieces of a jigsaw or ingredients mingled in the baking of a pie. Words like *window* and *gold* emerged between *carnival nights* and *dancing feathers*, which were slotted between *where the nights are always blue*, and then her eye fell on the final line: *The rose has withered and crumbled away, but in the courtyard he will find her another. Always red – red for devotion.*

'What are you going to do with it?' she asked.

'Attach it to the mast of my Sorrela boat and sail into a new story,' Eloura said, as though it was as easy and ordinary as pouring tea from a pot. For her, it probably was.

Stories are sails, thought Liddy, imagining it billowing out in the wind. 'What's a Sorrela boat?'

'A boat made of sorrowing stars,' replied Eloura.

Liddy helped her carry the other two sails to the table. Then Eloura picked up the pages from another pile and spread them out before her, like a deck of fortune cards. *What will they reveal this time?* wondered Liddy with a small tremble of anticipation.

'How many stories will you spin?'

'Three,' replied Eloura, closing her eyes and running her fingers across each page in turn, sensing somewhere beyond the story. 'Always three stories and three sails.'

'What is the next story?'

'Feel for yourself,' replied Eloura, handing her one of the pages.

Just like before, Liddy lifted it to her nose and breathed it in. Instantly it felt as though there was sand in her lungs and she pulled it away for a moment. It smelled of a dry, dusty land that had none of the beauty of the last place.

'It reminds me of a desert place,' she said, handing it back with a grimace.

Eloura lifted the page to her face. 'It is a growling place of chaos and metal. A place of shimmering tin roofs that sing in joy when the rain comes once a year. I can hear a pipe, and the bare-footed boy who plays it is covered in so much dust that it is no longer possible to tell the colour of his skin. The pipe once belonged to an old snake-charmer, and the boy thinks it has the power to conjure wishes. So he spends all day sitting in the dirt, staring at his reflection in the bottom of a saucepan, hoping that if he plays long enough, then the face of his mother will appear there. It has been so long that he's not sure if he'll recognise her. While everyone else is praying for rain, he is praying for his mother to come home.'

'Please find him,' whispered Liddy.

Eloura nodded. 'I will.'

'And the third story?' asked Liddy, hoping it was at least a little less sad than the others.

'Ah yes, the third story,' said Eloura with a heavy sigh. 'That story is the furthest away and will take the longest to reach. It's in a place of bustling markets, with trinkets and teapots and perfume in little corked bottles, fruit liquor and bags stuffed full of spices and nuts.'

'And teapots like that one?' queried Liddy, nodding at the one on the table.

Eloura smiled. 'Exactly like that. I can never resist a pretty teapot.'

'What else can you find there?' asked Liddy, her mind filling with delight.

'There are oranges too big to hold in your hand – a single bite will leave your whole arm drenched, and there is cheese so soft that it will crumble in your fingers before it reaches your mouth. All around, kilim rugs billow like colourful sails. It's like the market is a ship, docked there to share its discoveries.'

Liddy longed to be there. Sometimes words can only take you so far.

'It sounds beautiful, doesn't it?'

Liddy nodded. 'What story will you find there?'

Eloura picked up the third pile of pages. 'One of a granddaughter all grown up, who never got the chance to thank her grandparents.'

'Thank them for what?' asked Liddy.

'For saving her and her mother from the angry fists of their son. After the grandparents helped to smuggle them across the border, they were forever lost to each other and there was no way back after that.'

The sadness of all the stories was suddenly too much, and Liddy fell quiet. There was some comfort in knowing that Eloura would find them and bring them here. That they would at last have the chance to say the words they needed to say, but there were so many stories, so many wishes still waiting, and it was impossible to grant them all.

'Can I come with you?' asked Liddy, surprising herself. More than anything she wanted Eloura to take her to all these places, so they could explore them together; to taste the oranges and feel the bumps of the bluestone cobbles beneath her feet, and to swim in water that shone bright as a shattered jewel. Besides, the Keymaker had made it very clear he didn't want her there.

Eloura shook her head. 'Your story is here.'

Liddy couldn't help but feel the sting of disappointment.

'Will you bring me something back then?' she asked.

'I always do,' replied Eloura, looking at the teapot.

'And what if the people refuse to come?'

Eloura looked at her with a raised eyebrow. 'They always come.'

Liddy grew wistful, thinking that people could be surrounded by all the beauty in the world and not see any of it. Instead they retreated inside themselves for so long that they became trapped there. Eloura had described grief as being locked in a room. Is that why Vivienne had suggested the Keymaker should make his own key? And if so, what had put him there? Thoughts of him distracted her yet again.

'Well, I should leave you to write your sails,' said Liddy, watching Eloura begin to sift and sort through the pages.

'I will see you before I go,' said Eloura. She was kneeling above the second sorrowing-star petal, and her hair fell over her shoulders and down her back like glittering silver.

'How will you sail your boat out of a lake?'

Eloura lifted her head and her eyes shone with mischief and knowing. 'When is a lake not a lake?' she asked.

Liddy frowned. Her father used to give her riddles to solve, but she was never very good at them.

'When it's filled with sorrowing stars,' replied Eloura, solving it for her. She tipped her head back in open-mouthed laughter and Liddy could see the bright eye of a cat tattooed on her tongue.

Liddy had one last question.

'Who is the woman with copper-coloured hair?'

Eloura wasn't listening; the story had taken her attention.

Liddy raised her voice a little. 'The woman with a bone-white face, and eyes fierce enough to rip out your soul – who is she?'

Eloura lifted her head, and her face was dark and inscrutable. She waited a beat too long before answering.

'A woman like that belongs on the other side of the door.'

CHAPTER 26

Attack

Trundling back through the library, Liddy found herself in a section called *Loss*. Guided by fate, she let her fingers brush along the narrow spines until, for no particular reason, she stopped and tilted one of the books out to read its title: *Bluebells and Bird-Boxes*. She was about to let it drop into her hand when she heard a small thud at a nearby window. Pushing the book back in its place, she hurried to discover the source.

Through the glass, she could see a tiny bird lying on the lawn. Its head was turned towards its wing, its eyes were closed and it wasn't moving. *Poor little thing, it must have flown into the window,* she thought, rushing from the library, hoping to find that it was stunned and nothing more. By the time she got outside, both Ben and Vivienne were standing on the path, and the bird was cradled in the crook of Vivienne's arm.

'I was in the library and heard it fly into the window,' said Liddy, in case there was any doubt about what had brought her there in such a rush.

Vivienne cooed softly into the bird's feathers with practised murmurs. There was such tenderness in the way she lightly brushed her cheek against its wing until its rapid, shallow breathing steadied, and it looked around with alert and blinking eyes. What Ben had said about her saving creatures was true. Her instinct to protect lay deep under layers of ice, but it was still there. Perhaps animals were simply easier to trust, since they never share our secrets.

'Is it okay?' asked Liddy. She knew that birds often died from fright alone.

'It will be. It just needs a moment to find its bearings, that's all.'

Ben took his cap in his hands and twisted it in worry. 'It's not a good omen, though, is it? A bird flying into a window foretells a death.'

'A death is always coming,' replied Vivienne bluntly. She stretched out her arm and, in one swift motion, the bird lifted itself into the air and flew into a nearby tree.

Ben did not look reassured by the bird's recovery.

'Superstitions serve us well, but we must choose them wisely. After all, different birds foretell different things, do they not?'

Ben nodded slowly and replaced his cap. 'Aye.'

'And that was a sparrow, which promises heart-healing. All will be well.'

Vivienne brushed a few small feathers from her arm and then turned to leave.

'What about salt?' called Liddy.

Vivienne's head whipped round, and her eyes narrowed. 'What did you say?'

'Well, it's another superstition, isn't it? People line their doorways with salt to prevent witches and demons entering. It's said to keep away the evil eye.'

Vivienne looked quickly at Ben and then back at Liddy. 'Some people also say that spilled salt is a sign of treachery and lies, which is why we must be careful what superstitions we put our faith in.'

Liddy felt like she was being accused of something, but Vivienne was now striding away. She turned back to Ben, who was still standing on the path.

'I found the nursery this morning,' she said, with deliberate calm.

'I knew the bird hitting the window was a bad omen,' he muttered.

'It's such a morbid place, especially for a nursery. Pitiful even.' Liddy tried to sound light-hearted and thought it best not to mention the poppet she'd found stuffed up the chimney. 'Everything is thick with dust and the walls are—'

'You shouldn't be in there,' he interrupted, and there was fear in his eyes.

Liddy was undeterred. She had been there too long not to have the answers she sought.

'Was the nursery meant for Vivienne's child?'

He shook his head.

'But the girl in the square – she's Vivienne's daughter, isn't she?'

Ben walked over to the wall of the house and leaned against it. He lowered his head to the ground, his face hidden beneath the rim of his cap. Liddy wasn't sure if he was going to speak again, but was thankful when he did.

'It was the bandit I told you about,' he said softly. 'The one I saw her with in the kitchen. She never spoke a word of it to anyone, but nine months later she carried a little bundle in her arms. She held her like a gift, and I suppose in a way that's what she was.'

'A baby girl?' asked Liddy.

Ben nodded. 'That's right, a baby girl.'

'And that's why she sits in the square, isn't it? She's waiting to see her daughter?'

Ben pursed his lips. 'It's the only way.'

'But why?' asked Liddy, leaning against the wall beside him. 'Why did she give her away and why doesn't she just take her back?'

'Because it's not safe here.'

'What do you mean, it's not safe?' Liddy frowned, remembering the salt and the poppet and the strange green wallpaper ripped from the walls. His words were an echo of those Vivienne had spoken to her brother. 'Did something happen in the nursery?'

Ben turned and looked at her, his eyes filled with sorrow. 'That was merely the beginning.'

Suddenly they were both alert to the sound of footsteps and there in front of them, as though conjured out of the air, stood Vivienne.

'What has happened to the potatoes? Have they sprouted legs and run away or simply buried themselves back in the ground?'

Ben mumbled his apology and pulled himself away from the wall. 'I will fetch them now.'

'It's my fault,' said Liddy. 'I was asking Ben about the house.'

'They won't peel themselves, you know. Not while you're out here idling in the sun.'

Liddy straightened as she saw Ben come hurrying back along the path with his barrow full of potatoes. 'No, of course not. I can help.'

A few minutes later Liddy and Vivienne were sitting in the silence of the kitchen, with a mountain of potatoes on the table between them. Liddy watched how quickly and assuredly Vivienne used her knife to create endless spirals of skin that fell into a bucket at her feet. Liddy felt useless in comparison, as her knife did nothing but snag and scrape, gouging out big chunks of flesh. Her feelings of frustration intensified when she realised that Vivienne had peeled half a dozen potatoes to her three.

'What do you think of Raphaelle?'

It took Liddy a minute to realise who she was referring to; he was the Keymaker to her, distant and aloof, known only by his craft. She stared at her own pitiful pile of peelings, trying to think of what answer to give. She closed her eyes. What should she say? That she couldn't stop thinking about him. That whatever room he was in, she wanted to be there too. That at night she lay in bed imagining what his body might feel like pressed against hers. She could say so many things, but the pause had grown too long, and when she opened her eyes again, Vivienne was staring at her with a bemused look on her face.

'I see,' she replied, with a look of satisfaction.

Could she read minds as well as objects?

Liddy felt herself blush furiously and quickly dropped her eyes to resume her peeling. After a while she found her words. 'Your brother seems like a complicated man.'

Vivienne gave a short, sharp laugh. 'Well, yes, I suppose he is.'

'He doesn't want me here?'

'What makes you think that?' she asked, her interest piqued.

Liddy shrugged. She didn't want to admit that she'd overheard their conversation in the nursery.

Vivienne sighed loudly. 'The problem is that my brother doesn't know what he wants.'

If anyone had seen them sitting there, they would have been mistaken for friends, casually sharing their desires and intimacies like schoolgirls. When Liddy looked back up, Vivienne was watching her with shrewd and thoughtful eyes, challenging her to continue. Feeling awkward, Liddy gripped her knife more tightly, refusing to reveal the truth of her heart.

'I think he seems ... stricken.'

'Stricken?' Vivienne leaned forward, willing Liddy to say more.

'Yes, like a tree destroyed by lightning. Still there, but forever changed.' *Like you*, she wanted to add, but bit her tongue instead.

'Trees and lightning. Quite the poet!' exclaimed Vivienne, and Liddy wasn't sure if she was being teased.

'Why do you care what I think of your brother?'

Vivienne didn't seem offended by the boldness of her question and continued her methodical peeling.

'Finding your way back from grief can be a weary journey. Some never return.' This time her voice was cracked with emotion.

'What do you mean? What grief has he suffered?'

Vivienne waved away Liddy's questions with her hand and a furious shake of her head.

'Is that why you want him to make his own key?' The words were out before she could stop them.

Vivienne's head snapped up and there was a sharp cry as the knife slipped from her hand and clattered to the floor, then all Liddy could see was a rush of blood spreading over Vivienne's hand, as if she had slipped it inside a scarlet glove.

Before Liddy could help, Vivienne was already at the sink, holding her hand under the cold tap.

'I'm sorry, I—'

'Nonsense,' replied Vivienne impatiently. 'It's not your fault; besides, it's nothing more than a nick.'

From the pool of blood on the floor, it was anything but a nick. Liddy picked up a rag and began to wipe the stone slab clean.

'Leave it!' cried Vivienne, finding a strip of gauze and wrapping it tightly around her finger. 'I'll do it.'

Snatching the rag from Liddy's hand, she bent down and dabbed at the stain on the floor until all traces of it had disappeared. Finally she stood up, and the blood-soaked rag looked like a ripped-out heart in her hand. In the other one, she held the knife and there was something quite terrifying about the image.

'What I'm really asking is ... could you ever love my brother?'

At first Liddy was too astonished to speak. Is that what Vivienne had wanted all along? A wife for her brother? And why *her* – a woman she had never met until a few weeks ago? She couldn't find the words to make a sentence. Vivienne stood quiet and hopeful. Liddy sensed that the next words she spoke had the power to change everything.

'I'm not sure he will let himself be loved.'

Vivienne closed her eyes, as though in pain, and nodded. It wasn't the answer she had wanted, but neither was it the one she had feared. 'Ah yes, I suppose you are right;

loving someone is the easy part, but allowing yourself to be loved – well, that's another matter altogether.' Then she exhaled deeply, as though she was about to release a long-held secret. 'Whatever you might think of him, my brother wants to be loved.'

Liddy slid onto her stool and waited. Even if Vivienne was right and he did want love, then his cold dismissal of her in the nursery left her in no doubt that he didn't want it from her. What was it that had convinced Vivienne otherwise? What had she meant on that first night when she'd found Liddy's shawl and said she was glad? Glad of what? Had it really all begun with a box of marchpane?

'My brother is—' Vivienne faltered and pressed her fingers to the gauze, before flinching and letting go. 'He is lost.'

'And I'm some sort of map?' asked Liddy, with a teasing tone of her own.

'No, not a map – a key,' she replied. Her face gave nothing away but exhaustion.

'Why is he lost?'

Vivienne's face remained composed, but her whole body stiffened as she lifted her hand to her chest and seemed to clutch for the heart within. 'I suppose you must know,' she sighed.

Yes, I must, thought Liddy.

'I am too tired for such stories today,' she said, dropping the knife in the sink. 'Perhaps tomorrow I will feel a little better. I will tell you everything then.'

At that moment the door swung open, slapping the wall. At the top of the stairs stood the Major, with an empty bottle in his hand. As usual, his eyes were glazed as he tried to bring the room into focus. He stumbled forward, lost his footing and almost fell to the floor.

'Which of you ladies is going to get me a drink?' he slurred, tipping the empty bottle upside down and shaking it violently to emphasise its emptiness. 'There's not a single drop left.'

He lurched into the room and Vivienne stepped forward, quick to assert order.

'Perhaps I could get you a glass of water?' she suggested.

'Water!' The Major spat out the word and laughed as though a joke had been made. 'Am I a horse?' He took up imagined reins and, with his knees bent, began to gallop around the kitchen in a ridiculous, unsteady pantomime display, neighing as he circled the table. 'Giddy-up, giddy-up!' he chortled.

Liddy watched in disgust and disbelief.

Several times he banged against the counter and his elbow caught a saucepan, knocking it to the floor in a spinning clatter. He narrowly missed the bucket of soaking potatoes beneath the table, and Vivienne was quick to drag it away from his feet. Then his burst of energy ended abruptly and he slumped, panting, over the table, exhausted by his own mockery.

Liddy's eyes shifted to Vivienne, who remained impervious, with her hands on her hips as though she was dealing with a fractious child who refused to go to bed.

'In that case, you will have to remain thirsty.'

Liddy was impressed by Vivienne's calm demeanour; her refusal to give in to his demands.

The Major growled and recovered enough of his senses to stagger across the kitchen and into the pantry. There was a clanking of pots and pans and then the sound of something smashing onto the floor. Over the clanging and banging, they could hear his incoherent ranting.

'I must ask you to stop this foolishness at once,' called Vivienne, but the scuffles continued. Moments later the Major reappeared, and his face was puce from alcohol and fury, like a pomegranate about to burst from its skin. He lifted the empty bottle and launched it angrily against the wall. Liddy shrieked and was just in time to shield her head from the flying shards of glass. Vivienne stood calm and unwavering, with a look of mild disappointment on her face. He lurched forward again and pounded his fist on the table in a final demand, which rattled the shelves, and this time even Vivienne flinched. 'Perhaps if you went to bed – got an early night ...'

But the Major wasn't listening. He had finally found his focus and, when Liddy looked up, he was staring right at her.

'This is all your fault,' he snarled, each word bringing him closer, until she could feel his sour, angry breath on her cheek. It made her stomach clench.

'How?' she asked, trying not to breathe him in. 'How is it my fault?' She took a step back and then another, attempting to escape from the unbearable, cloying intensity of him, but he followed. She felt his whiskers scratch her face as she turned her head away.

'Making me think I wouldn't see my boy again.' There was venom in his words now and spittle frothed and bubbled in the corners of his mouth.

'Please,' cried Liddy. 'I didn't mean it. I would never—'

He lunged at her then and the force of his attack cut off her words and sent her tumbling backwards. For a drunkard, he moved remarkably quickly, and without warning he had her pinned by the wrists against the wall. Damp and clammy, he pressed harder against her until she struggled to breathe.

'Get off me!' Liddy cried, striking out with her foot in the hope that it would find his shinbone, but she missed. She squeezed her eyes shut, as though not seeing him would somehow make the Major disappear.

Then the weight lifted, and her wrists were released. Gasping, she caught her breath and slid all the way down to the floor, where she wrapped her arms around her knees and felt the hot, angry spill of her tears. When she lifted her head, the Major was being dragged by his collar across the kitchen and thrown onto the steps. The Keymaker towered over him.

'Get up,' he demanded.

The Major held his arm over his face, bent at the elbow as though to block an imminent blow. His feet grappled against the stone as he tried to push himself further away, but all his fight was gone. He curled himself into a pathetic ball, eyes closed, whimpering like a beaten dog.

'Get up,' cried the Keymaker again and this time, when the Major didn't obey, he clutched a fistful of his jacket and hauled him to his feet. The man's face was pitiful as he blubbered and whined, but there was nothing he could do to defend himself. Liddy just wanted it to stop. The Keymaker's anger was almost as terrible as the Major's.

'Raphaelle!' cried Vivienne, her voice full of warning. But the gravity of his face quickly silenced her.

'How dare you hurt her,' he said, thrusting the man against the wall. A crack rang loudly in her ears. Then the Keymaker pinned his elbow against the Major's neck, and Liddy heard the suffocating gargle of a windpipe being slowly crushed.

'Enough!' This time Vivienne pulled her brother's arm away, and the Major dropped to the floor. 'Have you lost your mind? This man is a foolish drunk, but nothing more. He means us no continued harm.'

The Keymaker noticed her hand then, wrapped in blood-soaked gauze, and his eyes blazed, ready to attack again.

'It wasn't him,' she said, moving to shield the Major. 'It was my own mistake.'

'This man is a bully,' he raged, but he dropped his arm and stepped away.

'And what does that make you?' She glared at him, before kneeling to help the Major to his feet.

The Keymaker looked at her in appalled disbelief. 'You're blaming me for this? For what *he's* done?' He began to pace up and down like a fettered animal, running his fingers through his hair as though he would find the answers there. He was too wild to approach. 'In the morning he must leave.'

'No!' cried Liddy, from the back of the room.

The Keymaker frowned and his voice grew incredulous. 'This man attacked you, and you want to let him stay?'

'I provoked him,' replied Liddy, ashamed. 'This morning in the drawing room I – I told him that he didn't deserve to see his son again. It was cruel of me, and I shouldn't have said it. It doesn't excuse his actions, but I am at least partly to blame.'

The confusion on the Keymaker's face deepened. 'But he could have killed you. If I hadn't been there ... This man is no longer welcome in this house.'

A sudden wild laugh came from near the top of the steps where Vivienne was now standing. The Major was beside her, groaning and rubbing his neck, which had already begun to darken into a throttled bruise.

Vivienne descended a single step, bringing her almost level with the Keymaker.

'Oh, dear brother,' she said in her calm, knowing voice, 'you have got this all wrong – you are not here to rescue her; she is here to rescue you.'

If there had been confusion on his face before, it was now replaced with a look of complete bewilderment.

'Rescue *me*?' he scoffed. 'And who is it that I need rescuing from?'

Vivienne paused and slowly fixed him with her sombre stare. 'Ravanna.'

The name took his breath away, as though he had taken a punch to the stomach. Vivienne turned and climbed back up the steps, but before she had reached the top, the Keymaker had barged past and was through the door.

Vivienne looked at Liddy. 'There is a monster in this house, but it is not the Major, and it is not my brother,' she said.

The Major was barely conscious now, mumbling his apologies and rolling his eyes as though he was lost in some fevered nightmare. Liddy couldn't bear to listen – whatever his actions, he didn't deserve to be thrown from the house.

'This can be undone,' she reassured Liddy, before helping the bleary-eyed Major through the door.

Liddy was left alone in the kitchen, trying to make sense of everything. Something told her that whoever Ravanna was, her hair was as bright as copper and she wore gloves of lavender blue.

CHAPTER 27

Defence

*H*ow dare the Keymaker punish the Major by sending him *away, especially after I explained my part in what happened?* thought Liddy. The raging sense of injustice would not leave her and it propelled her towards the Keymaker's room. The feeling burned so fiercely that, instead of knocking politely on the door, she burst straight in.

At first she couldn't see him. The room was dark and still. She sensed him, though; a beating heart, the rise and fall of a shadow on the wall and then, as her eyes grew accustomed to the gloom, familiar shapes emerged: a chair, a table, an upturned crate and last of all his face, twisted in anger above the flickering flame of a candle. Behind him the molten edges of the furnace door glowed an angry

293

red. The sense of injustice that had ignited her to confront him dwindled away, and as she stood there in the room, the only thing she felt was a sense of embarrassment.

He was sitting at a small open bureau where the candlelight revealed a neatly organised row of objects. It was the sole sign of order in the otherwise storm-tossed room. *He must be working on another key*, she thought. She strained to see what lay before him, but a small draught kept sending the candle flame into a wild dance, whipping its light across the room.

Still he didn't look up, too preoccupied by the objects to care that she was standing before him. With her fire now quelled, Liddy wasn't sure if she should turn around and tiptoe from the room or disturb him from his strange musings. Still undecided, she watched him run his fingers over each object, lifting them closer to the light for inspection. She hoped they were the Major's taglocks, and that the Keymaker had decided to make his key after all. The thought of the Major leaving without getting the chance to say goodbye to his son turned her blood cold. She couldn't let that happen, so instead of tiptoeing away, she stepped slowly forward.

'He made a mistake,' she said. Her voice sounded lost in the dark and the Keymaker still didn't look up. Was he too absorbed in his work to hear her? Or was it that he was too angry to speak? Liddy cleared her throat. 'The Major isn't a bad man ... He drinks because he can't do anything else – it gives him comfort.'

Instead of replying, the Keymaker lifted one of the objects up and held it in the palm of his hand, like some tiny creature he was trying to warm back to life. Curious to know what would provoke such tenderness from an otherwise cold and distant man, Liddy took a step closer. The object caught the light and she could see it was a ring with a sapphire at its centre, surrounded by a halo of diamonds. Not the kind of ring that would bind a father to a son, but rather one that would bind a husband to a wife.

'Do you think everyone should be forgiven so easily?' His voice was deep and steady and she was relieved that his anger, like hers, had faded.

She heard the voice of her mother exclaiming that *some sins are too grave to go unpunished*, and then the voice of her father advocating clemency in his wise and gentle tones. He had the softer heart of the two and, as she pondered his question, she realised that she had inherited the latter.

'Yes, I do, if it is truly sought,' she replied.

'But how can you ever know such a thing?' She could hear sadness in his words and felt she was on the edge of discovery.

'Trust,' said Liddy softly.

He gently placed the ring back inside the bureau and closed the lid on his secrets. Standing up, he moved towards her until he was almost close enough to touch. Liddy's arms remained pinned to her sides – the only part of her that moved was her heart, which thrummed so loudly she was sure he could hear it. She uttered a silent prayer for it to quieten, but instead it danced and quivered.

The Keymaker took a step closer, then another. Time stopped. They gazed at each other for an enduring minute and then he lowered his head ever so slightly, as though he was going to kiss her. Trembling, Liddy wondered if she would let him. His eyes moved slowly, taking in the contours of her face, and he lifted his hand as though to stroke her cheek or brush away a strand of her hair. Almost. He looked like he was remembering something or trying hard to forget, but what came next wasn't a kiss or a touch; it was a question. 'Why do you forgive so easily?' His dark eyes were full of resistance.

Liddy felt the crush of disappointment as he moved his head away. It took her a moment to recover. 'And why are you so cruel?'

'Me!' he exclaimed, in disbelief. 'By your own admission, you were the one to threaten the Major with not seeing his son, and now you come here and accuse *me* of cruelty.'

Liddy felt a flush of shame. Her words might not have carried the same authority as his, but still they had the power to wound.

'But it's not just the Major you will punish.' Her words caught his attention. 'What about his son? Doesn't he deserve to know that his father is sorry? That if he could go back and change it all, then he would. That he is proud of him.'

The Keymaker remained silent, unmoved. What had happened to make him so empty of compassion? Liddy grew impatient.

'Besides, it is not up to you – Eloura is the one who decides; you told me so yourself.' She turned his own words against him, just as he had done to her, and felt a small glimmer of satisfaction. Still he didn't respond, and Liddy's impatience turned to anger.

'Vivienne was right – you are no different from the Major. He's out there drinking because it's all he believes he has left, while you're in here hiding away, too afraid to live. You've both given up.'

Something in the Keymaker's eyes flared. 'What do you know about giving up?' he demanded. 'Whatever you think it is, you're mistaken. You are lucky that you only see what's in front of you. I envy your peace. You come here – a foolish girl with your trays of marchpane. You know nothing at all.'

'I know that cruel words won't make you feel better,' she said evenly, determined to keep the hurt from her voice.

Exhaustion seemed to overtake him and he rubbed his temple, before turning away as though her words had been too much for him to bear. The silence hung between them and the gulf widened.

Her voice, when she spoke again, was quiet. 'Please make his key. He suffers enough.'

The Keymaker had already withdrawn into the shadows and she couldn't be sure if her words had reached him or not. He was more remote than ever. Suddenly the candle flame was extinguished and all that remained was the distant blaze of the furnace quietly simmering in the dark.

CHAPTER 28

Ravanna

Brightness roused Liddy from her sleep. The light that fell through the window was luminous and ethereal, more snow than sun. It landed on the counterpane in a block of silver, yet the rest of the room stayed dark. Sighing, she realised she had forgotten to close the shutters and had invited in the moon. It must still be night. Pulling back the covers, she walked to the window, ready to shut out the light.

Outside, she saw neither moon nor snow, only a strange white shimmering that illuminated the whole lake from beneath and rose like mist, touching the edges of the garden. It was spellbinding. She gently rested her elbows on the ledge and settled her head in her hands to admire the view. It was just like Ben had explained, the day he rowed her across to the island – the sorrowing stars shone in the dark. It looked like a thousand moons had dropped from the sky, or perhaps they were fallen stars waiting to grant wishes. It was the most mesmerising thing she had ever seen. Under the water they had looked like giant lily pads, and there had been no hint of the magic they held – even Ben's descriptions hadn't made them sound this beautiful.

She would probably have gazed at them all night long if she hadn't spotted a figure standing on the edge of the lawn. Liddy instinctively stepped back, for fear of being seen, and it took her a minute or two before she found the courage to look again. The figure turned his head to follow something in the trees and it was then that she knew who it was. She had grown so accustomed to unpicking his features in the dark that, even from this distance, she knew the slope of his shoulders, the shape of his face and the outline of his tousled hair. But what was he doing standing in the garden in the middle of the night?

Nothing happened for a long time and then the soft, sweet chimes of music reached her ears. Something must have disturbed the keys hanging from the branches. But the night held no breeze, and all in the garden was still.

The Keymaker began to move towards the trees, and Liddy tried to keep sight of him. A few moments later he stopped again and waited. Surely any visitor to the house would approach from the opposite direction, climbing the steps from the jetty and onto the lawn. It didn't make sense for anyone to come the other way. He was almost out of sight, so she unlatched the window and pushed it open for a better view.

Then she saw it, a sudden flash of red, just like before. A burning flame appeared through the leaves, then it was gone again. The Keymaker must have glimpsed it too, as he began calling out to the dark. She couldn't hear what he said, but it sounded like a single word, repeated over and over. A moment later the flame was back, and this time it moved quickly, vanishing, then reappearing, then vanishing again behind the leaves. It looked like the trees were on fire. The Keymaker ran towards them, but soon the thick brambles smothered the flame and whatever had been there disappeared. She thought he would return to the house then, but to her horror, he plunged into the thorns in quick pursuit.

Liddy gasped. She knew it hadn't been a flame she'd seen in the trees; it was the woman in the red dress with her trail of copper hair blazing behind her, ready to burn.

Backing away from the window, Liddy turned and flew downstairs and into the garden. But when she arrived, he was gone. It was strangely quiet; no footsteps, no sound of the keys, no hunting owl. It was hard to believe that, only a few moments ago, the Keymaker had been right there on the lawn. It felt as if she'd woken from a dream, or perhaps she wasn't awake at all. She followed the path in hurried little steps until it curved right, through the lemon trees and towards Ben's potting shed. Instead of following it there, she stepped off the gravel path and picked her way through the brambles towards the iron railings and the neglected garden beyond. This was where he'd disappeared.

In her haste Liddy had forgotten to grab her coat or a shawl to keep her warm, and the cool night air felt damp against the flimsy cotton of her nightdress. She had at least managed to push her feet into a pair of slippers. She'd also forgotten to bring a candle, thinking the light from the sorrowing stars would be enough, but when she left the path, the light refused to follow.

Still she found her way, clamouring up the incline, which was steep and precarious in the dark. She lost her grip several times, sliding almost to the bottom. She tried to pull herself to the summit using tufts and weeds, but it was hard to see what she was reaching for in the dark and she winced in pain, realising she'd clutched at some nettles by mistake. Her efforts were hampered further by the wet mud that threatened to swallow her whole, but luckily it only claimed one slipper. From somewhere above came the loud cry of a vixen, just like the one she'd heard in the city. Perhaps there were foxes here, after all. With thorns caught in her nightdress and thistles clinging to her hair, Liddy finally made it and stood, panting, at the top. Ahead was the ridge where the three skeleton trees stood and beyond them, through the endless thickets, was the long drop to the lake. The looming shape of the house seemed further away at night, and the nursery window was smothered in darkness.

She scoured the shadows for any sign of the Keymaker, but there was nothing there, and the sole sound was that of her own breathing. As she moved, a twig snapped beneath her foot, disturbing the quiet. The sound of it was strangely amplified, making her gasp and pause. There came the ruffle of something like the unfurling of wings, but its source remained obscured. Moving forward once more, she finally spotted the Keymaker. He was kneeling beside the two graves she had seen from the nursery window. In her haste to reach him, she stumbled on the stones, crying out, but somehow managed to steady herself before hitting the ground.

The moon must have escaped from behind a cloud because suddenly the garden was brightly lit, and she saw him staring back at her with fear in his eyes. She must have appeared wild and out of place, with her one bare foot, her mud-splattered nightdress and half the garden caught in her hair. She could forgive him for thinking he'd seen a ghost.

He scrambled to his feet, but his fearful expression remained unchanged, and when she called out to him, his anguish seemed only to grow. Surely he knew who she was now. She began to pick her way, more carefully, through the stones, glad of the moon to guide her, but she hadn't got very far when she heard him call out in a strange, strangled voice that didn't seem like his own.

'Ravanna! No! Leave her alone!'

The Keymaker ran towards her with one arm outstretched, but he was too far away to help, and Liddy felt something grip her wrist, so agonisingly tight that she cried out in pain. She was pulled sideways and a woman's face surged towards her, more bone than flesh. Liddy recognised the eyes at once – the same as those that had watched her through the leaves, but this time they were filled with a fierce satisfaction. The mouth was a gaping black hole, fetid and foul, as though something was rotting deep within, and Liddy felt a putrid breath, cold against her cheek. She screamed, twisted free and ran – everything becoming a blur. Her only impressions were of fire and darkness and decay.

She ran blindly, without direction, tripping, stumbling and falling. Jagged stones hindered her at every turn and brambles tore at her skin like little teeth. But she couldn't stop, she wouldn't – the fear of what lay behind her numbed the pain and propelled her forward. She was almost at the ridge when a cloud snatched the moon away and its light was taken from her once more. The sudden dark was disorientating. She hesitated, desperate to see where she was, but the darkness was thick and unnatural, unlike any she had ever known. Spinning round, Liddy saw the silhouettes of the three trees before her and scrambled towards them as though they could somehow tell her the way. Her lungs burned as she finally pressed herself against one of the trunks. She listened for the Keymaker's voice, but either he had fallen silent or he was too far away for her to hear. She waited for her ragged breaths to steady, but before she could calm them, a copper flame hurtled towards her and Liddy screamed in terror once more.

Then she was falling down the bank towards the water.

Thickets and brambles and nettles ensnared her. The ground beneath her turned to mud, soft, squelching, slurping mud that pulled her down further. In a panic, Liddy felt herself sinking and flailed her arms, trying to find something she could hold on to, some way of pulling herself free. But the sprawling dark made it impossible to see and her strength was fading. She knew the lake could be no more than a few feet away, yet none of the sorrowing stars were shining.

Like an unexpected wish, the moon reappeared, and Liddy could finally see where she was. There was mud everywhere. A movement drew her attention and she watched in terror as something began to crawl out of the water towards her. Ravanna – or whoever, *whatever* it was – dragged her way up the muddy bank like a half-drowned creature, getting ever closer. Her face was twisted in a snarl of utter contempt and her eyes were burning, loathing, boiling cauldrons of hate. Liddy desperately reached for a clump of bulrushes to pull herself free of the mud and away from the creature, but she was held fast. Exhausted and bruised, she sank deeper instead, her limbs too heavy to move. For the first time she wished the moon would disappear so that she could hide in the relief of darkness, but it kept shining, and all she could do was close her eyes. The same smell as before crept over her, a reeking, rancid rot that made Liddy retch into the mud. Then she felt something on her face, the toying tap of fingers as they scuttled over her cheeks and began to push their way into her mouth.

She screamed and screamed, writhing in absolute terror until, out of nowhere, she felt a pair of arms wrap around her waist, pulling her free.

'I'm sorry. I'm so sorry.' She heard him breathless beside her. His hands were sweeping the hair from her eyes, and she was no longer sure whose tears stung her face. 'Please forgive me.'

'Raphaelle,' she murmured, reaching out for his hand.

With a loud gurgle, the mud finally loosened its grip on her legs and, as it slowly slid away, so too did everything else.

CHAPTER 29

Secrets Revealed

Liddy tried to open her eyes, but her lids felt too heavy. At first she couldn't remember much of what had happened last night, just flashes of something terrible. She tried again and saw a blur of dark shapes and heads huddled in whispers. Then the trees were on fire, and out of the flames appeared a face with eyes she would never forget. She tried to scream, but her mouth was full of mud: thick and bitter and choking. *Ravanna!*

Liddy's arms and legs writhed in panic and she realised she had become twisted tight between her covers. A hand pressed gently upon her shoulder, calming her, and she felt the touch of a soft blanket, warm against her chin, as though someone was tucking her into bed. Whoever it was meant her no harm, and she fell back against the pillow. The blanket carried the scent of violets, a reassurance that Vivienne was close. There was another smell too, like a pine forest. She wondered if a window had been left open somewhere and the mountain air had drifted in, or if it meant that he was here too.

A door shut and the voices faded away. Liddy slept deeply. When she opened her eyes again the room was empty apart from the cat, which had sprawled itself across her feet.

'I really do need to find out your name,' she said, stroking its head until it began to purr.

Liddy had no idea how long she had been sleeping, but the weakness in her body had lifted and her aches were now merely niggles. Pulling herself free of the covers, she stood in front of the mirror and gasped at her reflection. Although it seemed that someone had tried to wash the mud from her hair, it was still matted in thick clumps. Her face was a trellis of red scratches and her left eye looked bruised. Four deeper lines ran down her cheek like the claw marks of a wild creature. At some point her lip must have been split, because it was swollen and cracked. Lifting her nightdress, she could see more cuts and scrapes across her legs and knees, and a deep-purple bruise blooming up her thigh. Rolling back her sleeves, she examined her arms and saw that they too were covered in cuts and blotches. Surprisingly, nothing hurt too much and, after washing her hair in the bathroom, she was able to dress with only the smallest discomfort.

The cat stretched itself across the bedspread with a pretty squeak, more mouse than cat, and watched her thoughtfully. Liddy took a moment to warm her fingers in the long, thick fur of its back. 'I'm fine,' she said. 'Thank you for asking.' Then she dropped a kiss on the cat's head and went downstairs.

In the kitchen Vivienne was standing with her back to the door and a pan in her hand, the contents of which she nearly spilled to the floor when she saw Liddy standing there. 'You're out of bed,' she managed to say.

Liddy wasn't sure if it was said as a complaint or out of concern. Then she remembered the reassuring hand on her shoulder and the extra blanket and knew that Vivienne wanted her to recover.

'I'm feeling much better,' she insisted with a small smile. 'It looks worse than it feels.'

'I see.'

Taking a seat, she watched Vivienne pour water into a cup with a shaky hand. She seemed frailer somehow, and Liddy felt a small lump fizz in her throat. She had so many questions, but she was too afraid to ask them, in case they blew Vivienne away like a ball of dust.

'Thank you,' she said instead.

Vivienne looked at her in surprise. 'Thank you? For what?'

'For taking care of me. I know you were there in my room.' Then Liddy was stuck by a terrible notion: what if it hadn't been Vivienne, but somebody else who had peeled away her clothes and soothed her wounds? What if it had been Raphaelle?

'Yes, I was there,' she replied after much hesitation, and Liddy felt a little rush of relief.

Vivienne placed a cup of warm lemon water in front of her, along with a breakfast plate, and sat down. 'Your fever lasted three days.'

'Three days!'

To have lost so much time was unthinkable. As Liddy ate, she tried to swallow not only the mouthfuls of food, but her questions too. In the end there was only one that she couldn't keep from her tongue.

'Who is Ravanna?'

She expected Vivienne's usual quick dismissal or perhaps some pretence about not knowing anyone with that name, but Vivienne simply closed her eyes, bowed her head and answered with the truth.

'She was my brother's wife.'

Deep inside, Liddy had known it all along, or at least she had suspected it. The word 'was' troubled her, though, suggesting that Raphaelle's wife had gone away somewhere. Yet that couldn't be, because Liddy had seen her twice, and the last time Ravanna had tried to kill her.

'Was?' she queried tentatively.

'She died,' Vivienne replied, without lifting her head.

'Died? But that's impossible. I saw—'

'What you saw was her soul, trapped without release, and it is my brother who keeps it here. It is not right, not right,' she said, her words a fast-flowing torrent of despair.

A ghost? thought Liddy. She had never believed in ghosts, but what other explanation could there be for the woman in red who vanished so suddenly and without trace? It was just as Eloura had said: *A woman like that belongs on the other side of the door.* Liddy was convinced that had it not been for Raphaelle, she would have surely drowned in the mud.

'Why did she try to kill me?'

'Without a reason to move on, my brother refuses to make his own key. Your arrival could change all of that. Perhaps Ravanna knows it too.'

'My arrival?' Liddy laughed at the absurdity and felt a sharp twinge in her side: a painful reminder of the damage that had been inflicted. 'So I'm here to make your brother forget his dead wife? To chase away her ghost.'

Vivienne looked at her sharply. 'Ravanna is dangerous and until she is gone, this is not a safe place. It is why—' She paused.

'And yet you invited me here?' accused Liddy, narrowing her eyes. Anger grew at the thought of being used as bait. *So much for making marchpane.*

'Yes,' Vivienne replied quietly, without further explanation or apology.

'And you haven't once mentioned the danger I've been in?'

'No,' she said, unable to meet Liddy's eye.

Liddy had no idea what to say to that, and she could no longer ignore the rumbles in her hollow stomach or the plate of food sitting in front of her, so she began to eat, allowing the silence to resume. Vivienne's head was still lowered as though in silent prayer, feeling the weight of the burden she carried. Liddy watched her, curious, cautious, a little angry, but most of all confused.

When she had finished the last mouthful, Vivienne rose swiftly. 'Follow me,' she said, moving towards the door.

'How did Ravanna die?' called Liddy, refusing to obey until she knew more of the story.

Vivienne stopped sharply, as though she had been pulled by an invisible rein. Liddy couldn't see her face, but her spine stiffened and her answer came in a jittery whisper. 'It was an accident. A terrible, terrible accident.'

There was something so brittle in the way she spoke that it made Liddy tuck away the rest of her questions. She would ask them later.

Vivienne led them past the wide curving staircase, along the corridor towards the library. Liddy would have thought that was their destination, had Vivienne not continued straight past the large carved doors and up the narrow staircase, with its dark, claustrophobic panels. Liddy rested her hand against the wall, closed her eyes and waited a moment for the dizziness to pass. She was not yet fully recovered. When she looked up, Vivienne was no longer there.

Reaching the landing, Liddy could see that Vivienne was already inside her room. The door had been left open, but without an invitation to enter, Liddy waited on the threshold. Vivienne moved within like a sleepwalker. She stopped below the shelf filled with toys and trinkets and games. Looking round more carefully, Liddy noticed something strange about the room that had been hidden from her last time by the dim flame of the candle. In the daylight she could see things more clearly. With its shelves full of playthings, its frilly curtains at the window and its rosebud walls, this room belonged to a little girl, not a woman. Especially not one as cold and austere as Vivienne Castellini.

'Do you recognise her?' Vivienne asked, lifting the lid off a glass box and gently pulling out the doll that lay within.

It was the same doll that had given Liddy such a peculiar feeling when she'd first seen it. Still standing on the threshold, she took the question as an invitation and stepped forward to lift it from Vivienne's outstretched hand. Immediately she felt a tingling sensation. She tightened her hold and the feeling slowly subsided. The doll looked as if it had been restored, and lovingly so. The tip of its nose was slightly chipped, and one of its fingers was discoloured and a little shorter than the others, but it was still a beautiful doll. She turned it over, admiring the bright-blue colour of its dress and the little hand-woven slippers tied around its ankles with small strips of ribbon.

Crowning its head was a halo of flowers, and endless chestnut curls tumbled around its face. Turning it back over, Liddy noticed that a large square had been cut out of the side of the dress. Too neat and precise to have been made by mistake.

'It is—' Liddy frowned, trying to find some sense in what she was about to say.

Vivienne smiled and waited.

Liddy looked again at the doll in her hand and then her eyes widened. 'But—' she faltered and the words fell away.

This time the memory shone bright. She was a child again – holding her father's hand along narrow streets and eating bread as fluffy as clouds. She saw the toy shop in the village, and heard her own voice begging, then her mother's impatience and her father's kind surrender.

Then she remembered the crying, the hours of searching and her cousin Tabby lying next to her in the dark, whispering words of consolation. Could this really be the doll she'd lost all those years ago? And, if so, what was Vivienne doing with it?

'Don't you remember losing her?'

'I remember losing a doll, yes, but – this can't—'

'I found her,' replied Vivienne.

She took the doll back and carefully laid her in the glass box, tucking in all the frothy layers of her dress before replacing the lid.

'Where did you find her?'

'Right here on the island. She must have floated across from the village. I pulled her from the water.'

'But I don't understand.'

'She was badly damaged, and I thought about taking her to the toymaker and asking for his help in restoring her, but then I decided to do it by myself. I painted her face and washed her dress, and I rinsed her hair with vinegar to bring back the colour. See how it shines?'

Liddy was stunned; nothing she heard made any sense. Why would Vivienne have gone to all that trouble to restore a lost and broken doll? A quick calculation told her that Vivienne would almost have reached adulthood when Liddy had visited the lake and would certainly have been too old to be interested in dolls. But part of her knew it was true. The first time she'd seen the doll, it had brought a niggle of familiarity; and then outside the village toy shop, the half-memory came again. She had buried the thought, which was too absurd to be real.

'But how did you know—' Before she finished her sentence, she remembered Vivienne's gift: the ability to sense things by holding objects. The power of psychometry. It hadn't all begun with a box of marchpane, but with a doll lost many years ago. *What secrets has the doll revealed to Vivienne?* she wondered. 'You've been waiting ... all this time?'

'Yes.'

'And you knew I'd come?' she asked in a daze.

'I didn't know – not for sure, but yes, I hoped you would.'

'Why?' asked Liddy, slowly lifting her eyes in another challenge for the truth.

'I do not have much time left and I need to know that my daughter is back safe, where she belongs.' Vivienne paused. 'It is time to bring her home.'

CHAPTER 30

The Keymaker's Loss

Liddy shook her head, wondering if this was some strange game, or a trick.

'I don't understand,' she said. 'What has any of this got to do with your daughter?'

'All those years ago, when I held your doll, I knew you were the one to save us, and this house. I just didn't know from what. I could never have imagined the tragedy that would follow – nobody could.' Vivienne turned away; the memory was a difficult one and she needed a moment to compose herself before continuing. 'I had no idea how to find you of course, not until much later when Ben brought back that box of marchpane. He usually kept it for himself, but, for whatever reason, on that day he left it on the kitchen table for me to find.'

'Fate,' said Liddy quietly.

Vivienne gave a small smile. 'Opening it returned me to the day I found your doll – the feeling, the connection, the hope – and I knew instantly it was one and the same. For all those years I didn't know how to find you, and after the ... accident I began to think I never would. But my hope didn't go away, not completely.' She paused. 'Call it Fate, or Mira, or a miracle, but when I turned the box over in my hand, there it was.'

'My address,' whispered Liddy. The story had left her wide-eyed with wonder. She remembered how each of the boxes was neatly labelled with the name of their street and town. Her father thought it was important for people to know where the marchpane was made, especially if it was to reach distant cities, as he dreamed it would.

'That's how I found you.'

After that, neither of them spoke, and the minutes that followed were quiet and reflective.

'I know you have feelings for my brother,' said Vivienne at last. Her hand grappled along the edge of the dressing table; her own words had left her unsteady. 'I have seen the way you look at him.' She hesitated. 'And the way he looks at you. He has a kind heart – gentler than he reveals. He might be my brother, but I would not deceive you about that. Besides, he saves all his hatred for me.' She gave a short, sharp laugh, which left her coughing.

'But you'll happily deceive me about everything else?'

'Not happily, no.'

'Why does he hate you so much?' Liddy asked, wondering if it had anything to do with the reason she gave away her daughter. The two seemed to be connected.

Vivienne didn't reply, and Liddy watched the knuckles of her hand whiten with the strain of holding on.

'There is an old nursery above here, full of dust and forgotten toys; the wallpaper is half-clawed from the walls, and nobody is telling me what any of it means.'

'I have not deceived you as you think.'

'Well, I'm not here to make marchpane, am I?' said Liddy scathingly.

Vivienne moved her head a little from side to side. 'No, not entirely,' she admitted.

There was another long stretch of silence. The air felt taut like a bow just before the arrow's release. Slowly Vivienne lifted her fingers and pressed them to her lips, as though she wanted to feel the texture of the words before she spoke them.

'I have always been protective of Raphaelle, perhaps because our mother died giving birth to him.' She paused and sighed. 'You don't lose your mother and live the same life afterwards. I was the one who looked after him – an older sister taking care of her younger brother.' Vivienne looked thoughtful. 'Do you have a brother?'

Liddy shook her head.

'A sister?'

Once again Liddy shook her head. She had Tabby, but she imagined having a brother or a sister would be an entirely different thing. She had never thought of it until now.

'Perhaps you won't understand then when I tell you that the bond between a brother and a sister can be a complicated one, where both love and hate may exist together.' She stared into the middle distance. 'As a child, Raphaelle was always smiling; he was my little ball of sunshine, lighting up this house and everything in it. Then one day the darkness came, and after that we all got lost.'

As she continued, Liddy watched Vivienne shrink further into herself, and feared that she might disappear altogether.

'By the time Raphaelle brought Ravanna here, they were already married. She was undeniably beautiful, with her large shining eyes and hair the colour of autumn leaves. She had a dress in every colour imaginable and she wore each one like a queen.'

Liddy thought of the wardrobe in the nursery, full of faded glamour. Inside, the gloomy gowns were gathering dust and sorrow instead of swirling through the perfumed air of a ballroom. The thought of them being left to rot made her sad.

'She was delicate too, like a little bird he'd managed to tempt down from the trees, or a butterfly caught in a storm. I had no reason to disapprove of the union, or even to question it. Yes, Ravanna was highly strung and prone to tears, but it was clear that she cared deeply for my brother. What happened afterwards wasn't her fault; it was nobody's fault.'

'What did happen?' asked Liddy, barely above a whisper.

Vivienne sighed heavily, letting her shoulders droop further. 'One day I was folding away the clothes and the bedding, like I had done a thousand times before. But this time, as soon as I lifted Ravanna's nightdress into my hands, a wave of sickness ran through me that was so shocking it sent me retching towards the sink. I couldn't bear to look at it again, never mind touch it. I bundled it away and tried to forget what I had felt. But from that moment I knew something terrible was coming, something from which none of us could escape.' Vivienne closed her eyes and rubbed a spot on her forehead as though it hurt. 'In some ways it is worse knowing things too early than too late. Especially when there is nothing to be done.'

'What did you see?' asked Liddy, edging closer.

Vivienne shook her head and her eyes filled with fright. 'It was so dark, everything went so, so dark. Then there was so much green – enough to drown us all!'

Liddy frowned. Vivienne's words had become incoherent and rambling.

'I don't understand, Vivienne – who drowned? Did Ravanna drown?'

Liddy's words seemed to alarm her, as though she had just woken to find herself out of bed. Confusion crumpled her face.

'It started with the wallpaper,' she said, calming herself.

'What did?' asked Liddy, desperate for answers. Each word was like a shovel full of dirt digging closer to the buried truth.

'All of it. The madness. The chaos. The baby.'

The baby?

'Ravanna would sit in that wretched nursery, day after day, with the baby growing inside her. But it wasn't growing at all. The walls hissed their venom, spitting it out, but she didn't listen. She just sat in that chair humming lullabies, gazing at the cradle, waiting to welcome my niece into the world.'

'Ravanna had a baby?' *But if there was a baby, then where is it now?*

Vivienne made a sound like a half-stifled sob and turned her face away, but Liddy could see it reflected in the mirror: bereft and broken. There were no tears, perhaps there were none left to spill. Vivienne took another moment to steady herself and then turned her face back to the room.

'The birth was a difficult one and lasted for many hours. Raphaelle was tormented by the thought that the same thing would happen to Ravanna as had happened to our own mother. He is not a devout man and I have never known him to pray, but that night I found him on his knees, head tilted to the heavens, pleading for mercy. But, sadly, it wasn't meant to be.'

'They both died?' asked Liddy, horror-struck. Now she knew why the nursery left her feeling so morbid and melancholy. Death hung in the air.

'No, not then,' replied Vivienne quickly. 'It was only the baby at first. She never slept in that cradle, not even for one night. She never even got the chance to cry.'

Liddy understood then why Raphaelle shut himself away. Why he lived in the dark. Why he suffered. *How can someone ever find their way back from such a loss?*

'They chose it because of the colour – so cheery and bright, they said, perfect for a nursery – but it was such a terrible mistake.'

'The wallpaper?' asked Liddy, perplexed.

Vivienne's voice grew hushed as though the walls were listening 'It was laced with arsenic. There was poison in those trees, and in those hills, and in those greedy green garlands that covered the walls. Ravanna sat there hour after hour, and all that time she was breathing it in, not knowing what would happen. It wasn't enough to kill an adult, but it was more than enough to slowly stop a baby's heart from beating.'

Liddy felt nausea rise in her throat. She had heard rumours before of wallpaper being deadly, of how colours were mixed with toxic elements to enliven them, but she hadn't believed it to be true. It seemed nothing more than a conspiracy to keep homes less fanciful. But now she shuddered to think of the vivid floral patterns sprawling over her own walls.

'There was no recovery for Ravanna after that. How could there be?' Vivienne's face was sombre and foreboding. 'Raphaelle spoke to doctors who prescribed medication for her grief, but nothing helped. In the end he took her away to a sanatorium in the mountains. They were gone for months and, when they finally returned, I didn't need to hold her nightdress to see that the same darkness still haunted Ravanna.'

Gone for months, thought Liddy. 'Is that when – the bandits came?'

Vivienne didn't seem surprised that her secret had already been shared and she simply answered the question with a small nod.

'And then there was a second baby – *your* baby?' said Liddy, slowly slotting together another piece of the puzzle.

Vivienne pressed her hand to her chest as though to suppress her despair. 'I tried to hide it from them for as long as I could, and from myself. I didn't know how much I wanted her – not until she was in my arms. I would walk around the house wearing my coat and complaining of the cold, but a secret like that cannot be kept for ever.' She closed her eyes. 'The lies I told. So many lies, I should be punished for that alone.'

'But you told them to protect your brother and his wife. It's what anyone would have done.'

'Would they?' snapped Vivienne. 'What I should have been doing was protecting my baby.' Her hand slid from her chest, catching over her buttons until it came to rest on her flat stomach. 'Beatrice arrived in the first days of October. I remember standing at the window and staring at the wind as it swept through the garden, tugging, rifling, tearing, ready to snatch her away. I should have known it was a warning, but instead I chose to ignore it.'

'What do you mean? A warning about what?' There was still a missing piece in this strange, sprawling puzzle.

Vivienne's hands were tight little fists, as though she wanted to keep the rest of the story hidden inside them, but instead she released them and out spilled the rest of her story.

'One night I found Ravanna standing over Beatrice's cradle. She was holding a bunched-up blanket to her face, ready to smother her. About a week later I caught her furtively stirring something into Beatrice's milk. Another time she was standing beside her with a pair of scissors. Raphaelle refused to listen to my concerns, and I began to wonder if I had got it all wrong – if *I* was the monster, to think her capable of such wicked acts. There was always an explanation: an extra blanket to keep her warm; camomile to soothe her to sleep; scissors to keep her nails short so that she didn't scratch her face. I would perhaps have continued to doubt myself, if I hadn't gone into the nursery that day and found Ravanna with the poppet.'

Liddy thought of the poppet she'd found, with its burst pouches stuffed full of herbs and nail clippings. Her eyes widened as she realised who the poppet resembled, with its wild hair and dark clay face. Vivienne's fierce reaction when she'd snatched it so violently from Liddy's hand suddenly made sense. It was a wicked curse placed upon Vivienne's daughter.

'I knew what Ravanna was doing. She hadn't lied about trying to cut Beatrice's nails, but it wasn't so that she wouldn't scratch herself, it was because she wished her harm. If she couldn't have her baby, then I couldn't have mine. I tried to take the poppet, we struggled and' – Vivienne paused to stifle the rising sob in her throat – 'Ravanna fell from the window of the nursery.'

'But it was an accident,' said Liddy hurriedly. 'A terrible accident, just as you said.'

'Yes,' replied Vivienne, wiping her hands over her eyes as though she was trying to erase what she'd seen. 'It was an accident, but one for which I am still being punished.'

'But who would punish you for that?'

Vivienne looked up in astonishment, as though Liddy should have understood.

'My brother. He blames me for Ravanna's death.'

Liddy had sensed theirs was a past filled with secrets and suspicions, yet they were still bound by family loyalty. Perhaps that was what Vivienne had meant when she'd spoken of love and hate being able to coexist.

'I no longer know if he refuses to make his key out of devotion to Ravanna or because of his hatred for me.' She looked as if she could sleep for a hundred years and still wake up tired.

Liddy's face crumpled, and she had to stop herself from rushing forward and pulling Vivienne into her arms, a gesture that would not be welcomed. Words would have to do instead. 'He doesn't hate you. I'm sure he doesn't.'

Anger flared in her eyes. 'I lost my child too!' Her voice was suddenly frantic. 'I had to give her away. It was the only way I could keep her safe – it still is. I can never bring her back here, not unless Raphaelle makes that key and lets go of Ravanna's ghost.'

CHAPTER 31
The Sorrela Boat

Vivienne crumpled to the floor, her strings cut by the sharp blade of confession. Without thinking, Liddy rushed to her side and helped her over to the bed. She was shocked again by how light Vivienne felt – nothing more than small bones wrapped in a shroud. *How long has she been wasting away in front of us all?*

As Vivienne closed her eyes, her hand slipped from Liddy's and fell silently onto her chest. Liddy watched it rise and fall, relieved that Vivienne was still breathing, but every breath that came was a ragged, fluid-filled death-chant.

'My brother,' she murmured.

'I will find him,' Liddy said, glad of a reason to leave the room, but also hesitant. She wasn't sure that, when she returned, she would find Vivienne alive.

She moved quickly though the house, her mind spinning with confusion. The aches she thought she had escaped returned with a vengeance, making her stop and wince at every turn. At the bottom of the stairs she felt so light-headed that she was afraid she might faint, and she held on to the bannister until the feeling had passed. Finally she stood at his door, knocking for attention.

Raphaelle's voice called out almost immediately and the sound of it made her shiver. Only a few days ago he had pulled her from the mud and held her in his arms, his whispers soft against her ear. Had he been there in her room, sitting by her bed, as she'd imagined? She tried to force these thoughts from her mind, and the overwhelming feelings they brought. Everything was different now – she finally understood his grief – but as she lifted the latch, she felt less certain than ever about what she would find on the other side.

He was sitting at his table, lost in the grooves and whorls of the wood. *He was hurt too,* Liddy thought, noticing the bandage wound tightly around his hand and the deep scratch running the length of his jaw, a rivulet of red.

'Raphaelle!' she cried, saying his name for the very first time.

He looked up, like someone who has woken too quickly from a dream.

'You're awake!' he exclaimed. His voice was full of undis-guised relief. He rose quickly from the table and moved towards her, his expression a mixture of hope and concern.

But Liddy just stood there, shaking her head and biting back tears. He hesitated and she saw a deep frown appear on his face.

'What's wrong?' he asked, placing his hand lightly on her shoulder.

'It's not me,' she managed to say. 'It's Vivienne. She's—' The rest of her words were choked by tears.

Fear flooded his eyes, and he ran from the room.

By evening the house had calmed. The doctor had been summoned and had given Vivienne something to ease her discomfort, as well as a bright tincture that had to be spoon-fed to her at regular intervals. The trick would be keeping it down, the doctor had explained, and he was right. She spluttered out more than she swallowed, and the cloth they held under her chin did little to stop the sheets from staining a rusty brown. Now that the coughing had worsened, they were told to cover their faces. Washing their hands would help too, but better still to keep their distance, cautioned the doctor. Liddy understood then why it was that Vivienne stayed hidden, always hesitant for company, afraid of being touched. It wasn't for her own protection, but for the sake of others. A sacrifice.

Mostly Vivienne slept, but during the brief lucid moments when she opened her eyes, they blazed with renewed intensity and she looked more alive than ever. The doctor had also warned them to expect this, saying that it often happened to sufferers near the end and there could be no mistake: it was not a sign of recovery.

Liddy barely spoke to Raphaelle in the days that followed. Their hands brushed against one another as they passed in the doorway of Vivienne's room, but nothing more. He spent hours sitting by her bed, exchanging hushed words that Liddy couldn't quite hear. Every time she found him there, she would quietly move away, wanting to give them the space they needed to share their secrets and sorrows. The time to heal.

On the third evening she went in search of Eloura, hoping that she hadn't already left without saying goodbye. The library was quiet and dark as she walked between the stories, trying to find the turret room. Liddy got lost, as she knew she would, but when she heard the familiar flutter of wings she realised she wasn't alone. The owl watched her, its luminous yellow eyes gleaming, patient and wondrous. It settled on the shelf like a puff of dandelion seeds.

'Can you take me to Eloura?' She could hear her words floating high above her head. Almost instantly, the owl spread its wings and swooped in front of her and away. 'Hey! Wait!' she called, giving chase. Her feet released a myriad of echoes, and her breath sucked at the air. At last the owl settled on a new shelf and Liddy could see the tangled archway of the turret room up ahead.

'Thank you,' she called to the owl.

Its enormous eyes looked even more startled than usual and it swivelled its head, making Liddy laugh.

In the room sat a narrow boat. Its sides were small and salt-crusted; white and green, and white again as though it had been dipped in a landscape of snow and moonlight and meadows and hills. Stems bound everything together and sap sealed the gaps in between, as strong as caulking. Woven leaves created pouches brimming with seashells and sponges beneath tassels of seaweed, and there was a cluster of cracked barnacles clinging to the prow. Its hull looked deep enough to hold a bed and perhaps a small table, but not much more. The sails rose high into the turret, two already hoisted and one more to follow. They looked more like unravelled scrolls than ever: stories upon stories. Liddy imagined the boat gliding through the sea mist like an ethereal ghost ship, half-creature, half-vessel. Already she could taste the briny air and the summer-soaked oranges of distant unfamiliar lands. It seemed strange to crave what she had never known.

She heard a small noise and then Eloura appeared on the deck. The flow of her silver hair created the impression of gentle moonlit waters, frothy as the waves. Liddy was relieved that she hadn't left yet.

'Is it time to go?' she called, watching Eloura hoist and secure the final sail.

'Almost,' Eloura replied, giving one last pull on the line before turning round. 'What happened to you?' She frowned when she saw Liddy's injuries.

Liddy wasn't sure what to say, when she didn't really know herself. Eloura leaped down and stood in front of her. She was close enough for Liddy to see that the embroidered boat on her eye patch looked the same as the boat now tilting before her in the turret room. Two matching Sorrela boats.

'Those cuts need treating,' said Eloura firmly.

Liddy watched her slice into the stem of a sorrowing star at her desk, and then use the edge of a petal to dab at the bright silvery-white liquid that bubbled out like a large tear drop. It was the same colour as Eloura's tattoos. Was this how they had been made, with resin, not ink?

'Hold this to your face,' she instructed, handing Liddy the petal. 'Press it down, wherever it hurts the most.'

Liddy took the petal and held it to the corner of her mouth. At first the pressure made her flinch, but as she kept it there, the pain slowly ebbed away.

'Do you believe in ghosts?' she asked. Her voice was muffled through the thick petal.

Eloura took another and wrapped it around Liddy's finger, binding a cut that she hadn't even noticed was there. 'Ghosts take many shapes – some are real, others imagined. They can be wisps of a memory or a blizzard that makes us lose our way. Mistakes, regrets and losses have the power to haunt us, but they don't always mean us harm.'

'Well, this one definitely did,' asserted Liddy. 'And it had the unmistakeable shape of a woman, and a name too: Ravanna.'

Liddy unravelled her story from beginning to end, without stopping. How it had begun all those years ago with her lost doll, and then later with the marchpane Ben had brought back to the house. As the words spilled from her mouth, she was reminded once more of childhood fairy tales. At their heart hid something vicious and dangerous; a cruelty that made her want to pull the blankets right up to her chin and beg for the candle to burn a little longer into the night. Never did she imagine that she would come face-to-face with such darkness. The wolves in the stories were real.

'Do you blame Vivienne for what happened?' asked Eloura.

Liddy shook her head. There was no one to blame, and no one who deserved to be punished. Loss can turn an innocent heart into one of such bitter cruelty.

'Blame doesn't ease the suffering.' Eloura looked across the room to her boat and her gaze lingered there, taking her mind far away.

'Do you think it's ever the other way round – that the living can haunt the dead?' asked Liddy.

'That is entirely possible, yes. Sometimes ghosts appear because we invite them, and they stay because we can't let them go.'

Eloura's eyes returned once more to the boat, and Liddy wondered how it would reach the water; its mast was almost high enough to spear the stars, and its sails, even when folded away like wings, would be much too wide to fit through the tangled archway.

'How will you get the boat out of the turret?'

Eloura smiled, full of knowing. 'When is a turret not a turret?'

Liddy laughed; this time she had the answer. 'When it's on the Lake of Sorrowing Stars?'

'Exactly,' she replied, clapping her hands together. 'These walls fall away to create a slipway right down to the lake; from there the boat simply glides right onto the water.

Liddy couldn't imagine the walls collapsing all around them, like a stage set folding away at the end of a performance, yet if Eloura said it could, then she had no doubt it was true. There was magic in the patterns that swirled across her skin and seeped into her blood.

'When are you leaving?'

'Under the light of the new moon, following its phases until the story is full and the teller of it can be found.'

'But what about the Major?' asked Liddy, suddenly remembering Raphaelle's refusal to make his key. Was there no hope for him?

'There is time,' Eloura said. 'But it must be soon.'

'Why did you bring the Major here?' Of all the stories in the library, Liddy imagined there were many others more deserving of forgiveness.

'Why do you ask? Because he drinks too often from the bottle?'

Liddy shrugged. 'He just seems so ... unforgiving.'

'Everything inside him is broken. The alcohol smooths the sharp edges and makes it less painful to breathe for a while. It is regret that pulls the cork from the bottle – not because he craves what's inside, but because he wants to escape. You do not have to agree, but you cannot blame someone for not wanting to feel their pain. Grief is being lost in familiar places. It is not seasonal. It doesn't bloom brightly in the sunshine and wither away during the winter months. It is evergreen, and it is entirely your own.'

Liddy stayed quiet and thoughtful, and her mind turned to Raphaelle. It was so hard not to think of him and his loss.

'Besides, I have brought thieves and murderers here before; villains who wield daggers and knives, not bottles.'

Liddy's eyes widened in shock. 'Murderers!'

'You have to know more before a true judgement can be made. A single word, such as *murderer*, is simply a title. To understand the story, you must first turn the pages. Forgiveness can change everything.'

'Have you ever refused someone's story?'

Eloura shook her head. 'Just as they are not mine to choose, neither are they mine to refuse.'

'But what if Raphaelle won't make the Major's key?'

'Then you must convince him. The sorrowing stars do not blossom for ever; once they are taken from the lake, their shine begins to fade and so too does the chance to say goodbye. A lost chance can be so much harder than never having a chance at all. That is where the roots of regret take hold and never let go.'

'He won't listen. He—'

Eloura took Liddy's hands in her own and held her gaze. In a moment she became a mother, a sister, a friend, all the women she had longed for in her life.

'Raphaelle has always been stubborn. His loss has cursed his heart into a deep and sombre sleep – like lilacs under snow – but things are stirring now. Don't you see? You have roused him, and his heart is beginning to wake.' Liddy nodded, although she didn't see, not really. Raphaelle might have dragged her from the mud and saved her from the clutches of Ravanna, but anyone else would have done the same. Did he look at her differently now? She didn't know.

'It's not just the Major's key you are waiting for, though, is it?' Eloura squeezed her hand in a gesture of reassurance.

This time Liddy shook her head and bit her lip, trying hard to control her feelings. 'Has Raphaelle ever asked for help ... to make a key of his own?'

Eloura shook her head sadly, as though it was something she too had wished for. 'Raphaelle's heart has always been full of love, but in his grief he has forgotten how to release it. The time has come for you to remind him, Liddy.'

Eloura smoothed a strand of Liddy's hair behind her ear and smiled. It was the same simple movement that Raphaelle had made on that night, and it filled her with the hope that maybe, just maybe, he did feel something for her after all. Her stomach flipped like a creel of fish being freed back into the ocean.

'How do you know so much?' asked Liddy wonderingly.

Eloura smiled that all-knowing smile of hers, the one so full of wisdom and kindness. 'The house shares its secrets with those who are willing to listen,' she replied.

As she was leaving, Liddy looked back at the boat: a salt-worn, storm-tossed vessel whose colours had faded in the rain and lightened under the sun. Liddy admired Eloura for crafting something so beautiful, and even more so for sailing alone into so many sad stories and rewriting their endings. Her eye caught on a long tendril that weaved purposefully between the white and green of the boat's side to form a word. Calligraphy made with sorrowing stars, thought Liddy, as she began to follow the swirling letters until the word emerged: Mira.

CHAPTER 32

Bluebells and Bird-Boxes

Liddy climbed the stairs to Vivienne's room in search of Raphaelle, but when she peered in, she was surprised to find the chair empty and Vivienne alone. He had barely left his sister's side since her collapse, entering in the evening and staying until the early hours. She'd watched him through the open door, sitting close to the bed. In sleep, his head fell forward onto the covers and Vivienne's hand would rest on his back, still the protective sister.

Liddy was more determined than ever to convince him to make the Major's key, especially now that she knew he'd made them for less deserving guests. Vivienne was asleep, her arms resting by her sides and her hair unwound around her pillow, as if she was floating in water. Liddy looked up to the doll on the shelf and marvelled at how it had brought her here. *One loss to heal another*, she mused. A rusty rattle filled the room, and she turned to see that Vivienne was watching her with round, glassy eyes.

'Will you save my girl?' she rasped, dipping back into the shallow dreams of half-sleep. 'Will you bring my little Bea back?' Then a single solitary tear rolled down her pale face and she closed her eyes and turned her head away, saving Liddy from making a promise she couldn't keep.

Leaving the room, Liddy made her way through the house until her hurried feet brought her to Raphaelle's door. She hesitated, imagining him somewhere behind it. She didn't know what she was going to say, not exactly, but there was too much to lose by staying silent. She knocked once on the door, and his voice, when it came, sounded husky from lack of sleep. She found him sitting in the gloom, slowly twirling something between his fingers, like a magician about to make something disappear into thin air.

'How is Vivienne?' he asked. He sounded so weary. The only movement came from his fingers and the flicker of his eyes.

Liddy took a step closer, then another, until all that separated them was the desk.

'There is no change. I'm actually here about the Major.'

'What about him?' There was sudden threat in his voice.

'To ask you to make his key.' Liddy paused, expecting some response, but none came. 'Don't you think he deserves his chance to say goodbye? For his son to know the truth – that his father was not ashamed of him, only that he was blinded by pride. I know you have made keys for lesser men.'

Raphaelle just continued to sit there, silent and still, an infuriating, impenetrable wall. Whatever he had been twirling now lay clutched in his palm.

'Don't you see you're his only hope? There is no one else – no one else but you to make his key,' she cried, slamming her hands flat on the desk. A pot rattled somewhere in the shadows. 'His mistake is not for you to forgive.'

She was close enough to see the expression in Raphaelle's eyes and, to her surprise, she realised it was not one of reproach, but one of amusement. Was he toying with her? This only fuelled her irritation further.

'If you won't make it, then maybe you should teach me how to, instead. I mean if it's too much effort for you,' she said boldly. She lifted her chin in the defiant way she'd seen Vivienne do in the village.

'You?' A burst of spontaneous laughter filled her ears.

'Yes. Why not me? It can't be that difficult, if someone like you can manage it,' she replied, trying to believe her own words.

'Maybe next time,' he replied. Then he uncurled his fingers to reveal what he had been hiding.

In the glow of the furnace Liddy saw that it was a key. The unexpectedness of it left her baffled. Then longing leaped over logic and the words sprang from her mouth before she had time to think.

'Your key?' she exclaimed.

Immediately his smile faded, and Liddy realised her mistake.

'It's the Major's key,' he said quietly.

Words clotted in her mouth, and she couldn't find a way to break them apart.

'Take it,' he said, thrusting it towards her, his smile now a scowl. 'That's the key you wanted, isn't it?'

'Yes ... I— Thank you,' Liddy managed to say. It was what she wanted, and yet at the same time it wasn't. Tentatively she took it from him.

As their fingers touched, a calmness settled in the room. The key was still warm from Raphaelle's touch, like a living, breathing thing. As she clutched it in her fist, she no longer felt anger or dismay, only relief.

'I'll tell the Major I've got his key,' said Liddy, trying to find something else to say; some reason to keep her in the room.

He nodded and returned her gaze for a moment too long.

'Letting go is hard,' she said softly.

'How would you know?' he said, but his voice was gentle and without accusation. 'You've never had to let go of anyone.'

'I never had much of anyone to hold on to ... until now,' she confessed. Holding him with her eyes, Liddy saw the sudden flash of understanding in his own, before she turned and left the room.

When she reached him, the Major was snoring loudly in his chair, with a half-empty bottle resting in his lap. Liddy kicked his boot and he woke with a grunt and a smack of his lips. It took him a moment or two to recover his senses and to realise where he was – that brief, blissful moment of forgetting. Sighing, she realised she couldn't stay angry with him; she couldn't even dislike him really. She felt only sympathy for the mistakes he'd made, the losses he'd suffered and the life he could have had. The amber liquid sloshed in the bottle like a melted sun ready to burn as he woke, and Liddy reached out her arm to take it from him. Before she could do so, however, he grabbed her wrist and stared at her with cold, hard disapproval. She quickly slipped her other hand into her pocket and retrieved the key.

'It's time to make an exchange,' she said.

His fingers fell away, and his eyes shone with trembling astonishment at what he saw. She lifted the bottle without further protest and swung it behind her back.

'You must do this sober.' Her voice was kind but firm. 'You will want to remember it. You will *need* to remember it, and it cannot be done otherwise.' Then she held out the key and, with a shaking hand, the Major took it from her and folded it away in his palm. When he unfurled his fingers a moment later, he looked surprised to see that it was still there.

'Hope is real,' said Liddy and then, in case there was still any doubt, she added, 'This is your chance to say goodbye.'

The Major's body shuddered forward and he dropped his head in his hands, but it wasn't enough to stifle the huge racking sobs that filled the room, like a rabble of birds released from a cage. Liddy had an urge to fling open all the windows and doors, but instead she sat down beside him and listened to the sound of his grateful tears.

After the Major's huge release of emotion, the house felt like it was closing in on her. Its rooms were claustrophobic and its walls were too confessional. There was a strange liminal feel to everything, one of restlessness and longing, as if it had been holding its breath for too long. In an upstairs room a woman lay hoping for forgiveness and reconciliation; in the darkness below her, a man was tormented by indecision and doubt; and somewhere in between them sat a man holding his head in his hands, weeping at the thought of seeing his son for one last time. Liddy sought escape from it all in the garden.

Beyond the gate, towards the beginnings of the chestnut wood, she found Ben. He was halfway up a rickety old ladder, screwing a bird-box to the trunk of a tree.

'Hello,' Liddy called, wading through the grass.

He greeted her without turning round, his focus firmly on the task. Something made her pause, but she wasn't sure what – only that there was an inkling of something familiar. She was growing used to such feelings by now. Was it the way Ben held the bird-box so gently in his hand, as though it was already full of hatchlings? Or was it the bird-box itself, so intricate in design, with a petal-shaped roof and a diamond peephole? Perhaps it was the bluebells that surprised the shadows, or the bench that had been put there for someone to sit on and wonder. It wasn't until she got closer that she noticed there was a small plaque nailed to the front of the box, its metal glinting in the setting sun. Shielding her eyes, she read the single word inscribed upon it: Rosa. The name meant nothing.

'What's wrong?' asked Ben, climbing down from the ladder to notice the puzzled expression on Liddy's face. 'Isn't it straight?' He looked back at the box to see if it needed some readjustment. His eyes weren't what they used to be.

'Who is Rosa?' she asked.

'The woman I should have married,' he replied, not missing a beat.

'Should have?'

'Her parents didn't approve. They had already decided on the sort of man they wanted their daughter to marry, and it was someone with a lot more money than me.'

'So the woman you loved married someone else?'

'Yes.' He looked so sad, remembering what he'd lost and what might have been. 'She had no choice – she had to do as her parents wished.'

Things haven't changed that much, thought Liddy, remembering her lucky escape from Jack Heathcote.

'She gained a husband, a title and a new country. I never heard from her after that.'

A title? The inkling that Liddy had earlier was beginning to take shape. 'What sort of title?'

'I believe it was Chamberlain. Yes, that's right: Lord and Lady Chamberlain.'

Liddy gasped as the shape became clear. 'Ben, I think I know her. I know Rosa.'

He looked at her in disbelief. 'No,' he replied, shaking his head. 'That's impossible.'

She wasn't sure if the story she was about to tell would bring comfort or despair, but she told it anyway, right there on the bench in the golden light of evening. The story of a woman who gazed endlessly at her garden, and yet it was something else that she saw. A woman who kept bluebells in a vase by her bed and refused to take down her broken bird-box because it reminded her of the man who had made it for her; the man she loved before, and now, and ever after. When she had finished, Liddy let the words settle and they both sat still for a very long time, silently watching the pollen drift over the garden.

Ben was the first to speak. 'There are so many Rosas in the world – how did you make the connection?'

Liddy smiled. There had been so many little clues sprinkled in front of her that she should have seen the connection from the beginning. The way Lady Chamberlain spoke wistfully of a faraway place, and of the love she'd left behind. There was no doubt in her mind that they were one and the same.

'Marchpane,' said Liddy. 'Vivienne mentioned that sometimes there is a box of marchpane waiting with the books.'

Ben nodded slowly. 'And it always arrives on my birthday. I always thought it a strange coincidence.'

'Lady Chamberlain – I mean Rosa – was our customer!' she exclaimed. 'She was the one sending you the marchpane. It was her gift to you.'

His mouth opened a little and his eyes widened in wonder. She reached across for his hand and lifted it gently into her own.

'Don't you see – she never forgot you.' Liddy felt her own eyes brim with tears.

'All this time,' he murmured, not daring to believe it.

Liddy remembered the story she'd found in the library, the one she had been about to read as the poor little bird had flown into the window – *Bluebells and Bird-Boxes*. *Find my story*, Lady Chamberlain had said. Liddy hadn't understood it then, but she did now.

Ben sat turning and folding his cap in his hands, as though he was no longer sure what he was holding. 'I built her a swing right over there,' he said, gesturing a little way into the wood.

'So she was here? On the island with you?' asked Liddy. The idea had seemed unbelievable at first, but as she looked around, she could easily imagine Lady Chamberlain drifting through the long grass down towards the lake with Ben beside her, her vibrancy undiluted by time.

'Her father came to help repair the roof of the house after a storm. I still remember the day he brought her here.' Ben was lost for a moment in wistful thought. 'I thought she was the most beautiful girl I had ever seen, stepping out of that boat. She walked right up to me and shook my hand, not caring that I had soil under my nails and dirt on my cuff, despite her dainty white dress and parasol. She smiled and told me her name was Rosa. I must have been about seventeen and she was a couple of years older; I suppose it made all the difference at that age. I was gangly and awkward as she glided elegantly around the garden, asking me the names of all the flowers. She'd lie in the grass with her eyes closed, trying to guess the birds from their songs.' He laughed. 'She never could, and I'd have to tell her.'

'Have you been the gardener here all this time?'

Ben nodded. 'It's all I've ever known. I learned from my father, and he learned from his. It goes back generations. I know the difference between an edible mushroom and one that will give you stomach cramps, or worse; I can grow tomatoes as big as planets and remove the sting of a nettle or a bee. I could tame a fox if I wanted to – though of course I never would. Foxes should always be wild and free.'

'And you can make bird-boxes,' Liddy added, looking back towards the tree. 'Beautiful, beautiful bird-boxes.'

'That I can.' Then he sighed. 'But none of it was enough for her father. What use is a man who cannot read or write? Someone uneducated, penniless? He did not want that for his daughter. Providing a home for a bird is not the same as providing one for a wife.'

'But you *are* educated,' Liddy insisted. 'Just in a different way.'

Ben looked towards the lawn. 'Every day she came here, telling her father that she wanted to explore the gardens, that she loved the smell of the wildflowers and the sound of the birds. We fell in love right here.' Suddenly his face clouded. 'But she was never going to be allowed to marry a gardener.'

'You are far more than that,' she replied, resting her hand on his arm. 'Besides, someone once told me that gardeners have the most sensitive souls.'

Ben smiled. 'Strange – someone told me the exact same thing.'

'Did you get to say goodbye?'

'I said it every time she left; I knew that one day I'd never see her again. That's why I gave her the bluebells – something to remind her of the garden, and of me. I even gave her a bird-box, exactly like the one up there.' He looked sadly at the tree. 'But when the time finally came, I still wasn't ready.' He raised his hand and pressed a finger to the corner of his eye. 'Do you know why I've never left? It's foolish, really.'

Liddy shook her head. 'Why?'

'Because I thought if I did, she wouldn't be able to find me.'

Then he fell silent again as though he had run out of words, or perhaps it was just that he no longer wanted to share them. Years of sadness could not stay hidden for ever, but neither were they fully comfortable in the light. Liddy tried to give him some space by watching the bees rise and fall between the yellow poppies like musical notes.

'I found her story in the library,' she said after a while. 'I'm sure I'd be able to find it again. If you like, I could show you.'

Ben turned his head in astonishment. 'Her story's been in the library all these years and I never knew? Are you sure?'

Liddy nodded.

'I'd not be able to read it anyway,' he said bitterly, turning away. Liddy could feel the disappointment pressing down on him.

'I could help you,' called a voice from close by.

They both looked up to see the Major walking towards them. He must have overheard their conversation, or at least part of it, and Liddy felt slightly irritated by the intrusion. As he approached, she realised how alert he was – she was so used to seeing him slumped in a chair that she was a little taken aback.

'I used to teach soldiers to read and write in the army,' he explained hesitantly. 'Nothing too formal, just the basics, but enough for them to be able to read the letters sent from their wives and mothers back home. I'm a bit rusty now, but I still know my way around the alphabet.'

Ben seemed to tense, his face uncertain. 'You would really do that?' he asked.

'Yes. I understand the pain of loss, and its destruction. Grief is a ghost,' he said quietly, before turning away and heading towards the lake.

The unexpectedness of the gesture touched Liddy. Eloura was right: forgiveness really could change everything. In that moment she didn't know who would be helping who more.

Ben turned to her. 'I'd like you to show me where Rosa's story is – but not yet, not until I can read it for myself.

CHAPTER 33

The Key

That night in bed, despite the dark sky and the late hour, Liddy was restless. Perhaps it was the excitement of discovering Ben and Rosa's story, or the relief of knowing the Major had finally been given his key. It had been such an extraordinary day and she wasn't quite ready to leave it all behind. Her sorrowing star glowed from the dresser. Its stem was now weighted with leaves and the bud had burst wide open, releasing the sweet scent of pears and lilacs into the room. Soon it would be too big for its pot, she mused.

With a pillow behind her, she took out Lady Chamberlain's book and began to read. The poems within spoke of longing and regret and eternal hope, and she read each word with new meaning. Yes, she'd understood them before – semantically – but she hadn't *felt* them, not in the way that Lady Chamberlain had. Now as she sat reading and rereading every line, her cheeks grew hot and damp with tears. At the back there was a small handwritten inscription that she had never noticed before. She squinted, trying to read the words so faded by tears and time:

B,

I will love you through separation. My heart has nowhere else to go.

R

A knock at the door pulled Liddy back to the present. She frowned: who was knocking so late? *Vivienne?* she thought in a panic and hurried to answer it. But the person standing on the other side of the door wasn't Vivienne, it was Raphaelle.

'What's happened?' she asked in alarm. 'Is Vivienne okay?'

'Yes, yes,' he replied. 'I've just left her sleeping.'

Wearing only her nightdress, Liddy was suddenly aware of her own body. Raphaelle seemed to sense it too and dropped his eyes, allowing her time to grab her shawl from a hook on the door. She wrapped it quickly around her shoulders and turned to see what had brought him to her door.

'I believe Vivienne has told you that she has a daughter; her name is Beatrice.'

Liddy nodded, wondering what was coming next.

'Then you must also know that four years ago she removed her daughter from this house and left her outside a convent for foundlings, in the belief that it was a safer place.'

Liddy had known, but she hadn't realised how much time had passed. Four years of waiting and watching and separation, not knowing if she would be with her child again. Liddy couldn't imagine the anguish, and wondered why Vivienne hadn't simply left the house and taken her daughter with her. But sometimes choices aren't really choices. She had no money, no contacts, no way of providing for herself, let alone an infant. People were suspicious of her and her gift, and wouldn't have offered their help. The doll had given her hope that the separation would be a temporary one, and faith was her anchor.

'Yes, I have seen her daughter pass through the square on her way to church,' Liddy replied. 'Beatrice is a beautiful child.'

'It is Vivienne's wish that she is brought here before—' His words broke off and it took him a moment to rearrange them again. 'I need to bring Beatrice back here, where she belongs.'

He spoke so formally, as though he was afraid of there being any intimacy between them. Still, she felt the flutter of possibility. If Beatrice was to return safely, then that could only mean one thing: he was ready to make his key.

'However, a man arriving on the doorstep of a foundling home might arouse suspicion. The last thing I want is for rumours to spread.'

'I could go with you?'

Raphaelle's eyes softened in relief.

Liddy remembered the way Vivienne had looked at her when she'd spoken of bringing her daughter back. Her face had been so full of anguish and pain and desperation.

'I will help you bring her home,' she said.

'Yes.' He paused. 'Thank you, it would please Vivienne very much.'

But what would please you? Liddy wondered, keeping her thoughts to herself.

Giving a quick, sharp nod of his head, he began to back away, his eyes still fixed on her. 'Goodnight then.'

She heard the reluctance in his voice, as though he had more to say but didn't know how to say it. Then, after a moment's hesitation, he turned and walked away down the corridor.

'Wait!' she called, desperately trying to think of a reason to bring him back.

He turned without speaking, waiting for the reason to present itself.

'I just ... I mean, how can you bring her here unless ...'

'Unless?' he questioned, taking a step closer.

'Well – unless it's safe.'

'It will be,' Raphaelle replied. Then, walking towards her, he reached into his pocket and retrieved a long metal object. Even before he held it up for her, she knew it was a key. And this time it belonged to him.

Liddy stopped breathing, unable to tear her eyes from it and what it meant. She tried to stay calm, but her heart was dancing, and she was afraid it would waltz right out of her chest if she didn't press her hand down and keep it there. When she finally looked at him again, he was smiling – a small flicker at the corner of his lips, which in turn lifted his eyes. Anyone else would have missed it, but not Liddy; she had come to know his face better than any other. He dropped the key back in his pocket and, in doing so, his fingers slowly brushed against hers. How had he got so close?

Away from his room, the dark, damp chaos that normally surrounded him had slipped away, and his skin carried the now-familiar scent of pine trees. She could feel the heat of his body pressing against hers, making her breath catch in her throat. He must have heard it, as he let his hand fall back to hers and their fingers became entwined.

'May I?' he asked, lifting his other hand towards her waist.

Liddy closed her eyes and moved her head to make a small shuddery nod. His fingertips came to rest in the shallow dip of her spine; such a pulse-quickening touch that it made her flinch. An involuntary movement, but one he immediately misinterpreted as fear. He pulled his hand away sharply and stepped back; she felt the draught come between them. There was a hurt expression on his face.

'I thought—' he faltered.

But before he could finish his words, Liddy reached to pull his face gently back towards her. 'And you were right,' she whispered.

She felt the muscles of his jaw ease against her palm and then he slowly turned his head and kissed her wrist. Leaning closer, Liddy finally put her lips to his. Neither one of them broke away after that – not for a very long time, not until after they had fallen backwards into her room and onto the bed. When they finally pulled apart, they lay for a while in silence, each watchful of the other; cautious, shy, still wanting.

'Can I stay?' asked Raphaelle quietly, his breath warm on her skin.

Liddy smiled and tenderly tucked a curl behind his ear. 'I would like it if you did.'

He moved his head and kissed her fingers and then, leaning across the bed, he blew on the candle to extinguish the flame. The rest of the world disappeared and, with shining eyes, they slipped away together into a delicious liquorice dark.

CHAPTER 34

A Socket Full of Stars

Waking to an empty bed, Liddy suffered a moment of panic. Had last night with Raphaelle simply been a dream, her mind filled with illusions and moments imagined? But no. There was a cup of tea, still warm, by the bed – she wasn't imagining that. Who else had left it there but him? It had all been real. Lifting the cup to her lips, she could barely drink for smiling. She wished he had been here when she'd woken up, but took pleasure in wondering if he had stood there and watched her sleep. She decided not to look for him straight away – everyone needed time alone, especially him.

To distract herself, she made a batch of marchpane, pressing in the petals, as Vivienne wanted. Humming, Liddy moulded each one into the shape of a heart, a reflection of her internal musings. She could still smell Raphaelle on her skin and taste him on her tongue, and the memory of last night brought a rush of fulfilled desire.

While she baked she listened expectantly for the sound of footsteps, or the lifting of the latch, the opening of a door, but no sound came. She hoped he didn't regret last night and hadn't changed his mind about using the key. After all, having a key wasn't the same as slotting it into a lock. Little waves of panic began to surge.

Unable to wait any longer, she left the kitchen and went to his door. After a flurry of unanswered knocks, she knew the room was empty. He wasn't in the kitchen – she had just come from there – nor was he in the library, and when she climbed the stairs to Vivienne's room, she saw that she was alone and sleeping. As she stood wondering where else Raphaelle could be, the rhythmic creaking sound of the rocking chair came from above and she knew at once where she would find him. Until he turned his key in the lock, the ghost wouldn't be released.

Liddy spent what was left of the morning in search of the Major, who had vacated his favourite armchair. Eventually she found him with Ben, sitting on the terrace of the upper lawn, their heads lowered in concentration. At their feet a large stone held several flapping papers, in danger of flying away. As she walked towards them, she could hear the Major sounding out consonant clusters: *ch, sh, str*. True to his word and quick to keep his promise, the Major was teaching Ben how to read.

The crunch of her feet on the gravel broke their focus and their heads rose in unison. On a sketchpad lying across his knee Ben had written each letter of the alphabet and he was beaming at his achievement.

'I've brought you some marchpane,' she said, placing a plate of hearts on the table. 'They are mixed with petals from the garden. Vivienne says they can help ease sadness and heal an aching heart.'

'It's true,' assured Ben.

A hopeful look spread across the Major's face. Picking up one of the hearts, he popped it into his mouth and chewed slowly. For a moment or two he sat quietly as Ben continued to fill the page with more letters.

'How's our student doing?' asked Liddy.

'He's a quick learner,' said the Major, full of praise.

Ben smiled. The compliment encouraged him to turn the page and hold out the pad for Liddy to see where he had written his name again and again in big, shaky, wonderful letters.

'That's fantastic!' she exclaimed.

'Turn to the very first page,' he said, eager for her to see what was there.

Liddy took the pad and flicked back to the beginning.

'I wanted it to be the first thing I ever wrote,' he announced proudly.

Although Ben was an old man, Liddy saw an innocent boy before her, full of life and excitement and unwavering optimism, and she felt her heart break a little. And even though she knew what the word would be, she read it anyway: *Rosa*.

Handing the pad back to Ben, Liddy quickly wiped her eyes, grateful that neither Ben nor the Major passed comment. Instead they moved on to mapping vowel combinations, and Liddy realised that she hadn't mentioned why she'd been looking for them in the first place.

'Eloura is expecting you this evening,' she said. 'Come to the library after supper with your sorrowing star and your key, and everything will be ready.'

'This evening?' the Major asked, sounding hesitant.

Ben reached out and patted him on his back, but it wasn't in the same triumphant way the Major had done to him only minutes before; this was the comforting touch of a friend.

'I was thinking,' said the Major, 'I could stay here afterwards and help you with your reading. Perhaps we could get through some of those stories in the library. We could read them together when the rain keeps you from the garden.' He looked at Ben for acceptance.

'Ah, yes – but I'm always in the garden, especially in the rain,' replied Ben, with a mischievous look in his eyes. 'But in the evening, when the garden is dark and the birds all fall quiet, it's then that I'd like to join you.' He smiled.

'Excellent,' announced the Major, as though he had just brokered the deal of a lifetime. 'There's a lot more learning to be done until then. Let's get back to it.'

Liddy headed down and out into the garden until she could no longer hear the babble of syllables over the humming of the bees. She found a spot in the shade of a large tree and flopped onto the grass. Her thoughts returned to the night before, and to Raphaelle. She had barely slept, and smiled at the reason why. She couldn't imagine anyone else feeling what she felt; not Tabby, and certainly not her parents. She wondered what they'd think of him – Tabby would surely protest that Raphaelle was far too old for her, and her father would think him too sullen, but it was her mother's voice that echoed loudest in her head; *beware of broken wings*, she'd say, as though loss had transformed him into a flightless bird. Liddy pushed all the voices from her head and listened instead to the only one that mattered – her own. She was right where she needed to be. Maybe it was the soothing sound of the bees, or the warmth of the sun, or the fact that she had only had a few hours' sleep that made her so drowsy. She closed her eyes and, when she opened them again, it was almost dark.

That evening in the library the Major appeared, clutching his sorrowing star like a candle. Its glow was weak and the petals had begun to curl in on themselves, shrivelling away like rolls of tobacco paper. Liddy could see it shaking in his hand and felt the enormity of what was about to happen.

They stood waiting by the fountain for Eloura to arrive, and she emerged from between the bookshelves as if by magic. Her hair had been plaited in mercurial rows over her head, and the ends secured with glittering stars that clicked together every time she moved. Liddy had never seen her wear her hair that way before – it was spell-binding. Gently Eloura took the pot from the Major's trembling hand and dug out the sorrowing star. He wiped his hands on his trousers, and Liddy saw beads of sweat bubbling on his forehead. When Eloura had finished, she handed the plant back to him as clumps of soil fell from its dangling roots like black rain.

'You must throw it into the fountain now,' she instructed, placing the empty pot on a small shelf behind her.

The Major stared into the water for a long time. 'What if he doesn't want to see me again?' he asked in a sudden panic.

Eloura stepped closer and her eyes shone with kindness. 'It doesn't work that way.'

'I'm just not sure I—' The Major cut himself off with a nervous sigh.

'I promise you, there is no risk in saying goodbye.'

After a moment of fearful fluster, the Major dropped the sorrowing star into the water and watched it disappear in small, silent ripples.

'Now I need the key,' said Eloura.

Taking it from his pocket, he gave it to her, and they watched as she moved towards the large carved door.

Standing on her tiptoes, she pushed the key into an object on the side of the boat carving; it looked like a small round medal. *There must be a different lock each time*, thought Liddy, *all of them connected to one of the taglocks*.

The Major looked alone and afraid and, because there was no one else, Liddy took his hand and held it in her own. They all waited for the click, and when at last it came, the Major puffed out his cheeks and advanced towards his own private battlefield with as much bravery as he could muster.

'Wait,' cried Liddy, rushing forward. She wanted to tell him how proud she was, but instead she wrapped her arms around him and hoped he could feel the words she was too shy to say.

'Thank you,' he said quietly.

She pulled away as the door creaked open. This time it wasn't sunlight or birdsong or the smell of summer that drifted out; instead it was a dark, curling fog and the sound of gunfire, so loud they all jumped in surprise and the candle flames began a wild chase over the walls.

The Major faltered for a moment before continuing to move towards the door. 'I'll see you soon,' he said with a note of false cheeriness. 'Tell Ben to keep practising those letters. I can't get through all those books on my own.'

'Don't forget your persimmon,' said Eloura. He caught it as she threw it towards him. 'It will help you to forget the sadness.'

More smoke billowed out and, by the time it had cleared, the Major was gone.

'Do you think he will really come back?' asked Liddy, as the door closed behind him and Eloura turned the key in the lock.

Eloura nodded. 'I think it is his intention, but the shadow cast by war is a long one and it follows many men home. It may be a while before we see him again.'

'Did you say that once a person dies, their stories die with them?'

'That's right,' she replied.

'So the words just ... disappear?'

'As soon as the heart stops beating, the ink dries up and the words fall away. It means they have found a different kind of peace.'

'But what about the people they leave behind? What if they never get the chance to read the story before it disappears?'

Eloura stood before Liddy and took both of her hands in her own. 'The stories here are not meant to be read by those who appear within their pages. Reading them can only bring healing to the one who wrote them.'

She didn't really understand, but she nodded anyway. She also knew she wouldn't give up; if the Major wasn't there to help Ben, then she would be the one to do so until he returned.

'Tonight brings the beginning of the new moon,' Eloura said, still holding Liddy's hands. 'And you know what that means, don't you?'

'That you're leaving,' Liddy replied quietly. So much had happened that she had stopped counting the days and had forgotten to watch for the changing shape of the moon. A cold panic washed over her as she realised that Raphaelle only had a few hours to bring his key and unlock the door. What if he wasn't ready? What if he really had changed his mind? Who knew how long Eloura would be gone? Reading her thoughts, Eloura pulled Liddy towards her in a motherly embrace and held her there for a long, long time.

'Don't worry, he will come,' she whispered softly into her hair, and Liddy's heart settled like a baby bird back in the warmth of its nest. 'The only thing you must do is make sure he brings your sorrowing star with him.'

'Mine?' she asked in surprise, her words muffled in the fragrant lilac folds of Eloura's dress. She had almost forgotten about the sorrowing star in her room.

'That's right.' Eloura stifled a yawn. 'I think I will sleep now for a while. The journey is long, and I must leave with the dark.'

'Just two more things,' said Liddy quickly.

'Well, I already know the first one,' said Eloura, laughing. 'You want to know why Raphaelle needs to bring your sorrowing star with him.'

Liddy nodded.

'Because you were always there in the story, and you were always part of the ending.'

Liddy thought back to Vivienne and the doll she had found so long ago. *It is strange, the things that connect us,* she mused.

'And the second thing?'

'Second thing?' asked Liddy, confused.

'Yes, you said there were two things.' Eloura shook her head and laughed again.

'Oh yes, I was going to ask if I will see you again,' said Liddy, 'but I think I already know the answer.'

'And what is it?'

'Yes.'

Eloura nodded her head, slow and sure. She was full of sleepiness. 'After the old stories have been erased by the wind and the salt and the sun, I will return anchored by the weight of the new ones. But there is always a part of me here, waiting.'

'Until the next story then,' said Liddy, feeling that sudden ache you get on the edge of goodbye.

'I like that,' said Eloura, her eye shining with a thousand smiles. 'Until the next story.'

Then she lifted the eye patch and adjusted it over her other eye, and what Liddy saw was so astonishing it made her gasp out loud. Instead of an amber-coloured eye to match the other one, the socket was full of slowly swirling silver stars. Eloura laughed at the shock on Liddy's face. 'They help me find my way,' she said, by way of explanation. 'The world is vast, and I am easily lost.'

'They're beautiful,' she whispered, unable to look away.

It wasn't until she felt something brush against her legs that she finally averted her gaze and saw the cat poised at her feet.

'Eloura, what if he walks through that door and never wants to come back?' asked Liddy, but there was no answer. When she turned her head to look, Eloura was no longer there.

Sometimes we must find our own answers.

CHAPTER 35
Night Swim

A few hours later Liddy decided to resume her search for Raphaelle and found him outside the library. It was impossible to believe that only several hours ago he had seen every inch of her, and her of him; that his hands had been in her hair and on her skin. Standing there with her sorrowing star, she felt shy and awkward. Gently he took it from her hand and placed it on a small shelf behind him, his every movement magnified. There was a tiny freckle on his cheek and another on his temple. In the intimacy of the previous night she hadn't noticed them – small and round, two midnight specks. It was strange how in the near-dark she saw so much more, things she had never noticed before. The long sweep of his eyelashes, the moon edges of his mouth and the dark curve of his neck. She committed it all to memory, just in case it would be lost.

Her thoughts took her to a place of doubt and fear, but before they could seize her completely, his arms wrapped around her and she pressed her head to his chest. The scent of his skin was stronger now, like an alpine forest in the rain. In her ear she heard the fast beat of his heart. It was a sound to steady her own – one of desire, not regret. She leaned back and pushed the curls from his brow, and the lines beneath her hand instantly smoothed away. Vivienne had been wrong to think she was there to save Raphaelle from Ravanna; it was his own internal ache, the one deep in his soul, that needed to be soothed. She was not there to rescue him, only to give him the strength to rescue himself.

'You will see her,' Liddy said nervously. They both knew who she meant.

'Yes,' he replied, his eyes more serious.

'And you will remember ... how it was.'

He frowned.

'And maybe then you won't want to return – here ... to me.' She didn't look at him when she spoke those final words, too afraid of the reply that might follow.

'Don't you understand?' Raphaelle said, gently tilting her chin up to meet his eyes, dark and expectant, watching her.

Liddy shook her head. Her mind was a confusion of thoughts.

'My life has been full of misery and hopelessness. I have been so ... glum.' The last word made him laugh a little, as though it was too small to express the years of his suffering. 'I am not leaving you. I will find you as soon as I return.'

Liddy's eyes prickled with tears and she bit her lip.

'I am going so that I can return,' he said.

He pulled her back towards him and she sank into his warmth. Love is such a delicate thing, and a heart is far too easily crushed.

'No more hiding, no more shadows.'

'No more half-lives,' murmured Liddy.

'No more half-lives,' he repeated.

Then his lips met hers, and nothing else mattered. The kiss was a silent conversation, saying far more than words ever could. After the longest time, they finally pulled apart. Liddy noticed that the marker above the door had shifted to the thinnest sliver of moon, barely visible. A new beginning.

She remembered what Eloura had told her: *There is no risk in saying goodbye.*

'Go now,' she whispered.

Then she felt his hand slip from hers, and by the time the library door opened, she had already turned away.

Raphaelle had promised to find Liddy once he returned, so she'd waited expectantly in the kitchen until the dying embers of the fire had left the room too cold to linger.

Now, in her room, it was getting late and still he hadn't come. In a sudden burst of impatience, Liddy blew out the candle and lay in the dark, pretending to herself that she would try to sleep. She was alert to every sound the house made, but there was nothing aside from the draught and an occasional creak.

When he'd left she'd felt reassured, but now as she lay alone, she wasn't convinced that he was ready to let go of anyone but her. She closed her eyes and prayed she was wrong.

After midnight Liddy pulled on her boots and her coat and went into the garden. It was surprisingly warm as she walked across the lawn and she could smell jasmine and the trailing scent of lilacs in the air. The dark created a different world, telling a story of its own. A row of fir trees became a turreted castle, and the rose bush resembled a slumbering dragon.

Further down the garden, where the field sloped towards the lake, the chestnut trees became soldiers, and little winged creatures swung between them like pendulums. The bats were wide awake and ever-playful.

Once she reached the lake, Liddy stopped and sat spellbound by the sorrowing stars. They glistened and pulsed with light just below the surface of the water. She had only ever seen them at night from her window, and up close they were truly enthralling. Swirls of pollen drifted over the water and she felt soothed. Above her was the very beginning of the new moon, like a bright flame in the blackened grate of night. She wondered where Raphaelle was and what he was thinking. Had he even used his key? Was it already tied to the branch of a tree, or had he let it melt away in the furnace?

She had seen him enter the library, but that didn't mean he had found Eloura or unlocked the door. He could quite easily have crept back to the burrow-like safety of his room once Liddy had left, and she cursed herself for not going to see if he was there. She tried to busy her mind by guessing where his keyhole would be, and the sound and colour that would have spilled out once the door was opened. She could hear the soft sound of a lullaby in her head, so real that it could have been coming from the trees. After that she couldn't imagine anything at all. Wrapping her arms around her knees, she rocked backwards and forwards and listened to the murmurs and rustles of the garden behind her: the secret flutters and the tinkle of keys. The night sparkled. She decided to stay there until morning, until the shimmer of the sorrowing stars had faded away and the sun brought a different light.

'I thought I'd find you here,' called a voice from behind.

She closed her eyes and smiled. When she opened them again, Raphaelle was sitting beside her and had taken her hand in his own. Neither of them said anything for a long time, their thoughts keeping them quiet.

'How did you know where to find me?' she asked eventually.

'Because this is where it all began,' he replied. 'This is the spot where Vivienne found your doll.'

Liddy thought of all her tears and tantrums after losing it – if only she'd known then where it would take her. She wanted to ask so many questions, but not tonight. She would save them for another time, another place. Tonight he had returned, and that was the only answer she needed.

Suddenly Raphaelle was on his feet and pulling her up with him.

'Let's go in,' he said, with an excitement she'd never heard before.

Liddy laughed. 'In where … the house?'

He rolled his eyes. 'No, not the house – the lake. Let's go swimming in the stars.'

Liddy shook her head, still laughing.

But Raphaelle was already pulling off his clothes and running towards the water.

'Come on,' he said, dipping in his toe. 'It's not cold.' He crossed his arms over his chest and quickly rubbed his shoulders in mock shudders, but she could see that he was smiling. 'Okay, well, maybe it is a bit.'

It wasn't the cold that made her hesitate. It was her sudden shyness at seeing his naked body, its contours clearly lit by the glow of the sorrowing stars. Slopes and curves and angles that had seemed to fit so perfectly against her own last night. She closed her eyes, remembering.

He turned his head and reached out his arm towards her. 'Come on,' he urged.

Liddy wavered. Part of her wanted to follow him into the water, and the other part wanted to stay hidden beneath her clothes. Last night their desire had been wrapped up in darkness – it had been felt, but not seen. She heard a small splash and watched as Raphaelle dived into the lake and disappeared. Taking her chance, she quickly slipped off her clothes and followed him.

It was colder than she expected, but as she waded deeper, the petals wrapped around her thighs like silk. Swaying beneath her, she could feel the thickness of their leaves, strong and supple and full of magic. It was beautiful and dream-like – she felt caught between two worlds. Scanning the lake for Raphaelle, she saw the dark shape of his head in the distance. She bent her knees and let the water take her. When she surfaced, his arms were holding her and his body was pressed against hers, safe and warm. He lifted her up and spun her round, and her scream turned to laughter as she flung her head back to watch the dizzy blur of dancing light. It felt like a never-ending carousel. He was laughing too, and she realised she had never heard his laugh before. It was as deep and warm as hers was light and gentle and their notes mingled and drifted away into the garden.

'Look, it's Eloura's boat,' said Raphaelle, holding her steady as he pointed at something in the distance.

Liddy could see the silhouette of the sails, like giant scrolls against the sky, each one telling their stories to the wind. She whispered her goodbye, knowing that even though it couldn't be heard, it would be felt.

Shivering, she slid back down into his arms and her mouth found his. Then all she could hear were the keys gently tinkling from the trees in the darkened garden. A reminder that there was always hope.

CHAPTER 36

Little Bea

The next morning they climbed the stairs to Vivienne's room. Her face turned to greet them as they entered, alert as a bird. Liddy breathed a sigh of relief, but the room was unnaturally warm and gloomy, a small gap in the curtains permitting a long blade of light to enter. It sliced through the dark, capturing the swirling dust motes, making her think of germs and disease.

'Shall I open the curtains?' asked Liddy, about to cross the room.

'No,' said Vivienne sharply, pulling her blankets all around her. 'There's nothing out there I wish to see.'

Can't she feel the cloying warmth? The sickness in the room? But Liddy fell back.

'It is done,' said Raphaelle quietly.

'Done?' repeated Vivienne.

'Yes. I will need papers for Beatrice, if I am to bring her home.'

Vivienne's eyes widened and her mouth fell open in a gasp of disbelief as Raphaelle explained their plan. When he had finished, her cheeks were flushed and her eyes shone with fire. It was as though whatever light had been missing inside her had finally been found and fuelled.

'So, you forgive me?' She sounded like a small, redemptive child.

'There is nothing to forgive.'

Liddy was not surprised by the quiet that followed. By now she had learned that sometimes people escaped to a silent place when the words were too big, or perhaps when they weren't big enough. It was Vivienne who finally spoke, directing Raphaelle to a drawer where he would find the documents relating to Beatrice's birth.

'You will look after her for me, won't you?' Vivienne's hope-filled eyes looked first at Raphaelle and then at Liddy.

Liddy took a small step closer to the bed. 'Of course we will,' she replied. 'You don't need to worry. Beatrice is coming home and we will keep her safe.'

Her words brought solace and peace, and the pain that had been etched on Vivienne's face for so long slowly slipped away.

'I think I would like it if you opened the curtains now,' she said, slowly turning her face towards the window in anticipation of what she might see there.

The foundling home was nestled in the shade of a large convent, half-hidden under the enormous trees that surrounded it. Liddy was grateful for the shadows after the long, steep climb up from the village. Raphaelle had asked several times if she wanted to stop and rest, but she knew that if she did, she might never continue. It wasn't only the documents that Vivienne had given them; she had also insisted they take the doll, without explaining why. Liddy clutched it fiercely to her chest.

The walls of the home were old and crumbling and there was no sound from within. Other than the chirping song of the occasional cicada drifting down the hillside, the place seemed to be completely deserted. Engraved in the stone above the door Liddy read the words *Casa del Trovatello*. Raphaelle stepped closer and pulled on the chain, and a mournful clang echoed deep within. A minute passed and then another, and Liddy's eyes wandered along the wall until they fell upon a hatch-like opening in the middle of an archway. A pair of blue cherubs had been painted in each of the spandrels and inside the hatch there was a wooden barrel. It was crib-shaped for comfort, or perhaps to convince the mother that she was merely tucking her baby into bed. Liddy lifted her eyes to the small bell hanging in solemn silence above it. She wondered how many hesitant hands had pulled on its chain, and she imagined the hearts that broke every time the chimes rang out across the rooftops.

Her sad thoughts were interrupted by the sound of the door slowly opening. A small, squat woman appeared before them, with a round and smiling face. She stepped back and began wiping something from her hands with a cloth; it looked like paint. Raphaelle explained their purpose and she pulled the door wider, admitting them without question. She led them along a cloister, from where Liddy could see a small courtyard filled with about half a dozen children. They stood at easels, brushes in their hands and paint pots balanced on walls, poised in creativity. She slowed, trying to find Beatrice among them, but none of the faces were familiar.

The woman stopped outside a large door. 'Please wait here,' she said, before disappearing inside.

On the other side of the courtyard, Liddy noticed a small girl sitting high on the branch of a tree, swinging her long brown legs in the air. She couldn't see the girl's face through the leaves, but she felt sure she had just found Beatrice. Her heart thrilled.

The door opened again, and they were ushered into a small, well-polished office. A gentleman in a suit sat behind a desk and he rose to greet them as they entered. He introduced himself as Signor Silveri, the founder of the home.

'Well, I must confess this doesn't happen very often,' he said merrily, patting his tie and sitting back down.

'What doesn't?' asked Raphaelle.

'That a child is reclaimed. It makes a change – and a pleasant one at that.'

Raphaelle and Liddy sat down opposite him and they ran through the formalities, providing descriptions and dates, which Signor Silveri carefully wrote down on a pad. He glanced though the papers they'd brought, seeking confirmation.

'Her name is Beatrice,' blurted Liddy, unable to wait any longer, 'but I think you call her Neve.'

'Yes,' said the woman. 'The children are given new names when they arrive – usually it's something connected to when or how they were found; it might be a particular saint's day, or a day of the week or month, even the weather; sometimes it can be the colour of the blanket they'd been wrapped in. When Neve arrived, she was covered in snow.' She frowned. 'It was strange because it hadn't snowed here for months – I remember, because I was the one who found her on the doorstep.' The woman shook her head. 'She was too big to fit in the crib, poor thing!'

Liddy knew it hadn't been snow that she'd seen that day, but pollen from the sorrowing stars. Such an easy mistake to make, and one she herself had made before she had come to understand the stars' magic.

'Can we take her now?' Liddy asked, trying to keep the impatience from her voice. She felt the weight of Raphaelle's hand on her knee and bit her tongue.

'So . . . the child you are here to collect is definitely Neve?' Liddy could hear the scepticism in the man's tone.

'Yes, that's right,' replied Raphaelle.

Signor Silveri said nothing more, he simply leaned back in his chair and looked at them both with quiet, appraising eyes. Liddy could feel her knees begin to shake beneath her skirt and wondered why it was taking so long. The woman had fallen quiet in the corner of the room, awaiting further instructions. 'It's just that neither of you . . . bears much resemblance to the child,' he said at last. 'And we need to be certain she is yours to take. I'm sure you understand.'

'Of course we understand,' replied Raphaelle abruptly, edging forward on his chair, and this time it was Liddy who placed her hand firmly on his knee. He heeded her warning and slid back.

Signor Silveri hadn't finished and seemed to be thinking very carefully about what he wanted to say next. 'It's simply that the child is so much darker than either of you.' But as he spoke, his eyes were focused only on Liddy, and she knew she was the one being judged.

'I am in fact Beatrice's . . . Neve's uncle,' asserted Raphaelle. 'She is my sister's child.'

Signor Silveri continued to stare at Liddy. 'And you are?'

Liddy knew she was supposed to say something, but she wasn't quite sure what it was, and when she opened her mouth to speak, no words came out.

'This is her aunt,' said Raphaelle.

'So if you are her uncle and you are her aunt, then where, may I ask, are her parents?'

'Her father is dead,' he replied without hesitation. 'And her mother is not well enough to come here herself.' He took the birth certificate from his pocket and slid it across the table. Signor Silveri's eyes flickered down and he studied the paper for a moment.

'Is this all you have?' he asked, sounding unconvinced.

Raphaelle nodded. Clenching the muscles of his jaw, he waited.

Signor Silveri raised his eyebrows and gave a heavy sigh. Then he rose from the desk and went to a large cabinet. The drawer rolled open and they could hear the soft swish of paper as his fingers searched for answers.

'Neve – or should I say Beatrice – is not the kind of girl to be interested in dolls, I'm afraid,' said the woman, gesturing towards Liddy's knee. 'She much prefers to be outside, in the company of animals and trees.'

Liddy looked down at the doll lying in her lap. She had forgotten it was there.

At that moment Signor Silveri pulled a slim file from the cabinet and, as he did so, something fluttered out from between its pages and landed on the floor near Liddy's foot. It was small and blue, as if someone had snipped out a square of the summer sky, only it wasn't a square of the sky. Liddy recognised it at once. Picking it up, she carefully matched its edges against the missing piece of the doll's dress; it was a perfect fit.

'This is our proof,' she said, holding up the doll for them all to see.

'Sister Lucia,' said Signor Silveri, 'please fetch Beatrice.'

When she was first brought to them, Beatrice was understandably quiet. Her face remained unchanged as Signor Silveri explained what was about to happen. She looked neither pleased nor upset by the news. *As inscrutable as her mother*, thought Liddy. It was only when she caught sight of the doll that there was a sudden flicker in her eyes. Beatrice stepped closer and, instinctively, Liddy held it out for her to take. The nun looked surprised, especially after professing that Beatrice was not the sort of child who played with dolls. Liddy knew it wasn't the doll itself that interested her; it was the story that it told. Beatrice closed her eyes and buried her face in the doll's hair, and they all waited. Finally she lifted her head and looked straight at Liddy, leaving her with no doubt that she was Vivienne's flesh and blood.

'Can we go home now?' she asked, as though it was the most normal thing in the world.

'Of course,' replied Liddy, releasing a long-held breath.

The further away they got from the foundling home, the more curious Beatrice became, gazing at the birds in the sky and brushing her fingers against the leaves of the trees. She stopped to smell some wild yellow flowers growing by the side of the road, and from there she skipped the rest of the way down the hill in pursuit of a bumble bee.

In the square, Sebastian was outside the shop, wiping tables. He looked up at the sound of their footsteps. Before Liddy could stop her, Beatrice was running towards him, smiling. She stopped just in time to avoid a collision and, breathless, held out one of the bright-yellow flowers from the top of the hill. After a moment of uncertainty, Sebastian lifted it from her fingers. Liddy struggled with the thought of telling him about Vivienne, but when she looked at his face, it was filled with a sad sort of wonder. He already knew. She promised herself that she would bring him flower-petal marchpane as often as she could, in the hope that it would be enough.

CHAPTER 37
Letting Go

Vivienne stood at the window, her eyes glistening with the tender love of a mother watching her child at play. She could hear little Bea's laughter float up from the garden. She wished she could hold on to that sound for ever, but she could feel herself slipping away. She rested her head against the glass to steady herself and let the cold penetrate her skin; it soothed her, but only a little. She knew she must soon let go, that holding on would only cause more pain, but still she could not make herself look away.

Raphaelle was chasing Bea round the rose bush, with Liddy running the other way, ready to catch her. At the last moment Bea darted out between them both, narrowly missing Ben and his wheelbarrow. He shook his head, but he was smiling. Kind, old, loveable Ben – how she would miss him too. Liddy reached Bea first and they toppled onto the grass together in a fit of giggles. Raphaelle was there as she tried to roll away. There was so much laughter. So much love. Vivienne smiled because, after all this time, she felt it too. Watching them mended her heart and broke it, all at once. She had waited such a very long time for Bea to come home, but it was like a dream arriving on the cusp of morning. A beautiful, brief and haunting dream that filled her heart with bliss and sorrow.

She could never be part of the happiness she saw – it was too late for her – but that did not take away her joy at knowing that Bea would be safe and loved. She trusted Raphaelle and Liddy to tell her daughter who she was. Memories last longer than lived moments, and the stories they told each other would outshine everything. Despite that, it was hard knowing that she had to leave so much behind, with so much left to say. That she would have to take all that love with her. But she knew she would live on in the house, in little Bea, in her brother and in Liddy. They would protect her daughter and love her as if she were their own. It was enough.

'Goodbye, my little one,' she whispered, unheard. Her breath left a misty circle on the glass, slow to clear.

Finally she lifted her head, and the world went dark one last time.

*

Six weeks after Vivienne's passing, Liddy was sitting with Bea down by the water.

'This was your mother's favourite place,' she said. 'In a way, it's where we met.'

Beatrice smiled. 'Then it will be mine too.' She stood up and stretched her arms wide, spinning round and round until she tumbled, dizzy, back to the ground.

'She wanted you to have these.' Liddy reached in her basket and pulled out three cloth-bound books. She handed them to Beatrice, who hastily untied the string that kept them closed. 'I found them yesterday in the drawer.'

Inside were the names of animals: bats, foxes, mice, rabbits, fish and birds. There were dozens and dozens of them, dated in neat rows, and written next to each one was a short description of both the injury sustained and the treatment provided. Ben had been right about Vivienne rescuing unfortunate creatures, and she'd kept a log of them all.

'It says here that she found a vixen with a wound to its neck.' Beatrice looked up in amazement. 'And she made it better again.'

'Yes,' said Liddy, 'she had a habit of saving things.'

'Then she must have had a very kind heart.'

The words made Liddy sad and she quickly wiped away a tear before it fell, hoping Beatrice didn't see. 'She was the kindest person I've ever known, and she loved you so very much.' Then she stood up. 'Come on, let's see how Ben is getting on with that swing he promised you.'

About a month after the Major had left, he sent word that his return had been delayed. He had given no explanation, but Liddy wasn't surprised by the news. It was like Eloura had said: sometimes recovery takes longer than you think. He mentioned bringing his son's painting, and hoped no one would mind it being displayed in the library. Liddy had smiled, thinking what a perfect place that would be.

When Ben finally came to open the pages of *Bluebells and Bird-Boxes*, no words had remained, and the pages crumbled into the palms of his hands, leaving behind nothing but silver dust-like particles. Liddy had been devastated at his loss, but Ben had simply lowered his head and said it was okay – he didn't need to read the words, because he already knew the story. He'd sat in the stillness of the room for a few hours, remembering, and then taken the dusty remnants out into the garden and released them like tiny dancing stars. Watching them swirl and settle among the flowers, he'd said, 'It's where she always wanted to be.' The pollen would always remind Liddy of snowflakes, each one unique and special and flawed, just like the stories they came from. Liddy had given him Rosa's poetry book and now Ben had something of hers to keep. When the time was right, he might ask Raphaelle to make him a key of his own.

Eloura was still far away. All the phases of the moon had come and gone and come again, and Liddy thought she must be beyond this story and inside the folds of another. After the passing of the first full moon Liddy had searched the horizon, hoping to see the dark shape of the Sorrela boat, the wink of its small light, but there was nothing there. The water was as endless as the stories that spun from this world and reached far into the next. She knew this wasn't the beginning, nor was it the end, because all stories connect and overlap. In their many layers they offer comfort and refuge and hope. Stories are friends, lovers, mothers, fathers, a hand in the dark, a shelter in a storm. Stories are infinite and vast; they change and they survive. Liddy knew that one day she would see the Sorrela boat again and it would bring with it more stories to share, and maybe a new teapot as blue as Neptune, or an orange as bright and warm as the sun.

Until then, all she could do was wait.

EPILOGUE

*E*verything has been painted and the windows are left open more often than they are closed. The fragrant susurrations of the garden drift in and swill out the rooms, and for a while it feels as though my walls have completely fallen away. The nursery is a beautiful golden colour now, and the last of that terrible green wallpaper has been scrubbed away. When the evening light comes through the window, the room glows like the inside of a treasure chest, and there is no salt pile to cross when you enter.

Even though the days are shorter now, and there is a chill in the air, Beatrice still prefers to be outside. She helps Ben gather the fallen leaves and collects the eggs each morning; she plants new herbs and gathers strawberries in her skirts, although most of them are gone by the time she reaches the kitchen. She smiles guiltily as she tries to loosen seeds from her teeth.

This evening, when Liddy and Raphaelle call her in from the garden, there is no response. After a quick search they find her and Ben untangling a poor rabbit's foot from a wire fence. Bea is flushed with excitement as they release it and watch it bound away through the long grass. Then she rushes through the twirling stardust, impatient to add her very first entry to Vivienne's ledger. Halfway up the lawn, she pauses for a moment to look up at the window of Vivienne's room, as though she can see something that no one else can. I do not give up my ghosts so easily. She lifts a small carved owl from her pocket, looks at it and smiles. Then she is running again towards my open door.

The song of a vixen rises over the treetops and, higher still, a single star appears, but the light does not shine from above; it comes from the lake and the sorrowing stars beneath its surface that are starting to quiver.

At the back of the house stand three trees; once bare and black, they have now begun to stir. On one branch there is something small and round and bright as the sun. Soon there will be others just like it, and the flowers and leaves will flourish.

Raphaelle reaches for Liddy's hand and she gently rests her head against his shoulder. They do not notice the vixen hiding in the leaves, as she sits quiet and still, watching them before she slowly turns away. Dusk gathers them in and, with stardust in their hair, they follow little Bea through the garden towards my lamp-lit windows.

The trees are chiming.

The sorrowing stars are shining bright.

And finally, after all this time, I can breathe again.

ACKNOWLEDGEMENTS

My thanks to Ariella Feiner for her continued support and guidance. Thank you to Sam Bradbury and the whole Del Rey team for their ideas, insight and creative design. Thank you to the 'Glossip Girls' for a lifetime of memories and many more to come. I'm so grateful that you keep inviting me to the party, knowing that I probably won't show up. Finally, thank you to Agapios, Dawn, and Becky, who were there when it mattered, and to Char for all the cake.